Back to Me

QUIBLINGS: BOOK 2

KATIE DUGGAN

Book Cover Design & Illustration by Paige Moreland

Editing by Cheyenne Duhon & Jenn Allis

Scene Break Artwork & Family Tree by: Emily B. Rose

Peony Graphic by: Paige Moreland

1st edition 2024

Paperback: 979-8-9906598-5-8

Contents

Content Warnings

While *Back to Me* is, at its heart, a romantic comedy, serious topics are included as well. Life is funny, and life is tragic, and I hope I was able to marry these two facts in a sensitive, and empathetic way.

Back to Me features graphic, consensual sex, low blood sugar crash, ableism, emotional abuse and resulting trauma, depression (episodes in past, symptoms in present), religious bigotry, alcohol consumption, and food policing and diet culture (explicitly denounced by main characters).

There is also mention of past trauma including: homophobia and disowning due to homophobia, going no contact with family, religious trauma, and fatphobia.

While it is my biggest hope that *Back to Me* brings joy and healing to my readers, I understand that may not be the case for everyone. If you think it may be too much, please take care of yourself and your brain first.

If you have thoughts that are overwhelming and need someone to talk to, please call 988 if you are in the U.S.

If you are outside of the US, a fantastic resource to find resources is:

https://www.therapyroute.com/article/helplines-suicide-hotlines-and-crisis-lines-from-around-the-world.

You and your wellness are the most important.

For readers like me, who search specific keywords on their e-reader to get to the good parts sometimes: I hope this makes it easier on you.

And for those who want to avoid the smut: please know that while the following chapters are the ones with graphic intimate scenes, sex and pleasure is discussed freely in *Back to Me.*

Chapter 8
Chapter 23
Chapter 25
Chapter 26
Chapter 33
Chapter 34
Chapter 35

Playlist

While writing, I curated a playlist of songs that related to Jo, Hunter, and their love story. The lyrics may not always directly apply, and listening to the playlist is not necessary for the enjoyment of *Back to Me*.

Songs are listed below, and you can scan the QR code below to be taken directly to the Spotify playlist.

You can also find the playlist called "Back to Me by Katie Duggan (Quiblings 2)" on my Spotify profile (Katie Duggan).

Quinn Family Tree

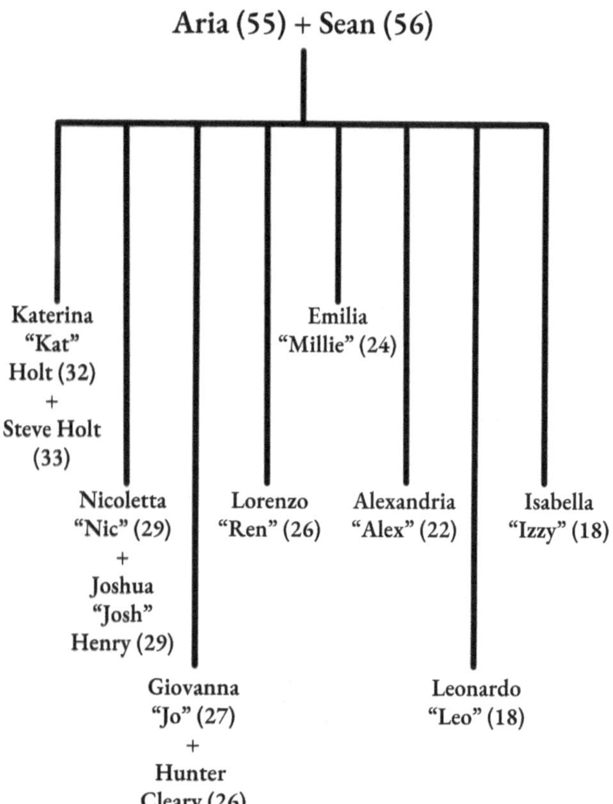

To those who feel like they're simultaneously too much and also not enough: we are the perfect amount for the right people. They're looking for someone who is our exact grade of sparkle.

And to Sarah, the Jo to my Nic, who doesn't quite get what I write about, but who gets me and loves me without conditions. I'm totally okay with you only reading this part of the book.

"You'll never get away from the sound
Of the woman who loved you."

-Stevie Nicks

Prologue

Jo

Twelve Years Ago

Playlist: August | Taylor Swift

"I don't want to go," I whine. "I'm fifteen. I should be able to make this decision for myself."

"We'll go to Queenie's after," my dad promises, bent over to tie Leo's dress shoes.

I let out a huff. "Fine. But you have to let me have a sip of beer."

My dad straightens and squeezes my youngest brother's shoulder. "All set, buddy." He turns his head to me. "You know that only happens on Football Sundays. It's not football season, Joey. But you can get a milkshake, if you're feeling well enough. Just make sure to check your blood sugar after Mass."

Mass. Blood Sugar. Words that remind me my life isn't mine. That I live under my parents' roof and and under the control of Type 1 Diabetes' whims.

That I'm not my own person.

I guess that's the case for most sixteen-year-olds. But it's one thing to have to do what my parents say, it's another to have a chronic illness pulling the strings.

"If you really don't want to go, maybe you have a stomachache?" Dad suggests with a playful wink.

"Will you bring me back something from Queenie's?" I ask hopefully, pushing away the strands of hair that fell into my face.

"Not if you want your mom to think you have a stomachache. It's just an hour."

Technically he's right. Mass is just an hour. An hour including prayers to a god who hasn't answered my prayers. An hour in a building with pamphlets titled: "The Sacrament of Marriage: God's Plan For Men and Women." An hour surrounded by people who shake their heads and whisper about how downhill the country is going since gay marriage is legal in Connecticut. The feelings of shame and self-hatred caused by that hour last much, much longer.

But I really want Queenies.

"Okay," I agree reluctantly.

We only live a few blocks from Our Lady of Hope, and since it's nice out, Mom insists we walk.

"You need sun, Nicoletta Jane," Mom insists to my older sister who, for the third week in a row, refuses to come to Mass.

Nic wrinkles her nose. "I'll just get more freckles, no thanks. Text me when you're on your way home and I'll be ready for Queenie's."

I spin furiously toward my dad, who at least has the decency to look guilty. "So she gets to skip church and go to Queenie's, but I don't?"

"Joey." Dad rubs his hand over his face, an exhausted look on his face. "Can we discuss this later?"

"It's always later," I snap. "And then even later. And then it gets forgotten, and we never talk about it." Angry tears sting in my eyes, and I hate it.

"Oh my god, Jo," my eldest sister, Kat, hisses, rolling her eyes. "Grow up."

"Stay in your lane, Kat. Let me be the parent," Dad says firmly, giving her *a look*.

"Jo," he says gently, turning his head back to me. "What's going on? You're acting-Alexandria!" And just like that, I'm forgotten and his attention lands on one of my seven siblings. "Look both ways before crossing the street, Jesus Christ." He's gone, speeding toward my younger sister, Alex, who apparently experienced a brush with death.

I swipe at my eyes, feeling Kat's judgmental gaze still on me. "Just because you're in college doesn't mean you're better than me," I mumble as we trail after everyone else on the walk to church. I'm in such a sour mood I can't even enjoy the beautiful day. Hydrangeas are blooming in our neighbors' lawns, and the smell fills the air. It's warm, but not uncomfortably hot, and I should be happy.

Key word: *should*.

"I'm better than you for lots of other reasons," Kat says simply.

"Fuck off."

She gasps and stops short as I continue to walk. "I'm *so* telling Mom and Dad you said that," she threatens, quickening her pace to catch up to me.

"Fine. I don't care," I snap, increasing my speed to get away from her. "Tell them."

"I will," she promises from behind me.

"Okay."

"I'm gonna do it, Jo. You're gonna be in so much trouble." I can hear her heels *click-click-clicking* on the sidewalk behind me as she tries to catch up to me again.

"Great."

Upon our arrival at Our Lady of Hope, Dad holds the door open for all of us while Mom wrestles Izzy's scooter from her.

"I want to ride it when we go to communion!" my seven-year-old sister whines, engaged in a vicious game of tug-of-war over her beloved yellow scooter. Personally, I agree with her. That would liven up Father Gilligan's service for sure.

Finally, the nine of us are seated, Izzy's scooter folded up on the end of our pew next to Dad, my youngest sister pouting between Mom and Leo.

Ren, who's a year younger than me, leans into me. "Why didn't Nic have to come?"

I grit my teeth. "Because she's Nic."

"Because she's a selfish brat," Kat mutters.

My brother and I openly glare at Kat as she unfolds the kneeler. Despite our annoyance for Nic right now, our dislike of our eldest sister and the "holier-than-thou" attitude she brought home after her freshman year of college is stronger.

Mom reaches over to me and strokes my hair. "Why don't you say a prayer, love?"

My stomach churns at the thought. "No, thanks."

Despite staring straight ahead toward the sanctuary, I can see Mom glance at Dad out of the corner of my eye.

As the seven hundred year old cantor announces the opening hymn, my eye is drawn to someone on the other side of the aisle.

She's sitting next to Mr. and Mrs. MacIntyre, an older couple who lives down the street from us, and wearing a sunshine yellow sundress. Her blonde curls dance over her shoulders like a waterfall, and a kaleidoscope of colors from the stained glass windows reflect onto her skin. As she stands for the opening hymn, she gathers her hair to one shoulder, exposing the skin covered only by the thin strap of her sundress.

I try to sing, to blend in, but my mouth is dry.

I'd had crushes on girls before this. I knew I was gay. But I had never felt this undeniable draw, this unignorable *need* for anyone before.

I stare at her for the entirety of the service. After mass, she follows Mr. and Mrs. McIntyre as they greet us outside the church.

"Hunter," Mrs. McIntyre says, pulling the girl forward. She has sparkling blue eyes that make her look like she's keeping a secret, and long blonde curls I want to tangle my fingers in. "This is Giovanna, she's your age and lives down the street."

I opened my mouth to correct them, to remind them yet *again* that I go by Jo, but Hunter speaks before I can.

"Giovanna," she says slowly, like she's tasting each syllable. She has a southern accent, so there's a lilt to her pronunciation of my name. It's the best sound I've ever heard. Her shimmering lips turn upward in a coy smile. "That's a pretty name."

I knew right then and there that Hunter had the ability to change everything, and she did. She changed my life, changed me.

And at the end of the summer, she broke my heart.

I never expected to see her again, and I didn't.

Not until she came strolling back into my life twelve years later, and made me as hopeless as I was at fifteen.

Playlist: Here You Come Again | Dolly Parton

June 17th, 10:36am

From: Jo Quinn <JoQuinn@me.com>
To: Hunter Cleary <Hunter@HunterClearyPhotos.com>
Subject: Tyler Boyle and Nellie Castro Wedding

Hi Hunter,

Tyler Boyle passed on your email address as a potential photographer for their wedding, and I wanted to reach out as their event planner and co-ordinator. We've finalized the date as November

13th at The Hilton in Jersey City. I know it's a long shot, and that you may not be available, but if there's any chance you are, please let me know.

Best,
Jo

June 17th, 3:21pm

From: Hunter Cleary <Hunter@HunterClearyPhotography.com>
To: Jo Quinn <JoQuinn@me.com>
Subject: Re: Tyler Boyle and Nellie Castro Wedding

Howdy Jo,

Thanks for reaching out! It must be fate that I have the thirteenth open, as I wouldn't want to miss Tyler's wedding for anything! They were just texting me and telling me how excited they were to be working with you, and how talented you are! Thanks for making them so happy!

I look forward to working with you,
Hunter <heart emoji>

You may be wondering how I found myself back in the closet at a gay wedding.

Picture it: after corresponding with a wedding planner for months about an event you're photographing, she turns out to be your ex. That you hadn't seen since you were fifteen years old.

What else was I supposed to do but hide in a closet?

At least this time, there's cake.

I know, I know. You're thinking, *"But Hunter, how didn't you recognize the name?"*

I called her Giovanna that entire summer, and she'd signed her name 'Jo.' It makes sense when you say it outloud—because Italian pronunciation is weird—but not when you *read* it.

So when Jo Quinn, Tyler's wedding planner, turned out to be Giovanna Quinn, the first girl I ever kissed, I was a little taken aback.

I think she was, too.

I'd tried to keep it together during the ceremony and reception, to not stare creepily at her. But it's hard—she's still so dang pretty. She still has long, wavy brown hair that my fingers slid through so easily whenever she touched me—

I bargained with myself, claiming if I focused on taking photos of the wedding party, I could lust over the way her ass filled out later on.

We made eye contact a few times, which she was always the first to break. Maybe she's wondering what I look like naked now, and that's why she has to look away. Because I certainly wonder about *her*.

Jeez, maybe MawMaw and PawPaw were right. Maybe these homosexual inclinations do make me a deviant.

As the reception continued, I realized Giovanna wasn't the only blast from the past at the wedding. Her older sister, who mostly kept to herself that summer, is also a guest. Her parents, too, somehow looking like they haven't aged a day. I made a mental note to figure out a way to casually inquire after their skincare routines, but maybe that's not the best idea. During Nellie's best friend's toast, I accidentally made eye contact with Mr. Quinn. At first, I thought he didn't recognize me, which would be the best case scenario.

It's been twelve years since he saw me, and it'd be horribly embarrassing if he *did* recognize me, considering what he walked in on.

No such luck, however. His eyes widened, and his fist clenched so tightly that the champagne flute shattered in his hand, causing everyone in the hall to panic.

He was fine. I overheard him claiming that it was already cracked.

Now I'm sitting alone in a broom closet, hiding away from my past and ready to enjoy the cake, which Tyler themself made. After tasting dozens of wedding treats during my career, I can confidently say nothing is better than their confections. I've been lusting after it like it's Giovanna Quinn's ass all day, and if anyone's earned a sweet treat, it's me.

The cake doesn't disappoint. The chocolate is rich and creamy, and there's a slightly spicy kick that surprises—

"*Dagnabbit,*" I hiss, fumbling my plate as the closet door opens, light filling the small space. I try in vain to catch the plate before it falls to the floor, to no avail.

"Shit, sorry." My shoulders tense at the familiar voice. "Didn't realize this closet was taken—"

"Giovanna," I look up and meet her eyes before my mental filter can stop me.

"Hunter." Her eyes widen. "Sorry, I'll just—"

"Grab me another piece of cake and you can invade my safe haven," I joke.

She seems to mull it over before leaning forward to hand me her plate. "Deal," she says, already heading for the door.

I tentatively take a nibble of the cake after she's left. Part of me is worried she won't come back, and gosh. It's so silly, but I think I'd rather have her company, hear what she's been up to, than this cake.

No, that's ridiculous.

The cake is phenomenal.

When the door opens with a click a few minutes later, I almost fumble my plate again after convincing myself she wasn't returning.

"Thanks for letting me crash your cake eating party," she says, sitting on another upturned bucket. "I'm starving, and Tyler's been talking about the recipe for months—"

I moan, and Giovanna's head snaps up, eyes narrowing as she looks at me. "Tell me about it. Everything Tyler makes is amazing, but this is their tastiest creation yet."

Giovanna clears her throat and pulls out her phone, tapping on the screen.

Well. I guess that's that. She doesn't want to talk to me and I should leave—

"Sorry," she says. "I need to check my blood sugar so I can take the correct amount of insulin. Carbs can fuck it up like a bitch."

"You don't have to prick your finger anymore?"

She glances up at me, a soft smile slowly spreading on her face. "You remember that?"

I can't help the blush that spreads across my cheeks. Maybe this isn't something I should remember. Maybe it shouldn't have left such a lasting impact.

"No, I don't," she replies, saving me from responding with my awkward truth. "Not as often, at least." She finishes whatever she's doing on her phone, then takes out a smaller, rectangular device. She taps at it for a few seconds before shoving it back into her pocket and picking up her fork. She takes her first bite of cake, her full lips wrapping around the tines of the fork. My mouth is dry, and I can't help but remember everywhere her lips have touched me.

"Oh, god," she moans, and I want to walk into traffic. "You're right, this is *amazing*."

"Told you," I wheeze, gripping my own fork so tightly the metal digs into my flesh.

Giovanna looks up and meets my eyes as she takes another bite of the cake.

I truly would pay good money to drop dead right now.

"This was an interesting way to find out that your last name isn't MacIntyre," she says, arching a full eyebrow.

I laugh nervously. "Yeah, MawMaw and PawPaw are my mom's parents. My last name is Cleary. It was also an interesting way to find out you go by Jo now."

She's silent as she chews and then swallows. "I've always gone by Jo. You're the only person in the world who ever called me Giovanna regularly."

I stare at her. "I could swear I remember your dad calling you Giovanna."

"Right. Because he walked in on me eating you out." She says it so casually, and I choke on my bite of cake as the memory rushes back.

I slap my chest a few times before I stare at her, mouth ajar. I'm not one to be without words, but right now, I'm speechless.

"Oh," I finally say, clearing my throat. "That—um, yeah."

Giovanna seems to sense my discomfort and blushes. "Sorry, that was weird," she pokes at her cake. "Pretend I didn't say anything."

How the actual heck am I supposed to pretend she didn't bring up the fact her face has been between my legs?

"Sure." Agreeing is easier than explaining that to her.

The energy is tense between us as she slowly drags her fork across her plate. "So," she says, breaking the awkward silence.

"So," I echo.

There's so much I want to tell her. About how I cried when my grandparents sold the house that winter because I wouldn't get to see her again. About how I still have the pictures we took on my old digital camera that summer. How photographing her in Port Haven made me fall in love with photography and changed the trajectory of my life. How I finally, *finally* came out. How happy I am to see her again. How much I want to get to know who she is now.

"I should go." It's easier to leave than put myself out there.

For a moment, I think her face falls, but then it's back to that same cool, unaffected expression. "Right, photographer and all that."

I swallow as I get to my feet. "Yeah. Photographer and all that."

"It was nice to see you again, Hunter," she says quietly, eyes glued to her plate.

"It was good to see you, too," I tell her earnestly. "The wedding is beautiful; you should be really proud."

She still doesn't look up, but there *is* a slight upturn to her lips. "Thank you. Take care of yourself, alright?"

"You too," I echo, a strange emptiness filling me as I open the door. Like any other time I've run into a former hookup, this should mean nothing.

But it doesn't *feel* like nothing, and as I close the closet door behind me, images of that summer play in my head like a movie.

Chapter 2

Jo

Four Months Later

Playlist: I Can Do It With A Broken Heart | Taylor Swift

Bodice Ripper Book Club Group Chat

Josh: Don't forget! Book club at my place, 7pm! Decaf Earl Grey is being provided for those of us who don't like caffeine after a certain time. <book emoji>

Jo: jfc, of course you're careful about not consuming caffeine at night

Josh: Yes, Josephine, I'm taking that as a compliment. You know I take my sleep seriously. <sleeping emoji>

Jo: still not my name

Nellie: she definitely didn't mean it as a compliment

Jo: she's right

Jo: i didn't

Josh: Thank you, I'm aware. Anyway, I'm done being harassed, bring whatever food you want. I'll have charcuterie. Bye. <waving emoji>

"Who the *hell* died and made you king of book club?" I yell, slamming my book on the coffee table.

"My *parents*." Josh yells back.

"Josh," Nellie says calmly. "Babes. You can't keep pulling the Bruce Wayne tortured orphan shit when Nic's not here. It's not fair that she doesn't get to see you being a little bitch."

He ignores his best friend's quip, continuing to glare at me with his creepy blue eyes.

"It's not that I don't like Tessa Dare," I explain, "but you've chosen her books for every meeting and it's not fair. There are so many other talented romance authors out there, and you know that. I don't know why, as Nellie said, you're being such a little bitch about it."He scowls at me, stroking his blond beard like a conniving villain. "Fine. What do you want to read next month?"

I cross my arms over my chest and lean back against the couch. "Something gay."

"Yes," Nellie says, pointing at me. "*Yes*. I love gay shit."

Nellie and Josh work together in the English department at NYU, and the three of us started a historical romance book club a few months after he started dating my sister, Nic, last summer.

Josh sighs melodramatically, like he's not also queer. "*Fine*. Cat Sebastian and Alexis Hall have some good rep."

"And Erica Ridley," I add. "Also Adriana Herrera."

Josh's face suddenly brightens. "Oh my god, I forgot she wrote that sapphic one."

"See, lil' guy," I tease. "It's not so bad to give up control once in a while." He blushes. "Oh my god, shut up. I do *not* want to know."

"Good idea," he mutters, rubbing the back of his neck.

"You know what we should read?" Nellie interrupts. "Monster smut."

We stare at her.

Her head pivots between the two of us. "What? It's good!"

"It's a historical romance book club."

"You were literally just telling Josh we need to branch out."

"Right, on authors and representation. The fact that we read historical romances is what makes it a historical romance book club."

Josh pulls out his phone. "Maybe there's a historical monster romance?"

I don't know why I'm surprised that he's able to find not one book, but an entire series. We choose one with a marble marquis, which sounds bizarre, but Nellie and Josh both are thrilled by it. We agree to a sapphic historical romance for June. A pride month win for the gays, which is all of us.

"Hey, Jo?" Josh asks as Nellie and I start getting our things together. "Would you mind staying to help me clean?"

I groan overdramatically and drop my bag to the floor. He rolls his eyes.

Bothering Josh is one of my favorite hobbies. Since he and Nic started dating last summer, he quickly became a cherished member of the family.

I always wanted more brothers, mainly so I can remind them who runs the show. That's how it goes with Steve, Kat's shitty husband. But Josh, unfortunately, is a really good guy. He loves Nic a disgusting amount, and it's annoying how naturally he fits in with the rest of us, like he's always been part of the family.

"Okay, I'm heading out," Nellie says.

"Sounds good. Text me when you get home," Josh answers as he carries empty plates into the kitchen.

Nellie throws her arms around my shoulders. "How are you feeling?" she whispers.

My heart sinks. I've been trying not to think about the fact I was supposed to be getting married this weekend. I hadn't mentioned it to anyone until Nellie and I grabbed impromptu drinks last week after work. I had one too many glasses of merlot and spilled.

My ex-fiancée, Kelsey, and I met at work last year. Our relationship felt like it was out of a romance novel. Girl meets girl at work, girls sneak around at work. Girls have sex and fall head over heels for each other and move in together and get engaged and everything feels *right*. Everything feels like it's exactly how it should be.

Until girl comes home from an event one weekend to an empty bedroom, except for the bed they'd shared and an envelope with her name on it.

And *other* girl goes on to fuck their boss and get promoted to the jilted girl's dream job.

But hey, that's Hollywood.

Except it's definitely not, this is New York, and this isn't a movie. It's my life, and even though she left almost a year ago, I still hate myself for falling so hard, so fast. For going all in and losing myself in the process.

It's been a year of therapy, and throwing myself into my job to prove that I'm capable of *something* at least, even if I'm not capable of maintaining a relationship. Add controlling my chronic illnesses and simply existing into the mix, and you have one burnt out Jo Quinn.

But I want to find myself again. To *feel* like myself again. It's almost like I can't remember what I liked before Kelsey, who I was before her. I'm just a hollow shell of afters.

"Jo?" Nellie prompts, leaning away and searching my face. "You okay?"

I force a smile. "Yeah, sorry. I'm just tired."

"You don't have to lie to me," she says softly. "You don't have to lie to any of us. We're here for you."

"Thanks," I say, averting my gaze. "If I need anything, I'll let you know."

"Hello!" The front door opens and I hear the soft thud of my older sister, Nic, kicking her shoes off in the foyer.

"In the living room, Nicky," I call out just as Nellie speaks again.

"I don't want you to start isolating yourself now that Nic's moving in with Josh."

Ice fills my bloodstream. "What?"

Nellie eyes widen as she takes a step back. "Shit."

"Fuck," Nic agrees from the doorway.

I meet her eyes. "You're moving out, Nicky?" I ask, hating how my voice cracks.

Nellie is saying something, but I can't hear her. I'm staring at my sister, whose deep brown eyes are wide as she stares toward the kitchen. The floorboards creak and I know Josh is back in the room.

I try to breathe in, but it feels like there's a pile of bricks on my chest and my lungs are caving in from the weight.

"We were going to talk to you tonight," Nic mumbles, twisting her hands. "I didn't—Jo, where are you going?"

I don't know where I'm going, all I know is this room is closing in on me and I need to get out.

I love Nic, and I love Josh for her. I love their relationship, and I love that it's at a point where they want to move in together. Nic barely ever sleeps at home anymore, anyway.

It has nothing to do with me.

And yet all my brain can focus on is the fact that Nic wants to leave, too. That I can't maintain a healthy relationship, even with someone who's more like my best friend than my sister. Even she found something better and is leaving me behind.

I know it sounds ridiculous, but my mind has grasped onto this thought process. That Nic isn't moving out because she and Josh love each other and are in a committed, serious relationship, but that she's moving out because-

"Jo!" Josh calls after me. "Come on, let's talk."

I hear him, but it's like his voice is coming through a voice modulator. It sounds distorted and fake.

The only response they get is the slamming of the door.

Chapter 3

Jo

Playlist: Hello | GROUPLOVE

Nic: jojo i'm so sorry

Nic: we were going to talk to you about it when nellie left

Nic: promise

Nic: josh made this dorky ass powerpoint and everything

Nic: please text me back

Nic: i'm sorry

Nic: i love you

Nic: jo?

Delivered.

"So you just left?"

"I just left." It's the day after I walked out of Josh's house and I'm doing virtual therapy on my bed with Alena, my therapist of two years.

"Why?" Alena asks, tilting her head.

I want to tell her to stop psychoanalyzing me, to stop asking questions and trying to get in my head.

But I guess that's what my twenty dollar copay is for.

"I got so anxious," I admit, shame creeping in my body like a thick, humid fog. "It felt like everything was closing in around me, like everyone knew about this big thing that impacts me...except for me."

She nods thoughtfully. "Did it remind you of Kelsey moving out?"

"Yeah. And I know it's not the same thing at all—"

"But your trauma doesn't," she interrupts and I glare at her through my laptop camera.

"I don't *have* trauma," I remind her. She's my therapist, she should know I'm perfectly fine and untraumatized.

She sighs. "Right. Let me know when you're ready to talk about your need to not have trauma."

"That's not fair," I argue.

"You're right. Your refusal to recognize that your relationship and subsequent breakup were traumatic. You're never going to move on and heal, and that isn't fair."

I stare at her, mouth agape. Alena's constantly calling me out on bullshit, but never to this extent.

"That's—I'm fine. Great. Wonderful," I stammer.

Alena's eyes search my face, and I know she doesn't buy it. Luckily, she seems to cut her losses and not push it.

"You mentioned that you skipped work today, too," she continues, glancing down at her notes.

"Yeah, I just needed time to take care of myself after last night."

"How have you done that?" she asks, scribbling something on a notepad.

"Done what?"

"Taken care of yourself."

"I've taken my antidepressants, and I came to therapy…" I trail off.

I've been in therapy and on antidepressants consistently for almost twelve years. Ever since my sophomore year of high school, when my parents dragged me to a psychiatrist who prescribed me Prozac and referred me to a therapist.

I was diagnosed with Major Depressive Disorder, meaning depression isn't just an emotion for me, but a constant part of my life. I've had several depressive episodes throughout my life, times where I'm so tired and low I can't get out of bed for days. Times when I have such low interest in life that I forget to brush my teeth for weeks. Medication and therapy help these episodes happen less frequently, but there's only symptom management, not complete eradication.

"And I'm so glad you didn't cancel your appointment today, Jo," Alena says softly. "I think you need to process this news."

"Yeah. And not rehash the past," I say pointedly.

"You control these sessions. You know that. But do you honestly think your reaction to the news has nothing to do with Kelsey?"

I groan and slump against my headboard. "I guess not."

"Why is that? How does this remind you of what Kelsey did?" she asks, chewing on her pen cap.

"Do we have to do this?"

"No. We don't *have* to do anything. But I think it would be helpful." Alena pauses. "Why are you so averse to talking about it?"

"Because it's selfish. Because I should be so happy for Nic. Josh is so great and she's never been happier and I'm—" I inhale shakily. "And I'm alone. I'm so alone."

I haven't cried since before Kelsey left, but I have that heavy, squeezing feeling that usually precedes tears. The feeling that makes breathing hurt. With one deep breath, I could crumble to pieces.

Then what good would forcing myself to go to therapy today do?

"How did it feel to get the news from Nellie?" Alena asks softly.

I shudder as a chill spreads in my chest. "God, it felt awful, like I was the only one out of the loop. Like reality wasn't real. Maybe I would've taken it better if Nic had been the one to tell me, or if it weren't two days before I was supposed to get married."

She nods thoughtfully. "That's a lot. And I'm so happy you're going to book club and aren't working overtime, but I want to see you heal. You're not going to do it in this protective bubble you've created. It's a valiant attempt to protect yourself from the harm you experienced in the past, but that same bubble is keeping the good stuff from getting to you."

"I feel trapped," I admit. "I know I put myself in this bubble, but I can't figure out how to pop it."

"Baby steps. You coming to therapy and taking your meds is a great start." She taps her pen against her mug. "How are your other symptoms? Any fatigue or struggles with hygiene?"

I shrug. "Not more than usual."

Alena nods thoughtfully. "How do you feel about calling Nic and asking to do a movie night? Tell her you're not ready to talk about it yet, but that you want to spend time with her. "

"That still feels too big. Too hard," I sigh.

"Then go smaller. Text her. Send her a TikTok or a meme."

I try to stay present for the rest of my therapy session, but I can feel myself dissociating in an attempt to not feel the uncomfortable feelings that have been following me around since yesterday.

When we end the session, I do what Alena suggested and text Nic.

Jo: hey

Jo: sorry i freaked

Nic: don't kill me.

Jo: what did you do

Nic: you weren't answering my texts so i called your office and left a message

Jo: ok

Nic: kelsey called me back

Jo: what the fuck?!?!

Jo: she shouldn't have access to my voice-mail

Nic: she said you didn't go to work and i got worried it was because of me and may have mentioned that…

Nic: jo, why didn't you remind me about tomorrow?

Jo: fuck

Nic: we would've waited to bring it up if we knew, promise.

Jo: i know

Nic: if it's too much i can stay at josh's and it's no big deal, but if it's okay with you, i'm feeling a hankering for miss congeniality and ice cream

Jo: ugh

Jo: fine

Nic comes home after work, and we watch Miss Congeniality and eat ice cream.

"When are you moving out?" I finally find the courage to ask halfway through the movie.

Nic swallows her mouthful of ice cream. "I'm not."

I freeze, spoon halfway to my mouth. "What the hell do you mean you're not?"

"Josh and I talked about it and agreed we should wait until our lease is up. It's a short walk and I'll still stay over—"

"Nic, don't be absurd. You two want to move in together, and that's okay. I'll be okay."

Nic digs her spoon into her ice cream. "He's willing to wait longer, and I am too. You're important to us, JoJo."

"It's not that you're moving out, it's that I feel so trapped. I'm still the me Kelsey left, and you're a brand new Nic. You're doing such great things and I've never seen you so happy in your own skin and I—"

My big sister scooches closer to me and puts her head on my shoulder. "I understand," she says softly. "I wish I had remembered it was harder than normal this week for you, we could've made plans to distract you. Do you want to go out tomorrow?"

"I didn't want you to know or make plans. I don't want to be a—"

Her head snaps up and she glares at me. "Don't you dare say burden."

I shut my mouth.

"You're *not*, JoJo. You're in pain and that makes you a human, not a burden."

"I'm so happy you and Josh found each other," I whisper, trying to swallow the lump that's grown in my throat. "I just feel so alone. And I don't know how I'll afford rent when you move out."

Nic glares at me again. "You really thought I'd leave you high and dry like that? I'm insulted."

Nic may be evolving, but she's still the no-bullshit menace I grew up with.

"Anyway, do you remember Hunter Cleary? She's Tyler's friend from college and was the photographer at the wedding. The McIntyres' granddaughter, the one that spent that summer with them when we were teenagers? She's looking for a place to live, and obviously it's up to you, but Nellie and Tyler suggested it. They think it would be a good match."

I stare at her, slowly closing my mouth after it drops open. Luckily, Nic is too focused on digging into her marshmallow swirl to notice.

My run-in with Hunter at the wedding had been unexpected and uncomfortable. She couldn't get out of the broom closet fast enough when I'd finally mustered up the courage to talk to her.

Plus, she'd looked so pretty and poised and I probably looked like the elusive troll that lives under the Brooklyn Bridge.

Nic doesn't know we hooked up that entire summer. No one, except my dad, knows. Poor guy walked in on us having sex and then dragged us to Planned Parenthood to get tested for STIs and have an employee talk to us about safe sex practices. I wasn't out at the time, and I was so scared he would out me. My family is relatively religious, and though half of us are out as queer *now*, I was the first one to officially come out that fall.

Dad never told anyone about Hunter and I. He did what he thought was right to make sure I was safe, and that's it. My parents aren't perfect by any means, but I'm grateful for how my dad handled that particular situation.

"I have Hunter's number, and she's available this weekend to see the place." Nic's voice is hopeful, and god. I want her to be happy so much. I want *me* to be happy, and I know holding her back from living with Josh isn't going to make me any happier.

I sigh. "Fine."

Chapter 4

Hunter

Playlist: Better Angels | Marcus Mumford

Hunter: hey jo, it's hunter cleary. nic gave me your number so we could set up a time for me to stop by your apartment, i hope that's okay.

Jo: thank goodness you told me who it was, i'd never have guessed with you calling me jo.

Hunter: haha, i figured since that's what you go by, it makes more sense for me to call you that. is that okay?

Jo: you calling me giovanna doesn't bother me, but neither does you calling me jo.

Hunter: hmmm okay. maybe i'll call you jo for now and then BAM when you least expect it, i'll drop a surprise giovanna.

Jo: …ok.

Hunter: umm anyway, does tomorrow at like 6pm work for me to stop by to see if it'll work out?

Jo: can you do saturday or sunday?

Hunter: i have a wedding i'm shooting on saturday, and a super extra baptism party on sunday. maybe next week.

Jo: no let's just get it over with. tomorrow at 6pm is fine.

Hunter: okay, great! I'll see you then! <smiling emoji>

Seen at 9:24pm.

"Are there any rules about pets?" I ask Giovanna as we stand in her kitchen. I'd shown up at her door at six on the dot, after watching the clock all day to make sure I'd be on time, and she gave me the quickest apartment tour known to man. It's only 6:04 and I feel like I've already overstayed my welcome.

She eyes me. She's barely looked at me since opening the door, so this honestly doesn't feel as awful as I think it should. "Nic didn't mention you have a pet."

"Oh, I don't," I clarify. "Yet. I want one, though."

She thinks for a moment. "Our neighbor has a dog and two cats, so I guess not. I'm not a big animal person, but as long as you take care of it and shit, I guess it's whatever."

I nod, taking it as close to assent I'll get from her. "Cool, thanks. One last question."

"Shoot."

"Do you not want me to move in? I need you to be honest with me."

That gets her attention, and she looks up at me, startled. "What makes you think I don't want you to move in? I don't care."

"I don't mean to pitch a fit, but you're acting very much like you don't want me to move in. If that's the case, say the word and I'll be out of your hair."

"Fuck, I'm sorry. It's not you—I'm having a shit day. I was supposed to be getting married today."

She says it as casually as she mentioned oral sex at the wedding, but this is somehow even more jarring.

"I beg your pardon?" I wheeze.

"Yeah. Um, we ended things like a year ago but it's still hard, you know?" She tries to smile, but her eyes are full of sadness.

Before I can stop myself, my arms are around Giovanna's shoulders, squeezing her tight. "God, I'm so sorry."

She awkwardly pats my back. "It's okay."

"No, it's not. It sucks."

I feel her body relax, little by little, against mine. I try not to think about how soft her breasts are pressed against mine, how she smells like peonies and champagne. "You're right, it sucks."

I hug her until she seems to remember that she wants to be aloof and pulls away. "I uh, I actually really needed that," she admits sheepishly. "Thanks."

"Anytime. Literally, if I'm your roommate."

There it is, a ghost of the smile she teased me with at the wedding. I vow to myself that when I move in, *if* I move in, I'm getting as many of those smiles as possible. I'll put a penny in a jar every time she smiles at me and once I have a hundred dollars, I'll—*fuck. What can you buy for a hundred dollars in New York?* In Georgia I could treat her to a night out, but in Brooklyn, I don't know, maybe I could swing a slice of pizza for us to share.

"Do you want to talk about it?" I ask, prepared for her to refuse and tell me it's none of my business.

Giovanna surprises me yet again. "No. But maybe I need to." She lifts her eyes to meet mine and be still my heart, I'd forgotten how they're swirls of burnt caramel, a deep Christmas green, and warm milk chocolate.

I lean my elbows on the counter and rest my chin in my hands. "I'm listening."

"I need wine for this. Do you like merlot?" She walks to the refrigerator and opens the door, peering inside.

"Do you have moscato?" I ask.

She glances over the refrigerator door at me. "Hun, that's basically juice, not wine."

Hun. My heart pitter patters at the nickname she'd called me so often all those summers ago. The name she'd moan when I licked her inner thigh—

"Merlot's fine," I wheeze, shaking off the sudden feelings of want I have for her.

Focus, Hunter. I mentally admonish myself. *Giovanna is about to be your roommate. And your friend if you don't fuck it up. Gay people can just be friends even if they fucked twelve years ago.*

Jo pours two glasses of wine, and we make our way to the living room. We sit on a dark green velvet couch that reminds me of the green flecks in her eyes. I hope she'll keep it when I move in. If I move in.

Then, she pours out her heart as abundantly as she poured the wine. She talks about her ex-fiancée, Kelsey, and how blindsided she'd felt when she moved out, leaving only a note on Jo's dresser. Kelsey called their vendors to cancel the wedding, and left Jo to inform their guests. Then Kelsey was promoted at work when Jo was more qualified. Finally, as the cherry on top of a shit-sundae, Kelsey announced a relationship with their boss just days after the promotion.

It all happens so fast, and before I know it, I'm on my second glass of wine.

"You should curse Kelsey out. Or set her on fire," I tell Giovanna, noticing a slight slur to my words. *Oops.*

She doesn't look at me. "I can't." "Why not?"

"I just...I can't."

"Fine. Then you should quit and give them hell and tell them–"

"Tell them what? Tell them they suck and then what? I'm out of a job and—" she inhales shakily. "It doesn't make anything better."

"Is it a healthy work environment?"

She barks out a laugh. "Oh, absolutely not. It's awful, especially now. I never wanted to work there long term, anyway."

"You didn't?" She shakes her head. "What do you want to do?"

"Same thing I'm doing now, but I want to move back to my hometown. Open my own firm, one that plans with and for the queer community. Port Haven has, surprisingly, become quite inclusive and accepting of the LGBTQIA+ community nowadays. More and more affirming organizations and queer couples are popping up in the area, with a need for event coordination. I want to be the one to provide that service in my hometown."

She pauses and blushes, looking down at the empty wine glass in her hand. "I know it's silly. I don't have the money to open my own firm—"

"Yet," I interrupt.

She looks up at me again. "What?"

"You don't have the money to open your own firm *yet*. Just because it isn't possible right this very second doesn't mean that it won't ever be. I have faith in you, Giovanna."

She blinks at me, stunned. "You do?"

Aw, heck. Maybe I went too far. Maybe I scared her and now I'll have to look for housing again.

"That means a lot, Hun." She looks down at her wine glass and trails her index finger around the edge. "You're the first person I've said that out loud to, you know. I've thought about it, dreamed about it, but it always feels both too big and too inconsequential to say out loud. Who knew all I needed was two glasses of merlot and a night with my potential roommate?"

"Potential roommate, huh?" I tease.

"If you want to move in, I'm down. I was sort of worried it would be weird, with our history and whatnot, but it isn't. It almost feels like we stayed friends and never lost touch." She takes another sip of wine.

Well, that makes one of us. Unless she means we stayed friends and I realized twelve years later that I still find her incredibly beautiful and can't help but wonder if her lips were as soft as they once were—

Hunter Lillian Cleary. Stop lusting over your future roommate, you horndog.

At least my inner voice is able to keep me in check. Sort of.

"I'm in," I blurt out, before I can overthink it.

Maybe this is one of those situations where I *should* overthink it.

Chapter 5

Jo

Playlist: Port of Call | Beirut

It takes exactly two weeks for Nic to pack and be ready to move out. On moving day, she and Josh come over after work, Nellie and Tyler joining us later that night to help. We ordered pizza and packed up every trace of my sister from the apartment. All her knick-knacks and the touches that made this apartment feel like *ours* for the past few years are packed into boxes and labeled. We load up the U-Haul, Nic gives me a squeezing hug, and then she's gone.

All I can think about is the last time I felt this lonely in this apartment. The last time it was so quiet I could hear the pitter-patter of my upstairs neighbors' dog's paws on the floor.

I know I'm not losing Nic, but I *am* losing the relationship that we had as roommates, the relationship we cultivated by sharing space, just the two of us.

I wake the next morning to knocking on the front door. When I shuffle through the apartment and open the door, I find Hunter standing on the rainbow doormat holding a plastic container and wearing an obnoxiously big smile.

"Mornin', roomie!" she says, her voice far too chipper for 7:44 am, and I fight the urge to slam the door in her face.

"Fhgbajrda," I grumble back, holding the door open so she can get in. "Let me get your keys so I can go back to sleep."

Hunter pouts. Like sticking out her lower lip, *pouts*. "You're not going to help me move in?"

"I wasn't planning on it. Do you need me to?"

"I don't *need* you to, but I thought it would be some good roomie bonding time!"

I stare at her. "I've seen you naked, Hunter. I think we're plenty bonded."

The plastic container falls to the ground as her mouth drops open in shock.

And I feel bad, so of course I end up helping her move in.

A few weeks later, and there's a record player set up in the living room, with vinyls of every genre and generation. Taylor Swift, Fleetwood Mac, The Four Seasons, Olivia Rodrigo, Dolly Parton...speaking of Dolly Parton, there's a cross-stitched pop-art pillow with her face that smiles at me now from the couch. It's a little disturbing.

Hunter set up her computer in the spare room, which I've always used as a library, to utilize as a home office. There's a large amount of glittery and pink mugs scattered around the kitchen, as well as magnets from cities all over the American south stuck to the refrigerator. My personal favorite is the one from Savannah that proudly declares the city's apparent support of Dolly Parton for US president.

It's a little disconcerting how quickly she's comfortable in the apartment. I haven't adjusted to the changes as quickly as her.

At first, things seemed like they were fine, but lately, she's been leaving her dishes in the sink for days at a time. She forgets her keys, and one morning, I woke up to find a spoiled gallon of milk that she'd left on the counter overnight.

One Tuesday after work, I come home to Hunter sitting on the ground outside the door, a sheepish smile on her face.

"Do you have a keychain you could use or something? So you don't lose your keys?" I ask, turning the key in the lock.

She shrugs as she gets to her feet. "Nah, they'll turn up."

My eye twitches. "I think I have a lanyard or something you can use if that would be helpful."

She looks at me questioningly as I push open the door. "Helpful for what?"

"Helpful for keeping track of your keys."

Hunter's face falls in such a dramatic way that, before I saw it, I thought it was only an expression that could be captured in animation.

"Oh." Her voice is quiet and eyes are focused on the floor. "Sorry. Didn't think about how it must inconvenience you. The lanyard might be helpful."

I stare at her as she shuffles into the apartment. "What just happened? Did I say something wrong?"

I'm so confused. Her sunshine is nowhere to be found, and instead it feels like there's a dark, heavy cloud covering her beams of light.

She continues down the hallway towards her room without looking back at me. "I'm fine."

"Okay, listen." I close the door and follow her. "I'm one of eight children and only date women. You can't possibly think I'm going to fall for the 'I'm fine' bullshit you're trying to pull—"

Hunter sniffs loudly and looks up at me, eyes watery, and I freeze.

I awkwardly pat her shoulder. "Lighten up, buttercup."

She bursts into tears.

I retract my hand like I've been burned. "Oh god, oh shit, oh god, what do I do?" I ask.

I've never been especially good at physical touch or comfort, except with Nic. Maybe it's both our prickliness canceling each other out, but otherwise, I'm not good at saying the right things, at giving people what they need.

"Hunter," I hiss, wringing my hands. "Hunter, what do I do?"

The only answer I get is continued sobs into her hands.

What would Hunter do?

Suddenly, I find myself taking three steps forward and wrapping my arms around her, the same way she did for me the night she visited the apartment.

I feel her stiffen for a moment, but then her arms wrap around my middle and she softens into the hug.

"I'm sorry I said the wrong thing," I tell her quietly, after letting her cry for a few minutes. She smells like magnolia and the air right after it rains, fresh and soft.

She sniffs. "I'm sorry that I'm such a big baby," she murmurs, her breath hot against my neck. I can't control the shiver that wracks my body.

"You can talk to me, too, you know. I don't want to make you cry."

Hunter pulls away and wipes at her eyes with her hands. "I'm sorry. I know I'm a shitty roommate. I'm trying to be better but it's always so hard when getting used to a new environment. Nothing feels normal yet. I still feel like I'm out of place, just a fish out of water flopping around."

That's surprising. From my vantage point, Hunter seems like she's adjusted to the move and new space effortlessly.

"I have ADHD," she continues. "I was diagnosed a year after we met, which was pretty lucky. Way too many women go under the radar for way too long."

"Izzy and Leo have ADHD," I blurt out. "My youngest sib-lings."

She meets my eyes, her own puffy and red-rimmed. "Really? It's comforting to know you have experience with it. Maybe I should have told you sooner, but I like to think I have it under control. I mean, I own my own business." She picks at her cuticles, and I remember her doing that as a teenager too. The nights we spent at the beach and she'd open up about being scared to ever come out, picking at her nail beds until she'd bleed.

"But it's been hard lately. My brain feels like it's being pulled in ten-billion different directions but I don't know where any of those directions lead to." She takes a deep breath. "So I...I don't know. I try to push back and block out the noise and obviously that's not working and it's impacting you as well as me, and I'm really sorry."

I feel awful. I hadn't realized that Hunter has ADHD, but it makes so much sense. I should have tried to be understanding, tried to work with her brain instead of just calling her out. I know what it's like to have a brain that functions differently than what's considered the norm.

"I didn't mean to be an asshole. I was frustrated you kept losing your keys and I should have gotten all the facts before saying anything."

"Another part of ADHD that nobody really talks about is the rejection sensitivity and emotional dysregulation that comes along with it. Sometimes it's debilitating. Like when you offered to help me with my keys, you weren't rejecting me or doing anything cruel. But my brain still hyperfocused on the fact I was fucking up. That I wasn't good enough."

Hunter's voice grows quieter with each word until it's barely above a whisper, her eyes fixated on her hands. "Criticism is especially hard for me, and that doesn't mean I should be exempt from criticism or anything like that...it's just something I'm constantly working on."

I think about the time when, that summer, Hunter had cried because her friends had gone to a movie she'd been excited to see without her. I didn't understand, considering she wasn't home for the summer. But she had been devastated, and said it felt like they'd taken a knife to her heart. I wonder if she'd felt like she was overreacting then, and couldn't figure out why she felt this way. After all, she wasn't diagnosed yet.

"I'm sorry," I say honestly. "That sounds difficult."

"It is, but it's not always a negative thing, you know? I'm me because of ADHD, not in spite of it. But it for sure makes things more difficult. Because my brain sucks at making dopamine, organization and being on time are uphill battles. It's embarrassing; it always seems easy for everyone else."

"I have Major Depressive Disorder, so my brain sucks at making serotonin." I'm not sure why I'm telling her this, but I want to. I can see how harshly she's judging herself and I want her to know I'm not. "And my Type 1 Diabetes means my pancreas sucks at making insulin. I have to take medication to help those organs do things that seem easy for everyone else, too. I'm not trying to invalidate your experience...but I can relate to the way you feel."

She exhales heavily, staring down as she picks at her sparkly pink nail polish. "I try so hard. And then I forget to try because I'm exhausted from trying all the time. God, that probably sounds ridiculous..."

"It doesn't," I assure her. "I understand."

She looks up again, eyes puffy and soft. "I don't like that." I stare at her, not understanding. "I don't like that you understand what it's like to judge yourself too harshly."

"Ah. I think everyone does, in one way or another."

"I still don't like it."

We sit in silence for a beat, and though it's awkward, it reminds me of the quiet hours spent together that summer—the touches, the glances, the knowing smiles.

Why the fuck am I longing for that? Why do I want her to look at me with that same twinkle in her eye that was there just before she'd kiss me?

I'll unpack that with Alena another day.

"Is there anything I can do to make things easier?" I ask instead.

She's still picking at her nails. I want to take her hands in mine, rub my thumbs over her skin and tell her it's okay to feel however she's feeling.

"If I forget to do something, could you remind me? Maybe we can make up a chore chart or routine or something?"

I smile softly at her. "Yeah. I'm happy to do that. It's gonna work out, Hunter. You're not a bad person, or a bad roommate, and we'll figure out a way to make things easier."

She smiles at me, and her mouth is all wobbly and crooked, lips puffy and the tip of her nose red.

"Thank you," she says, lowering her hands. "You didn't have to be so nice, but I appreciate that you were."

Maybe I'm a shitty person for what I say next, but at least I can acknowledge it.

"I've seen your tits, Hun. I can't not be nice to you."

Her responding blush and gasp make it all worth it.

"Oh my *god*," she whines. "You gotta stop that."

"Stop what?" I ask innocently.

"You know what."

"Do not."

She narrows her eyes. "I know what you're doing, Giovanna Quinn. Don't forget that I've seen you just as naked." Her eyes trail down my body and I awkwardly shift. "I remember how your eyes darkened whenever you were turned on, and that one freckle on your inner thigh..."

Oh, god. Abort mission, I repeat, abort mission.

"I remember what you taste like when—"

"Okay!" I interrupt, taking a step back from her. "I get it. I played dirty."

She smirks. "You always were a dirty girl."

I slap my hands over my face. "I get it. I'm sorry. I'll stop."

She chuckles and takes two steps toward me, placing a hand on my shoulder as she presses a kiss to my cheek. "Thanks, Jo," she whispers, her warm breath tickling my ear.

And then, as suddenly and chaotically as she reappeared in my life, she's gone, her bedroom door closing as I stare in bewilderment.

Chapter 6

Hunter

Playlist: Girls Like Girls | Hayley Kiyoko

I tried to be quiet when I made myself come last night. I tried to be quiet as images of Giovanna Quinn kissing her way up my thighs ran rampant in my mind.

I tried to be quiet when I came all over my favorite vibrator—a hot pink rabbit that's lasted since college—biting the pillow in an attempt to muffle my moans.

I didn't even need to use 4Play, my go-to audio erotica app. I tried a morning oral audio by Clementine, a best friend's brother audio by Sky , even a rough enemies to lovers audio by Talia.

None of it was necessary—my imagination was better. So I tried to be quiet while I was overwhelmed with sensation, imagining Giovanna leaning over me, guiding me. I tried to be quiet because otherwise, that would make for an awkward morning: Me walking into the kitchen when Jo's drinking her tea. Making eye contact as she smiles, that annoying as hell, knowing smile. She'd know somehow, I just know it.

Instead, what happens is somehow worse.

I'm awoken at 4:54 by a blaring fire alarm.

"Dagnabbit," I mutter, swinging my legs over the edge of the bed and getting to my feet.

There's a violent banging on my door moments later. "Hunter!" Jo hollers. "Get out!"

I try to shoo away the butterflies I get from the fact she doesn't want me to burn to death.

I grab my robe off its hook on the closet door, pulling it on over my shoulders and tying a bow at my waist before opening the door.

Jo's dark waves are piled messily on top of her head in the most enticing bun. She wears an oversized t-shirt with photos of Alice Cullen on it, and green plaid boxers that somehow don't hide her curves.

I open my mouth to inquire about her garment of choice but before I can, she's dissolved into hysterical laughter. The sound pops in the air like champagne bubbles, making me feel all warm and fuzzy.

I force myself to scowl and fold my arms across my chest, the movement causing Jo's bubbles of laughter to stop. "What are you laughing at?"

"What *aren't* I laughing at?" she asks, smirking.

"If I die a fiery death, I'll sue."

"Just...tell me where you got the robe, at least. You look like Martha May Whovier from *The Grinch*."

"No need for flattery, Giovanna," I say breezily, reaching out and wrapping my fingers around her wrist as I squeeze past her in the doorway. I try not to think of how close our faces are, how our bodies are pressed together, curves on curves and soft on soft. "If we survive this I'll send you the link so we can be twins."

Jo chuckles to herself the entire time it takes for us to exit the building.

I, heroically, do not slap her.

It's still pretty chilly out, so while Jo shivers and thumbs through a well-worn paperback, I'm toasty, grinning to myself as I scroll through Taylor Swift thirst TikToks to distract myself from the alarms. It feels like the firefighters are taking *forever* in the building, and our neighbors are grumbling.

"Is that...Taylor Swift?" Jo asks, leaning over to look at my phone screen.

"Mmhmm."

I watch out of the corner of my eye as Jo raises an eyebrow appraisingly. "Damn. I didn't realize she was hot."

"Aren't you gay? She's a damn babe." Jo hums to herself, and looks back down at the book in her hand. "What are you reading?"

She lifts the book so I can see the cover better. "Beverly Jenkins."

"It's a romance?" I ask, even though it is obviously a romance. The cover model's six pack puts Henry Cavill's to shame.

"Mmhmm. Historical."

"I like that Netflix show, Bridgerton, but I'm not a big reader."

"But you don't get the full experience without reading the books!"

I stare at her. "Wow, you're one of *those* readers."

"Oh god, that was obnoxious, wasn't it?" Giovanna brings the book up to her face and hides in it.

It's quite possibly the most endearing thing I've ever seen.

"Extremely obnoxious." I fight back a smile. "Unbelievably gatekeepy gamer bro of you."

She gasps dramatically and lowers the book just enough that I can see her eyes. "You take that back!"

I shrug. "Sorry, can't. Mama didn't raise no liar."

She smiles at me, and I make a mental note to put another penny in my Giovanna Quinn's Smiles Fund.

"I'm sorry, it's just true. Bridgerton as a show is great, but reading it gives you a deeper experience of the story."

"Hmm, interesting." I mull it over.

"You can borrow any of my historical romances, as long as you're not violent towards them. Blonde literacy is important to me." She's wearing a shit eating grin now and hell, I'm putting aside a whole dollar for that one.

I gasp theatrically and thwack her on the arm with the sleeve of my robe. "You are such a little shit, Giovanna Quinn!"

"Um, I'm taller than you," she reminds me, like we're not standing next to each other.

"Being a little shit has nothing to do with your height and you know it."

She smirks at me and I swear, every small upturn of that pretty mouth of hers makes my heart pitter-patter.

Finally, around 6:15, we're given the clear, and are able to return to the apartment. I'd normally go back to sleep, but being with Giovanna has me wired, and she has to get ready for work soon.

"How do you like your eggs?" Jo asks, getting a frying pan from a cabinet.

"Scrambled with cheese," I tell her, hopping onto a bar stool. "And Sriracha."

She gives me a look. "What do you think this is, Queenie's?"

I gasp. "Oh my god, I forgot about Queenie's."

Queenie's was the diner in Port Haven that Giovanna's family, and my grandparents, frequented. That summer, we'd grab milkshakes and sweet potato fries late at night and sit giggling at the sea wall.

"The food is as delicious now as it was then." She opens the refrigerator and pulls out a carton of eggs, a bag of shredded cheese, and a bottle of Sriracha. I bite my lip, fighting back a smile. "Their sweet potato fries have gotten even better, if you can believe it."

"I can't." I watch her hands as she cracks the eggs, the motion of her wrist as she scrambles them. They're such lovely, talented hands—

"You should come back to Port Haven with me some time. We could get root beer floats and sweet potato fries and—"

"Strawberry milkshakes," I correct, my face reddening when she lifts her eyes to meet mine. "Sweet potato fries went best with strawberry milkshakes."

"You remember that?" Her voice is quiet.

"I know it's probably pathetic, but I think I remember everything about that summer." I feel foolish admitting how much of her had stayed with me, shaped me.

Her smile is slow to build, a whisper in the dark. It's my favorite Giovanna Quinn smile yet, and I want to call the whole mission quits after this, because a thousand of her other smiles don't measure up to this one.

"I do too, for what it's worth." She looks back to the stovetop and sprinkles shredded cheese into the pan.

Little does she know it's worth everything.

That Summer
Jo

"Miss Jo, here's your milkshake and fries." Derek, my favorite waiter at Queenie's, slides my order across the table to me.

I force a smile at him. "Thanks, D."

I pick up a sweet potato fry, dip it into the strawberry milkshake, and pop it into my mouth before repeating the actions. Sometimes, I hate summer. All of my siblings are home and loud and I just want to stay in bed and hide, but they make it impossible. When I need to get away I come to Queenie's alone, using my dogsitting money to buy some peace and quiet. Quiet compared to my family's home.

"That looks bizarre."

My neck snaps up at a southern drawl from above me, making eye contact with clear blue eyes framed by the darkest, thickest eyelashes known to man. She's wearing a pink sports bra and shorts, and her skin is shimmering from a light sheen of sweat.

I want to lick it off.

"Sorry," she says, keeping her eyes on mine. "I shouldn't yuck your yum."

I blink at her.

"I'm Hunter? We met after church yesterday?" she says, shifting her weight between her feet.

I know who she is. That's exactly why I don't know what to say. I'm able to manage a nod in response.

"Do you...do you mind if I sit?" she asks, motioning to the empty booth across from me.

I shake my head, words still not coming to me.

She sits and folds her hands in front of her as she leans forward. "So," she asks seriously. "What's good here? Besides that atrocity, of course."

"I thought you shouldn't yuck my yum." Oh, now I find my words. And they're ridiculous.

Hunter's eyes brighten and she straightens her back, clapping her hands with delight. "She does speak!"

Wordlessly I push my food and milkshake across the table. She looks at me dubiously. "Try it," I encourage, motioning my head towards the plate. "That's the best Queenie's has to offer."

She looks doubtfully at the food, but picks up a fry, and dips it in the milkshake. She pops it in her mouth and chews, her eyes widening as she swallows.

I lean back in the booth and cross my arms with a smirk. "I don't want to say I told you so, but..."

"Oh, hush. That's exactly what you want to do." She picks up another french fry, and repeats the dip before eating it again. "God, you're a genius. This is so yummy."

I wave to Derek. "Hey D? Think you can bring us another milkshake and side of fries?"

Chapter 7

Jo

Playlist: What Was I Made for | Billie Eilish

Quiblings Group Chat

Kat: Happy birthday, Nic! <celebration emoji>

Nic: thanks kat!

Leo: nic's birthday was like two weeks ago

Kat: Haha, very funny. I know it's April 13th.

Jo: it's 100% march 25th

Kat: then why isn't she the one correcting me?

Ren: probably because she's trying this thing where she's nice to us now.

Nic: aww! you noticed!

Nic: and yeah my birthday was the twenty fifth, i just didn't want to be an asshole.

Kat: Does this mean I used the wrong date for my password?

Nic: i guess?

Izzy: hey kat when's my birthday.

Kat: Same day as Leo's.

Millie: someone buy this woman a calendar with all of our birthdays. We're so inconsequential to her that she can't be bothered to remember.

Kat: First of all, not what I said. Second, there are seven of you to keep track of.

Alex: aw, i miss you guys sometimes.

Alex: i especially feel it when you all gang up on kat.

Kat: I tried, okay? Sorry I'm not perfect.

Nic: i really appreciate the sentiment kat

Jo: okay nic moves in with josh and becomes nice this is fucking bizarre

Nic: it's that good good dick every night.

Ren: can you not?

Leo: hey totally unrelated but do you think josh would be okay with stelly and i staying over a few nights??? <prayer hands emoji>

Alex: josh has big dick energy, am i right?

Millie: nic.

Millie: NO.

Nic: let's just say i can barely walk today
<smirking emoji>

Millie: what the FUCK did i just say???!

Ren: <vomiting emoji>

"Jo? Do you mind joining me in Becky's office?" Kelsey asks, sticking her head into my office.

Yes, that Kelsey.

I sigh, but don't look up at her, instead continuing my email to the DJ for the event I'm coordinating next weekend. Once again, I'm working through lunch, but I'm planning on eating soon. "What's up?"

I can hear her roll her eyes, somehow. "Jesus. Can you do what I ask for once? I know you're dealing with shit but there's no reason—"

I stand up with enough force that my desk chair crashes into the wall behind me. "I'm coming." My teeth and fists are clenched, and I hate how much she's able to still get under my skin, how perfectly her criticism still hits the target.

I follow her into Becky's office, trying to breathe deeply like the YouTube yoga gurus always say. I've been trying to force myself to like yoga. It hasn't worked. Maybe because I haven't found an

"Everyday Flow for When You Still Have To Work With Your Ex-fiancée" video.

"Ah, Jo, come in," Becky greets me, lowering her glasses.

"Hey, baby," Kelsey coos, walking behind the desk and bending down to press a kiss to her girlfriend's cheek.

I expect my Pulitzer Prize for not vomiting on my boss's office floor any day now.

"Hi, Becky," I say stiffly, clenching and unclenching my fists. "Kelsey said you wanted to see me?"

Becky looks up at Kelsey as she straightens. "Did you tell her?"

My ex shakes her head in response. "No, I wanted to tell her together."

My eyes dart between the two of them. "Tell me what?"

Kelsey bites her lip, and then squeals, lifting up her left hand and wiggling her fingers.

On her ring finger sits a big ass, princess cut diamond ring.

What.

The.

Fuck.

"We're engaged!" Becky exclaims as she gets to her feet, wrapping her arm around Kelsey's shoulder.

"You're engaged," I echo back, hoping my voice sounds more excited than I feel. The reality is I feel numb, empty. "You wanted to see me to tell me...you're engaged?"

"Um, thank you!" Kelsey says, rolling her eyes at me. "But no, that's not the *only* reason we wanted to see you."

"Jo, you know what an asset you are to Coffey & Co., don't you?" Becky asks, eyes still on her girlfriend.

No, her fiancée.

What is the correct answer to a question like that? 'Yes' sounds cocky. 'No' sounds insecure. A simple, "Thanks," is what I settle on.

"Kelsey and I want to be married by the end of the summer. And while the wedding is of course the main focus, we want several celebrations leading up to it. And I think you know you're the only one we can trust with such complex, important events celebrating our love."

I feel lightheaded.

"We of course would pay you a generous flat fee for everything. One hundred grand. That's around what you make in a year, isn't it? And you'd still be paid your regular salary in addition, of course. Though your regular workload would be reduced so you'd be able to prioritize our events. We'll delegate any conflicting events to other coordinators and planners…"

"You're asking me to plan your wedding?" I interrupt.

"Of course, Jo!" Kelsey says it like it's a good thing.

What sin did I commit to earn this special brand of hell?

"Do you think that's appropriate, considering our past…relationship?" I look at Kelsey, whose expression doesn't change.

"Do you think a past fling would impact your ability to perform your job?" Kelsey asks, tilting her head to the side. Her face is innocent, like she didn't verbally slap me across the face.

Kelsey and I had been engaged. For several months. We hadn't disclosed it at work, but it had been real. I still have the ring I got for her, the ring she'd left atop a note when she blindsided me by moving out.

I swallow hard. "No, that…it won't impact anything. I have a girlfriend, anyway."

Becky gasps and clasps her hands together excitedly. "Jo, really? That's wonderful. You deserve someone wonderful."

"Thank you, it's serious," I stammer. "We are deeply, deeply in love."

Maybe it makes me a bad person, but I like how taken aback Kelsey looks. Like I caught her off guard, the same way she caught me off guard. When she lifts her eyes, I avoid her gaze, intently staring at my Nonna's garnet ring on my pinkie. Whenever I wear it, I think about how much she'd hate that her openly gay granddaughter wears her beloved family heirloom.

"What's her name?" Kelsey asks, voice even.

"Hunter. We met through mutual friends."

If I'm going to lie, I may as well use partial truths. Hunter did move in with me, and we did run into each other because of mutual friends. She is, however, most definitely not my girlfriend.

"I'm so happy for you, Jo." I'm not able to label the tone of Kelsey's voice. It's not congratulatory, I know that much.

I force myself to meet her gaze. "Thank you."

"It's nice to see you serious about someone."

It feels like my heart is being put through a wringer, followed by a blender. It's bloody and gory and painful as hell. And she's just so casual about the fact she's pummeling a vital organ.

"So, you want me to plan your wedding?" I reiterate, looking back down at Nonna's ring. Next to it sits a Claddagh my Granny got me from Ireland for my sixteenth birthday. On my middle finger is a simple twisted band. I try to focus on these details, rather than what's happening in this room.

"Of course, Jo." I can hear Kelsey's smile in her voice. "Who else would we trust with our special day?"

I squeeze my eyes closed and inhale shakily. *Their* special day. It was supposed to be *ours*. But apparently all we were was a fling.

"I'll consider it," I say, forcing my eyes open and meeting Becky's. "*If* the salary increases by twenty percent." I don't know where the gall comes from, but I do know that I deserve to be paid more for going through this bullshit. "Considering that you're hiring me because of my skill set, I think we can agree that what I'm asking for is more than fair."

They look at each other. I fight the urge to scream, and send them every invoice from every session I've ever had with Alena. I can tell Kelsey isn't happy with my demands, but honestly? I'm not happy with her. Period.

"Of course, Jo," Becky finally says, looking at me. "We're more than happy to meet your request."

"Great." My voice wavers, and I lower my gaze. "I'm not feeling so great, I should go."

Kelsey sighs. "Is it your blood sugar again? You can be so careless with that."

My stomach contorts. "Careless. Yes. Me. Right. Um, thank you for the opportunity, and I'll look over the contract when I receive it."

I walk as quickly as I can out of Becky's office, making a quick pit stop in my own to grab a bottle of honey from my desk drawer. When I get to the unisex bathroom, I shut and lock the bathroom door, then slowly slide down it to the ground. My body shakes as I flip the lid of the honey bottle and lift it to my lips. The sticky sweetness is a stark contrast to the way I feel.

I want to cry, to have some outlet for this all-consuming pain I feel. But I can't seem to cry, and I don't understand why.

Why did Kelsey agree to marry me? Why did she waste her time on me if I mean so little to her? If I'm so unimportant, why did she make me believe I meant something to her?

I've truly never felt so small, so worthless and unlovable in my entire life, and I hate that someone who couldn't care less has this much power over me.

I just want to be loved the way Josh loves Nic. The way Nic loves Josh, and Tyler and Nellie love each other. The way my parents love each other.

The way I loved Kelsey.

But I feel so empty, so lost. Any strength I'd felt before is gone, and I feel like a hollow shell being whipped around by a merciless ocean.

Except I'm me. The ocean is my life.

And I feel like I'm drowning.

Chapter 8

Hunter

Playlist: Red Wine Supernova | Chappell Roan

Giovanna Quinn has somehow proven to me that she can further ruin my life. Who does she think she is, letting her floral scent linger in her home long after she left for work?

And worse still, introducing me to historical romances?

She was right, dammit. *The Viscount Who Loves Me* is as good as Bridgerton Season 2, if not better. I have three batches of images from a wedding this weekend to edit. But I've been hanging out pants-less in the living room while I kick my feet and squeal at Kate and Anthony's banter.

I hope my client, a bride claiming to be Paris Hilton's third cousin, understands why her photos are late.

The room grows quiet as the current Taylor Swift album comes to an end, the final notes echoing in the room. This time, I don't get back up to start it again, or put on another record.

Because right now, it's getting *juicy*.

I'm on my stomach on the couch, and slide my hand under my belly, tracing the waistband of my cotton thong with my fingertips. My vibrator is in my room, and I could easily move there...but I don't want to. I want to use my fingers and imagine that Jo's touching me the way this viscount is touching his wife.

So I do.

I slip my fingers beneath the fabric and shiver as my thumb grazes my clit. Has Jo done this very same thing while reading a scene like this? Maybe this exact book, on this very couch?

The thought makes me squeeze my thighs together, trapping my hand between them as my hips rock. I grind my center against my hand, chasing shamelessly after my high. And just as I think I've found it, the apartment door opens.

I throw the book towards the kitchen with all my might as I spring to my feet, meeting Jo's tired eyes.

"I asked you not to be violent with my books," she sighs, shutting the door behind me.

"Oh, Jo, I'm so sorry. You just scared me and why are you looking at me like that?"

Her eyes are wide, and she finally blinks when she realizes I'm addressing her. "Where the hell are your pants?"

"Uh," I respond, all intelligence gone. "Didn't wear any today. Since I was home alone." I peer at the microwave in the kitchen. "Wait, you're home early. I thought you got off at five?" Why is she home two and a half hours earlier than usual?

"Feeling sick," Jo mutters, avoiding my gaze as she shuffles into the kitchen. She pulls a granola bar out from the pantry and rips the wrapper with her teeth.

I swallow. "Oh. I'm sorry. Is there anything I can do?"

"No," Jo answers, peering at me out of the corner of her eye as she chews. "Well. Maybe put on some pants."

And then Giovanna Quinn blushes, and I want to burn every pair of pants I own.

"I can do that. Do I need to put on a bra too?"

Her gaze immediately falls to my chest.

Mission accomplished.

Am I a bad person for trying to seduce her while she's not feeling well?

Maybe I *should* go back to church.

"I mean—" Jo wheezes, and I bite my lip. "A bra might be breast—best."

This is every dream I never knew I had come true.

I salute her. "Aye aye, captain. Sorry. I don't know why I said that. Or did that. It seemed like a good idea at the time." I awkwardly start shuffling backwards to my bedroom.

"Okay," Jo says weakly as she leans against the counter. "Whatever you say, honey."

Did she call me *honey*?

That certainly doesn't help the ache between my thighs right now.

I make an unintelligible squeaking noise and push my bedroom door open, quickly closing it behind me. I walk to my bedside table, grabbing my pink rabbit vibrator out of the drawer before climbing onto my bed, spreading my legs, and moaning as I push the toy inside me. I turn my head and clench my pillow between my teeth as the ears vibrate against my clit, slowly moving the shaft inside me so it rubs against my g-spot.

I can be quiet. Giovanna's right out there and—

Giovanna.

She's so pretty—so fucking pretty—and I want to remember what she tastes like...everywhere. I want to know what kind of marks those long nails of hers would leave on my skin, what noises she could coax out of me.

What noises I could coax out of *her*.

My release is blessedly muffled by the pillow, like I'd hoped. But once I come down, I don't move, staring at the ceiling as my chest heaves, an all-too-familiar feeling of shame washing over me like a wave.

What the fuck is wrong with me? No, what the fuck is wrong with *her*? What is it about her that has me so undone? This isn't my fault. This is all—

"Hun?" Jo's voice is muffled through the door and I jackknife into a sitting position.

"Y-yeah?" I stammer, face burning red.

"I didn't mean you couldn't come out." Her voice is shaky, and I frown, unable to stop myself from worrying about her.

I cope with my worry the way I know best—by covering it with humor. "I already came out, thanks."

She's silent for a beat before exhaling deeply. "That's a good joke."

"Thank you," I beam, pleased as punch at her affirmation.

"Would you mind coming out again? Of the room that is. Unless you want to disclose your sexuality to me, which you don't have to. It's totally personal and none of my business—"

In the fifty-thousand years it takes her to ramble, I'm able to climb out of bed, pull on a pair of yoga pants, and stride across the room. She stops short when I open the door.

"Oh," she says, blinking at me in surprise.

"Easy as pie," I tell her. "Also I identify as bisexual, with a preference for pretty girls."

I watch her bite that pillowy, pink lip between her teeth, in an attempt to stifle the quiet laugh that escapes anyway.

This one? Worth at least a dime.

"I'm a lesbian," Jo says.

I smile softly. "It must feel cathartic to say that out loud, huh?" I wonder if she knows what I mean. If she knows that I play back her telling me how broken and wrong she feels for her attraction to girls. How she prayed that she would wake up and think boys were cute the way her sisters and friends did.

She meets my gaze, her brown eyes flecked with green and gold immediately hypnotizing me. "Yeah. It feels good to be okay with myself."

I attempt to swallow the lump in my throat, but the mass of emotion on my chest makes it impossible. "I'm glad, Giovanna."

"When did you come out?" she asks, averting her gaze. "You don't have to tell me, actually. I shouldn't have asked—"

Before I can stop myself, I reach out to her, taking her soft hand in mine and squeezing gently. "It's a long, kind of emotional story. Not one that I'm adverse to telling you, just not right now. Is that okay?"

Giovanna nods. "I—yeah. Of course. I'm sorry. I got distracted. I actually wanted to ask you to come out—" I open my mouth to make another goofy joke. "Of your bedroom," she says pointedly, arching a perfect brow at me.

The Italian gods blessed this woman with such annoyingly expressive and full eyebrows.

"I wanted to ask you to come out of your bedroom so that I could talk to you about some stuff having to do with my diabetes," she continues.

I hope she can't tell I'm lusting over her eyebrows. Her *eyebrows*. I'm pathetic as hell.

"I realized I never gave you the 'my roommate's a Type One Diabetic' orientation."

At this moment, it occurs to me that my rabbit is in plain sight, and the smell of my arousal is likely lingering in the air.

"That sounds amazing!" I exclaim loudly, taking a step forward and causing Jo to stagger back as I pull the door closed behind. "I'd love to know *everything* about your diabetes!"

Giovanna eyes me suspiciously. "Okay?"

"I just have to go pee real fast."

"Sure," she mumbles in response, turning away and shuffling towards the living room. I quickly pop into the bathroom and close the door behind me before sitting on the closed toilet.

I inhale shakily. What the *fuck* is wrong with me? What is it about this woman that has me so unable to control myself and my desires? She's all I can think about, all I *want* to think about right now.

Maybe I need to go to therapy more often. Or to go back to church. Repent of the sin of being way too attracted to Giovanna Quinn. It has to be a venial sin, at least.

After I pee and clean myself up a little, I wash my hands and that unwelcome wave of shame crashes over me again. Like the waves in the ocean, when you think it's gone, there's always another one to follow.

She can never know what I think about her. How much I want to touch and taste her again. She'd be disgusted by me. Just because she likes women doesn't mean she likes me, *and* she's still healing from a traumatic breakup. Who the hell am I to come in and have any impact on that?

"Okay, I'm ready for Type 1 Diabetes 101, professor," I announce in a forcefully cheerful tone as I enter the living room.

Jo is sitting cross-legged on the couch as she scrolls on her phone. She looks up at me and smiles gently, patting the couch next to her.

Why is her motioning for me to sit next to her giving me goose-bumps? I need to move out. Or cease to exist.

Whichever affects my credit score the least.

I walk to the couch and sit next to Jo, keeping my eyes on my thighs as they expand against the cushion.

"Okay, so," she says, not reacting to my anxiety. "This is my omnipod, which gives me my insulin. I used to have a pump with tubing, but this is what I use now." She untucks her blouse and lifts it just enough to show a sliver of her smooth skin and a rectangular device on her lower belly.

"Whoa, you're a robot."

"Yup, machinery keeps me alive. How much do you know about diabetes?"

I shift uncomfortably in my seat. I should have done research on my own time. It wouldn't have been hard, but I didn't, and I feel like I should have. "Not a lot, just what you told me that summer."

"What do you remember?" she asks.

I think about it. "You have to test your blood sugar levels, and they affect how much insulin you need."

"Exactly. I used to have to test my blood sugar by doing finger pricks, but the machines win again, because now I have this bad boy."

Jo pulls off her suit jacket, and points to a device on her upper arm. "This is a CGM—continuous glucose monitor—and it does exactly what the name says: continuously monitors my glucose. It serves the same function as the finger pricks, and I can look at my levels on my phone. It's so much better. Also, there's an emergency medication called glucagon that I keep on hand. I'll show you where I keep it, in case I don't wake up." She shoots finger guns at me, like she didn't just hint at her mortality. "It's the same premise of an epi-pen, but diabetics use it to inject glucagon..."

"Glucagon?" I interrupt, brow furrowed.

"It's sort of like a liquid sugar that will quickly bring up my blood glucose in the case of severe lows."

"No." I pause for a moment. "Yes. Does your pod automatically deliver insulin?"

"Sort of. I have to input the carbs I've eaten for it to work." She pulls out a device that looks like a little phone out of her pocket.

"This is my PDM—personal diabetes monitor. If my pod falls off, or isn't properly attached, then I have to administer manually, and I use my PDM to do that. But it lets me know when that happens, there's an alarm that goes off when it thinks it isn't working the way it's supposed to.

"So you take insulin when your blood sugar is low?" I ask, trying to keep track of everything she's telling me.

She shakes her head. "No, I'd take it when it's high, or when I'm eating something high in carbs."

Damn, that's a lot. Nick Jonas never mentioned that in his Disney Channel PSA.

"If my blood sugar gets too high, and my pod isn't working," Giovanna continues, "or I don't have enough insulin on hand, that can be an emergency, but it's not a daily worry."

"How do you know if you're low?"

"There's an alert that my phone plays when my CGM senses a low, but I usually feel it first. I feel achy and tired, and I shake a ton," she tells me, and I notice she looks uncomfortable when she says this.

I nod. "Noted. What helps when you have low blood sugar?"

"Fast acting carbs. I keep little bottles of honey around, you may have noticed them." She digs in her leather tote bag and pulls out the most *adorable* little honey bear.

I squeal. "That's *adorable*!"

"Adorable *and* functional," she answers. "It's an easy way to get those carbs, so I always keep some in my office at work, at Nic and Josh's, in the bathroom, in my bedside table…"

"You're more prepared than a Boy Scout," I tease.

She smiles cautiously. It's strange how I feel like I can label her smiles now. There's this one, the cautious one, where her smile is crooked and unsure. It's a polite smile, a smile that fulfills social expectations more than reflects joy. "Gotta be. It sucks but…" she inhales shakily. "This kind of runs my life. I know it inconveniences and impacts the people around me. I try to handle it on my own as much as possible so it isn't inconvenient for you…"

"Inconvenient for *me*?" I interrupt her before I can remind myself people don't like when you do that. "None of this is . I want to understand it better so that I can be more supportive. As a roommate."

Gosh, if only we were the type of "roommates" that women throughout history were. The "roommates" who exchanged lusty, longing, lyrical correspondence. The "roommates" who were only really roommates because historians decades later decided so.

But we're just roommates. And that's all we'll ever be.

Jo shifts, her shirt riding up a bit and my gaze is immediately pulled to the soft roundness of her stomach.

Sure, we'll only ever be roommates, but it doesn't hurt to look.

"I'm not ignorant, Hun. I know that it's inconvenient for other people," she says.

I stare at her, mouth gaping like a fish. I know my ADHD impacts her, but she would never allow me to say this stuff to her.

"Who made you feel like this?" I ask curtly, balling my hands into fists. I'm ready to fight whoever made Jo Quinn feel like less than the fucking treasure she is.

Her brow furrows as she looks up from examining her nails. "Huh?"

"Who made you feel like an inconvenience?"

"No one. I just am."

"Your ex-fiancée?" Her eyes dart to the floor and I know I've found the answer. "I hate her."

"You don't know her."

"I know you. And that's enough to know I hate her."

"Okay, I think that's all you need to know. About diabetes. For now," she says shortly as she stands.

"I'm sorry, I think you deserve–"

Jo cuts me off with a deep sigh, running a hand through her hand and pulling at her roots in frustration. I know she's had a hard day, and it's not my business, but I hate that she's been made to feel like her body is a burden on the people around her. Especially the people she loved. Maybe still loves.

"I can't do this today, Hunter."

"Sorry," I say in a small voice. "You're right, it's not—"

"I'm going to my room. If you're going to read my books, please don't throw it." She turns and walks to her room, avoiding my gaze the whole way.

Playlist: Change (Taylor's Version) | Taylor Swift

Leo: have you talked to nic

Jo: no

Jo: why

Jo: what did you do you little shit

Leo: nothing!!!!

"What did he do?" I call as I let myself into the brownstone.

"Jesus—knock next time!" Nic shrieks from somewhere in the house. I freeze and cover my eyes with my hand.

"Lock the door if you're going to have wild sex on the main floor, you animals. Hi, Josh."

"Hey, Jo." His voice is muffled, like there's something in his mouth—

Nope. Not entertaining that image.

I awkwardly wait in the foyer for a good three minutes, waiting for the all-clear to continue further into the house.

"Okay, come in!" Nic shouts, and I follow her voice into the living room.

"I need your help," I announce. "And I know what you're going to say but—" I freeze, looking around the room. "Is that a new couch?"

Nic groans melodramatically and Josh sighs. He looks at my sister with a distressed expression, immediately telling me everything I need to know.

"Leo and Stella?" I gasp in horror, my hand flying to my mouth.

"Leo and Stella," Josh confirms dejectedly.

"Fucking dipshits," Nic grumbles, crossing her arms over her chest.

"I thought we agreed to never let them step foot in our home?"

"You and I did agree to that, yes," Nic confirms, turning and pointedly looking at Josh, who seems to be looking everywhere but her.

"Goddammit, Joshua." I pinch the bridge of my nose, trying to breathe deeply.

"Okay, I was trying to be nice? I don't understand how the fuck he broke it," Josh says, eyeing the couch. "I'm bigger than him and we've—"

"I'm not above slapping you across the face right now," I inform him.

He scowls at me.

Nic giggles. "Joshy came home to the poor couch totally trashed. And he didn't know what to do, and since I was in Greenwich on Friday and Saturday for a work conference, he called and asked me to come back early to yell at them for him."

"Did you?" I ask, reluctantly invested in the horror film slash sitcom of our lives.

"No! Josh handled it like a big boy all on his own," Nic says proudly, squeezing her partner's shoulder.

I try to cover my laugh, but fail miserably. "So you yelled at Leo over speakerphone like the time he broke mom's car window and told them they had to be gone by the time you got home?"

"Yeah," Nic admits sheepishly.

Josh throws his hands into the air. "I fucking tried! But he apologized so sincerely and...what are you doing here, Jo?" Josh asks in a way that tells me he's desperate to change the subject.

It works, and Nic turns towards me, wordlessly arching a brow.

I roll my eyes. "I'm getting lunch at some fancy French bistro down the road."

"Fancy French bistro? Oooh, is this a date?" My sister asks hopefully.

I wince, and her face falls. "Not the right thing to say," she says quietly.

"No, no it's fine. I get it." It doesn't really feel fine.

"I'm sorry."

"It's okay, really. It's just a business lunch." I take a deep breath. "Promise you won't get mad."

Josh and Nic's eyes are immediately on me. "Have a seat, ladies," Josh says, motioning towards the couch.

I eye the new sofa suspiciously. It *does* look comfortable, but, unfortunately, I know without a doubt that they were naked on it less than ten minutes ago. "No, thanks. I'll stand."

Nic grabs my hand and pulls me down onto the couch with her. I shudder.

"Want some tea, JoJo?" She's using the sickly sweet tone she only uses to get what she wants.

"We have Earl Grey and English Breakfast," Josh offers.

"Earl Grey with oat milk. And a drizzle of honey."

"So what am I not getting mad about?" my sister asks, rotating her body so she's facing me.

"I took on a new side project—a big one. It requires weekends and overtime."

She purses her lips. "I thought you and your therapist agreed it was best if you cut back on overtime?"

I wince. "Yeah. We did. But I couldn't say no."

"Why the hell not?" my sister exclaims, a baffled expression on her face. "Saying no at work is my new favorite pastime. Well that and tying Josh—"

"Stop," I interrupt.

"Okay."

"This is where I need you not to get mad," I say, hands fidgeting in my lap.

She narrows her eyes at me, "I thought you taking on a ginormous project was what I wasn't getting angry about. Which I did amazing on, by the way."

"No. It's, ugh. I'm just gonna say it okay?" I cover my face with my hands.

"Itskelseyandbeckysweddingandeventsleadinguptothewedding."

I spread my fingers and peek out at Nic, who stares at me in confusion.

"What?" she asks, tilting her head to the side.

"What?!" Josh shouts as he storms back into the living room, two steaming mugs in his hands. "Josephine, tell me you didn't say what I think you said."

"Not my name."

"My god, you did." He looks at Nic. "She's planning Kelsey and Becky's wedding and the events leading up to the wedding."

My older sister laughs. "No she's not. You must have misheard." She looks at me expectantly.

I examine my nail beds.

Thwack.

"What the *fuck*, Nicoletta?!" I screech, rubbing the side of my head where she'd walloped me with a throw pillow.

"No! You don't get to say what the fuck! *I* get to say what the fuck! And what. The. *Fuck*." She punctuates each word by smacking my shoulder with the same pillow.

Josh puts our mugs on the table and pulls the pillow from Nic's grip. "Let's keep the violence to a minimum, Buttercup."

"Thank you, Josh," I say, glaring at my sister.

"She needs to be in one piece when we kill her," he continues.

I throw my hands in the air. "You assholes dating is the worst thing to happen to me."

"Oh, not being left by your literal fiancée who broke your heart into a billion pieces?" Nic glares at me, her hands balling into fists. I scoot back a smidge, just to be cautious.

"That's not fair," I argue. "It's not my choice."

"Is she blackmailing you?" Josh asks, sitting on the other side of his partner and peering over her shoulder at me.

"No...she's offering me a *lot* of money."

Nic eyes me suspiciously. "How *much* money, exactly? It better be at least six figures otherwise—"

"They offered me one hundred thousand and I was able to negotiate to one hundred and twenty," I interrupted. "In addition to my regular salary."

They blink at me wordlessly for a moment.

"That is indeed a lot of money," she finally says.

"It's enough for me to start my own firm in Port Haven like I've always wanted to. To get away from them forever. For the queer community in our hometown to know they're loved and supported, the way I didn't. I'm not being rash, or masochistic."

My sister's face softens, and she reaches out to cover my hand in hers, squeezing gently. "Oh, Jo. I'm sorry. That is what I sounded like, isn't it? That's not fair."

I swallow hard. "I don't even know who you are anymore, Nic. Since you started dating Bruce Wayne over there you're like...nice."

"Bruce Wayne?" Nic asks, tilting her head to the side. "You mean...Josh?"

Josh coughs into his fist, attempting to hide his smile. "Don't worry about it, Buttercup," he tells his girlfriend. He wraps his arm around her shoulder and pulls her into his side, pressing his lips to her temple. Nic simply glows at his attention—it's adorable. And yet I still feel a twinge of jealousy in the center of my chest. "We just love you, Josephine—"

"Still not my name."

"—and we're worried about you," he continues, like I didn't say anything.

"You've come so far," Nic adds, thumb rubbing circles on the back of my hand. "And I know you don't see it, but you *have*. You've put in so much work and I know how strenuous every single day at the office is. I don't want that pain amplified even more. I don't want her to hurt you more." Her voice cracks, and my chest aches.

"Kelsey acted like we were nothing." I don't know why I say it. Maybe it's because as annoying as the two lovebirds are, they *do* care about me. "She told Becky all we had was a fling."

"A *fling*? Oh, fuck that," Nic growls, dropping my hand and getting to her feet before. She strides purposefully across the room towards the foyer. "She's fucking dead."

Josh looks at me in panic. "She's...kidding. Right?"

"Oh, Joshy." I pat his knee. "You've been dating her for a year and know what she's capable of. Go catch that tiny, violent girlfriend of yours and bring her back before we have to post bail."

Josh rushes out of the room and moments later re-enters the room, Nic thrown over his shoulder. She's kicking her feet, and I grin when I see she had already gotten a shoe on.

"You can't stop me from killing her," Nic argues as she lands back on the couch with a bounce. She crosses her arms over her chest as she scowls up at Josh, looking like a petulant toddler.

"I can delay it," he answers, sitting next to her and rotating her so that her back is to him. He pins her arms behind her back, and she smirks at him over her shoulder. He blushes.

"Oh, how the tables—" Nic begins.

"Nope," I interrupt.

"Sorry."

"It's fine. I need to get going anyway." I stand up. "Now you freaks can get back to being gross."

Her face falls. "Jo. Don't go. Joshy will give you the money."

Josh sighs. "I probably should be mad that you're trying to pimp me out as a sugar daddy, but she's right. Josephine—"

"I swear to god, you are risking your ability to father Bruce Wayne Junior."

"—I'll give you the money you need," he finishes, ignoring me again.

I swallow hard. Due to tragedy in his life, Josh has enough money that honestly, he could probably support my entire family without working again. He works because he loves it. He's such a loser.

"Thanks. That's thoughtful of you, but I want to do it on my own."

I swallow and force myself to look at my sister, meeting her eyes that are so similar to our mother's. Where I have flecks of green in my eyes, Nic has pure, milk chocolate-colored eyes. "Why?" she asks. "Why do you want to do it on your own?"

"I want to prove myself."

"To who?"

"To *me*. I know it sounds ridiculous, but I have to prove that I'm capable and worthy of at least a *part* of my dreams."

"Goddammit, Josephine." Josh releases Nic's arms to wipe at his nose. Is he...crying? "You're so fucking capable and worthy. Is this really going to do anything to make you truly believe it?"

"I don't know," I admit. "I just know I have to try."

They exchange an annoying, knowing couple glance. Kelsey and I could never do that, say things without saying them. There was never a secret language or an intuitive way with her, and I thought that meant we were mature, that we communicated by talking like adults.

Maybe it just meant we were never in sync.

"Okay," Nic says slowly, breaking eye contact with Josh. "I get that. But we're here for you okay? And if Kelsey does *anything* to hurt you, I'll wait until Josh can't stop me."

I don't doubt it. I'm lucky to be on her good side.

She gets to her feet and stands on her tiptoes, wrapping her arms around my neck. I blink in confusion. I can't remember the last time Nic initiated a hug. This is *so* not like her.

Except it is. It's *just* like healing and content Nic. I'd never gotten to know that version of her before, and it's a little disorienting now, to be honest.

I wonder what parts of myself I haven't gotten to know, which parts of myself are waiting to be unlocked with the healing and hope and growth and joy I hope are ahead. Maybe that's what Nic and Josh see in me, the parts that are like the sun peeking out from behind the clouds on a dreary day. Maybe they can see it better than I do, because they've unlocked those own versions of themselves with their own healing.

"I love you, JoJo," Nicky whispers in my ear. "Don't tell the others, but you're my favorite sister."

I hug her back. "Love you too, Nicky. Thanks for caring about me enough to be ready to commit murder."

"Literally always."

I peek over my sister's shoulder at Josh, who's wiping away at more tears. I roll my eyes. "Get over here, dumbass."

Josh springs to his feet wrapping his long arms around both of us. "Am I officially a Quibling?" he whispers excitedly.

"Yes," I sigh, knowing it's going to go to his head, but also knowing he's earned it after today.

"I've always wanted a big family. Here's to making all sorts of dreams come true." He squeezes my shoulder.

Maybe I'm making the wrong choice, and maybe Nic and Josh still think that. But it's *my* choice. *My* attempt at reclaiming what I've always wanted for myself after over a year of so much pain.

My chance to find out if they've been growing pains all along.

Chapter 10

Jo

Playlist: Homesick (with Sam Fender) | Noah Kahan, Sam Fender

Jo: hey

Leo: what

Jo: i talked to nic

Leo: okay well it wasn't as bad as she made it sound

Jo: did you cry when she yelled at you

Leo: there's nothing shameful about crying!

Leo: please don't tell mom and dad
<prayer hands emoji>

Jo: i'm holding on to it until i need something from you

Leo: fuck that's even worse

Jo: oh, i know <devil emoji>

By the time I leave the brownstone, I'm already five minutes late for lunch. This doesn't bode well for me—Kelsey does *not* like tardiness.

After that weird little love fest with my sister and her boyfriend, I find myself thinking about Hunter for some reason. I haven't talked to her for four days, since I came home early. When I'm home, she's usually hidden away in the library editing, or out on a shoot. But yesterday, I came home to a clean kitchen and an India Holton paperback with a 3 post-its listing her thoughts stuck crookedly to the cover. This morning, it was an Eva Leigh mass market. It made me smile; she's uses a pink pen and an abundance of hearts and exclamation points.

As I walk to the bistro, I pull my phone out of my pocket to text her my own thoughts on the two books, but am surprised to see she's called multiple times in the past few minutes.

I start to type out a quick response as I approach the restaurant, but when I look up, my eyes meet a pair of blue eyes I know all too well. Kelsey and Becky sit at a table facing the window, and while Becky is looking at the menu, Kelsey is looking right at me. I inhale shakily and drop my phone into my tote, deciding to text Hunter back later.

As I walk to their table, I realize this place is out of my price range. The waitstaff wears crisp white button downs with a vest and tie, and they carry plates with the tiniest portions. But Becky, Ms. "Comes From Old Money," is paying.

Now I can't help but wonder how much Kelsey's ring cost. When I proposed, I had saved for months—okay, one month, which is months in lesbian time—to afford a ring off Etsy. She'd seemed to love it, gushing over how much it meant and how sentimental it was...but maybe sentimental wasn't as good as I thought. I knew she liked nice things, but I genuinely thought she liked me more.

"Jo!" Kelsey waves from the table, the light dancing off her gaudy ring. I try to smile, but it's pained. Her engagement ring, at least two carats, is a stabbing reminder of what she wanted, and who I was never able to be.

Becky is a two carat diamond, and I'm a random ring off Etsy.

I nervously wave back, careful to avoid waiters and trays as I make my way to the table. *I can do this. I can do this. I can—*

"You're late." Kelsey scowls at me, tapping her perfectly manicured fingers on the table. "I hope it won't happen again. You wouldn't want us to dock your pay for tardiness."

I try to swallow, but my throat is too dry. "Right, I'm sorry. It won't happen again."

Becky looks up from the menu and playfully elbows her fiancée. "She's kidding, right babe?"

Kelsey laughs, the same way she used to laugh at my jokes. "Right. I'm just *so* excited to get to work." She claps her hands together, the noise echoing in the buzzing restaurant.

"Is someone else joining us for lunch?" I ask, motioning to the place setting next to me with my head.

Suddenly, both sets of eyes are on me from across the table. Kelsey's eyes sparkle in a way passersby will call playful. But I know her, and that sparkle is mischief. "Jo freaking Quinn," she says, Cheshire Cat grin in place, too. "Why didn't you tell us your new girlfriend is Hunter Cleary?"

I understand all of those words individually, but not put together. "Huh?"

"We booked Hunter Cleary as our photographer, and imagine our surprise when she arrived—" Becky begins to say.

"On time," Kelsey interjects, and I wince.

Becky shushes her, waving her hand dismissively. "Imagine our surprise when she arrived and we told her you were our event planner...and she wondered why you hadn't told her."

Hunter? My *girlfriend?*

I laugh nervously. "Hunter Cleary?"

Kelsey nods, her smile unwavering. "Mmhmm. We were taken off guard when Hunter referred to you as her roommate."

I want to forget the way my full name sounds in her mouth. When Hunter says it, it's warm tea and sunbeams. When Kelsey says it, it's like I'm being pelted with hail. She, like my mother, only used my full name when she was upset.

"Snookums! There you are!" The very second Hunter's southern accent cuts through the tension, I feel my entire body somehow tense and relax at the same time. I jump up from my chair and spin to face her.

She's wearing a hot pink sundress with white cowboy boots, blonde curls flowing over her shoulders as she walks towards me.

She's beaming, and unlike Kelsey's smile, hers meets her eyes. I feel boring as hell in my black suit. I only wear eyeliner and mascara, but her signature pink gloss makes me want to try a signature color, too.

She's so unapologetically Hunter, and it makes my chest ache. She's all woman, and somehow still the girl I loved so long ago. How she is able to harness both is beyond me.

But then I remember where I am, where *we* are. That she's at my business lunch and that Becky and Kelsey think we're dating.

My hands begin to tremble, and my throat is dry. "Hunter," I somehow manage to croak, feeling the color drain from my face.

She steps towards me, my back to the table, and then reaches out and cups my face between her hands. "I'm going to kiss right next to your mouth," she whispers. "It'll look real to them, okay?"

I stare at her silently, because what the hell am I supposed to say in response to that?

"Okay?" she prompts. "I'm not doing it until you consent, but we need to move fast if you want it to be believable."

What the *fuck* is happening right now.

I nod, feeling like my brain's lost connection to my body. "Okay," I whisper back.

Hunter leans into me, lips brushing softly at the corner of my mouth before pressing firmly to my skin.

Her lips are soft and pillowy, and I fight the urge to turn my face to find out if she still tastes like bubblegum and tequila, the way she did during our first kiss.

After a few seconds, she pulls away. It had to have only been a few seconds, though it felt so much longer.

And yet, it felt too short, too. This woman is turning my existence into a walking contradiction. "Hey," she says, smiling up at me. "Surprise, baby."

Surprise, indeed.

Hunter is here. At my business lunch with my ex-fiancée and her current fiancée–my clients.

What the *fuck*.

"I didn't realize that surprising you would put you into shock," she says with a wink as she pulls out my chair for me. "Sit down."

I obey, trying to avoid looking at Kelsey and Becky, but it's hard when I can feel them staring at us.

"You two are so sweet together!" Becky squeals, clapping her hands together.

"I didn't realize you knew Jo would be here," Kelsey says to Hunter. Her voice has changed, but I can't put my finger on it.

Hunter scoffs as she sits beside me. "You didn't realize that I know where my girlfriend is on a Sunday afternoon?" She nudges my leg with her knee under the table, subtly motioning to her lap with her head. Her phone is unlocked and open to a list on the notes app.

> -We met as teenagers, reunited at Tyler & Nellie's wedding and have been dating since.
> -We decided I'd move in when Nic moved in with Josh
> -I like being spanked. This might be TMI and not matter but my god your ex has already asked me weirdly invasive questions, and I wouldn't be surprised if she quizzes us on our sex life.
> -We'll talk more after.
> -You got this, snookums.

I swallow and look back up, where Becky and Kelsey are looking at me expectantly across the table. "Huh?"

"I was just saying, snookums, I didn't realize Kelsey was your ex." Hunter takes my hand in hers and squeezes gently. It feels like I grabbed a livewire, heat and sparks running through my entire body. I want to pull away, to run away from all of this.

"That's why I was confused when that was the first thing she mentioned about you. I know how much you love surprises, so I didn't tell you we were working together. Your surprised face is the cutest ever." She widens her eyes and opens her mouth, recreating my surprised face, I suppose.

"I'm just...confused that Jo didn't tell you we dated," Kelsey says in that same, unidentifiable tone. Hunter squeezes my hand tighter, and I can feel her tense as well. It's strange how this comforts me. Not her discomfort or unhappiness, but the shared tension at Kelsey's words. It makes it a little less lonely.

Kelsey takes a sip of water just as Hunter speaks again. "Oh, I mean...it's not like you two were engaged or anything, right? She'd mentioned a recent fling that she regretted. I didn't realize it was you!"

I stare at Hunter as Kelsey chokes on her water. Hunter smiles sweetly and brushes a drop of water from her cheek. "Have y'all ever tried escargot?" Hunter asks casually, picking up the menu.

After a minute or so, Kelsey is able to speak coherently. "I didn't...Giovanna Quinn, should you be eating that? Doesn't it have too many carbs?"

I freeze, the dinner roll I'd gotten for myself halfway to my mouth, face reddening.

"What did you say to her?" Hunter asks, voice rough and ragged. Gone is the sickly sweet smile, and it's replaced by glaring eyes and pursed lips. Her cheeks are pink and she looks *pissed*.

Holy fuck. Hunter's always hot, but angry Hunter is really something else.

"I asked if she should be eating those carbs." Kelsey's eyes are shooting daggers at Hunter, and for the first time, I realize how similar the two of them look. Blue eyed and blonde, though Kelsey's a natural brunette. What the fuck did Hunter Cleary do to me all those years ago that made my type specifically women who look like her?

"She has diabetes, if you didn't know. I didn't see her check her blood sugar," Kelsey continues.

"Of course I know she has diabetes. But maybe the question should be whether or not *you* should be eating your roll." Hunter says cooly.

"I'm not diabetic," Kelsey responds, a forced smile plastered on her face.

"Oh, with the way you were talking about it, I assumed you were just projecting your own issues onto Jo. Do you make a habit of policing your vendors' food choices?"

"Of course we don't!" Becky answers. "Kelsey didn't mean harm, she's just looking out for Jo's health."

"Jo's an adult who manages her own diabetes. She knows her body and making comments on what she decides goes into her body is both ableist and fatphobic. What a shame." Hunter pouts. "I'd hate for Coffey & Co's business to suffer because you allow your employees to treat vendors this way."

I stare at her as the following silence echoes around us. Holy shit. Hunter is more than sparkles and glitter and soft, fluffy things. She's a goddamn firework. Fuck with her in the wrong way, and she's an explosion capable of destruction.

I look at Kelsey, and know she's holding back her anger. I can tell she wants to snap, and so can Becky.

"Babe, can we talk?" Becky says, getting to her feet.

Kelsey is silent as she stands and follows Becky toward the restrooms.

Hunter drops my hand and I flex mine, the absence of her touch jarring.

"You could read the note?" Hunter stage whispers, rotating her torso so she's facing me.

"Yeah…what the fuck is happening right now?"

"I never got a chance to apologize for what I said and I wanted to make things right. So I said we were dating."

"Back up." I am *so* confused by this whole situation. "How did you know I was planning their wedding?"

She shrugs, staring at her hands as she picks at her peeling sparkly silver nail polish. "I didn't. They reached out to me about shooting the wedding and, hell, I had no idea you worked for Becky. When I emailed you for Nellie and Tyler's wedding, I thought you worked for yourself. Your email address didn't say anything different."

It's true. I'd taken on Nellie and Tyler's wedding as a side project because I liked them so much.

Hunter continues rambling. "And they said they liked my work, and asked me to photograph the events leading up to the wedding, and I had no reason to say no. Then she mentioned you were their coordinator when I got here, and I got excited and told them you're my roommate and Kelsey was all like 'you're dating my ex?' and I didn't know what to say so I said yes."

She inhales sharply and my brain spirals in an attempt to keep up with her rapid-fire info dumping before she piles on even more. "I knew she must have reason to think we were dating, and I had a feeling I should just agree, especially considering she's your awful ex and I tried to call you but you didn't answer and I wrote the note in the bathroom so we would be on the same chapter, if not on the same page—"

"God," I groan, sinking low in my chair and rubbing my hands over my face. "This is a fucking mess."

"I'm sorry," Hunter apologizes, and I peek at her through my fingers. She looks so defeated, and it makes my heart hurt a little. I miss Firecracker Hunter.

"It's my fault, not yours. When they offered the gig, I realized the payment would be enough to get a fresh start and start the firm I'd always wanted to. Then Kelsey referred to our engagement as a fling, and I realized Becky doesn't know we were engaged because we hadn't disclosed it at work. God, I don't know why I said it, but I said my girlfriend had moved in, and your name was the first I thought of. I didn't think it would ever matter."

Hunter's quiet for a moment, and her silence is unnerving as hell. "That makes sense," she says.

I peer through my fingers again. "No, it fucking doesn't."

She's staring at her hands clasped in her lap, and shrugs her shoulders. "Maybe not, but I get it. Do you want to tell her the truth?"

I think about when I met with Kelsey and Becky about planning their wedding. How easily Kelsey had referred to me as a fling, as *nothing*. The way my heart hurt so fucking badly that I hoped it would stop beating altogether.

"What do you think?" I ask. "I didn't mean to rope you into this, but I did. This isn't just about me anymore and it involves and impacts you."

"I don't like her." Hunter looks at me, blue eyes clear as the ocean. She has an intense look on her face, but it makes me feel safe. Secure. I slowly lower my hands from my face, keeping my eyes on her. "Kelsey. She's...I don't know. I get a bad feeling about her, and I'm never really wrong about these things. I hate how she makes you feel, so if you can use her to get what you need, do it." She bites her lip, and I can see the wheels turning in her head.

"You can say it," I encourage.

Her brow furrows. "Say what?"

"Whatever it is you're currently trying to decide whether or not you should say."

She blushes. "I'm that obvious?"

"Maybe just to me. Because, you know. We're roommates."

Hunter giggles. "Speaking of, Kelsey asked why I referred to you as my roommate, and I told her it was an inside joke about women from history who were obviously lovers but historians refer to as roommates. Just so you know."

I can't help but smile. "I like that."

"Anyway, I'm just going to say it, and I'm so sorry in advance if it's harmful. But I don't think you see it."

"See what?"

"Kelsey's power over you. She knows the impact she has on you, and she revels in it. She likes watching you scramble to appease her and saying things that make you second guess yourself and feel ashamed. Like that bread shit?" She scoffs and rolls her eyes, leaning towards me. "*That's* why she can never know the truth, and why you need to run as soon as this is over and never look back."

I stare at her, speechless. Nic and Josh insinuated the same thing, but I thought they were biased. Hunter has no reason to say this to me, not when I'm certain Kelsey and Becky are offering her a pretty penny.

"Thank you," I whisper hoarsely. "I think I needed to hear that."

Hunter reaches out and takes my hand in hers again, squeezing in such a comforting way it makes me want to never break contact. "I know." Her voice is soft, kind. "You deserve the truth, Jo, even when it's painful. I hate that it isn't the norm for you, hearing the truth."

"So you want to pretend we're dating? You'd do that for me?" I ask, wanting to clarify that we're actually continuing with this bizarre plan.

"Of course I would." She blinks at me, and then blushes the prettiest shade of magenta. "I mean…it doesn't really matter to me, and it'll help you. So why not."

I have a list of reasons why we shouldn't do this. We should come clean and I should quit my job and change my name and run away.

"Okay," I say, swallowing.

She sticks her hand out. "Fabulous. They're coming back, so act quickly."

I take her hand in mine, pushing away the sparks that feel like they're igniting my entire body.

She pulls me in and presses her lips to my cheek.

"So sorry about that," Becky says as she and Kelsey take their seats across from us at the table.

I look at Hunter out of the corner of my eye as she crosses her arms over her chest. "I assume we aren't expected to tolerate discrimination if we sign the contracts?" Hunter isn't playing around, she's getting right to business.

"Absolutely not." Kelsey smiles that same empty smile. "I apologize for my lack of professionalism."

"It wasn't only unprofessional," Hunter fires back. "It was discrimination, which is illegal. How am I supposed to trust that you'll treat my girlfriend and I with the respect we deserve?"

"Hun…gah!" I yelp in pain as she digs the heel of her boot into my foot. No one else at the table seems to notice.

"I just want to know what you'll be doing to make this a safe and healthy work environment, and what you'll do to earn our trust," Hunter clarifies.

What is she doing? I told her I needed this money and she's going to ruin everything and…

"I apologized," Kelsey bites. All pretenses of a smile are gone and she's back to scowling at Hunter. "What else do you want me to do?"

"Prove your apology isn't empty. To be completely honest, the fact you're fighting against this shows me that you aren't taking what I said seriously and I don't see a need stay any longer," Hunter says, standing from her chair and holding her hand out to me. "Come on, snookums."

"We'll increase your compensation. Both of you," Becky says, standing also. "Name your price."

"Fifty percent increase. Each," Hunter says smoothly, sitting back down and reaching for another dinner roll.

"You have yourself a deal," Becky agrees, returning to her own seat as well. Kelsey's eyes dart between the three of us. I avert my gaze and look at Hunter, who happily butters her roll before taking a bite. The butter smudges on her lip, and the tip of her tongue sneaks out and licks it away.

Why the hell is Hunter Cleary cleaning butter off her lips so hot?

"Fantastic," she says while I leer at her mouth. "Can we expect updated contracts by the end of the day tomorrow?"

"Absolutely," Becky promises. "Again, thank you for your understanding."

"Of course." Hunter's mouth is full of dinner roll. She turns to me and grabs my hand, which is tightly clenching the napkin on my lap, before swallowing loudly. "Giovanna was telling me the other day how happy she was that her ex was able to move on. I just want to support Kelsey's efforts." She winks at me, and that's when it hits me.

Hunter Lillian Cleary is a mastermind.

God, that's hot.

Chapter 11

Hunter

Playlist: Lady Killer | Maddie Zahm

"What. The fuck. Is *that*?"

I scowl at Jo, who stands in the doorway, her hand on the doorknob after walking into the apartment. "Stop! You're going to make her feel self-conscious."

"Good. It's hideous."

"Her pronouns are she/her, asshole. And she's beautiful." I roll my eyes as Jo shudders. "What happened to the Giovanna who chased after me with a horseshoe crab?"

"That's different," she says simply, finally stepping all the way into the apartment and closing the door behind her. "I was in control of that situation. And that was the same day you let me go under your bikini for the first time. I felt confident and unruly."

I stare at her.

"I mean, maybe it was the same day," she stammers, cheeks flushing. "Could have been. I don't remember."

"Okay." I duck my head so she doesn't see how tickled pink I am from her accidental revelation.

She shuffles into the living room, stopping around five feet away from where I sit cross-legged on the floor. "What is it?"

"Don't you mean *who* is *she*?"

"No, I don't."

I sigh and open the front of the terrarium, gathering my new best friend in my arms. I turn to face Giovanna as I cradle her to my chest. "This is Dolly Parton. She's a bearded dragon and I would die for her."

"Gross."

"Jo! She can hear you!" I glare at her.

"Good," she retorts, but she shuffles six inches closer. "She's terrifying. I can't believe you did this."

I ignore her. "She's a gentle creature. She likes cuddling and being petted. Did you know bearded dragons are super social? I didn't until I saw a TikTok and I knew I needed one." I press a kiss to Dolly's head, following it with a scratch that she happily leans into. "See!"

"I see a fucking monster."

"You're such a dick."

She shrugs. "Just don't expect me to take care of her."

"I don't. I wouldn't. She's my baby." I meet her eyes. "I'm a single mom now. As Reba would say, I'm a survivor."

She scoffs, turning and walking back into the kitchen. "Dramatic much?"

"Very, very much."

"At least you're self aware." Jo pulls a can of soup out of the pantry and pours it into a bowl. "What does that thing even eat?"

"'That thing' has a name. How would you feel if I called you 'that thing?'"

She laughs, and it's so loud and jovial that I startle. My god. I haven't heard her laugh like that in twelve years.

It's my new favorite sound, the rough and raw cackle followed by a snort.

Her eyes widen and she slaps a hand over her mouth. "Oh my god, I'm sorry."

I stare at her, confused. "Sorry for what?"

"Laughing like that. I know it's ugly..."

Ugly? Try goddamn *magical*.

I shake my head. "No, I'd never think that about your laugh, Giovanna. You know, that laugh is one of my favorite memories from that summer? You laughed like that when you felt so happy you burst."

"Still an ugly sound."

I ignore that comment. "You feeling free and uninhibited could never be ugly."

"Says the person who thinks that a bearded dragon is an ideal pet," she mumbles, punching in some numbers on the microwave.

I sigh and stroke my index finger along Dolly's spine. "Don't listen to her, Dolly. I love you, even if mean ol' Aunt Jo doesn't."

"There's no way in hell I'm that *thing's* aunt."

"She can call you mommy if you'd rather." Jo snickers and I narrow my eyes at her.

"Stop."

"You started it."

"Right, and now I'm asking you to stop it."

Her laugh grows again, and hell. I'll say things with slight sexual innuendos for the rest of my days if it allows me to earn her laughs. "You're ridiculous, do you know that?"

I smile softly at her. "I do."

"Enough deflecting. What do bearded dragons eat?" she asks, retrieving her soup from the microwave and leaning against the counter.

"Fruits, veggies…" I trail off, looking nervously at her.

She blows on a spoonful of soup before speaking. "It's bugs, isn't it?" She closes her mouth around the spoon, and I can't look away.

"It's bugs," I confirm.

"Swell," she mutters after swallowing. "As long as you're going to be the one to take care of her."

I try not to take any notice of the fact that she referred to Dolly as "her," but it makes me unreasonably giddy.

"Of course. You're her cool, fun, single, wine aunt. Not her other mom."

Unless she wanted to be.

God, I want her to want to be.

"The lesbian dream." She smirks while stirring her soup.

"Are you an aunt? Don't you have like eighty billion siblings?"

"Yes. That's correct. I have ten times the amount of humans on this planet as my siblings," she says dryly, taking another spoonful of soup.

I laugh loudly, delighted by her sarcastic sense of humor. And maybe I imagine it, but I swear her smile grows a little. Maybe she likes making me laugh, too.

Or maybe I'm centering myself in something I certainly shouldn't be. Maybe she's like everyone else and likes making people laugh. Maybe she feels validated by it.

I hear Jo moving out of the kitchen and towards the living room. I try to keep my breathing even. Why the hell do I have this reaction to her? It must be because we had sex. We were each other's first everything, after all. Maybe all that nonsense my grandma told me about giving away a piece of you by having sex is true. Maybe Jo's kept a piece of me in her pocket for twelve years, and maybe I've kept a piece of her. Maybe they're just trying to get back to their rightful owners.

Or perhaps those little pieces of us loved the sex so much that they're fighting to get back to one another so they can have more sex.

That must be it. Cuz damn. Fifteen year old me had her mind and back blown out by Giovanna Quinn's fingers and tongue.

That's all this is. A sexual, magnetic attraction. That's why I can't look away, why I tally every smile and hate that she feels like she lost herself.

I can admit she's attractive. Her hair, the color of dark chocolate, falls in soft waves over her shoulders. Her eyes, which she claims are brown, actually have specks of gold and green that shimmer when she smiles. Then there's her body. When Jo and I were together that summer, she'd been curvy—all luscious breasts and thighs I could never get enough of. I'd spent twelve years imagining what Giovanna would look like if I ever was lucky enough to see her again. Countless versions of her existed in my imagination, and none of them measured up to reality. She's tall, around four inches taller than my five foot three, and all ass and tits and hips and belly.

I was raised doing cotillions, and taught to groom my body in traditionally feminine ways. To keep my body at a size deemed acceptable by my mother and grandmother, which, considering I started wearing a bra at age ten, was an impossible standard to meet. I was taught how to apply makeup in a way that was "classy, not trampy," and how to behave in a way that brought honor to my family.

Despite trying and trying, I could never be just right. I was too big, too loud, too boisterous. I always showed ADHD traits, which, even after my diagnosis, my family didn't understand why I couldn't control.

In college, I met Tyler, and realized that maybe the idea of femininity and gender expression I was raised with wasn't fact. Like maybe thinness and being a stay-at-home wife and mom weren't the only *good* choices I could make. I had to figure out who I was, what I liked, not who I *should* be, or who I should be attracted to, because my family decided based on the genitals I was born with.

And honestly? Thank God I did because right now Jo's body has me feeling a certain type of way. Not that I've seen much of her, but what I have seen drives me crazy. She has stretch marks visible on her upper thighs when she sits on the couch in sleep shorts, and on her cleavage when she bends over in a lower-cut shirt.

I want to feel all of her, to become an expert in her body and know where every mark, roll, and dip is. I want to—

"Hun, did you hear me?"

"Yes," I lie, peering up at Jo. When did she get this close?

She raises a full eyebrow.

I sigh. "No."

"I was saying, Dolly Parton isn't as horrifying up close."

I gasp in offense. "I know I fudged a few stitches but—"

Jo laughs, another one of those hearty laughs and I have no idea why she's laughing, but I need to find out so I can make sure it happens again.

"I'm so sorry." Her laugh bubbles down to a sweet giggle. Why the heck am I keeping a collection of the times I've made her smile when I should be bottling these laughs? Lining the pantry with little mason jars filled with the sound, labeled with the date and cause for laughter.

"I'm sorry," Jo repeats. "I literally just said this was going to be a problem, and came up with a solution for it. That's on me. I'm talking about the little monster."

I beam up at her. "You called her by her real name!"

"Right, and look what happened when I did." She gestures toward the cross-stitched Dolly Parton pillow on the couch. "You thought I was mocking your artistry."

"Right. Because you'd never do that," I tease, uncrossing my legs and getting to my feet as I carefully balance my child in my arms.

Jo furrows her brow. "I wouldn't. I'd never make fun of something you worked hard on."

Well. Now I wish she *would*, because goddamn, that sentence has my stomach aflutter.

"Oh," I say softly, moving to put Dolly Parton back into her terrarium and kissing her one last time on her little head.

"Are you busy tonight?" Giovanna asks, her long fingernails tapping on the side of the bowl.

"I should be editing, but I'm also almost done with the last Spindle Cove book, so I'm definitely reading instead. Why?"

She's never asked what I'm doing before. We're friendly, but we're not friends. I wish we were, but she's so guarded, and I don't blame her. She's experienced hurt from people she'd trusted

"I was thinking maybe you could teach me to cross-stitch?" she asks, continuing to tap her nails on the bowl. "Or maybe we could kind of get our story straight for Becky and Kelsey? In case they ask something we haven't discussed, we should..."

"...be on the same page," I finish. "You really want me to teach you to cross stitch?"

She shrugs. "Yeah. The stuff you make is pretty and...I don't know. I need hobbies. I feel like I have no personality anymore, like

I have no idea what I like. Everything I liked and did was because Kelsey liked and did it first and now…"

"Now you need to figure out how to get back to yourself," I say softly.

She meets my eyes. "Now I need to figure out how to get back to me," she agrees.

I smile at her as I get to my feet. "So let's get you there. Starting with learning to cross stitch."

We should not have started with learning to cross-stitch. While Jo's quest to rediscover herself is noble, I don't think cross-stitching is part of it.

"Fuck!" she yells, forcefully throwing her embroidery hoop onto the coffee table. She grabs her glass of merlot and slumps against the back of the sofa, taking a generous sip. "This isn't as easy as I thought it would be."

I eye her over my own embroidery hoop. Dolly Parton—the bearded dragon—is sleeping in my lap. "You saw my human Dolly Parton pillow and assumed it was easy to make? That took me a year."

The guilty look in her eyes tells me it's a good thing when she doesn't answer. "I like to be good at things."

"That's a unique thing that only you feel," I say dryly as I reach to place my own project, a crossed-stitched bearded dragon wearing a pink cowboy hat, on the table and pick up my glass of moscato. I've begun to keep the fridge well-stocked with "juice wines," as Jo calls them.

"Hey!" she says, scowling as she playfully pushes against my thigh with her foot. I glare at her and put my fingers in my wine glass, flicking the liquid at her. She gasps. "Did you flick wine at me?"

"And if I did?" I ask, sticking my tongue out at her and biting down on it. I savor the way her eyes are immediately on my mouth.

Though, to be fair, there are several of Giovanna Quinn's body parts I'd rather have on my mouth.

"If Dolly Parton weren't sleeping on your lap, you'd *so* be paying for that." Her voice has dropped to a dramatic whisper, like she doesn't want to wake up the creature she once called a little monster. While she has yet to touch said little monster, I know it's just a matter of time.

"How would I pay for it?" I ask innocently, fluttering my eyelashes at her. "You'd be making me wet too?"

Jo's face contorts, and a pained gargling noise like a car with a dead engine comes from her mouth.

It takes me a few seconds too long to understand it's because of what I said.

"Oh, gosh. Not like...horny wet," I stammer, cheeks heating in a way that puts Savannah in mid-July to shame.

"Don't say horny," she groans, cheeks so pink I'm sure they give my own complexion a run for its money.

"Sorry. Aroused."

"That's worse! How is that worse?" She sounds tortured by this.

"I don't know! What am I supposed to say?" I hiss.

"Just...stop talking, Hunter."

Shame flows through me like molasses in summer: fast and thick. Childhood memories of grown-ups telling me I talked too much, too fast. That what I had to say didn't matter. That I was meant to be seen, not heard. That I was embarrassing them in front of their friends.

You talk too much, Hunter Lillian. You are too much.

"Wait...Hunter. Come back to me." Jo's voice is distant and distorted, like we're on opposite ends of a tunnel. Her hand tightens on my forearm. "You're pulling away, I can tell. Tell me what I said wrong so I don't say it again."

It feels like my brain and my body slowly reconnect, like the wiring had come loose. I turn my head and make eye contact with Jo.

"It's not important," I mumble, desperately wanting to look away, but not being able to.

"Yes, it is," Jo argues, her thumb rubbing patterns on my forearm. "I said something that made you feel like you needed to pull away. Was it when I told you to stop talking?"

I nod. "Yeah. That's something I heard a lot growing up."

Her eyes search mine. "And it brought you back to that?"

I duck my head, trying not to cry. "Yeah. I'm in therapy and it shouldn't bother me...but it still does sometimes. It's so silly, I—"

"When Nic told me she was moving in with Josh, it reminded me of when Kelsey left me." She says it quietly. So quietly that part of me wonders if it's in my imagination.

She continues when I don't respond. "I felt like...she was leaving like Kelsey did. Even though it's not the same situation at all, right? Like the only similarity is someone moving out of the shared space. The reasons are completely different and Nic is still my sister and friend. She wasn't leaving me. She was moving in with her amazing boyfriend and I *knew* that..."

"But it's like your heart doesn't."

"Yes!" Our eyes meet. "But it's like my heart doesn't. I'm sorry. I didn't mean to make it about me..."

"Stop that. You didn't." I place my hand over hers on my arm. "You were just telling me you could relate. And it was helpful."

She smiles softly. "Because you could empathize with my situation, it forced you to be kinder to yourself?"

"I mean, I guess. Like when you were talking, it made so much sense. I'd never judge you the way I was judging myself."

"I know. It's a trick Nic taught me. It's helpful, when I remember to do it, that is." Her eyes drift downward. "Can I hold her?"

"Dolly Parton?"

She nods.

I narrow my eyes. "I thought you said she's a little monster."

"She can be a little monster *and* I can want to hold her," she argues. "Think about babies. They're the definition of little monsters. And I want to hold and snuggle them all the time."

"Yeah. You can hold her." I gently place Dolly Parton into Jo's arms, fighting a smile.

"Oh, goddammit," Jo says miserably, stroking Dolly's spine with her index finger.

"What?" I ask, scooching closer to her. "Do you hate this? Do you want me to—"

"I think I like her, Hun. This is a disaster."

I laugh, loud and boisterous, and Jo laughs too, not stopping until she lets out a snort. Her eyes widen and I squeal with joy, pointing at her in glee and bouncing up and down.

"Giovanna fuckin' Quinn, you snorted! You snorted and—" In all my excitement, I fall off the couch, my head narrowly avoiding my glass of moscato and the corner of the coffee table. Jo's laugh is immediate, as are her snorts, meaning my laugh returns, too.

I don't know how long our laughter lasts, but when we finally have a handle on ourselves and our laughter, I'm wiping away tears, and Dolly is side-eyeing me.

"You're an awful influence." Jo chuckles, shaking her head.

I climb back onto the couch, stretch out my legs, and place my feet in her lap. "Just for you" I say, remembering the time during mass I put my tongue between two of my fingers and she snort-laughed during Father Gilligan's homily. "Your laugh is fucking awesome."

Jo scoffs. "It's obnoxious is what it is."

"So? I'm obnoxious. What's wrong with being obnoxious? Use that trick Nic taught you!"

She bites on her lip. "Kelsey got annoyed by my laugh on our third date when we watched Miss Congeniality. But my god, that movie is so fucking funny."

I narrow my eyes. "Isn't Sandra Bullock literally shamed out of laugh-snorting in that movie to conform to traditional feminini-ty? And isn't that supposed to be a bad thing? Jo...you know how you said you wanted to get back to being you again?"

"Cross-stitching isn't helping."

"Right. But you laughed the way you used to," I say gently, knowing how easily this could scare her off. "You snort-laughed and it was fucking fantastic."

She peers at me timidly. "You're not just saying that?"

"I'm not. That obnoxious noise that came from your mouth and/or nose was incredible."

She rolls her eyes. "Thanks so much."

We fall into a comfortable silence, with human Dolly Parton's *Here You Come Again* album playing quietly in the background. Jo petting bearded dragon Dolly Parton, occasionally cooing at her like the baby she is, me with my feet in Jo's lap, leaning back on my elbows and enjoying the comfortable calm.

I never really had friends until college. Tyler was one of the first people I met at Yale, though we both dropped out of pre-law after a semester, them to pursue culinary arts and me to change my major to business management. It was the only way I could

think of to have my parents not cut me off and still move forward towards my actual goal of being a photographer. I took
photography electives, was in the photography club, and when
I graduated, I took a soulless job at an office in my hometown,
shooting weddings on the side.

I always knew I wanted to move to New York, so I lived with my
parents and put up with them until I'd saved up enough money
to leave. I came out at dinner with my grandparents, where they
swore to never talk to me again. And yet, they still call me from
a burner phone once a month to leave a scathing voicemail about
how another one of their church friends heard about my "affliction."

If wanting to kiss pretty girls is an affliction, I hope I'm never
cured.

That Summer

Hunter

"This is the skin of a killer, Bella," Edward Cullen's tortured voice says from Giovanna's laptop.

I toss a handful of popcorn into my mouth. "Yeah, Edward's hot, but like...Jacob's abs."

I feel Giovanna shift next to me from her spot on her bed. "He does have abs, yes."

It's been a week since I arrived in Port Haven, and I've probably spent ninety percent of my time with Giovanna. I probably would have done so, even if she wasn't a bad bitch, which she is. MawMaw and PawPaw are always complaining about something and asking me what my favorite mystery of the Rosary is.

The answer to that *is* the real mystery.

"Don't you just want to lick him?" I ask her, eyes on Edward and Bella.

She sputters. "Edward?"

"No, silly. Jacob. Don't you wanna lick his six pack?"

"Not even a little bit."

I feel her shift again. "Well, you're probably the only girl in the world who doesn't."

She laughs, that loud laugh with a snort. "I promise you I am not. Lesbians exist."

I roll my eyes. "Right, but like...I don't know any. Do you?"

When Giovanna doesn't respond, I turn my head to look at her. She stares at the screen, but her eyes are glassy, like she isn't paying attention. "Giovanna?"

She snaps out of whatever strange trance she was in. "Right, uh. Sorry."

"Do you know any lesbians?" I ask again.

She inhales deeply. "Me. I...I like girls."

I stare at her. "Like...like that?" I point to her laptop screen. "Like how Bella likes Edward?"

She nods, staring at her bedspread. "Yeah. I like girls the way everyone else seems to like boys."

"Oh!" I say, not sure what else to say. "That's okay! Girls are so pretty, so I get it."

Giovanna lifts her eyes to mine. "Don't...don't tell anyone, okay? No one knows. You're...you're the only one who knows."

I furrow my brow in confusion. "Why would I tell anyone?"

"You don't think I'm a freak?" she asks.

I bark out a laugh. "For liking girls? Giovanna, I told you I wanted to lick a fictional werewolf's abs. If anyone's a freak, it's me."

Giovanna laughs again, loud and clear. "You're not a freak. You're just...straight."

I break eye contact and look away. "Yeah. I'm just straight." I've never said I am straight out loud before. Where I come from, everyone is just straight. If they aren't, they are an abomination. But Giovanna is so nice and makes me laugh...she could never be an abomination.

I reach out and squeeze her hand, jerking back when it feels like I've been electrocuted.

What the hell?

"I, uh. I think we missed some of the movie," I stammer, feeling my face heat. Suddenly, I don't really care about tasting Jacob Black's abs.

I want to taste Giovanna. To kiss her and be close to her in a way I've never wanted to be close to anyone before.

"Right," Giovanna murmurs, staring at her hand. I wonder if she felt it too, the electricity I felt in my bones. "The movie."

The two of us are silent for the rest of the night, eyes trained on her laptop screen.

Chapter 12

Hunter

Playlist: Oontz | MICHELLE

"Hunter, what's your love language?" Kelsey's question feels like it comes out of left field.

I look at Jo. Jo looks at me. We're over two weeks into our fake relationship, and the four of us are sitting at a fancy, barely lit steakhouse in midtown. Kelsey had texted me earlier today telling me she and Becky were meeting with Jo for lunch to talk about initial plans, and that I should surprise her and make it a double date.

I, obviously, immediately texted Jo to tell her to work on her surprised face, instead of the look of pure horror that she'd worn when I surprised her at the bistro.

Instead of looking like someone had pulled out a machete in front of her and told her they were killing her entire family like last time, Giovanna blinked three times at me before saying, "Oh, wow! It's Hunter! I didn't know Hunter was coming here!" in the most flat tone I've ever heard in my life.

I clear my throat in response to Kelsey. "Why?"

Kelsey shrugs her shoulders. "I was thinking, I know Jo's are quality time and physical touch." She looks between Jo and I, a skeptical expression on her face. "Well, it was physical touch when we were together, maybe not anymore."

Becky is in the bathroom, otherwise I would have punched her jerk of a fiancée. I want her to see it when it happens.

"Mine is words of affirmation, and Giovanna is so good at affirming me," I say instead of resorting to physical violence. I take my fake girlfriend's hand beneath the table, squeezing gently. I reach for a dinner roll with my free hand, and only let go of Giovanna's hand to butter the roll. I wordlessly offer her half of the roll as a consolation prize. She takes it tentatively, worriedly glancing at Kelsey out of the corner of her eye.

"Love languages don't usually change from partner to partner," Kelsey says coolly.

I force a smile. "Okay."

"I'm just...I'm worried Jo doesn't feel comfortable to be herself with you, Hunter," Kelsey tilts her head to the side, a small smile on her lips. "No offense."

"Much taken," I say, popping a piece of roll into my bread. "Like, there's no way that statement *couldn't* be insinuating something unkind about me, so why wouldn't I be offended by that?"

Kelsey blinks in surprise, and I raise a challenging eyebrow. Blondie must not be used to someone who bites back.

She composes herself and looks at Jo, reaching over to her and clasping her hand. I feel a volcano of envy bubbling beneath my surface. "I know things ended weird between us, JoJo—" Giovanna inhales sharply at the familiar nickname. "—but I still care about you. If you ever need to talk, I'm always here for you."

I feel bile rise in my throat. I'm getting to know Jo. Not as well as, and not in the way I'd like to, but enough to know she subconsciously still wants Kelsey's approval.

"Thank you, Kelsey," Giovanna answers, eyes pinned on the carpet. "But um..." She lifts her eyes to mine, and I smile encouragingly. "I think Hunter and I are just fine."

I want to scream. Jump on the table and cheer because I know how hard that must have been for her. I make a mental note to grab her a bottle of that merlot she's so into on the way home.

"I want you to be as happy as you were last year, as happy as I am now." Kelsey says innocently, hand still on Giovanna's.

Damn, homegirl isn't backing down, and it's pissing me off. Giovanna isn't mine, but she also isn't Kelsey's and it's fucking *weird* that Kelsey is trying to show ownership over her ex while her fiancée is in the bathroom.

I take Giovanna's hand in mine under the table again, this time intertwining our fingers together. I squeeze her hand, and though Giovanna's eyes stay on Kelsey, she squeezes back.

"I think I'm learning that happiness doesn't look the way I thought it would," Giovanna answers, turning her head to look at me. There's a half smile on her face, just for me.

I lift our entangled hands to my mouth and press a kiss to the back of her hand. I can feel Kelsey's eyes on us, and I know that's the point. For her to see and to make her believe that this is real.

But this moment is solely for Giovanna, and I hope she can feel that.

"What did I miss?" Becky says, sliding back into the booth next to Kelsey.

"Not a thing," I say, winking at Giovanna. Her half smile becomes a three-quarter smile, at least.

No one can ever say I wasn't a good roommate, and like any good roommate, I will have my praises sung by historians in the future for being such a devoted friend. And I'll shake my fist at them from hell for getting it right for once.

Damn, I'm still alive and I'm already angry at hypothetical historians for interpreting my fake relationship correctly.

Jo reaches for and takes another roll from the basket, Kelsey's eyes following her. I know she's biting her tongue to keep from saying what she wants to, to keep from saying bullshit about Jo's food choices.

I like knowing this discomfort exists for her.

After our fifteen million year-long business lunch with the brides from hell, Giovanna and I are outside the restaurant. I'm surprised when she starts walking with me to the subway instead of going with Becky and Kelsey towards their office.

"You're not going back to work?" I ask.

"I actually have therapy today." She's staring down, like she has a crucial exam on the exact coordinates of each crack in this damn sidewalk. "Can I hold Dolly during my appointment?"

I bite my lip to keep from giggling. Giovanna still likes to pretend that she hates Dolly Parton, but I've caught her holding her while singing "Jolene" multiple times in the morning. She's even fed Dolly her buggy breakfast. She's like a dad who swears up and down he doesn't want any pets, and then is obsessed with them when you actually bring home said pet.

"Of course you can," I say as we continue to walk to the subway station. I'm grateful I'm with Jo, because public transportation and the different subway lines are still overwhelming.

"It doesn't mean I like her," Jo says, and I'm unsure if she's trying to convince herself, or me.

I try to fight my grin, and fail spectacularly. "Of course it doesn't."

Chapter 13

Jo

Playlist: The Archer | Taylor Swift

"You've got to be fucking kidding me," Alena says, blinking in disbelief.

"Nope." I scratch Dolly on her nose as she happily snuggles into me. Hunter can never know, but dammit, I'm fond of this little monster.

"You're pretending to date your ex-girlfriend to convince your ex-fiancée that you're over her while planning her wedding?"

"Not exactly," I argue, avoiding looking at the laptop set up on my bed. "Hunter and I never defined the relationship back in the day. So she's not *technically* my ex-girlfriend."

I can see my therapist rubbing at her temples in my peripheral vision. "So you cancel three weeks of appointments and this is what you get yourself into."

"See, this is why I canceled the appointments." I glare into the camera. "I knew you wouldn't get it. Nobody gets it." I pause for a moment. "Except for Hunter. She gets it."

Alena takes a deep breath, like the ones she usually tells me to take. "You have to understand why I'm concerned, Jo."

I bite my lip. "I do. Nic and Josh tried to convince me not to plan the wedding, too. But the money would change every-thing...you have to understand *that*."

Her face softens. "You're right. I do understand that, *and* the idea that you're putting yourself willingly into a situation with your ex is concerning."

"But I'm not dealing with it alone," I remind her. "Hunter's in it with me."

"I don't buy it," she says, crossing her arms.

"What do you mean?"

"I mean you're getting enough money to be able to start the business of your dreams, but what is Hunter getting out of it? Why is she agreeing to this madcap plan that should only stay in historical romances?"

That perks me up. "You read historical romance?"

"Yeah, you talked about them enough, and I got curious. You're right. About historical romances, not this situation," she clarifies, because god forbid she insinuate I was right about this situation.

I smirk at her. "You're welcome."

Alena rolls her eyes. When Nic started bugging me about going to therapy, she'd helped me find someone LGBTQIA+ affirming. I'd liked Alena right away because I knew she wasn't going to let me bullshit myself out of things, that she'd push me. She's also a chronically ill Latina woman, so she *gets* how my chronic illness affects every aspect of my life in a way most people don't.

I regret picking her now, though.

"Don't think you're getting out of this. What is Hunter getting out of this arrangement?" she repeats.

"I don't know," I admit, realizing I haven't thought about it. "Maybe she's trying to make up for that summer."

"What about that summer?"

I swallow the lump in my throat. "I don't want to talk about it."

"You and I both know the things you *don't* want to talk about are the things you *should* talk about." Her voice is gentler.

I begin to pick at the peeling burgundy nail polish on my left middle finger. It's keeping me from flipping my therapist off, which is probably for the best. "I fell in love with her," I admit. I've never said it aloud before. "With Hunter. I was fifteen, so it was only like...unimportant teenage love..."

"First loves are impactful, and not at all unimportant. Don't invalidate yourself or your experiences," Alena says. She lifts her favorite mug to her mouth.

"Hunter told me at the end of summer that she didn't know if she was actually gay. She's from the south, her family's extremely traditional and conservative. Like her grandparents went to church with my family, and got mad when our priest said we should care about undocumented immigrants.

"I knew I was gay, so that broke me. Everything that summer had felt so real to me. And...and I thought it was the same for her." I try to swallow the lump that had grown in my throat while talking. "We decided not to exchange numbers or add each other on social media, and wait until next summer. She said if she still wanted me, she'd have me again, and consider coming out. But, her grandparents sold their summer house the following spring and we never saw each other again.

"It was my first real heartbreak. I thought she might try to reach out...ask her grandparents for my parents' number or something. But by then, I had already come out and Mr. and Mrs. McIntyre were looking at me with disgust, so I knew I couldn't ask..." I inhale shakily. "She was just...gone."

Alena nods slowly. "So you think agreeing to fake date you is some sort of atonement for your past?"

I shrug helplessly. "Maybe. Or maybe she's a nice person who wants to help me out."

"Nothing I say is going to change your mind, is it?"

"No."

"Your determination is admirable." She says it like she's being held at gunpoint. "I hope you know I don't want to see you get hurt, and I'm worried that this will harm you."

"And maybe you're right," I admit, feeling like it's being forced out of me, too. "Maybe this is a terrible decision and maybe it's going to hurt me." I take a deep breath. "But it's *my* decision. I've felt so out of control of my life since the breakup, and I know you think this is a bad idea, but I finally feel like I have some control over my life again, even if it's just this teeny tiny way."

Alena looks pensive. "I mean, there are literally dozens of ways for you to assert control over your life, but I don't think talking about them is going to make any difference."

"Probably not."

"Just...take care of yourself, okay? Does your family know about what you're doing?"

"No, and I'm not going to tell them," I tell her definitively.

"You're going to keep this from Nic?" She looks surprised, which is fair. Nic is able to read me and see through my bullshit even better than Alena.

I groan. "Fuck. I can't do that. But if I tell her, she'll yap."

"So maybe you should tell your entire family to keep that from happening."

I can see right through her. "What, so all of them can tell me that I'm making an awful decision and it's not just you?"

"No!" she insists unbelievably.

I roll my eyes. "I have a book club meeting tonight, so maybe I'll tell Nic then. Maybe even Josh and Nellie. God knows they've been dumbasses before."

"Okay," Alena says in a disbelieving tone.

After we end the appointment, I text the book club.

Bodice Ripper Book Club

Jo: bruce am i allowed to bring alcohol to book club

Josh: 1) "Bruce" doesn't have the same effect as "Josephine," but good try.

Josh: 2) I'd prefer you didn't.

Nellie: great boundary setting josh!

Josh: Thank you!!!! <smiling emoji> <thumbs up emoji>

Jo: okay well can i bring hunter.

Josh: Hunter?

Josh: Your ex-girlfriend/roommate Hunter? Sure.

Nellie: i'm sorry your WHAT

Nellie: EX GIRLFRIEND????

Nellie: WHY AM I JUST HEARING ABOUT THIS????

Jo: thanks a bunch, bruce.

Jo: she's excited to join us.

Jo: or she will be when i tell her she's coming.

Josh, Nic, and Nellie know me. They get me. Maybe I'm right and they'll all get it, and prove Alena wrong.

Okay, so I was wrong. Hunter sits next to me on Josh's loveseat, our thighs pressed together in a way that is not at all distracting, while Josh and Nellie sit on the new couch across from us. Nic sits on the arm, and all three are staring at us with gaping mouths.

"Close your mouth before you catch flies, Nicoletta," I tell my sister dryly, echoing our Nonna. It works though, all three of them shut their mouths.

"That is..." Josh says, looking nervously at Nic. "Certainly an interesting plan."

"Shut up Joshua," Nic growls, eyes fixed on mine. I shift uncomfortably. My sister usually isn't the biggest fan of eye contact, so when she holds it like this, I know she means business. "What the fuck is wrong with you?"

Hunter raises her hand. "I'm involved with this decision, too."

Nic ignores her. "What did Alena say about this?" she demands.

"She loved the idea!" I lie. "Said it's a great way to feel more in control of my life."

Nic studies my face for about two seconds before speaking again. "You're such a liar, JoJo. You're doing your lying face," she groans, grinding the heels of her hands into her eyes. "Joshy, tell her this is a terrible idea."

Josh looks my way, a panicked expression on his face. "I'm not getting in the middle of you two."

"Coward," Nellie grumbles. "I'll say it. Jo, what the *fuck* are you thinking?" She looks at Hunter. "I don't know you as well, Hunter, but considering everything Tyler's told me about you and the fact that you have nothing to gain from this, I have a feeling that you're getting strong armed into this."

"Hey!" Hunter objects. "I'm not a helpless damsel. I have just as much agency in this as Giovanna."

The three of them all stare at Hunter. "Did you...call her Giovanna?" Nic asks, confused.

I feel my face flush. It's an inside joke in my family, that we all hate being called by our full names. Mom decided we needed "strong Italian names" to balance out the Irish last name we inherited from dad. I think Dad should have fought against it, since most of us look Italian enough to make it obvious. But no, we all have obnoxiously long names that end in vowels. Katerina, Nicoletta, Giovanna, Lorenzo, Emilia, Alexandria, Leonardo, and Isabella. We all go by our nicknames, though: Kat, Nic, Jo, Ren, Millie, Alex, Leo, and Izzy. Unless, of course, Mom's mad at us about something. Then we get the full name and her Long Island accent comes out in full force.

Nic hates being called Nicoletta, but I've heard Josh call her by it multiple times. Which is, like, so gross. But also kind of cute. The man knows better than to call me Giovanna, which is why he started jokingly calling me Josephine.

I don't know what it means that I don't mind—hell, maybe even like—when Hunter calls me by my full name. Maybe it's the fact I have a crush on her–and I mean honestly, who wouldn't? She's all curves and curly blonde hair and laughter and smiles. Hunter is sunshine personified, like the solar system gifted her to the earth to make up for nighttime.

"Shut up, Nicky," I grumble, instead of addressing Nic's concerns. My sister throws up her middle finger.

"I want to be clear that I'm not being forced into this. In fact, I'm the one who suggested it," Hunter continues. "I couldn't just stand by when Kelsey was treating Giovanna like a possession. So, yeah. I suggested we pretend to date, and I'd do it again in a heartbeat."

I can't stop staring at Hunter. Her eyes are so blue, so clear. Her eyelashes are so unfairly long, the faint sprinkling of freckles across the bridge of her nose make her look so damn sweet, so unlike the woman who's repeatedly put my ex in her place.

I don't want to like her as much as I'm beginning to. I tried to keep emotional distance between us, but when I'm around her, it doesn't feel like my heart is entangled with barbed wire, the way it's felt for so long. Instead, my heart feels light and airy, like it's filled with champagne bubbles.

"I still feel like there are better ways." Nic's words bring me back into the present. "Like literally anything else."

I look at her. "Hunter was able to negotiate so that I'm getting even more money than the amount I told you before."

Nic and Josh's eyes widen. "Oh," Nic whispers. "Oh. That's an obscene amount of money."

Nic's eyes are darting between me and Hunter. I can tell that she's nervous, and I don't blame her. I was nervous about her and Josh when they started seeing each other. I didn't trust him when he stopped texting her and she was sad. Sure, his grandma was dying, but my big bad sister was *sad*. She also saw the aftermath of mine and Hunter's relationship twelve years ago, *and* mine and Kelsey's last year. I can understand why she's not thrilled about me working with both of them, and pretending to date one of them. My siblings and I are ridiculously protective of one another. I felt bad for Leo's girlfriend Stella when he first brought her to Sunday dinner a few years ago. She had seven of us interrogating her and the poor girl burst into tears over her plate of lasagna. Yet, she's somehow stuck around since then. She's a stronger person than I am.

"I'm a big girl," I say. "It's okay, I can make my own decisions."

"Thoughtless as fuck decisions," Josh mutters under his breath. I grab a piece of salami from the charcuterie board and throw it at him. It lands with a slapping noise on his cheek.

Nic barks out a laugh, covering her mouth with both hands while he glares at me. "Don't waste my charcuterie," is all he has to say for himself before peeling it off his face and popping it into his mouth.

"I think it's really cool that Jo has so many people who care about and are worried about her," Hunter speaks so quietly that I almost think I imagine it.

When I look at her, she's looking at Nellie, Nic, and Josh, a sad sort of smile on her face. She hasn't talked about her family at all, and I have no idea what her relationship with them is like. Does she FaceTime them on the Sunday evenings she can't make it home, sometimes hiding at events she's working, to see most of her family yelling over each other at a long table?

I don't know for certain, but something tells me she doesn't. Shame swirls in my stomach as she looks at the people who love me with such genuine admiration.

Nellie's face falls. "Hey, Hunter," she says quietly, "it's not that we don't trust you..."

"You just love Jo," Hunter finishes, and I notice her fidgeting with the hem of her blue floral sundress. It perfectly matches her eyes. "You've seen her get hurt and come out the other side after a lot of pain and you don't want that to happen again. I think that's beautiful, and I'm grateful she has people like you in her life." She smiles, but it's a watery smile, one that makes me think that it's something she hasn't experienced, something she wishes she has, too.

It makes my heart ache.

I clear my throat. "It doesn't really matter if you approve of this or not, it's happening. I'm just telling you because...well. I can't lie to Nic. And Nic has a big mouth. So I'm telling the rest of the family next weekend at Sunday dinner." I turn to Hunter. "Do you want to come, Hun?"

She looks taken aback. "Me?"

I roll my eyes. "No, the other Hun."

She sticks out her lower lip in a pout, and my eyes are immediately drawn to her mouth. She wears the same pink lipstick every day, and I wonder what it feels like. If it's creamy, or sticky. If it transfers easily or is one of those new formulas that claim to be transfer-proof. If I kiss her...

"I'm from Georgia, Giovanna. Everybody calls everybody hun."

I pretend I wasn't fantasizing about fucking up that perfectly applied lipstick with my own mouth, about how swollen her already full lips would be. "Ha, right," I say shakily, forcing myself to look at everyone else. All three of them look like they're fighting back smiles, like they could tell what I was thinking.

"What?" I snap, hoping to startle them out of their sudden goofy moods.

It doesn't work, not even a little bit. "Fake dating," Josh snickers, giving Nic a knowing look. "Do you think they'll be able to fool themselves too, Buttercup?"

I look at Hunter, who looks as confused as I feel. "It works just fine in romance books."

Josh and Nic are snickering to themselves, like there's a joke I missed the punchline for. Nellie, while not directly interacting with them, looks like she at least gets the joke.

I do not get the joke.

"Right, because how does that fake dating thing end in romance books? With the roommates simply going back to roommates?" Nic cackles at Josh's response and Hunter's cheeks redden as she ducks her head.

"You two should break up," I grumble. "You're annoying as fuck."

"Just let us know how it goes." Josh wipes a tear from his eye. "The fake dating thing."

"It's going to go great," Hunter insists. "This is real life, not a romance novel."

"Speaking of romance novels, can we talk about the marble marquis of our dreams?" I plead, digging in my bag for my copy of our monthly pick.

Nic's laughter cuts off suddenly. "And there's my cue," she says, hopping off the arm of the couch and pulling her phone from her waistband. "Have fun, nerds."

"Should I go, too?" Hunter asks me, nervously picking at the skin around her nails as Nic makes her exit. "I haven't read this one."

"Do you read historical romance, too?" Nellie asks.

"Jo gave me full access to her library after I moved in. I'm obsessed."

"Okay, well, stay then," Josh says definitively. "So you can give input for next month's book."

"Like you pay any attention to anyone's input but your own," I say. He takes a page out of his partner's book and gives me the middle finger.

"You want me to join your book club?" Hunter asks with uncertainty.

I look at her. "Yeah, Hun. That's why I brought you."

"Oh." She looks bewildered by this.

"You don't have to join if you don't want to," Josh tells her. "But we'd love it if you did. These two like to gang up on me and you actually seem like a reasonable human, so you joining would be advantageous for myself."

Hunter's laugh is so bright it makes me want to run headfirst into a wall. "As long as I'm not imposing."

I smile at her. "You could never impose." Out of the corner of my eye, I see Josh and Nellie exchange a knowing look, and my stomach sinks.

This might not be as straight-forward as I'd thought.

Chapter 14

Hunter

Playlist: Dips | Daisy the Great

Hunter: help.

Hunter: i'm supposed to shoot our favorite brides this weekend.

Hunter: on sunday

Hunter: in central park

Hunter: all my photographer groups say it's gonna be swimming with tourists so i told them that and they were like "oh well"??????

Jo: hahaha, that's becky and kelsey for you.

Hunter: wanna come to the shoot? it'll make kelsey's eye twitch and make her look ugly in her pics.

Jo: i'm actually coordinating a wedding at the boathouse, so if you're over there, i might see you.

Hunter: they want to shoot in multiple locations but wouldn't specify where besides starting at bethesda fountain.

Jo: yikes. they probably wanna wander and shoot where they decide is pretty that day.

Hunter: yeah, i'm gonna highly encourage them to choose three shooting locations and if we have time we can do more, but walking aimlessly around central park on a weekend with them sounds hellish.

Jo: tell them they're shooting at bethesda fountain, and the bow and gapstow bridges. Great photo locations, and if they don't like them, ask them to specify. If they don't, let me know and i'll get on them.

Hunter: i've shot at those locations before! They're close to one another, right?

Jo: yup. That's why i picked them. Less travel time means less time for you to have to talk to them.

Hunter: my god, jo. I could kiss you right now.

Hunter: i mean, i won't. Cuz that would be weird as fuck.

Hunter: right?

Seen by Jo Quinn.

"Okay, calm down," I say, wincing as Jo slams the door behind us and walks ahead of me. It's been a week and a half since book club, and today was the engagement shoot from hell. "It could have been worse."

I'm just saying that to be nice. It really couldn't have gone much worse.

"How? Please, tell me how it could have gone worse," Jo asks, stalking down the hallway to her room without looking back at me. I gingerly place my camera, Loretta, on the kitchen counter before jogging after her.

"Freak snowstorm," I offer.

Her bedroom door is open, which I take as an invitation to follow her inside. I realize as I look around that even though we've lived together for months at this point, I've never been in her room until now. It feels intimate. But she's not kicking me out as she pulls her black blouse over her head and—oh.

Oh.

I should leave, because I'm achy and turned on by the sight of her bare skin. The rolls and bumps of her back and hips, a single freckle on her right shoulder blade, the way her waist delicately curves inward with silver stretch marks etched into her skin.

"The freak snowstorm would have made for gorgeous pictures at least," Giovanna grumbles as she reaches behind her to unclip her bra. I watch in equal amounts of horror and lust as the black fabric falls to her feet.

Oh god, I think, feeling dizzy.

"Wait, what are you doing in here?" she yelps, spinning to face me and covering her breasts with her hands. Oops, I guess I spoke out loud. I understand what she's trying to do, but my god, her hands just create incredible cleavage. I want to lick—

"Get. Out," she seethes as her eyes darken. I'm both terrified and turned on.

"Yep. Got it," I manage to say, backing out of the doorway and pulling the door closed.

I turn and walk into the living room as images of what Giovanna's breasts would look like overflowing in my hands swirl in my mind.

I am no better than a straight man.

I squat in front of Dolly Parton's terrarium.

"Stop looking at me like that," I tell her.

She blinks.

"Yeah, I know I'm unhinged. Thanks for the reminder."

She stares at me.

"Okay, no. No, this isn't a bad idea. This is gonna go fine. I can control my lustful urges fine."

"Are you talking to the little monster?"

I screech and jump at Giovanna's voice, spinning to face her. She's changed into pajama shorts and an oversized I Love New York t-shirt. Her dark waves flow over her shoulders, like a chocolate fountain, and what a coincidence: I deserve a sweet treat.

"You call her little monster like you didn't feed her breakfast this morning."

Her cheeks flush pink, like she's embarrassed to be caught caring for Dolly. "Whatever. We need to talk about...the park incident."

"Yeah. We fucking do," I agree, crossing my arms over my chest. "Why did you look like I murdered your dog when we ran into each other?"

"Oh my god, I did not," Jo argues, scowling at me and mirroring my movement, crossing her own arms over her chest.

"Yeah, you did. And Kelsey's already texted me the most bullshit backhanded compliments." I pull my phone out of my back pocket and begin to read. "'Hey, I know dealing with Jo's moods and blood sugar is sooooo'—she used five o's there, by the way—'exhausting, and I can tell by the dark circles under your eyes that it's taking its toll on you. Also she doesn't seem to be herself when you guys are together. I'm here if you need me. Heart emoji, heart emoji, heart emoji, heart emoji, heart emoji.' That's right. *Five* heart emojis."

I hold my phone out to Giovanna, who takes it and quickly reads the message. "Wow. Five o's *and* five heart emojis. Her record with me was three."

"It's not funny! I can't tell which one of us she thinks is the bad guy in our fake relationship, but she definitely doesn't think we're happy."

"Why doesn't she think we're happy?"

I throw my hands in the air. "I don't know, Jo. Maybe because you act like you fucking hate me whenever you see me."

She looks taken aback. "No, I don't."

"You do! You didn't even acknowledge me when you bumped into us at the boathouse. You were so chatty with Becky and Kelsey and like...you barely looked at me. When you did look at me, it was like I was the last person you wanted there." I swallow, trying not to show how much it hurt. "We're supposed to be dating. That's not how people who are dating act towards each other."

"I was surprised to see you," she counters.

"You knew it'd be a possibility since we were both working in the park! *You* were the one who said it was a possibility, and you still looked at me like you got coal on Christmas morning. And let me tell you, Giovanna, I'm not just saying this as your fake girlfriend, I'm saying it as your roommate, your friend. That was weird as hell."

Jo's eyes meet mine, and I'm taken aback by the emotion in them.

"I don't know how to act around you." It's so quiet that I have to ask her to repeat herself. "You're my fake girlfriend, and I've never had a fake girlfriend before."

"I think the whole point is to *not* act like I'm your fake girlfriend."

"I'm your friend?" She asks, suspicion and what I think is hope in her voice.

"No, I help all my former lovers convince their ex-fiancées that they're over them," I deadpan.

A small smile curls at the edge of her mouth. "That's pretty on par with being sapphic."

I can't help but smile back. "Cute joke. Stop deflecting. I don't have ulterior motives and yes, we're friends. I shrug helplessly. "I'm helping you, but you've helped me, too. More than you'll ever know."

She eyes me with caution. "So you're just a genuinely kind person? Like this sweet southern girl shit isn't a facade?"

"What sweet southern girl shit?"

"The naming your camera and pet after country powerhouses. The 'y'alls.'" Jo's attempt at copying my accent makes me giggle, though the look on her face lets me know that's not the right reaction.

"Sorry," I say, forcing the smile off my face. "No. That's just me."

"Huh." Jo appears to ponder this. "You're as southern and sweet as tea."

"That is a *fantastic* metaphor. But you're forgetting that I can also be a bitch to the people who deserve it."

A small smile breaks across her face. "I thought it was a good one, too," she admits bashfully. "Anyway, back to business. You're not doing this to, like, break my heart again and leave me all sad and shit, right?"

"Not that I'm aware of?" The way she's insisting I can't just be doing this to help her almost has me convinced I have ulterior motives unbeknownst to me.

"Okay. Okay." She inhales shakily. "Okay."

"Since it's so okay, we need to find a solution to your ex-fiance thinking we're in a toxic relationship because of how you interact with me."

Jo groans and flops onto the couch. "How?"

"You stop acting like you hate me," I say, walking over to Dolly's terrarium and opening the hatch on the front. "Hi, princess," I coo, as she crawls into my arms.

I feel Jo's eyes on me. "How?" she repeats.

I turn around and walk to the couch, sitting next to her. "I think we need to practice intimacy."

She jerks away from me. "I'm not having sex with you."

I roll my eyes. "You read too many historical romances, Jesus Christ. Sex isn't the only type of intimacy that exists. Think of the stolen touches and kisses before the big event. The longing stares and words exchanged before they take their clothes off. All of that is intimacy, and you're absolute shit at it."

"Gee, thanks," she deadpans.

"I'm serious. The only way we're going to convince anyone is if we perform for them. And what do you do before a performance? You rehearse. So we're going to spend the nights you're not working getting to know each other."

Jo groans and lets her head flop against the back of the couch. "Goddammit."

"Okay, you know what? See, right there is why Kelsey thinks things are weird between us," I exclaim, cradling Dolly Parton closer into my chest. "You're acting like I said I'm going to pull out your teeth and burn all your romance novels."

She lifts her head, having the decency to look at least a little ashamed. "Sorry."

"It's fine." I shove my emotions into a box to deal with later and wave my hand at her. "But if you want to convince Kelsey and Becky that we're a thing, you have to figure out how to fake excitement and love around me. I think us getting to know each other and fostering a friendship would help that."

She ponders it for a moment. "That's it? I just have to pretend to like you?"

"Um, no," I say regretfully as my cheeks heat. "Giovanna, we gotta be physical in front of them. It's fucking weird that we don't. I can count on one hand the amount of times we've touched around them. We have to touch, hold hands...maybe even kiss."

I think that Jo's going to oppose again, but she's silent.

"Did you hear me?"

"Yes. Give me a second," she answers, chewing on her bottom lip. Finally she exhales heavily. "God, you're right. It's fucking weird that there's always like, a foot between us."

"A little."

She looks down at our legs, which are only a few inches apart. She and I both have thick thighs that expand when we sit, so that part of our bodies is closer than the rest. "It's not hard when it's just us."

"Maybe because this closeness we share as roommates is real?" I suggest. "Like we're not trying to convince anyone of anything. We just both sat on the couch. That's why I think it'd be helpful to do a little more at home."

"I keep wanting to argue that this doesn't make sense." She reaches out a hand out to scratch Dolly under her chin. "But none of this makes sense, does it? So why would fixing it make sense?"

I bite back a smile. "Fair point."

"We have to practice kissing?" Jo says, sounding nervous.

"A quick kiss every once in a while wouldn't hurt. We don't have to make out, or use tongue, or anything like that. But it'll sell us as a couple. Plus, with us both going to the bachelorette weekend, I think it'd be really weird if they didn't see us kiss for the entire weekend."

"Oh. You're going to hate me," Jo says sheepishly. "I asked for two rooms for the weekend in Port Haven. Told Becky that I wanted my own space to organize everything I needed, and that you needed your own to edit."

"You're not wrong. Having our own separate rooms makes it easier to do our jobs. But, I think that means we need to work on touching and being couple-y extra, extra hard."

"Okay," Jo says, her eyes on Dolly. "Where do we start?"

I shrug. "Like this." I hold our bearded dragon out to her. "Wanna hold her?"

Jo nods and takes Dolly into her arms. "My favorite little monster," she says, a soft smile spreading across her face.

As she cradles Dolly, I reach out and brush her hair off her shoulder. She tenses and looks at me, eyes wide. "Oh. Like *that*?"

I bite the inside of my cheek to keep from laughing. "Mmhmm. Like that. Let's put on a show or something and just sit here and platonically touch."

She places her hand on my thigh and I almost spring through the ceiling at her touch.

This was a *terrible* idea.

"Good," I croak. "That's good. How does it feel?"

"Like I'm touching your leg," she responds without even a millisecond of hesitation.

"Thank you, that's very helpful."

She's fighting back a smile, and she sucks at it. This woman wants to smile *big*. "I mean that it doesn't feel forced or fake."

"See! It can be as simple and straightforward as touching my leg."

We spend the rest of the night watching the 2005 *Pride and Prejudice*, during which Giovanna argues that Mr. Bingley is hotter than Mr. Darcy, which is the worst take I've ever heard in my life. Her hand stays on my thigh, and I try to regulate my breathing, to tell my body that this is practice and doesn't mean anything. So *stop* picturing Giovanna naked, for goodness' sake.

At one point, her hand slowly moves upward until she squeezes my inner thigh and my soul ascends to a higher plane.

"Is this okay?" she asks, not taking her eyes off the screen.

"Uh-huh," I squeak.

This isn't helping me not picture her naked.

Minutes later, she turns her body to me. Dolly is asleep on my lap, and Jo weaves her fingers through my curls, which are especially tangled after today's Central Park adventures. She cups the side of my head, and I slowly realize what's happening.

"When I said we should practice kissing, I didn't mean it had to be tonight," I whisper, mouth dry and heart pounding.

Jo's eyes are fixated on my mouth. *Stop that*, I want to scream at her. *But also don't stop. But stop. But don't. Kiss me hard, like you used to. But we're not who we used to be, so don't. But please do.*

"I think we should get it over with. The first time," she says, raising her eyes to mine.

"Right. Get it over with."

She pulls me closer to her. Her eyes search mine as she bites her lower lip. Her breath is warm on my face. "You're no Charles Bingley, but you'll do, Hunter Cleary."

She presses her lips to mine and I try to control myself, I promise I do.

But how do you control yourself when this fake kiss is making fireworks go off in your stomach? When your toes are curling and this soft, closed mouth kiss is the greatest kiss you've had in years?

I can't help it. I sigh and lean into her, head swimming.

And she immediately pulls away, eyes snapping open.

"What was that?" she asks, sounding panicked.

"Nothing," I answer, way too quickly for it to be nothing.

"You sighed. And leaned into the kiss." Giovanna scrambles to her feet.

I stand with Dolly Parton in my arms. "It's not my fault you're a good kisser." Maybe I can gaslight her into thinking this is her fault. "We can't kiss and *not* act like we're into it. That ruins the purpose of kissing altogether."

She runs her fingers through her hair. It's so thick and long and I want to see it splayed out around her as she moans my name and I kiss her everywhere I can reach.

"I guess you're right," she says slowly.

Holy shit. I'm a little concerned at how easy that was.

"Yeah. We need some movement. We can't just push our lips together and not move. That doesn't look real."

Though it felt incredible. What am I doing telling her we need to do more? Doing nothing was plenty to make me weak in the knees.

She nods. "Can we try again?"

"Yeah. Let me put the little monster away first." I motion to Dolly Parton with my head before putting her back in her terrarium.

I turn back to Jo and we lean into each other. We both still for a moment, lips a breath apart, breaths hot on each other. And then she's kissing me with the movement I'd demanded of her.

And it was a terrible idea, because I once again lean into this fake kiss that means absolutely nothing to us. But this time I moan.

Loudly.

Giovanna pulls away, eyes wide. "Was that..."

"A moan? Yep. Sorry. It just kinda happened."

"No, it's fine. Makes it really believable." She clears her throat. "I just wasn't expecting it."

"You and me both." I inhale deeply. "Are you open for some constructive criticism?"

"Only if you are," she answers.

"Is your constructive criticism that I moaned too loud?" I ask.

"Yes."

"Okay, well. Your hands were limply by your sides." I demonstrate the position I'm describing, raising my shoulders and straightening my back to drive the point in. "Like you were standing at attention, not embracing me in any way."

"Jesus." She rubs at her temples. "I promise I've kissed people before."

"I'm guessing when you usually kiss a partner, you're not so...in your head. When you're kissing, you follow your partner and intuition, right? With this, you're trying to kiss *right*. Not just kiss." I motion to the TV with my head. "So pretend I'm that goofy ginger dude...wait, you don't like dudes."

She giggles and that's it. Her giggle is my new favorite sound. "I wouldn't actually want to kiss him, but like...lesbians can have crushes on male fictional characters or celebrities."

I blink at her in surprise. "*Really*?"

"Mmhm. Doesn't make me less of a lesbian."

"Okay, well. Imagine I'm him." I'm thrown off by this information. I always thought that having crushes on men, fictional or not, disqualified you from being a lesbian. "Or if that doesn't do it for you, pretend I'm...a beautiful woman," I finish lamely.

"You are a beautiful woman," Jo says earnestly, a blush creeping down her neck.

"Just imagine I'm someone you want to kiss." My throat is dry, my voice quiet.

Her eyes meet mine again, soft and earnest. "I can do that."

She cups my face in her hands again. She stares at me for a moment, like she's drinking me in, or waiting for me to pull away. But then she takes my mouth with hers and my arms wrap around her waist on their own accord, I swear to god.

It's a good kiss. A really good kiss. There's the movement we'd been missing previously, and she runs her thumbs over my cheeks in a way that has me reminding myself this still isn't real.

Then, so lightly I think I imagine it at first, she opens her mouth, her tongue gently brushing against the seam of my lips.

I moan and lean into her again, one of her hands moving to grab at the back of my head. I open my mouth and our tongues meet, our kiss growing more frantic by the second until I force myself to pull away.

"Good work," I gasp. "A+ in kissing class today."

"Thank you." Her lips are swollen and her cheeks are pink. There's a stunned expression on her face, like she can't quite figure out where she is.

"That was fun," I blurt out. "Really, really fun."

She blinks a few times before delicately running her tongue over her bottom lip.

It's like she *wants* me to jump her bones.

"Really, really fun," she echoes.

"Yeah," I agree. "I think we nailed it."

"Nailed it."

"I'm going to bed. I'm tired." I fake a yawn, stretching my arms over my head to sell it.

"Sounds good," she says, suddenly averting her gaze. "Goodnight, Hun."

"'Night, Giovanna."

When I close my bedroom door behind me, I don't know what comes over me, but I'm screaming into my pillow as my feet kick excitedly.

I keep saying I'm fucked. That Jo's going to make me fall for her and I'm going to get hurt.

Now I know I'm wrong. I'm already gone.

Chapter 15

Jo

Playlist: This Kiss, Faith Hill

Hunter and I kissed a week and a half ago. A week and a half ago, I let myself believe I was worth loving, worth kissing passionately.

I didn't tell Hunter, but Kelsey had told me I wasn't a good kisser. I'm still not sure what that meant, and despite googling *how to be a good kisser* repeatedly, I never got it quite right.

There were never any passionate makeouts between us. Kissing felt like a chore, one I dreaded, because I knew she'd look miserable when we pulled apart.

Hunter has me thinking that maybe kissing isn't supposed to be like that. Maybe kissing is supposed to be enjoyable in itself.

Or maybe it's just her. She's Hunter, after all; being a hype girl and making people feel good is what she naturally does.

Or maybe it's me. Maybe she likes *me*.

No. I can't let myself think like that. If I think like that, I'm just asking to be hurt.

"Just thinking like that is asking to be hurt? Not any of the other stuff you're doing?" Alena asks innocently, taking a sip of tea.

I roll my eyes and reach behind me to adjust the pillows on my bed. "Do you not like this plan, Alena? Please, elaborate. You haven't mentioned it before."

She scowls at me as she dunks her teabag in her mug, lifting it up to the camera. "Read it."

I sigh heavily but read the words on the mug out loud. "I am a therapist. Let's just assume I'm never wrong."

"Bingo. And let's assume I'm *doubly* right about this, because you don't need a Masters Degree to see this is headed straight toward disaster."

"It's not!" I argue.

"How do you feel about Hunter?" Alena asks, taking a sip from her personal attack of a mug.

"Hunter?"

"Hunter. Your fake girlfriend?" she elaborates, lowering the mug.

Shit. That's a good question. How *do* I feel about Hunter? I haven't really let myself linger on that.

I chew on my bottom lip. "I think she's genuine. Like what you see with her is exactly what you get. She has no filter, which is sometimes annoying, but also refreshing as hell. Sometimes it's randomly saying something kind. Like today she told me no one brews Earl Grey like me, and it's silly as fuck, but that made me feel good? Nobody's ever really just...said nice things to say nice things to me before." I shrug.

"So she's your friend?" Alena asks.

"Yeah," I say slowly. "She is. We've been spending more time together to make it seem more natural when we're in front of Becky and Kelsey."

"And what happens when this fake relationship ends?" Alena asks, tilting her head thoughtfully.

I haven't let myself think that far in advance. I know it has to end, because that's kind of the point of everything. To sell it to Kelsey and Becky and move on.

But what happens when it ends?

After the cross-stitch fiasco, Hunter taught me to crochet. Who am I going to show my finished granny square blanket when I complete it if it ends?

"I don't know," I admit, picking at my cuticle.

"Will it hurt if your friendship can't continue? If you have to move on?"

"Who says that has to happen?"

"How else do you see the fake relationship ending?" Alena asks, raising an eyebrow. "Especially if Hunter thinks it's all fake. Ask her what her expectations are for after the wedding, when you no longer have to convince people you're dating."

I slump back against the pillows. "I hate that."

She smiles softly. "I know you do. But that's your homework this week."

I groan melodramatically. "Thanks, I hate that even more."

Alena chuckles. "If you liked what I told you to do, would I even be a therapist?" She takes another sip from her 'I'm always right' mug and I roll my eyes.

When my session is over, I grab my bag and ready myself for dinner and game night at Nic and Josh's. I knock on the office door before opening it and seeing Hunter in her natural habitat.

She's sitting in her desk chair, her left leg bent so that her chin is resting on her knee. Dolly Parton snoozes on the desk in her mini bed that I found on Etsy, and Hunter wears her ginormous noise-canceling pink headphones. She's humming along to what I'm pretty sure is a twenty-year-old Faith Hill song as she stares intently at the computer screen, clicking on different images, working her magic to make them just right.

Friends. Are Hunter and I friends? I don't really have friends, unless you count Josh and Nellie, and really I'm only friends with them through Nic. I work too much to let that happen, and I've forced myself to believe that my friendship is a burden due to my depression and diabetes. I also have enough siblings that I rarely feel the need to let anyone who doesn't share my DNA get too close.

But then there's Hunter, who somehow wormed her way back into my life. Who I tried to keep at a safe distance.

I think she's become a friend.

Hunter does a double take when she sees my reflection in her monitor. She spins in her chair to face me, lowering her headphones. "Hey! Is it time to go?"

I nod. "Just about. I can text them if you need more time."

She bites her lip and looks over her shoulder at the monitor. "I got distracted and spent most of the day reading and *finally* was able to hyperfocus like an hour ago..."

My heart sinks. "I mean...it's okay if you can't go," I say, trying to hide the disappointment I feel.

"No, I'm coming. I want to beat Josh's ass at Monopoly."

"I thought you liked Josh?" We've hung out with Nic and Josh several times since she joined the book club, and she and Josh seem to get along.

"Oh, I like Josh plenty. But if he gets the last word or wins you get cranky." She stands, gathering Dolly Parton in her arms.

I blink at her a few times. "No, I don't."

"Yes, you do. And it's kinda funny most of the time but we have the bridal shower from hell tomorrow, and I have to keep you from having a total breakdown somehow." She kisses the top of Dolly's head, making high pitched cooing noises as the reptile sleepily opens her eyes.

"Aw, so you're going to make him regret ever being born?"

She looks at me, a mischievous glint in her eye. "Worse."

I stare at her as she walks out of the room, stroking Dolly Parton's back the same way a supervillain strokes their hairless cat. "I don't know what that means. Also, are you *sure* it's okay if you don't finish your edits tonight?"

She shrugs without looking back at me. "I don't have any plans this weekend."

"None?"

"Well, the bridal shower...which I know you worked really hard on so I'm sure it's going to be great. So great."

"The theme is 'queer chic' and it's going to be ugly as fuck," I tell her. "But what about Sunday and Monday?"

She shrugs again. "Nothing. So it'll make editing easy."

"I think I mentioned it before, but I'm going to Port Haven for dinner on Sunday and a barbecue for the holiday on Monday. You should come."

"Do you think your family would mind?" Hunter asks. "What do they know about this weird ass situation?"

"I haven't talked to them, but they're used to extra people showing up without notice. I'm guessing Nic's told them we're fake dating, since she can't keep her mouth shut." I pause. "There's probably a secret group chat without me and everything."

"Oh," Hunter says, chewing on her lower lip as she mulls it over. "Are you sure I wouldn't be imposing?"

"Never. Aria DelPresti Quinn makes enough food for twice the amount of people she expects for an event. I'll let them know, but I'm certain they won't mind."

"That sounds kind of fun," Hunter says, seemingly shocked by her own answer. "I didn't realize you wouldn't be here. I was sort of planning to annoy you in addition to getting work done."

I smile softly at her. "You can annoy me in Port Haven. And sneak away to my room if you need to edit."

"Okay," Hunter says, pushing her shoulders back and pulling Dolly in tighter to her chest. "Okay, I'll come. That sounds fun." I grin at her. "It will be."

***

"That was *so* much fun!" Hunter squeals, bouncing down the stairs of Josh's brownstone.

I can't stop smiling as I watch her. She's charmed everyone, even Nic, though I doubt my sister will ever admit it. She's funny, clever, smart, and finally brought an end to Josh's reign as Monopoly champion.

"Did you have fun, Giovanna?" Hunter asks, spinning to look up at me when she reaches the bottom of the stairs.

"Yeah," I say honestly, reaching out and tucking a piece of her hair behind her ear. Her breath hitches, and I immediately pull my hand back.

"Sorry," Hunter says, biting her lip and blushing as she turns to walk away. I follow her, grateful that my legs are longer and it doesn't take me long to catch up to her.

"Why are you sorry?" I ask when I'm next to her. "I'm the one who touched you without consent."

"You have my consent," Hunter says quickly, her blush deepening. "I mean...I just know you don't like it when I react. But that was perfect, by the way. Casual intimacy, like we've been working on. I have to practice..."

I grab her wrist and turn her to me, her sapphire eyes widening with surprise. I feel my own doing the same. But, God. She's so pretty and joyful and...and I want to taste that. To inhale it, have it branded on my skin.

"We haven't practiced kissing again," I say. "Maybe we should do that before tomorrow. I wouldn't be surprised if an opportunity arose and we need to be ready."

"Should we?" Hunter asks softly.

My heart is pounding so hard it echoes in my ears. "Only if you're okay with it. I think more practice before tomorrow would benefit us."

Hunter slowly rises in height as she lifts herself onto her tiptoes, her nose brushing mine. My breath hitches, too, and who do I think I am, mocking her for her responses to our kisses when this is what she does to me?

"I'm okay with it," she says, her breath warm against my lips before hers touch mine.

For a moment, I lose myself in a fantasy. A fantasy where this isn't a ruse, and we're not kissing just to convince my ex-fiancée we're in love. We're kissing because she wants to kiss me, and I want to kiss her. We're kissing because her lips feel right against mine, and because this feels *good*.

One hand cups her neck while the other grasps her hip, pulling her body into mine until she's flush against me. She's so soft, so supple. I love how the soft parts of her body feel against the soft parts of mine, how we seem to melt together.

"Jo," she sighs before opening my mouth with hers. Our tongues find each other instantaneously, and touching her like this feels electric.

Our kiss grows deeper, more desperate. I like to think of myself as someone always in control, always keeping her cool. I always have been. I like restraining myself while making someone else unravel. I like the wait, the slow burn.

Or I did, until Hunter Cleary grabbed a fistful of my hair while her tongue was inside my mouth and made me forget my own name.

I force myself to break the kiss, taking a drastic step back that causes Hunter to stumble forward into me.

"Sorry," she mumbles, stepping back from me. "I got carried away again." She looks up, lips swollen and lids heavy. "You're a really good kisser, Giovanna. If that whole owning your own firm thing doesn't work out, you can totally make it as a professional kisser."

I laugh before I can try to stop myself. I've been noticing that happening more and more, me laughing or smiling without remembering to feel self-conscious to hide it.

How strange. I have to remember to feel self-conscious now, rather than it being immediate and natural. I feel like that's something Alena will love to hear next week.

"That's nice. Instead of being a street performer, I can be a street kisser for some extra cash. Set up a kissing booth in the Lorimer Street station."

Her hand is in mine, and she uses the leverage to spin my body towards hers, cupping my cheek and pressing up onto her tiptoes to kiss me again.

"What was that for?" I ask when she pulls away. My voice is shaking, and Hunter's eyes are squeezed shut.

"I wanted to know what it was like to kiss you mid-laugh. To taste your happiness before it slipped away. And now I'm making sure I don't forget it."

It should be weird, I know that. But Hunter squeezing her eyes closed so she'll remember what this short kiss was like has my stomach doing flips.

I smile and squeeze her hand, which seems to take her aback. She looks at our hands, as if she's surprised we're still touching, and maybe she is. This isn't the norm for us.

Maybe I wouldn't mind if it was.

Oh my *god*. Maybe Alena's right.

I clear my throat and pull out my phone. I notice that Hunter, unlike a lot of people, isn't bothered by this. She seems used to me pulling out my phone to check my blood sugar. And it's such a small thing, isn't it? But she gets this part of me in a way so many people haven't.

"There's a good ice cream place that's a little bit out of the way if you want to get some," I say, sliding my phone back into my pocket after seeing what I'd already suspected: my blood sugar is higher after eating Josh's homemade pasta. If we walk to the shop, my blood sugar should hopefully come down.

"I'd love to," Hunter says, a smile brightening her face.

Our hands brush as we walk to the shop, side by side. And though I want to grab hers and ask what the hell she's doing to me, I don't. Being with her, being her friend, is enough for now.

Chapter 16

Jo

Playlist: Anything But Me | MUNA

I look around the restaurant, at the bridal shower I've put my blood, sweat, and tears into putting together for Kelsey and Becky.

I hate it.

At first when they'd started talking about having a joint shower and their initial visions, I'd noticed a lot of similarities to the shower Kelsey and I planned for ourselves.

But then I pulled out "aesthetic queer celebration" out of my ass as a theme and they ate it *right* up.

It's so fucking ugly.

The center pieces are gerbera daisies, monochrome for each table. That part isn't too bad. What has me cringing is the pastel rainbows making it look like a baby nursery, and the rainbow layered mimosas whose colors blend together in half the time it takes to make them.

"Jo!" I turn and see McKenna, Kelsey's best friend and sorority sister waving at me. My stomach sinks. McKenna is Kelsey's maid of honor, and was supposed to fulfill that role at our wedding, too.

"Hey," I say uncomfortably.

"It's wonderful to see you," she tells me, running her hazel eyes down my body. "I haven't seen you since, what? Your engagement...uh. I mean, dinner. At the steakhouse?"

"Probably." My entire body is so tense that if I tip over, I'm shattering into a million pieces.

"I was so sad things didn't work out between you and Kels," she continues, not noticing my discomfort.

"Yeah." I look nervously around the hideous room, my eyes landing on Hunter, who's taking a picture of the presents that are beginning to pile up. "But everything works out for the best. Kelsey has Becky, and I have Hunter."

McKenna stares at me blankly, tilting her head to the side. Her platinum waves move with her. "Hunter?"

"Hun!" I call, waving her over frantically. This is our first test. Not only do we have to sell it to Kelsey and Becky, but we have to sell it to their families and friends, too.

Hunter comes over, a pageant perfect smile plastered on her face. "Snookums!" she squeals as I wrap an arm around her and pull her into me. I press a kiss to her temple, inhaling the sweet smell of her shampoo.

"Hey, Hun," I say, forcing myself to pull away. It's disconcerting how *safe* Hunter feels. "This is McKenna, Kelsey's maid of honor."

Hunter beams at a stunned McKenna as they shake hands. "It's great to meet you, darlin'!"

"I'm sorry," McKenna says, looking between Hunter and I after dropping her hand. "I didn't realize you'd moved on so quickly." Her voice is degrees colder from the warm tone she'd initially spoken to me in, like I've wronged her somehow.

"Kelsey did," Hunter says, eyes narrowing. "I'm not sure why you thought Jo wouldn't."McKenna looks taken aback by Hunter, the same way I constantly feel around her. "I didn't mean any offense. I just know Jo was devastated by the breakup."

She's not wrong, obviously, but I don't like knowing that Kelsey is telling her people that.

Hunter slips her hand into mine and squeezes tightly. It feels like she's transferring her gumption and courage to me.

"I'm not here as a guest, McKenna," I say firmly, proud that there's only a slight tremor in my voice. "I'm the event coordinator, and if you'll excuse me, I want to make sure Hunter gets a picture of the centerpieces."

I pull Hunter away, towards an empty table five.

"Christ. So Kelsey's people are just...other Kelseys?" Hunter asks, squatting to get the perfect angle .

"Pretty much," I agree, folding my arms over my chest. "Wait until you meet her Grammy. She's homophobic as shit and cried at our engagement party."

"Lovely," Hunter says drily, before standing again. "It's beautiful, Jo."

"What?"

"The event. It's really on theme."

She won't even meet my eye, the fibber.

"Shut up, I know it's ugly as shit," I snicker, nudging her with my shoulder. "Kelsey thought she was stealthy and suggested ideas we'd planned for *our* shower at first and I had to get her to drop that somehow, so I suggested gay aesthetic. It looks like Target during Pride Month."

Hunter barks out a loud laugh that gathers the attention of Kelsey's mom. I smile nervously and raise a hand in greeting.

"Oh, god. It's really…uh. Something. You nailed the theme."

"Thanks. They wouldn't let me hire a drag queen. Said it wasn't 'aesthetic enough,'" I say, using finger quotes.

"How the fuck is a drag queen not aesthetic enough for a gay themed wedding shower?" Hunter looks appalled.

"Excuse me!"

I wince. Hunter had the awful, no good fortune of saying that as Kelsey's grammy was hobbling by with her walker.

"Oh, sorry, ma'am. I was just—"

"Aren't you the girl that was going to marry my granddaughter?" Grammy interrupts, narrowing her eyes at me. Kelsey, who's talking to another guest, overhears, and sends a panicked looked towards us.

"Nope," I say quickly. "I'm the event coordinator."

For the remainder of the shower, person after person from Kelsey's life asks variations of the same question.

"You look familiar. Have we met before?"

"You and Kelsey were together, weren't you?"

"What happened between you and Kelsey?"

And each time, Hunter shows up panicking over some absurd, made up emergency that immediately needs my attention.

"Jo, do you have the games?" McKenna asks after brunch has been served and cleared.

"Yep." I dig through my bag and hand her the games Becky and Kelsey had asked me to create.

"Thanks for doing this," McKenna says, looking intently at the games in her hands.

I force a smile. "No worries."

She eyes me suspiciously, like she's trying to understand something, before walking towards the sound system and taking the microphone.

"Okay!" she says, voice echoing in the room and a bright smile plastered on her face. "We're playing our first game of the day, and I'm going to need the brides to come up to the front!"

I watch from the bar as Hunter intently follows Kelsey and Becky with her lens, capturing what I'm sure are beautiful pictures of terrible people in love.

McKenna explains the objective of the game: the brides answered questions about themselves and now will guess the right answers for their partner.

"Oh, this is going to be too easy," Kelsey giggles, crossing her ankles.

"First question: What is your fiance's favorite cocktail?" McKenna asks. Hunter crosses the back of the room, joining me at the bar as the brides scribble their answers on white boards.

"I want a drink," she whispers to me. "Everybody here is *awful*." She slips her hand into mine and squeezes, resting her cheek on my shoulder.

"You can drink, if you want to. It'll give the photos a lovely artistic blur."

"They don't deserve me at my artistic blur."

My cheeks ache from how big my smile is. "They don't deserve you at all. I hope they realize how lucky they are that you're working with them."

I can feel her eyes on me, but I'm too nervous to look at her. That was personal, honest in a way I know she feels, too. She brings a vulnerable side out of me and I should hate it.

I hate that I *don't* hate it.

"They're lucky to have you, too, Giovanna." Her voice is as soft as cashmere, and covers the buzzy noisiness of the room like a cozy blanket.

My breath catches in my throat and I shakily inhale. I don't know that anyone outside my family has believed in me the way Hunter so evidently does. It feels like magic.

"Um, no, tiramisu is not the right answer." Mckenna's voice pulls me out of my trance. I'm not sure what question they're on, but they're at least a few in.

"What? No, tiramisu is definitely your favorite dessert, Becks," Kelsey laughs, poking at Becky's calf with the toe of her heeled pump. "Remember when we went to that Italian place and you kept saying all the reasons your mom's is better?"

"You know what, I think I need that drink," Hunter says, spinning to face the bar. "Hi, can I have one of those gay-ass mimosas please?"

"Nope, I'm a creme brulee girl," Becky corrects, laughing nervously. "That's why I brought you to that French place on our first date."

"Oh," Kelsey blinks, looking confused. "That...sorry. I must be thinking of someone else."

"Mmhmm." Becky stares at the ground.

"Okay, next question," McKenna says nervously. "What is your fiancée's favorite movie?" There's silence as the brides write on their respective white boards. "Becky?"

"Breakfast at Tiffany's," Becky says, spinning her board around to show her answer.

"Correct!" McKenna cheers. "Kelsey?"

"Miss Congeniality." Kelsey spins her board around to face the guests.

My stomach drops, and the hair on my arms stands up. What are the odds Becky also loves my favorite movie?

"Sweet baby Jesus, this is disgusting." Hunter gags after taking a sip of her mimosa. "Can I just have the bottle of prosecco?"

"Um, no. That's not my favorite movie." Becky's voice is tight and clipped, the same tone it is when she's talking with an inept employee she's planning on firing. I don't blame her. I feel like people are turning to look at me, and I wish I could do something, anything, to turn this trainwreck around.

As much as I despise this event, it's going to fund my dreams. I have to make it work.

"No, it is. You laughed so hard at…"

"Wait–" Hunter whispers, the prosecco bottle halfway to her mouth. "Isn't that your favorite movie?"

"Shh," I hiss quietly. "Please don't make this worse."

Hunter shakes her head slightly, then tips the bottle back for a swig. "Bless her heart."

"Miss Congeniality isn't my favorite movie, Kelsey," Becky says, voice increasing in volume.

"It's one of them, right? You kept laughing at…"

"I think you're thinking of another coworker you fucked," Becky snaps.

A disconcerting silence falls over the room, and it feels like everyone's eyes are on me.

I want to throw up.

"I need a minute." Becky's eyes are still fixed on the floor as she gets to her feet and speed walks to the exit.

Hunter pushes the bottle into my lap. "I think you need this more than I do, Snookums."

That Summer

Hunter

"What if your parents find out we stole their booze?" I laugh, the sea breeze whipping my hair in my face. Giovanna is smarter, having pulled her waves back in a braid. She smiles wickedly at me, handing me the bottle of Jose Cuervo.

"They won't. They're too distracted by having too many kids around."

I giggle and take the bottle opener from her, popping open the top and taking a swig. I shiver as I swallow.

Giovanna and I waited until after midnight, making sure everyone else was asleep to sneak out to the beach. We're armed with a flashlight, our phones, and the bottle of tequila we stole from the liquor cabinet after dinner and hid in her dresser.

She shrugs as she swallows her sip before handing the bottle back to me. "Come on, it's not that bad."

I force myself to take another sip and shudder. "It *is* that bad."

She grabs the bottle from me and holds it above her head where I can't reach it. "Fine, I'll drink it."

"Give it back!" I complain, waving my arms above my head fruitlessly. She laughs, head thrown back and throat exposed.

Everything in me feels like it's on fire. My eyes linger down her throat, and to her breasts, which are covered by her purple sleep shirt. When I lift my eyes again, her smirk makes me blush a deep shade of red.

"Can I ask you something personal?" I ask slowly.

"Sure."

"How did you know you were gay?" It's been a few weeks since Giovanna came out to me, and I found myself thinking about it all the time.

"Oh!" She seems surprised at my question, which makes sense. I hadn't brought it up since she first told me. "I, um, I always thought the way my sisters and friends talked about boys was weird. I could never...quite relate. Like I liked when boys were funny, but I never like...I don't know, found them physically attractive?"

She shrugs, taking another swig of tequila. "I went on Tumblr and did some research, and then I looked in the mirror and said, 'I'm a lesbian.' It just felt right. *For the first time I felt like I understood myself."*

"How do you know when you like a girl?" I ask.

She pauses, and I'm grateful for the sound of the waves. I don't think I could survive complete silence at this moment.

"I think about her," she finally says. "A lot. And I notice little details, like...like how soft her hands look, or the way she bites her lip when she's concentrating. I want to be around her all the time, to touch her. To...to kiss her..." Giovanna's voice trails off at the end, and I take another swig of tequila for courage.

"Do you want to kiss me?"

Her head snaps up, eyes wide. "What?"

"Do you want to kiss me? Do you notice how soft my hands are? Do you...do you want to be around me all the time?" It's like I can't stop talking. It all spills out and what's worse *is I am dying to know.*

Is she thinking about me all the time? The same way I think about her all the time?

I can't see her face, but I see her putting it into her hands, shoulders heaving as she inhales. "Don't make me tell the truth, Hunter. I appreciate your friendship too much."

Butterflies swarm my stomach. "Do you want to kiss me?" I ask again, emboldened by tequila and her diversion. "Because...because I think I want to kiss you."

She lowers her hands and turns to me. "I...I've never kissed anyone before." Her voice is a whisper, barely audible above the crashing waves.

"I have," I answer simply. "Follow my lead."

I feel her move closer to me and I shiver, unsure if it's from the chill of the seabreeze or the warmth of her arm against mine.

"Yeah, honey," she says, voice a little louder. "Yeah I...I want to kiss you."

"Then kiss me, Giovanna." I can't believe I'm saying this. I'm not supposed to want to kiss girls, but all I know is how desperately I want to kiss this girl.

She cups my cheek, and I can feel her eyes searching. "Please," I breathlessly add. "Please kiss me."

Before I can brace myself, her lips brush against mine, timid and unsure. It is perfect, absolutely perfect. We move slowly, softly.

Until we don't.

Chapter 17

Hunter

Playlist: II Most Wanted | Beyonce, Miley Cyrus

Jo is silent the entire subway ride back to the apartment.

We survived the rest of the shower with minimal awkwardness. The brides finished the games with no more incidents, smiling fake smiles the entire time. The silence echoed as we cleaned and packed up after everyone had left.

Jo hasn't spoken since.

But she's clinging to my hand, and it gives me hope that she sees me as grounding. Comforting.

When we get off at our stop, she freezes in front of a liquor store.

"Yeah, I need some moscato, too," I say, and she cracks a teeny, tiny smile.

We're in and out of the store in minutes, still hand-in-hand while I hold the paper bag with our wines.

"Ugh," I say as Jo unlocks the door to the apartment. "I really need a shower to wash off that nastiness."

"Go shower," she insists, breaking her silence. "I'll feed Dolly."

She goes right to the terrarium and I go to the bathroom, stripping and stepping into a scalding hot shower. When I'm finished, I join Jo in the living room, dressed in a nightgown and robe, my hair in a microfiber towel. She's reclined on the couch, Taylor Swift's Red album playing at full volume as she brings the bottle of merlot to her lips. She's holding Dolly on her chest, and our eyes meet as she swallows.

"I couldn't be bothered with a glass," she tells me, motioning to the coffee table with the bottle. "But I got you one, in case you wanted that vibe."

I raise the uncorked bottle of moscato. "If drinking from the bottle is the vibe tonight, I'm game." Maybe it's silly, but knowing that Jo uncorked my wine when she very well could have just opened her own and left the corkscrew on the table for me.

I tap Jo's feet with my free hand. "Scooch."

She obliges, surprising me when she places her feet in my lap. I take an extra long swig of wine.

"You okay?" I ask, lowering the bottle from my mouth.

"Yeah," Jo says, as she brings the wine to her mouth. "Actually, can I be honest?"

"Of course, Giovanna."

She exhales and shakes her head, picking at the label on the wine bottle. "No. I'm not okay."

"I know." I cup her ankle with my free hand. "And that's okay."

"I hate how much Kelsey's still able to get under my skin. I didn't even realize what was going on at first. I didn't realize she was thinking of *me*. That she was listing my favorite movie, my favorite dessert. And that should be good because I barely think about her unless I have to for work." She inhales shakily and tips her head back, resting it on the back of the couch. "She really *is* just a client to me now. She has been, but there was still a lot of pain when they initially asked. It's still not great, but it's more of a dull, throbbing ache than the sharp stabbing feeling I'd been feeling.

"But in the end, it doesn't matter, because she's still able to shove her way into my life. Still able to hurt me."

"It *does* matter," I insist empathically. Jo lifts her head and meets my eyes. "Because at the end of the day, your healing is about you. Not Kelsey. And yeah, she sucks and I'm pissed she's able to get to you, but it doesn't undo the progress you've made."

"I'm happy you moved in, Hunter," Jo says quietly. "Not only because you agreed to an outrageous scheme to help me out. But because you're kind and you make me want to be kind, too. Because you adopted our little monster, and brightened up the kitchen with your tacky-ass magnets, and the apartment isn't quiet anymore, because you're always singing along to music."

I force myself to continue her massage and not kiss her. Because *not* kissing her after saying that to me is the hardest thing I've ever done.

"Thank you," I force out, refusing to look up at her. "I'm just glad I'm not making your life any harder."

"Shut up." I see Jo pointing her bottle of merlot menacingly at me out of the corner of my eye. "Stop being self-deprecating."

"Thanks, you fixed me," I say flatly, reaching for my moscato.

"You deserve people that are kind to you, including yourself."

My mouth is dry and my throat scratchy as I force myself to swallow the wine. "Look who's talking."

"God, you and Alena would get along so well," she groans.

I furrow my brow. "Alena?"

"My therapist."

"When did you start going to therapy?" I ask casually. She's mentioned therapy a few times, and I hope it's okay to ask about her experience.

"Oh. Um, the fall after that summer, actually. The therapist I saw then was the one who encouraged me to come out," Jo tells me.

"What was that like for you? Coming out?" I immediately regret asking about such a personal topic, my shoulders hunching over as I try to withdraw into myself. "Fuck, I'm sorry—"

"Terrifying," Jo whispers, and I force myself to look at her. She's staring at the spinning vinyl when she continues. "I was so scared. But I couldn't pretend anymore, and I was so afraid my dad would say something. Telling my mom was the hardest thing I'd ever done. She just stared at me, and asked if I was sure. Or if I wanted to talk to our priest about it...and I cried myself to sleep that night. She wasn't trying to be hurtful..."

"But she hurt you," I finish, tears stinging at the back of my eyes. "I'm so sorry."

She shrugs, still looking down. "She got over it pretty quickly. I don't think my dad ever told her that he knew before, but he did a lot of the, "*What would Jesus really do?*" shit with her. She ended up praying about it apparently and realized that Jesus would love their damn kid.

"It sucked, but she got there. As hard as it was, I'm kind of glad it was, because it paved the way for my sisters to feel safe when they came out. Like Nic just called my mom and dropped it on her one day last summer, and Mom reacted well."

"But she was only able to react that way to your sisters because you had to hurt first," I say, heart breaking for the girl I once loved, for the woman in front of me.

She finally meets my eyes. "Yeah. Something like that. And I've forgiven her, you know? She really does the work to unlearn the homophobia she was raised with, but sometimes it feels like I'm a teenager wondering if my mom's still going to love me. If I'm about to find out that her love is conditional upon me liking men."

"I think all of that can be true, you know?" I say slowly. "She can have hurt you, and be someone who is learning and doing better. That doesn't erase the harm caused. But I think, maybe, that's what makes it love—the desire to do better. To be better for those you love."

"What was it like for you?" she asks, taking another swig of Merlot.

I follow her lead and take a long swig of moscato before speaking. "My family disowned me. Kicked me out of the will, told me I'm no longer family...the whole shebang."

I hear Jo's sharp inhalation of breath. "What?"

"Oh yeah. My dad called Yale to yell at them for turning me gay, because his going didn't turn him gay, so the liberals must have ruined the school." I roll my eyes and scoff. "My family calls every once in a while to leave a voicemail quoting the bible and reminding me that it's not too late for me to turn from sin. I need to change my number—they're buying burner phones since I blocked them.

"But I knew that's what was going to happen, you know? That's just them. I stayed in the closet until I had saved enough money to move up here. Then I packed up my car, dropped it on them at PawPaw's birthday dinner, and drove all night. I haven't seen or talked to them directly since."

"Oh my god, Hun." Giovanna's voice is husky. "Why the fuck did you let me complain about my mom when you dealt with that?"

"Because what you went through still fucking sucks! And my experience doesn't negate that." I feel hot stinging tears at the corner of my eyes and angrily brush at them. "Just because my parents are terrible people doesn't make your pain not real. My therapist and I talk about that a lot, that so many things can cause pain and they're all valid. My experience doesn't lessen yours, and yours doesn't make mine worse. Our pain is independent of each other, and can co-exist."

"Did this happen recently?" she asks quietly.

I nod. "A month before Tyler's wedding."

She inhales sharply. "Oh my god."

"Yeah." My voice breaks as I shakily bring the bottle to my mouth. I take a swig and as I'm lowering the bottle, Jo shifts and her arms are around my shoulders. Maybe it's the wine, or maybe it's because of the topic of conversation. Maybe it's because Jo is initiating this embrace. Whatever the reason, I'm crumbling into her, sobbing into her chest.

"You deserve better," she says, cradling my head to her as I weep. "I'm so sorry they didn't love you right."

"No, that's what I say to you. I tell you that you deserve better," I tell her through my tears.

Giovanna breaks our embrace and cups my face in her hands. I want to scream, because my eyes are bloodshot and puffy and snot is dripping and her face is so damn close to mine. "If you get to tell me I deserve to be treated well, I get to tell you that, too. Because I hate your family for hurting you, but you're so fucking brave, Hun. You're so strong, and you shouldn't have been required to be. You should have been loved and celebrated and you know what? We're going to do that." She leans into me and presses a soft kiss to the corner of my mouth.

When she pulls away, she taps her phone for a few quiet moments before the opening notes of "I'm Coming Out" by Diana Ross start playing from her phone speaker. I laugh shakily and wipe at my tears with the back of my hand.

"You don't have to do this," I say.

"No, but I want to. I'm not letting you go another second without knowing how fucking beautiful it is that you're you." She grabs my hand and pulls me to my feet. "Go get dressed. Fanciest outfit you own."

I bite my lip. There's some part of me that desperately wants to keep fighting her on this, because this isn't worth celebrating. *I'm* not worth celebrating.

Giovanna senses this and points menacingly at me. "Tell your brain to shut the hell up. Why is it so easy for us to be dickheads to ourselves, but so compassionate to each other? This is me being a dickhead to you, for you. Go put on whatever ridiculous, flouncy gown I know you have in your closet. We're fucking it up tonight."

I can't help it, I grin through my tears. "I don't know which dress to pick."

"Oh my god," Jo rolls her eyes and I giggle. "I can't believe I was naive enough to assume you don't have multiple ridiculous, flouncy gowns. Go." She playfully pushes me towards my room.

After some deliberation, I choose a pink, sequined, floor length gown that I wore to a charity gala a few years ago. It's fitted and I look hotter than hell. Seems like the perfect choice for a forced, but welcome, celebration of my bisexuality.

There's a knock at my bedroom door as I'm putting on my favorite boots. When I open it, Giovanna's standing at my door, donning a white dress suit. The jacket is tossed over her arm and she's holding the corset top up to her chest with her other hand. "Hi. Can you fasten the back?"

I nod, speechless, and she turns around. My hands shake as I fumble with the ribbons, and she gathers her hair up to make it easier.

"Your fanciest outfit isn't black?" I force myself to break the silence.

She shakes her head, a strand of hair escaping from her grip. "Nope. I bought this for the wedding."

"What wedding?"

"My wedding. And since I'll never get to wear it..." she shrugs. She's not wearing a bra, and each time my finger brushes her bare back, I am inexplicably filled with even more desire. I want to run my finger along each back roll, to kiss up her spine and whisper everything I'm feeling–if I could even manage that. I feel drunker from the sight of her than the moscato, so weightless I could float away and take her with me.

"You won't wear it if you get married someday?" It's a struggle to keep my voice even, and even more so to stay on task and not linger on her bare skin.

Corset. She asked for help with the corset.

She barks out a laugh. "I wish, I fucking love this suit. But I doubt my hypothetical future wife would be thrilled if I wore an outfit I bought for a previous engagement."

I would! I want to scream. *I'd be honored if you wore this to marry me because you're so fucking beautiful and you love it so I love it and I don't care that it was originally for your wedding to someone else because it's* you.

"Oh," is what I say instead, tying a bow at the bottom of the corset. Because saying any of that out loud would be absurd. "Done."

She turns to face me and throws the jacket on, completing the ensemble. I reach out to fix it when it gets caught on her CGM, and I notice her omnipod outlined beneath the tight corset. God, she's so pretty I want to cry.

"You're like...a pink disco ball," she says, running a single finger down my side.

"Thank you." I choose to see her words as a compliment. "You're like...really pretty."

She lifts her eyes to mine and tucks a strand of wayward hair behind her ear. *How* is every move she makes the absolute hottest ever? It's like she wants to make a mess of me.

"Thank you."

I can't take my eyes off her. She's breathtaking, mesmerizing, and I don't want to forget how comfortable and confident she looks in this moment. After the bridal shower from hell and telling me about her mom, she still wants and chooses to celebrate me.

She's a goddamn miracle.

Giovanna takes my hand in hers and squeezes gently. "Come on, Hun. We have twelve years of celebrating to make up for, and we can't leave Dolly out."

Celebrate we do–scream singing along to Jo's "praise hayley kiyoko that i'm gay" playlist on Spotify. She spins me, and we both dance with Dolly. We drink our wine from the bottles, and she wows me by somehow not spilling a drop of merlot on her suit.

A goddamn miracle.

I have no idea how much time passes. All I know is I'm dizzy from spinning, the bottles are empty, and a slow song is playing. Her face is flushed pink, and she goofily bows and offers me her hand. "May I have this dance?"

I giggle and curtsy, immediately losing balance and stumbling into her. "Oof. Sorry."

"You okay?" Her voice is serious as she pats down my sides, like she's checking for damage.

I can't speak with her hands still on my hips, fingers molding to my curves.

Her eyes meet mine. "You're so pretty, Hun."

"No, you," I manage to wheeze out.

Her eyes drop to my mouth, and my heart is beating so fast I'm afraid of the gore it'll create when it inevitably beats out of my chest. "Do you want to kiss me, Hunter?"

"Depends on if you want me to kiss you."

"And if I told you I did?" She raises her eyes back to mine, so warm and comforting. "What would you tell me if I said I wanted to kiss you?"

"I'd tell you I do, too," I whisper.

"Thank God."

My back arches as I press myself to my toes and kiss her, long and hard, wrapping my arms around her. She moans into my mouth and it's the greatest feeling of my life.

For the first time, I was celebrated for simply being me out loud. For the first time, I feel like I've gained something after coming out. I got Jo back, got to hear her share the parts of her life I missed after that summer. We kiss while Taylor Swift plays in the background like a literal *dream*.

This is the best night of my life.

Chapter 18

Jo

Playlist: Casual | Chappell Roan

Quiblings Group Chat

Nic: everyone be nice today jo is bringing her fake girlfriend to dinner

Jo: why do i want to slap you

Millie: are you hungover?

Millie: you usually want to get physically violent when hungover

Ren: not true. she wants to get physically violent more often than that, she only SAYS it when she's hungover. otherwise it's all in the facial expressions.

Jo: you're all texting too damn loud shut the fuck up

This is the worst morning of my life.

"Is the city always this loud?" Hunter grumbles as we walk towards the subway stop.

I stop walking and dry heave. Who knew *sounds* could make you nauseous?

I'd woken up in the middle of the night curled up on the couch, my head in Hunter's lap. When I looked up at her, my stomach sank. We'd only kissed, and *fuck it*. It might have been the best kiss of my life, but I felt like absolute shit, not just because I was hungover.

Opening up to her and letting her open up to me and letting each other in enough that kissing seemed like a good idea at the time. But kissing her like that was a mistake. Maybe all of last night was.

Things with Kelsey had gone right so fast, and then wrong even faster. I can't do that to myself again. That's the thing—*I'm* the only one who can make sure I avoid a situation like that again.

I carefully removed myself from the couch and went to my room, where I spent hours staring at the ceiling, unable to fall back asleep.

When I came out of my room a few hours later, Hunter was gone. The living room looked incomplete without that mirrorball of a dress.

She eventually came out of her room in a floral sundress and her heeled white cowboy boots, just as I was checking train times to Port Haven for Sunday Dinner. right as I finished brewing coffee for our hangovers. Her eyes were puffy, and my heart sank as she gave me a tight lipped smile.

"Hey," I said.

"Hi," she answered, walking across the living room and squatting in front of Dolly's terrarium. "You gonna tell me we can't do that again?"

"I—um. I mean, that *can't* happen again."

She nodded curtly, staring intently at Dolly. "Yeah. Figured."

She didn't say anything else until she commented on the noise levels of the city.

I groan and stand up straight. I'm not surprised that she's kept walking without looking back, but I am surprised at the way I feel like I've been stabbed.

"Good morning!" Nic says in a singsong voice as we approach the subway station, making both Hunter and I wince. She's bouncing on her heels, her short curls bouncing with her. "Thought you cuties were gonna no-show."

Hunter grunts and kicks at a crushed Mountain Dew can in response.

My stomach lurches. Just last night I'd been telling her about my family's tradition of Sunday dinners. It'd started with my mom and her grandparents, and something that carried over when she married my dad. Growing up, we'd drive to Long Island for Sunday dinner at Nonna and Nonno's with various aunts, uncles, and cousins.

My grandparents died when I was in college and my mom decided to continue the tradition as a way for our immediate family to stay connected. Once I'd graduated, I began working more and more Sundays, and I was able to go to less and less family dinners. Everyone acts like it's a holiday when I'm able to attend. It's both annoying and adorable as hell.

Hunter had been so excited to experience Sunday dinner, since my family still spent Sunday evenings in Long Island that summer.

Josh and Nic exchange one of those looks where they say something without actually saying something. "Yeah, hang on a sec," Josh says, walking towards the crosswalk.

"Where's he going?" I ask.

"To cure you." Nic crosses her arms over her chest and raises an eyebrow. "What the hell happened?"

Hunter laughs hollowly. "I was wondering the same thing."

I grind my teeth. I have a headache. I'm nauseous. I barely got any sleep last night. Hunter's cranky and I know it's because of me. The three of us are silent until Josh reappears.

"Eat this, it'll cure the worst of hangovers," Josh hands Hunter and I each a bag.

"What the hell is this?" Hunter asks, peering into the bag.

"New York classic. Everything bagel with cream cheese, lox, onions, tomatoes, and capers."

"Gross," she says, wrinkling her nose.

He ignores her. "These helped me survive grad school before I got sober. You'll thank me later."

My blood sugar is a little low due to the lack of sleep I got last night, which is probably contributing to my poor mood in addition to the hangover. I tap at my PDM to make sure I give myself the right amount of insulin so that the carbs don't cause a spike.

Ten minutes and a full sandwich later, my belly is full and blood sugar balanced.

"I hate when you're right," I grumble as we wait for the train on the platform.

"She admitted I was right," Josh whispers excitedly to my sister.

Hunter's still silent, and it's making me uneasy. She stares blankly at the tracks, hands shoved in the pockets of her sundress.

I step over to her, and despite her still not looking at me, I open my mouth to speak. My words are immediately overpowered by the sound of the train approaching and I snap my mouth shut as the train comes to a stop. It causes a breeze, blowing Hunter's curls around her head. She looks ethereal and I hate myself for thinking like that because this is Hunter, my friend. That's it. Just because I'm a lesbian doesn't mean I have to date every single friend. Hunter is an objectively gorgeous person, but there are millions of objectively gorgeous people and I could be friends with all of them, probably.

Nic and Josh chatter amongst themselves the entire way to Grand Central, but Hunter continues to ignore me. She even goes as far as putting in a pair of earbuds, and I receive her message loud and clear.

We end up sitting in two rows across from one another on the train to Port Haven–Nic and Josh, me and Hunter. Hunter's in the window seat, earbuds still in place as she stares out the window once we're out of the Grand Central tunnel.

"Hey," I say softly, gently nudging her with my elbow.

She doesn't budge.

"Hun?"

She sighs and turns to me, pulling an earbud out. "I really need space right now, Jo. I'm hurt and I don't want to talk about it, okay?"

I stare at her. "Oh. Okay."

I'm a little floored and a lot impressed that she told me that. Kelsey would give me the silent treatment without explanation.

Hunter's face softens, and she chews on her bottom lip. Last night, I could taste the sweetness of the moscato on that lip. She whimpered and tightened her hold on me when I sucked on it.

God, what a fucking kiss. But I meant it when I said we couldn't do it again.

"I'll talk when I'm ready," she adds, like she's read my mind. "I'm not going to stonewall you or anything."

"Okay," I say quietly. It's not fair of me to expect her to open up when she's not ready, especially not when she never once pushed me when I wasn't ready.

We're silent for the remainder of the train ride until we arrive in Port Haven.

"How are we getting to your parents' house?" she asks as we exit the train and walk towards the parking lot.

I shrug. "Dunno. We all have each other's locations so one of the local siblings usually shows up at the station to give us a ride."

She nods. "Got it."

"Can we—"

"Not yet." She lowers a pair of oversized heart-shaped sunglasses over her eyes. "I'll tell you when I'm ready."

I inhale shakily. "Okay."

Nic and Josh are a few steps ahead of us, and my sister turns her head to look at me over her shoulder. "Which minion do you think Mom asked to get us?"

"I'm nervous it'll be Kat," Josh says.

Kat's our oldest sister, and probably the family member who will react the worst to Hunter and I, if there were a Hunter and I. But even Hunter and I faking it might cause some homophobic microaggressions. She told me she didn't think it would be appropriate for her and her husband, Steve, to come to my wedding to Kelsey because…I don't know? She hates gay people? Whatever.

"Wait, when did she get a minivan?" I groan as we turn the corner and the parking lot comes into view. Kat's leaning against a red minivan while her douchebag husband, Steve, paces on the other side of the car while on the phone.

"Wow, I didn't think you were actually going to come." Kat lowers her sunglasses to eye me as we approach the car.

"Fabulous to see you too, Katerina," I respond dryly. "This is my friend, Hunter."

"Is she an actual friend, or is it a fake friendship, too?" Kat asks.

I sigh and rub at my temples. "You're starting already? Really?"

"He's my real boyfriend," Nic interjects helpfully, lifting up Josh's hand. He waves awkwardly, like he hasn't spent hundreds of hours with my family.

"Hey party people!" Steve whoops, shoving his phone into his khakis. "Kept us waiting long enough." He slaps Josh's back with enough force that he whimpers.

Hunter looks at me with confusion in her eyes. I lean into her, her scent infiltrating my senses. She smells like magnolias, and the air just after it rains. It would be romantic if she weren't someone I need to keep my filthy paws off of.

"That's Kat's husband, Steve. He's sort of the worst. Sorry in advance," I whisper in her ear, hating that I notice how my breath blows her hair.

"When did you guys get a minivan?" Nic asks, eyeing the car like it's personally offended her. She's lived in the city long enough that suburban life gives her the ick.

"Last month. We're going to need it soon, anyway!" He wraps his arm around Kat and squeezes her into his side. She meets my inquiring gaze and shakes her head. My stomach sinks.

Kat and Steve have been trying to conceive since their wedding three years ago. Kat never talks about it with any of us, but every once in a while, Steve will drop a gross comment insinuating that he's rawdogging my sister at specific parts of the month.

"Speaking of," my asshole brother-in-law says, pointing his finger between Nic and Josh. "When are you two—what the *fuck*?"

"Oh, darlin', I'm so sorry, must've lost my balance there," Hunter coos, brushing at Steve's shoulders as he jerks away from her. Everyone else, meanwhile, gapes at her. I hadn't been looking at her when it happened, but out of the corner of my eye, it looked like she'd tripped into Steve. Except she hadn't been moving, and suddenly has perfect balance again. This woman physically threw herself into my douchebag brother-in-law to get him to shut up.

It was the hottest thing I've ever seen.

"Let's just get to the house and catch up there," I say. "You know Dad gets moody when he's left out of important conversations."

When we pull into the driveway, Josh and Hunter climbout of the van first, followed by Nic and I.

The front door to the house flies open, my younger sister Millie waving at us through the screen door. "The Brooklyn Quinns are here!" she says in an over-exaggerated Boston accent. Nic and I look at each other out of the corner of our eyes, dissolving into giggles when our gazes meet.

Millie scowls at us, as we ascend the front steps. "Hey, Mills," I wrap my arms around her while she keeps hers stiffly at her sides. "Good to see you."

"Don't act all nice after you and Nic made fun of my accent," she grumbles. "Dicks."

"Speaking of dicks..." I break contact with her and motion to the minivan with my head, where Kat and her worse half still sit. "Wait till you hear the bullshit our favorite brother-in-law said."

Millie's mood immediately perks. "Oh, say less. I mean...say more."

"He was trying to nose around into mine and Josh's relationship." Nic looks around, checking that no one is close enough to overhear. "I just know he was about to ask when we're going to settle down and get married. But then Hunter physically knocked some sense into him."

"Oh, that's fucking awesome," Millie says, smiling wickedly.

"Where's my hug?" Leo appears out of nowhere, arms lifted for a hug. He gulps and slowly lowers his arms at my death glare.

"Don't pull anything today," I warn him. I grin when Stella, his girlfriend, joins us and wrap my arms around her. "Hey, Stelly."

Josh and Hunter come into the house, and Hunter introduces herself. I realize she stayed behind to help Josh with our bags. Of course she did, she's thoughtful and kind.

She's the worst.

"And this is my youngest brother, Leo, and his girlfriend, Stella," I say to Hunter.

"Great to meet y'all," Hunter says brightly, hugging Leo and then Stella. "I'm Jo's..." she looks at me, and my stomach sinks as I realize she's not automatically finishing the statement with the word *friend*. "Hunter. I'm Hunter."

"Where's everyone else?" Josh asks.

"Izzy and Finn ran to the store to grab ingredients for the salad, and Ren has something today, so he's coming later," Leo tells us.

"And Poppy's closing the bookstore but she's going to try to stop by for dessert," Millie adds. Poppy, Millie's best friend, took over operations at her parents' bookstore on the boardwalk a few years back.

The front door opens, and Kat and Steve walk in. The chatter dies off eerily quickly.

"Does Sean have beer?" Douchebag grumbles, elbowing Millie as he shoves past her.

When I look at Kat to tell her to ask her man child to behave, my mouth snaps shut immediately. Her eyes are red and puffy. Hunter notices, too, and takes a few steps to the side, whispering something to my eldest sister. Kat's lip trembles as she nods and leads Hunter upstairs.

What the hell?

The newly arrived Quinns head to the kitchen to say hi to our parents, who are hard at work making enough lasagna to feed their army of offspring.

"Is that sweet Hunter girl here?" Mom asks after pulling me down to kiss my forehead.

Dad and I make eye contact as she bends over and opens the oven. He looks away immediately, rubbing his hands on his apron that says, "Wicked Pissah," and lists a bunch of classic New England foods spelt out in a Bostonian accent. He collects aprons, and this one was a gift from Alex, who will be the only sibling missing this week.

Poor Dad. I just know he's thinking about when he walked in on Hunter and I.

I clear my throat. "So I should probably tell you...uh, Hunter and I were sort of...seeing each other that summer she was visiting."

I'm surprised when Mom doesn't say anything. Aria Quinn is a stereotypical Long Island Italian and isn't known for being quiet when being presented with new, unexpected information.

Then she slowly straightens her back and shuts the oven door with a *thud*. "What." It's more of a statement than a question.

Luckily, Izzy and her best friend, Finn, just came back with the ingredients for salad, so everyone else is too busy chopping vegetables to pay attention to us.

"Uh. Yeah. Hunter and I hooked up. That summer. A lot." Dad snorts and I glare at him over Mom's shoulder.

Mom blinks at me, expression unreadable, and my stomach sinks.

"Oh my god...are you mad at me?" I say, trying to keep the disappointment out of my voice.

Her face softens. "Oh, Joey girl." She stands on her tiptoes and wraps her arms around my shoulders, pressing her lips to my cheek. "No, not at all. I mean. I don't love the idea of any of my children hooking up with anyone...I'm just remembering that fall."

My teeth dig into my bottom lip. The following fall, I was severely depressed and Mom dragged me to a therapist and psychiatrist to cope with it. My grades suffered, and I quit student government, which was something I'd adored the previous year. But with therapy, and antidepressants, the crushing weight of depression slowly lifted. My therapist scheduled a family meeting with my parents in November where I finally came out to them.

"Was that part of what triggered everything? The depression?" Mom pulls away and puts her hands on my shoulders, her eyes on mine. Everyone says that I have her eyes, but she and I always deny it. Nic and Kat have her eyes. I also have brown eyes, but not *her* eyes. Hers are purely brown, mine have flecks of gold and green in the irises. My poor dad's genes fought for their life with the three oldest Quinn children. Luckily for him, the next two kids, Ren and Millie, look more like him. Millie is his twin, if you ignore the tattoos and piercings.

"I mean...yeah. It was my first relationship and breakup and everything."

"And now you're pretending to date her?"

I groan and pull away from her, accidentally making enough noise that a few of the others in the kitchen look over at us. "Mom. I'm a big girl, I'm fine."

"I don't want her to hurt you again," she argues.

And what if I'm the one hurting her? What if I want to kiss her and I have nothing to give her because I'm an empty shell of a person who's broken beyond repair and she deserves everything good the world has to offer and that's not me? What then?

"Thanks," I say stiffly. "I'll..." I'm cut off by Steve banging on the window, making mom and I jump.

"I locked myself out," he yells through the glass, lifting a bottle of Guinness up. "I came out to get a beer from the patio and now I can't get back in."

"Good," I mutter under my breath.

"Giovanna Theresa!" Mom hisses, pinching my side and causing me to yelp. "Sean will open the back door for you, dear."

Shit. I forgot Dad was still right next to us.

Dad goes to let Steve back in—unfortunately—and a few minutes later, Hunter and Kat finally come back downstairs and go into the kitchen. Izzy and I are setting the table and discussing the mortality of goldfish.

"I had four this past semester," she says sadly. "Because they kept *dying*."

"That sucks," I empathize as Hunter shuffles into the dining room.

"Your mom told me to help you set the table," she says awkwardly. "I think she might dislike me more than your dad."

"Why, cuz you guys bumped uglies when you were in high school?" Izzy asks, looking between us.

"Izzy!" I snap, narrowing my eyes at her.

Hunter just laughs. "It wasn't ugly. But yes."

I can't help it. I blush.

Izzy snickers. "Ooh, I like her, Jo. You should keep her."

I blush deeper, and ignore my youngest sister. "Where did you run off to?" I ask Hunter, hoping I keep a casual tone.

"I asked Kat to show me the bathroom," she says breezily, reaching over me to grab a cloth napkin.

"Must have not been feeling well...you both were gone for a while," I say, straightening a water glass on the table.

"I needed some space away from the hubbub," she responds, taking the silverware from Izzy.

Izzy takes her leave, returning to the kitchen, and I lean into Hunter. "Is she okay?" I ask, hoping she knows what I mean.

"She'll be okay," she answers in a way that closes off any more questions.

We finish setting the table in silence, and the room gradually fills with my family and Mom's delicious food. Once we're all seated, I look around and notice three empty seats.

"Who's missing?" I ask. There are so many damn people in this family, it's easy to forget who's not there.

"Ren and Will," Millie answers, reaching into the center of the table for a piece of garlic bread. "They should be here soon."

"And Steve," Kat adds, looking nervously around the table. "He had to take a quick call."

My parents and Kat cross themselves, silently saying grace as everyone else chatters with each other. They, along with Steve, are the only practicing Catholics in the family. I see Hunter watching them and realize I should've warned her that some of my family still practices.

"Sorry we're late!" Ren strides into the room, his best friend, Will, trailing after him. Will recently moved back from California to be closer to family after graduating from Stanford Law. His older sister, Laura, is actually Finn's mom, and became Will's legal guardian when he was in middle school. They moved here with a five-year old Finn, who was in the twins' kindergarten class. Finn and Izzy have been inseparable ever since. Will and Ren became friends too, through Laura and Mom making the two introverts hang out with each other.

Ren bends down and kisses Kat on the top of her head. "Hey, Meow. Your husband told me to tell you he'll join us in a minute."

Kat's smile, which was genuine and bright when Ren first kissed the crown of her head, becomes obviously forced. When Ren was little, he exclusively called our family cat, Cannoli, and any other cats he encountered, "Meow." He started calling her Meow, too. He's done it ever since, and god bless the brainless sibling who dares to call Kat that. Only Ren gets away with it.

Leo. It was Leo who tried.

"Will!" My mom says, getting to her feet and embracing him before kissing him on both cheeks. "I'm so happy you're able to join us for Sunday dinners now. We just have to get your sister to join us, too."

Out of the corner, I see Ren sit next to Hunter, sticking his hand out to introduce himself. My neck rotates to them when I see her smile and blush.

Objectively, my younger brother is a good looking dude. He's the tallest in our family, with broad shoulders and a muscular build. He has mom's unruly, dark curls and dad's emerald green eyes. If he were famous, he would definitely be white boy of the month at some point.

"Hunter," I hear her say, her voice melodic and fuck why does she sound like that when she's talking to him?

Oh, god. Is she into him? She's bi, and they'd make a gorgeous couple and the prettiest babies and oh my god they'd ask me to plan their wedding, wouldn't they?

"Ren, have you met Hunter before? Jo's roommate?" Mom calls down the table as she serves herself more salad.

Ren gives her a lopsided smile and I want to stab his hand with the butter knife I'm gripping. "Ah, so you're the fake girlfriend."

Hunter laughs and that should be *my* laugh. "My reputation precedes me, then."

"Trust Nic to never keep a secret," Millie teases, popping a piece of bread into her mouth.

"Hey!" Nic says, glaring at her. Her face softens and she tilts her head to the side. "No, I guess that's fair."

Josh wraps his arm around her and kisses the top of her head. "You have many, many strengths, Buttercup. Secret-keeping is not one of them."

"Ren, Hunter was telling me earlier that she collects vinyls, too," Stella says. When the *hell* had she and Hunter talked?

Ren's face brightens. He teaches music at the elementary school, and music is his damn life.

I try to block out Ren and Hunter's conversation for the remainder of dinner. It's unbelievably hard, though. They keep laughing, and they talk so animatedly. I debate eating a spoonful of crushed red pepper, just to feel something.

After we've eaten, they both volunteer to wash dishes. Meanwhile, I chug the remainder of my wine, for obvious reasons. My brother is probably going to fall in love with and impregnate Hunter and then we'll have another roommate—the most beautiful damn baby ever.

"How are you, Joey?" Dad asks, sliding in the chair that was next to me, which was abandoned by Stella.

"Great," I respond. "I'm planning my ex-fiancée's wedding and fake dating the girl my dad walked in on me going down on when I was fifteen who's also my roommate and currently falling in love with my brother. Why would I be anything less than spectacular?"

Dad stares at me, mouth hanging open.

"You still in therapy?" he finally asks.

"Yep. So you don't have to tell me it's a bad idea. My therapist has been chastising me for months."

"Okay," Dad says uncomfortably. "Um, I'm gonna see if they need help in the kitchen."

I'm alone in the dining room, so I get up and make my way to the living room, where my mom sits with Kat to her left.

"Where's Steve?" I ask, sitting on Mom's right.

"Not sure," Kat answers stiffly, picking at her fingernail. "He didn't text me, but the van is gone. Must have been an emergency at work."

Everyone is lucky I only had one glass of wine with dinner, because I feel like exploding.

"Cool," I say instead, averting my gaze and looking around the room. Will and Josh are putting the china Mom insists on using for Sunday dinner back into the hutch, and Leo and Stella are snuggled up on the loveseat, giggling as they look at something on one of their phones.

Almost everyone else is in the kitchen cleaning up and *fuck* I feel like an asshole for not helping. While everyone else is talking to each other, Ren and Hunter come into the room. Hunter hasn't looked at me in so long and I fucking hate it.

My stomach sinks as their hands entangle and Ren motions to the stairs with his head. Hunter nods, her teeth digging into her bottom lip.

Oh my god.

Ren's taking her upstairs.

Are they...?

No.

I mean there's no reason for them not...

No.

They couldn't. They *wouldn't*.

But no one else noticed that they're climbing the stairs and I feel like the narrator of Mr. Brightside.

I want to scream. I want to cry. I want to beg for Hunter to choose me.

But what happens if she did choose me? I'm not the kind of person she'd want to be with. Sure, maybe she thinks she wants to be with me. But after a while she'd realize I'm broken and have nothing to offer and she'd leave.

That's how things work for me. People think I'm shiny and new and exciting and then once they get used to me and realize how much work I am, they *leave*.

I put my head on my mom's shoulder, trying not to cry. I haven't cried since Kelsey left. Since before then, really. When I'd read the note she'd left, I folded it back up in the neat little rectangle she'd left on my dresser and just sat on my bed, staring at the wall until Nic came home.

This time, I want to cry over someone who's not mine.

Chapter 19

Hunter

Playlist: Eightball Girl | Maddie Zahm

"This isn't going to work," I say, laying starfish on Ren's child-hood bed.

"Yes it will. Just relax and breathe. We'll make it work."

We're both silent for a moment before I hear him snicker. I roll my eyes and sit up. "Should I say that it's too big for good measure?"

Ren raises an eyebrow. "Oh, sweet summer child. It *is* too big."

"We're talking about your ego, right?"

"What else would we be talking about?"

I bark out a laugh. "I can't believe you think this is a good idea."

"It *is* a good idea. Have faith." Ren is cross-legged on the floor, plucking at a guitar he apparently has been keeping in his closet since high school.

"So she'll think we're boinking while you're playing guitar?" I ask dubiously.

"No. She'll think I'm *seducing* you with music before we boink." He grimaces. "It wouldn't be the first time I did that."

"Yikes."

"I know."

"How many chicks did young, seductive Ren Quinn get with that method?" I ask teasingly.

He eyes me. "I said it wouldn't be the first time I did it, not that it wouldn't be the first time it *worked*."

I sigh dramatically and flop onto my back. "This is ridiculous. She won't care."

"She's been staring at you all night," he counters. "Fifty bucks says she bursts through that door without knocking."

I roll my eyes. "I could use an extra fifty dollars. You're on."

He continues to tune the guitar before starting to strum the chords to "I Will Always Love You".

"Did you know Whitney Houston's song is actually a cover?" I ask, turning my head to look at him. He's ridiculously handsome. I've slept with men way less attractive than him, and now I'm realizing I never really felt anything. It's not that I don't feel *anything* for Ren, but I'm certainly not attracted to him. Not the way I'm attracted to Giovanna.

Maybe I'm *not* attracted to men.

"I'm playing Dolly's version, obviously," Ren says teasingly. His head is bent over and his curls are flopping into his eyes and I should find him so hot.

And maybe that's why I kept trying, why I found myself swiping through Tinder and hoping that maybe *this* one would give me the butterflies I'd heard so much about.

The butterflies I'd felt with Jo.

Ren starts to softly hum along and I feel tears pricking my eyes. There's something about that song that makes me feel like my heart is being put through the wringer, especially right now.

Thwack.

Ren's door flies open, slamming against the wall. He stops playing and I jacknife up to see Giovanna Quinn breathing heavily in the doorway.

"Hey," she says. I think she's trying to smile, but it just looks like she's baring her teeth. "What are you up to?"

I swallow, hearing Ren chuckle in the background as he gets to his feet. I can't stop looking at her.

She came.

Ren leans his guitar against the wall. "My job here is done. You can Venmo me."

He leaves the room, pulling the door behind him and winking.

Jo's looks between me and the door in confusion. "What just happened?"

"Jo," I say softly. "Why did you come up here?"

She narrows her eyes at me. "I asked first."

"Ren just left." I bite my lip to keep from smiling. "That's what just happened." Somehow, her eyes narrow even more. "We came up here to see if you'd follow us."

Jo blinks at me in surprise. "What?"

My mouth feels dry, but I try to speak anyway. "He said you couldn't stop looking at me. I didn't believe him. So he suggested we flirt and come up here...because it would make you jealous." I lift my eyes to meet hers. "Are you? Jealous?"

"Of what? You and my brother?" She scoffs and stares over my right shoulder. "Of course I'm not. There's nothing to be jealous of. What would I be jealous of? You fucking Ren? You can fuck whoever you want. I don't care."

"Jo."

"Don't make me say it," she blurts out, her eyes darting to mine.

"Why did you leave me this morning? Why did you say it couldn't happen again if you were going to come bursting in at the mere idea of Ren and I together? Why are you acting like I mean something to you when this morning you acted like I meant *nothing*?" There are angry tears in my eyes blurring her. She looks like a dream, fuzzy and unfocused.

It feels like a nightmare.

"You could never mean nothing." Her voice shakes in a way I've never heard from her before. "Not to me."

"That's not what leaving me this morning said. Or telling me something that meant a lot to *me* could never happen again. All of that tells me it means nothing—"

"I left *because* it meant something," Jo interrupts. "I ran because it meant a fucking *lot* to me and I've never felt like this and the last time I thought I meant a lot to someone this quickly, she fucking *left*."

My heart stops beating for a moment, I swear it does.

"I got scared, because I can't give you what you want, Hunter. I can't give you a relationship or love or any of that because I'm so goddamned broken."

"So you think running away is letting me down easy?"

She throws her hands in the air. "I don't know how to do this! I don't want to hurt you. I'm sorry I did. You have every reason to hate me and—*oof*."

My arms are wrapped around her, squeezing her because god, I couldn't even take space from her for a full business day.

Pathetic.

"I'm sorry she hurt you, in all the ways she hurt you." Then I feel something life changing. The best thing I've ever felt.

Jo wraps her arms around me too, and I'm surrounded by peonies and champagne.

"I'm sorry *I* hurt you," she says quietly. "That wasn't fair of me. I'll try to communicate when I need space like you did today." She rests her chin on my head, and god, this closeness feels so *right*.

I've never felt safe or more seen, or more loved than I do at this moment, in Ren Quinn's childhood bedroom, in the woman I love's arms.

I do, don't I? I love her.

Of course I do. Jo's the easiest to love. She's dark, stormy days when you get to stay inside and drink tea. She's a cozy blanket you find at the thrift shop that looks a little wonky, but is the softest thing you've ever felt. She's midnight walks along the beach with the waves lapping at your feet and the moon shining down on you.

I want her to love me too, and I know she can't. At least not yet.

Maybe someday. My heart whispers. *Maybe someday she'll be able to give you herself.*

But I don't have someday. Right now, all I have is her in my arms.

I clear my throat and pull away, wiping at my eyes. "I forgive you." She opens her mouth to say something, but I interrupt. "Kelsey mentioned your mom makes a mean tiramisu, and Ren told me she made it today."

"God, that shower was fucking wild."

I shudder. "Horrifying. But you know what's not wild *or* horrifying? Dessert. Let's go."

I open the door and Ren stumbles in, the fear of the Lord in his eyes.

"You little *shit*," Jo growls, lunging at him.

"I could barely hear anything!" Ren says, quickly like it's one word.

"You're dead meat." Jo stalks after him as he turns and runs back towards the stairs.

I can't help but laugh. It doesn't look or feel the way I thought it would, but I recognize it all the same.

Belonging.

That Summer
Hunter

I have never been more uncomfortable than I am sitting in a Planned Parenthood lobby with Giovanna Quinn and her father between us.

Okay, that might not be true. Around an hour ago when he opened her bedroom door without knocking might take the cake.

"Did you know gonorrhea and chlamydia are the most common STIs among high schoolers, but HPV is the most common among college students?" Mr. Quinn asks, flipping through the pamphlet he's reading.

"Please stop talking," Giovanna groans.

"Hi there." I look up to see a middle-aged nurse with a warm smile standing in front of us. "I hear we need to have a few tests done?"

"Yep!" Mr. Quinn says like he didn't ruin my life today. "These two here need to get tested, and also a conversation about safe sex practices."

"Da-ad," Giovanna whines. "This isn't necessary."

Mr. Quinn starts flipping through the pamphlet again. "Here's how this is going to go, Giovanna. You and Hunter are either going back with this nice nurse, or all three of us are going."

"Dad!" I can hear Giovanna's embarrassment somehow.

"Alright, guess we're all going," he says, getting to his feet.

Giovanna and I are on our feet immediately. "No, no we'll go," she says sheepishly.

Mr. Quinn sits back down. "That's what I thought."

We trail behind the nurse as she walks us back to the examination rooms. "Do you think he's going to tell my grandparents?" I ask Giovanna, finally verbalizing what has my stomach in knots.

She's silent for a moment before speaking. "I don't know what he's going to do."

"Do you regret it?" I can't stop myself before I ask.

She meets my gaze for the first time since her dad came into her room. Then she grins wickedly, and I feel myself blush from the tips of my toes to the roots of my curls.

"Never."

Chapter 20

Jo

Playlist: whywhywhy | Misterwives

"How are you feeling about this weekend?"

I groan at the question. Therapy had been going so well. Alena complimented me on using my coping skills and keeping up with care tasks and of course then she brings up what I'm dreading the most.

It's been almost three weeks since I brought Hunter to Port Haven. It felt like a turning point. There's no doubt about it—we're definitely friends. I wash the dishes after she cooks and then we end the night with Dolly on one of our laps while she cross-stitches and I crochet. I have ten granny squares she's going to help me make into a blanket and I feel unstoppable. It's a calm, comfortable friendship.

Or it should be. I still feel unsettled, like there's something unspoken between us.

"I'm dreading it." I pull Dolly closer into my chest. She snuggles her head into me, like she can sense my stress. "I don't want to deal with this anymore."

Kelsey and Becky have somehow become even more demanding over the past few weeks, and I've been living with a never-ending headache triggered by it. But I'm so close to my dream becoming reality. I've begun scoping out rental spaces in Port Haven, dreaming up business names. Thinking of the positive impact I can have on a community that once hurt me.

"Do you have a plan on how to cope when it gets overwhelming?" Alena has a new mug today, one she'd been excited to show off to me. It says, "I like my romance novels like I like my tea: hot and steamy."

"Yeah, Hunter and I have talked about it. She texted me a list of two dozen excuses we can use if I need to disappear for a while." A slow smile spreads across Alena's face and I narrow my eyes at her in suspicion. "What?"

"Nothing. You...your face brightens when you talk about Hunter. I've never seen that with you, except when you introduced me to Dolly Parton for the first time. It's nice to see you this way."

I jerk back. "You saw me like this when I was with Kelsey."

"No. It's different."

I stare down at Dolly, like she'll open her mouth and tell me what to say. Because what am I supposed to say? That Hunter's brought light to my life? That she's patient and seems to genuinely like me?

"Do you see yourself in a romantic relationship again?"

I hadn't. I shouldn't. There's no way I could keep someone invested enough to stay.

"I don't know. I don't know if it's realistic…but I think I want to be. One day, when I'm better."

"Better than what?"

"Better than the person Kelsey left."

Alena's quiet, and the sentence echoes in my mind.

"I think you use 'better' as something to hide behind," she says carefully, like she's tiptoeing through a minefield. "I think you focus so hard on all the things you perceive as wrong, or bad, about yourself. But we all have those things, and it doesn't make us less capable of a healthy romantic relationship."

"You're right," I admit.

"Oh my god, say that again. I need to get a recording for *my* therapist."

I roll my eyes. "You suck."

"In all seriousness, you don't need to be actively looking for a romantic relationship, but I want you to continue facing the things that scare you, and challenging what you believe. And right now, that might be the uncertainty of life, of love."

"It's so hard," I whisper.

"It is. But you've survived every single hard thing that you've encountered. You're working your ex's wedding for fuck's sake. You can certainly examine why you think you don't deserve love."

Somehow, that feels even harder than planning the wedding.

"At least we're not hungover this time."

Hunter smirks up at me as she plops down into an empty row. We woke up early to catch a train to Port Haven and set up for the bachelorette party. Becky heard about SandPiper Inn from a former client, and then became obsessed with my hometown. I guess she got Kelsey into it, too, because the wedding ceremony, reception, and the bachelorette weekend are all taking place there. We're reaching the home stretch of this thing: it's just the bachelorette weekend and the wedding next month.

The brides and bridal party are arriving in a limo later this evening, but I wanted to arrive early to meet with Audrey, who owns the inn, to make sure everything is set for the weekend.

I sit down next to her after putting my bag in the overhead rack. "That's true," I admit, wiggling anxiously in my seat. "This morning would have sucked tenfold if we were dealing with hangovers."

"I'm going to miss Dolly."

Goddammit. "I am too."

I'm acutely aware of how close Hunter and I are to one another. We're both blessed with, as my pediatrician uncomfortably told me when I was in middle school, birthing hips, and the only empty row we could find was a two-seater.

I can smell the faint floral scent of her shampoo wafting off her, and I want to get drunk off it, to bathe in it. To be so surrounded by it that I somehow turn into a walking, breathing flower.

"Jo? Did you hear me?" Hunter's voice is distant, like our hips and thighs aren't pressed together at this moment.

"No, sorry," I admit guiltily. "What's up?"

"We have separate rooms this weekend, right?"

"Yep." I know it's the right choice, and that we'll be able to play the roles of obnoxiously in love girlfriends just fine without sharing a room. But part of me wishes we *were*.

"I'm proud of you, you know," she tells me quietly.

I blink in surprise. "For what?"

"For keeping your head held high throughout this whole shitshow. Honestly, I'd be proud of you even if you didn't."

I'm taken aback. She thinks *I'm* brave? How can she think that when she's the most extraordinarily courageous soul I've ever met?

"It's you," I croak. "You're brave, and you make me want to be brave, too." It's true, she makes me want to be open and fearless and trusting. She makes me want to jump and trust that she'll catch me at the bottom.

She deserves someone who trusts her as much as she deserves someone who's trustworthy. She deserves the love and energy and sparkle she puts out into the universe returned to her.

I hate whoever that ends up being.

Because there will be someone who gives her that, who takes her precious, precious love and bravery and keeps it safe in their heart. Who doesn't squander it or take her for granted. Who climbs mountains to reach her and waits in the valleys to catch her.

I force a smile and look away, hating the pin prick feeling behind my eyes.

Chapter 21

Jo

Playlist: Too Well | Renee Rapp

"Okay, so check-in isn't until 4pm, but I figure we'll crash at my parents' until three-ish and meet with Audrey then, does that work?" I huff as we drag our luggage behind us on the train platform.

"Sounds good," Hunter says, sounding annoyingly less huffy than I am. "Who's picking us up?"

"I texted my mom and dad, so it'll probably be one of them."

It's not. I'm surprised when Millie's best friend, Poppy, is waiting in the parking lot next to her lilac beetle bug and holding a sign that says, "The baby's yours, Joe." above her head.

"Oh my god!" Hunter squeals, squealing and jogging to the car. "This is the prettiest vehicle I've ever seen in my life!"

"Thank you! You must be Hunter," Poppy grins at her, pushing a piece of light pink hair from her eyes. "I'm Poppy, Jo's baby mama."

"Oh my god, shut up." I roll my eyes. In high school, Poppy and I had both ended up with mono and quarantined at her parents' house. We'd spent the days watching Maury and Jerry Springer, and we counted eight episodes in that one month with men named Joe getting paternity tests. We thought it was the funniest thing in the world.

Hunter looks confused, but smiles and shrugs her shoulders. "Okay! Yeah, I'm Hunter, Jo's fake girlfriend. What do you think about having fake beef?"

"Ooh, adding to the lore. Love it," Poppy says, nodding seriously.

"What are you doing here?" I ask her as we put our suitcases in the trunk.

Poppy sighs heavily. "God, you're not going to believe this. After six years, I was finally caught by your parents."

"Doing what?" I ask, opening the passenger side door and pushing the seat forward so I can climb into the back seat.

"Jo, don't be silly. I'm shorter, you take the front seat." Hunter says, hip checking me out of the way and clambering into the backseat before I can object. It gives me a great view of her ass, and I want to reach out and squeeze it and oh my *god* what the fuck is wrong with me?

"Okay so you know how your parents have, like, that super expensive, snazzy espresso machine? Sometimes I sneak in and use it."

I close the door behind me as I sit down. "You break into my parents' home to use their espresso machine?"

"Hey, stop being so judgy!" Poppy shoves the paternity sign into my lap before pulling the door closed behind her. "I run into Ren and Millie at least a few times a week."

"You work at a hybrid bookstore and tea shop."

She checks that her seatbelt extender is secure before pulling it across her torso. "Right. What about books or tea has anything to do with access to an espresso machine?"

That's valid.

"Anyway," she continues, turning the car on. "Your dad came in this morning and was all, 'I'll let it slide this once if you get Jo and her fake girlfriend slash roommate from the train station.'"

"So now you won't be using the espresso machine?" Hunter pipes in from the back seat.

Poppy stares at her in the rearview mirror. "Who the hell said that?"

"There's a bag of mass markets for you in the trunk," Poppy tells me when we arrive at my parents' house.

"Thanks!"

"I'm impressed you were able to pack everything you needed into one bag," Hunter says, hoisting my bag out of the trunk before grabbing her own. It makes me giddy. She's so fucking cute.

"Oh, I didn't. I had the decor and shit mailed here, and to the inn." I slam the trunk closed and wave at Poppy through her rearview mirror. "This ain't my first rodeo."

I'm not looking at her, but somehow I can *feel* Hunter's smile. It's like whenever she smiles, there's an energy-shift. Like a handful of confetti is thrown into the air.

"I'll have to take you to a rodeo sometime." Her voice is so gentle and teasing and *safe*. "That way it *can* be your first rodeo."

I force a scowl at her as we walk up the driveway. "What makes you think I haven't already been to a rodeo?"

She laughs, bright and bubbly. "Um, everything about you?"

I can't help it, she makes me laugh, a loud, snorting laugh. It's jarring how suddenly and violently it hits me that I don't care that I'm snorting, that I haven't heard Kelsey asking me if I *had* to laugh so loud. Hunter grins brightly at me, like she's thinking the same thing.

"Tomorrow night *is* country night," I remind her when I stop laughing. "I rented a mechanical bull and everything."

"Well," Hunter says, smirking at me as she rings the doorbell. "Maybe you can borrow my cowboy hat. But you know what they say—wear the hat, ride the cowboy."

She blushes and I feel my cheeks heat, as well.

"Who says that?" I ask.

"Cowboy smut," she says plainly.

"Cowboy *what?*"

"Cowboy smut?" My mother says as she opens the door. "I've read some of that."

"Oh, Jesus." I rub my hand over my face in exasperation. "I do *not* want to know that about you."

She ignores me. "TikTok told me about this one with a single father and his nanny..."

"I read that one last year!" Hunter squeals. "I can't believe romance authors manage to make cowboys hot. They're actually the worst in real life."

Mom pouts. *Gross*. "That's a shame. They're so nice in books. And naughty." She winks, like a fucking weirdo.

I dry heave as Dad appears behind Mom. "Who's naughty?"

"Your wife apparently has a thing for fictional cowboys," I say, shuddering.

Dad smirks and teasingly nudges mom with his elbow. "Oh, I know. I love that your mother loves cowboys."

Mom giggles. Hunter awws. I gag.

Hunter and I spend a few hours at my parents' house, organizing the different decorations and things I'd sent here before we leave for the inn. "Audrey says we can start setting up the bridesmaids' and brides' rooms early, but our rooms won't be ready until later." I tell her, snapping a lid onto a plastic bin.

"That's fine by me." Hunter stretches her arms over her head and groans. "Did you notice your dad still hates me?"

I scoff. "My dad doesn't hate anyone."

It's true, my dad's never hated anyone.

But he does hate her and it's unbelievably disconcerting. Hunter's been her bubbly self and I see her slowly wilting as he refuses to give her his approval.

After he drives us to the SandPiper Inn, I confront him.

"I'll be right in, Hun," I tell her before she shuts the back door behind. I swivel my head and narrow my eyes at my dad, who at least has the decency to look sheepish. "Sean Quinn, calm your tits."

"Calm my *what*?"

"I get walking in on us was fucking weird and like I'm really sorry for traumatizing you but can you not be an asshole to Hunter? You're hurting her feelings and it's pissing me off."

"I was afraid of this." He sighs and turns his head slightly, staring out the windshield as Hunter walks into the inn.

"Afraid of what?"

"You still have feelings for her."

"What?" I sputter. "No I do *not*."

Do I?

"Do you remember how bad that fall was, Joey?" His voice is quiet, and he's still staring ahead. "You were failing your classes and barely left your room. I was afraid we'd lose you."

"That's not Hunter's fault. I was also deep in the closet and struggling with the knowledge you knew and no one else did.

I'm grateful for how you handled it, making sure we were safe and keeping it to yourself, but I lived in fear that one day you'd say something. That everyone would know and reject me. I was depressed and scared. I had finally met someone I could be myself with. I probably would have been depressed no matter how or when my first relationship ended."

"I don't trust her," he says, still not looking at me.

"I do. And I like to think that you trust me. So can you be nice?"

He looks at me from the corner of his eye. "You care this much?"

"Yeah. Hunter's my friend. You don't have to like her, just stop being a fucking asshole."

"I can't believe the way my damned offspring talk to me," he grumbles, shaking his head. "The disrespect."

I smirk and lean over, kissing his cheek. "Thanks, Pops. Here's your chance to practice."

He sighs long-sufferingly as Hunter walks out of the inn. He rolls down his window. "Bye, Hunter."

She stops in her tracks and blinks as she looks around. "Me?"

"Yes," he says stiffly. "Goodbye."

I roll my eyes. And here I thought we all got our dramatics from our mother.

"Thanks!" Hunter says, perking up. "And thanks for the ride, Mr. Quinn. Enjoy your weekend!"

"Don't you feel like an asshole for being mean to that sweet angel?" I tease as she walks to the trunk.

He grunts.

We finish unpacking the car and haul everything in the lobby.

"Jo!" Audrey, the owner of the inn, waves at me from behind the front desk.

"Hey! It's great to see you again, Audrey. Thanks for letting us set up early."

She waves her hand at me. "Oh, anything for you." She smiles and turns to Hunter. "I don't think we've met, I'm Audrey, the owner here."

"Jo's mentioned you! I'm Hunter Cleary, the photographer. You have a beautiful home. I mean place. I mean business." Hunter blushes.

Audrey grins and looks proudly around the lobby. "Thank you. It is my home, in a way. My aunt owned it and left it to me when she passed. Becoming the owner is the second best thing I've ever done."

"It's really spectacular," I assure her. "It feels new and classic at the same time."

She smiles sheepishly. "Thanks. Hunter, did Jo tell you I've known her since she was in diapers?"

I roll my eyes. "Audrey and Kat were best friends growing up, and she was always at our house being annoying with Kat."

I don't remember it that well, but I do remember that when in my early teens, Audrey stopped coming around. Kat stopped talking about her, and I didn't see her again until I came with Becky and Kelsey a few months back for a tour of the inn. I haven't asked her, but I guess she got married, because she has a different last name. Plus, now that we're both adults, she's way less annoying. I like to think I'd be monumentally less devastated if she and my older sister refused to let me play with them.

"Yep," Audrey affirms, flashing a quick smile. "So if you want to hear any embarrassing stories from her adolescence, let me know."

Hunter's eyes widen. "Oh my god, I would *love* to hear embarrassing stories from her adolescence."

Hunter and Audrey immediately fall into easy conversation, with Audrey telling her about the time my tongue got caught in my braces while my parents were out and Kat didn't have her license yet, so Audrey had to be the one to drive me to the orthodontist.

She gives a giggling Hunter and I the keys to the bridal party's rooms. "Sorry, we had one late checkout today, and I'd hoped you wouldn't mind if it was your room," she says as we climb the stairs to the floor the rooms are on.

"No worries!" Hunter and I say at the exact same time. We both freeze, and slowly turn our heads to face each other.

"Wait," I say slowly, a feeling of dread slowly washing over me. "Whose room?"

Audrey stops walking and spins around to face us, putting her hands on her wide hips. "Yours."

"Which one of us?" I ask.

"Both of you?"

"What?" Hunter squeaks. "No, no, we requested separate rooms."

"So we could have separate workspaces," I add. "Since you know, we're both working this weekend."

"I…one of the brides called to tell me that you had decided you wanted one room," Audrey stammers.

"Christ on a cracker," Hunter mutters. "I'm gonna kill her."

"Oh," I say, voice cracking. "That's fine."

"Aren't you two dating?" Audrey looks confused.

I don't blame her.

"Yep! We're actually hella in love." I wrap my arm around Hunter's waist and pull her into me. "Right, honey?"

"Right. Hella in love." She's staring blankly at the wall, and I think she's dissociating.

"We both plan to spend our nights working and we get too distracted by each other's bodies if we're in the same room," I blurt out.

Hunter makes a choking noise next to me, and I dig my fingers into her side.

"I'm so sorry, when I canceled the separate rooms, the extra was booked immediately." I have to give it to her, Audrey does genuinely seem to be sorry, despite the absolutely absurd situation happening in front of her.

"It's okay," I assure her, waving my hand at her. "Really. We'll make it work."

Hunter and I are silent as we decorate the brides' and bridesmaids' rooms. When we finish, our room is ready and Audrey brings us our key.

"Maybe we'll have separate beds!" Hunter says hopefully.

We do not have separate beds, and we stare at each other across the singular, king sized bed.

"What in the regency road trip romance is this bullshit?" I groan, rubbing my hands over my face.

"Well," Hunter says quietly. "At least it's a king."

"Could this weekend get any worse?" I complain, throwing my hands up.

"It's your ex's bachelorette weekend. I'm a thousand percent certain it's going to get worse."

She's not wrong.

"Okay, well…"

"Are you going to use the dresser?" Hunter interrupts, striding to her suitcase, which is leaned against the wall in the entryway next to mine. .

"Cool." She pulls her bag right in front of the dresser, squatting down to unzip it.

I just stare at her like an absolute creep. I stare at her hands, the way they move as she unzips the bag, then her lower lip which is clasped between her teeth in concentration. I have to force myself to look away as she straightens.

Thud.

I look back her way as something falls to the ground. Our eyes meet before looking down to see what fell.

"Oh my god," I choke out, just as Hunter lunges to grab the hot pink object from the floor. "Please tell me that's not what I think it is."

Hunter straightens her back again. "It's not what you think it is."

"Are you lying to me?" I ask, mouth dry.

"Obviously, Giovanna," she snaps, eyes meeting mine. "I dropped my fucking vibrator."

"Why did you bring a vibrator?"

"I was *supposed* to have my own room!" She brandishes the rabbit vibrator at me like a wiggly sword. "I don't know about you, but I have a feeling I'm going to need some stress relief this weekend, and I'm not ashamed of that!"

"I didn't mean to insinuate you should be ashamed of masturbating," I stammer. "I just...we're sharing a room now."

"Oh, I'm sorry. Was this inanimate object supposed to magically make its way back to the city when the plans changed? I'll have a talk with Reba later."

She named her vibrator after a country singer. That checks out.

"Now I can't use it, so be prepared for me to be extra cranky this weekend," she adds.

I nod absently. "Okay."

She bends back down and shoves it into the suitcase. "There. Safely stowed away. No more scary vibrator to get you."

As she finishes unpacking, I bring my toiletries to the bathroom. I look in the mirror, and yep. My face is flushed. Not surprising, considering I can't stop imagining what Hunter looks like when she uses her toy on herself. I wonder if she still giggles when she comes, if she's still strangely sensitive between her breasts, if she'd moan my name if I were the one using it on her…

"What's the plan for tonight?" Hunter asks, barreling through the doorway into the bathroom, and dumping her toiletries on the sink top.

"Everyone should be here by seven, and we're having a catered welcome dinner and karaoke in the event room downstairs. So I have to decorate and get ready…"

"Want me to help?" she interrupts.

"Oh no, I'm sure you have your own shit to set up."

She shrugs. "Not really. Just have to check the lighting, which shouldn't take long."

"Aren't you doing a photobooth?"

"Am I? Ah, shit. I forgot." She smiles sheepishly.

"If you can't do it, it's fine. I took care of all the accessories and backdrops, since they wanted specific theming."

"Oh, that's easy then." Hunter waves her hand dismissively. "Did you get box lights?"

"I did." I wanted to be sure we had everything we needed, and it's on Kelsey and Becky's dime, so why the hell not buy what she'd need? Hunter usually does event photography, so light boxes aren't a part of her usual equipment.

"Giovanna Quinn." I'm surprised when Hunter wraps her arms around my shoulders and presses a kiss to my cheek.

"What just happened?" I ask, eyes widened as I stare at us in the mirror. Her eyes meet mine in the reflection, and I almost collapse when she rests her head on my shoulder.

"I was going to say I was so happy I could kiss you. But then I decided to do it. Is that okay?"

"Yeah that's cool," I say, trying to keep my voice even. "Totally, totally cool."

"Okay. Yay," Hunter says, smiling at my reflection. Her fingers brush mine and for a moment, I let myself pretend this is real, like I did that summer. It's as if I see our past and our present in the reflection. Hunter and I are touching, for the sake of touching. Because I let myself love her, and she loves me.

God, how pathetic.

I clear my throat. "We should go over the itinerary before decorating."

She's still looking at our reflection, and it makes me want to keep looking, too. What is she thinking? Is she imagining the same things I am? Or is she imagining I'm a better woman, one who's worthy of her goodness? One who's not me.

"That sounds perfect," she says softly. "What do you need from me?"

Too much. I think to myself. *I need too much from you and that's why this can't happen. Why I can only pretend.*

"Just help decorating, really," I say instead, finally forcing my gaze away from the mirror. The reflection felt too real. A reflection of two women who love each other. A reflection of everything I've ever wanted, and everything I'll never have.

Chapter 22

Hunter

Playlist: I Will Always Love You | Dolly Parton

> *Ideas for stress relief that aren't masturbating*
> -take a walk
> -take a hot shower
> -listen to calming music
> -this is ridiculous
> -i just wanna masturbate
> -commit murder and hide kelsey and becky's bodies

Not one of Kelsey or Becky's friends can sing.

I know it's karaoke and that's not the point and I'm not supposed to care, but I'm one of two sober people in this room.

I fucking *care*.

After Sorority Sister Number Seventeen takes several pictures like it's 2016, complete with a solo sorority squat and duck face, Giovanna steps next to me.

"Having fun?" she asks teasingly.

"So much," I deadpan. "Too much, really." I turn to the makeshift stage where Becky's sister is singing a very pitchy version of "Silver Springs" by Fleetwood Mac. I shudder as I lift my camera and take a few pictures of her.

"Did you know Stevie Nicks cursed Lindsay Buckingham while performing this in 1997?" I ask Jo after taking a few pictures.

Her brow furrows and head tilts. "Who cursed who?"

I stare at her. "Stevie Nicks. Cursed Lindsay Buckingham." She shakes her head and I gasp. "Oh my god. Do you not know about the infamous Fleetwood Mac lore?"

"I have a feeling I'm about to find out."

I grin at her. "Later. There's videos that have to be a part of the presentation."

"Ren probably knows about it."

"Oh, that handsome brother of yours *definitely* knows about it."

I see Jo's body stiffen out of the corner of my eye.

"Handsome in an objective way," I blurt out, spinning to face her. "Like, you probably don't want to know this, but your brother is kind of the male beauty standard. Not handsome like 'oh he's so handsome I want to kiss his face.' Handsome as in tall and white and muscular with fluffy hair."

"You don't want to kiss his face?"

"Nope. Nope, nope, nope. I'd love to be his friend. But like the purely platonic kind. He's cool, but I usually only kiss people I'm attracted to, and I'm not. Attracted to him, that is." I'm rambling and I want to stop, but I can't. "Like he's objectively handsome, but that's it. Did I tell you I think I might be a lesbian?"

I slap my hand over my mouth, eyes widening as I watch Jo's do the same.

"I thought you were bi?" she asks, confusion evident in her voice.

I laugh nervously. "So did I. But uh, my therapist and I have been unpacking shit and I think my attraction to dudes is more compulsory than genuine attraction. But maybe I'm wrong. I could totally be wrong. I haven't been with a woman in twelve years..."

"Wait. *What*?" Jo takes a step back, and I want to slam my head into a wall because *why* the fuck can't I stop talking? "Twelve years?"

"I don't know why I said that," I groan, slapping my hand over my face. The room around us erupts in applause as the song comes to an end, and Kelsey takes the stage.

"Am I the only woman you've slept with, Hun?"

I peek at her between my fingers. "No. Yes. No. Maybe? Yes. Yeah. Um. Yeah."

"This is for my fiancée," Kelsey slurs from the stage. "I love you baby, and I always will."

The opening chords of Dolly Parton's "I Will Always Love You" fills the room..

"She's going to butcher my favorite song," I yell over the music.

Jo just stares at me.

"I made things fucking weird. I'm so sorry. Will you still let me tell you about Fleetwood Mac lore in the room?" I ask hopefully, pivoting my body to face the front of the room, getting some shots of Kelsey doing the worst thing a person has ever done to me.

"Since when has this been your favorite song?" Giovanna asks from behind me.

"What?" I ask, grabbing a few shots of the drunken bridal party singing along.

"Your favorite song was 'Jolene' that summer. When did this become your favorite song?"

I turn around so fast that I almost lose my balance. "You remember that?"

She ignores the question and takes a step towards me. "When did this song become your favorite, Hun?"

I open and shut my mouth, words not coming to me.

"Tell me. Please," she whispers.

"You know when." My mouth goes dry, heart pounding.

The fall after that summer, I'd cried myself to sleep listening to the song on repeat, thinking about how I'd been the one who told her Whitney Houston's version was a cover of Dolly's. Remembering how she hummed it in my ear when we were naked and wrapped around each other.

She stares at me, but only for a moment, because then she's angling my face and pressing her lips to mine. She tastes like the lime sparkling water she's been drinking all night, with a touch of buttercream from the cupcakes that were served.

I raise onto my tiptoes and wrap my arms around her shoulders as her hands run down my sides until they clasp my hips.

"Hun," she whispers against my mouth, her breath hot in my mouth. "Fuck."

"Yeah," I sigh. "Fuck."

She pulls away, just enough that the tips of our noses are still touching.

"Is this because Kelsey can see us?" I breathe.

Please say no. I beg whatever deity has a free moment. *Please, please say no.*

"No," she cradles my jaw, leaning in to press a gentle kiss to my left cheekbone. The relief I feel is palpable, like the deep breath you take upon breaking the surface of the ocean. "It's because you were brave enough to say what I wasn't brave enough to say in Ren's room." She kisses the bridge of my nose, my chin, the corner of my mouth. "It's because I've been trying to hold back, but I'm a fucking mess and I can't do it anymore."

"Then don't." I'm begging. I know I am, and I don't care if I'm pathetic. "Don't hold back anymore."

She bites her lip and looks at a still-singing Kelsey over her shoulder, making my heart drop.

But then she's pulling at my hand. "Come on."

That Summer

Jo

This summer flew by. School starts in two weeks, and Hunter is going home to Georgia in one. I could pretend I don't know which I am more upset about, but it would be fruitless. Hunter is still here, and I already miss her.

"Do you think you'll come back next summer?" I blurt, sudden and unprompted.

Hunter and I sit at the sea wall with strawberry milkshakes and sweet potato fries from Queenie's. She swallows before answering.

"I hope so," she says quietly, staring out at the sound.

"So you like Port Haven?" I hope my tone is casual.

She laughs softly. "I think you're trying to get me to say I like you."

"You caught me," I tease, poking her side. She squeaks and jerks away, shooting me a playful glare.

"Rude." She looks so pretty right now, the sun making her hair golden, her blue eyes even bluer. I want to kiss her.

But I can't. We're in public and it's the middle of the day. We've had to be more careful since my dad caught us. He's been acting weirder than usual, but I don't think he's told anyone, and he hasn't *brought it up to me. He also knocks for a full minute and announces himself twice before coming into my room now.*

But still, it's awkward. So we only get to touch each other on the beach at night. Which feels kinda reckless and dirty and fun.

"I do, you know," Hunter's soft voice, barely audible above the waves, breaks me out of my stupor.

"Do what?" I ask.

"Like you."

My responding smile is so big my jaw aches. "Me, too."

Chapter 23

Jo

Playlist: August - Recorded at Electric Lady Studios | MUNA

I've lost my mind. I must've. I don't know when or how, but I have an inkling it was when I realized Hunter's favorite song was her favorite because of *me*.

"Where are we going?" Hunter asks as I pull her through the lobby.

"You'll see."

I kissed her. Without waiting for prompting, and without reason, I kissed Hunter.

My Hunter.

It was fucking heaven, and she kissed me back, and she tasted so damn sweet, so fucking *right*.

I pull her out the front doors, making a right and heading towards the beach.

My head is swimming. I don't know what's happening to me, but I know I need her.

Port Haven Point is a tiny lighthouse—short and squat with a lock that's easy as hell to pick. Or at least it was when I was in high school.

"Giovanna Quinn, are you going to push me off the top of a lighthouse?" Hunter asks teasingly.

I look at her over my shoulder, raising a brow. For a minute I'm fifteen again, holding my girl's hand and laughing as we run along the shore. "Not unless that's what you're into, honey."

Once we reach the door, I face her, reaching into her hair to pull a bobby pin from her perfectly messy updo. Her eyes widen as a strand of hair falls into her face. I turn to the door, inserting the bobby pin into the lock. A little to the left, a little jiggle, and...

Click.

"Holy shit, you're a delinquent!" Hunter sounds both delighted and scandalized. "Why didn't you ever that summer?"

I push the rickety door open, nodding at her to enter first. "I didn't figure out I could break in until that fall. When you were in Georgia discovering your new favorite song, I came here to be alone."

Once we're through the doorway, I close the door and flip the light switch on. I step behind Hunter, wrapping my arms around her waist and pulling her into me. When I press my lips to her neck, her breath hitches and it's such a pretty noise that I have to hold back a moan.

"I always wished I'd found it sooner," I whisper against her neck. "That we had come here together, that it was ours. Maybe...maybe it's not too late. Maybe it can be ours."

I'm startled when Hunter pulls away from me, heart sinking beneath the floorboards like I'm in an Edgar Allen Poe story.

"Giovanna," she cups my face in her hands, eyes searching mine. "I need you to promise you won't pull away if we do this. I don't think I could take it if you left again, or said it was a mistake. Even if you're scared and regret it, promise you'll talk to me. Please."

I turn my head and press my lips to her palm. "I promise." It's the hardest promise I've ever made, but also the one I'm most committed to keeping.

"Kiss me," she whispers.

I do, tangling my hand in her hair, tilting her head back and kissing her with everything I have.

I don't know what will happen after this or in the morning. All I know is right this second, she's mine again. I can't give her what she needs from a relationship, but I can give her what she needs tonight.

I gently push her backwards into the room. It's a small space, with a spiral staircase painted with chipping navy blue paint. She whimpers when I press down on her shoulders, forcing her to lower herself to a stair.

"What are you doing?" she asks, leaning back against the stairs above her.

I raise a brow letting my eyes run over her body. Her face is so flushed, and I wonder if she's wet, if her nipples are straining against her bra. If she wants me as much as I want her. "I thought it was obvious."

She bites her lip and shakes her head.

I slowly begin removing the rings from my left hand, keeping my eyes on hers. "I'm fucking you on the stairs, honey. Where I can make you scream as loud as I want."

"Fuck." A shiver wracks through her entire body.

"Mmhmm. That's the plan." I shove my rings into my jacket pocket. I tug on her hip, until she's on her side facing me as I lower myself onto the stairs beside her.

"Hi," she says softly, reaching out and brushing a strand of hair behind my ear.

"Hi," I whisper back before leaning in and kissing her again. I take my time with her, savoring each moan and drinking in the way her fingers dig into the softness of my hip.

There's no way to make this comfortable, but I still put my arm behind her head as a pillow as we kiss.

"Is there anything I need to know before I touch you?" I ask her gently.

Hunter blinks up at me, blue eyes unfocused and shimmering. "Huh?"

"I really want to touch you. To make you feel good. But I need to know what you want, and for us both to feel safe."

"Oh!" Her eyes widen in understanding. "Right. I've been tested since my last partner and everything came back negative."

I nod. "Me, too. I was tested at my annual last month and everything is clear."

She exhales longly. "Good, cuz if Kelsey had given you anything..."

"Please stop talking about my ex." She giggles, and my face breaks into a soft smile. "Remember when my dad dragged us to Planned Parenthood after he walked in on us and made us get tested listen to a lecture on safe-sex practices? God, he'd be so disappointed I don't have dental dams on me..."

"Please stop talking about your dad." Hunter interrupts, grabbing the collar of my blouse and pulling me into her until we crash together.

"How do you want me?" I murmur against her. "You want my fingers? My mouth? You want to grind that pussy on my knee the same way you did the night we watched *FRIENDS* reruns?"

"Yes," she breathes, tracing the seam of my lips with her tongue. "Yes. Yes to all of that."

I smirk against her and gently bite her lower lip. "Dirty girl. You're so greedy."

She moans, and I feel her body moving as she rubs her thighs together. She's wearing a sundress with cowgirl boots, because of course she is. I slip my hand between her legs. "Keep them open for me, honey."

She's so obedient, so responsive. She spreads her legs as best she can, opening herself to me.

"That's my good girl," I praise her, testing out the waters.

She whimpers and I smile to myself. Of course she has a praise kink. Of course I fucking love it.

Then she surprises me by closing her legs, squeezing my hand between her thighs. I pull away from her. Her chest is heaving under her dress, lips swollen and cheeks tinged pink.

"Hunter. Legs open."

"Or what?" she asks with a wicked uptick of the corner of her mouth. "Legs open or *what*, Giovanna?"

"Oh, so naughty," I tease, reaching out to run my finger along her collar bone. "Legs open or you'll have to work for it."

She slings her leg over my hip and I smirk, slowly moving my finger down her sternum and over the softness of her belly. I slide it beneath her skirt, savoring the softness of the skin on her inner thigh. God, I want to make her scream my name until she loses her voice. To make her come so many times she...

She clamps her legs shut again.

I meet her eyes, and instead of the anxious expression I'd expected to see, she's smirking at me.

"Oops," she says innocently.

I bite back a groan. "Hunter."

"Yes, Giovanna?"

I don't even know what to say. She's all batting eyelashes and giggles and fuck, she's wrecked me.

I pull my hand from between her legs and dig my fingers into her hip, shifting so that I'm on my back against the stairs. She follows me, swinging both legs over my body and straddling my knee. Her hair's all mussed, and she looks down at me expectantly.

"I told you. You're going to have to work for it since you can't behave, honey. Fuck yourself against my leg."

She moans, eyes fluttering closed. "Giovanna," she whines, grinding her core against me. "You want me dead?"

"Never. I want you to come." I check my watch. "The party ends in twenty minutes, and I have to break down the room, so you better get going if you want to come."

"I hate you," she grunts, her hips moving in a circle, chasing the pleasure of friction from her lace panties against my thigh.

"No, you don't." I don't try to hide my smirk since her eyes are closed.

"No, I don't," she sighs.

"Play with your tits," I encourage.

Hunter opens her eyes to glare at me. "Stop telling me what to do," she whines.

I smirk and lean back on my elbows. "Okay."

"Fine!" she exclaims after *maybe* ten seconds, screwing her eyes closed again. She lowers the thin straps of her dress from her shoulders and tugs the bodice of her dress down. She then tugs down on the cups of her pink, lacy bra and dear god, she's perfect.

She grasps her perfect tits, and they overflow from her hands as she rolls her nipples between her middle finger and thumb. Her cunt is so warm against my leg, a radiating heat that is burning me alive.

"Giovanna," she gasps. Her movements are frenzied as a blush creeps up her chest.

"You gonna come for me, Hun?" I ask, breathless. She nods frantically, eyes still squeezed closed. "Use your words."

"Yes," she whimpers. "Yes, I'm gonna come for you."

I squeeze her hips, stilling her movements. She lets out a frustrated moan, opening one eye.

"Ask nicely."

She groans, and she can pretend she's annoyed all she wants, but I can see the way her teeth dig into her bottom lip, biting back her smile.

"Please, can I come?"

"That's my girl," I praise, one hand sliding beneath her skirt again. I groan when I feel the softness of her lace thong beneath my fingers, which I'm certain matches her bra. "Can I feel you come on my fingers?"

She nods enthusiastically. She's so worked up, so wet, that when I slip my hand beneath the lace, my middle and ring fingers slide effortlessly into her. God, she feels good. Her pussy squeezes around me, and I curve my fingers like it's muscle memory.

She rides my hand, frantic and fast and hard, and then she's coming. She's so fucking beautiful, mouth open on a silent scream as she squeezes my fingers. Her lips curl upward, and my heart flutters. She giggles a smiley, breathless giggle that's haunted me for over a decade.

"That's it, honey. God, you're beautiful, you're so, so beautiful." I'm overwhelmed, just from watching her, from feeling her.

She exhales loudly, eyes fluttering open as I pull my fingers from her and bring them to her mouth, tracing the shape and watching her lips glisten from her wetness.

"Clean up your mess, Hun." Her eyes are on mine as she opens her mouth and I place my fingers on her tongue.

Her lips close, I groan, throaty and loud. She smirks, swirls her tongue around my fingers, and releases them with a pop.

"Did you know you laugh when you come?" I ask as she pulls her bra and bodice up over her tits.

She peers up, looking shy. Imagine that. Hunter Cleary, shy. "No?"

"Yeah. Uh, you did it that summer, too. You're the only person I've ever seen who does."

"You looked?" And somehow I understand exactly what she means.

"Yeah, I looked," I say softly, reaching up and cupping her jaw. "You're something special, Hunter Cleary."

"No one's ever told me that before," she muses. "That I laugh when I come. I don't think anyone else ever noticed."

For a moment I let myself believe that it's because it's just for me. That this is something I can hold close to my chest and secret from the rest of the world.

"I wish they had. I wish someone told you how it's your best laugh. Do you... Maybe you can see it? I can show you?" I'm stammering at the end, cheeks red as I imagine supporting Hun in front of the mirror in our room as I fuck her with that pink vibrator she brought with her. Imagine our eyes meeting in the reflection like they had earlier, but this time, as she giggles and comes. Just for me.

"Yeah," she swallows and looks around. "How do you want me to touch you? I want to make you come before we face the wrath of Kelsey."

Kelsey. While we were here, Kelsey hadn't existed. It had been me and Hunter and our baggage from the past that really doesn't feel like baggage when I'm with her.

"So, um. I've learned a lot about myself over the past twelve years," I say slowly.

"Oh?" Hunter shifts on my lap. "Like what?"

I cup her waist in my hands. "Like sometimes...getting someone off is even better than me getting off. Sometimes, the longer the wait is, the better it is."

Hunter's eyes widen in understanding. "Oh! You...get off by not getting off."

I smirk. "Yeah. And I just...I like watching my partner when I make her feel good."

Hunter nods slowly, looking deep in thought. "That's helpful."

"Are you okay with that?" I ask apprehensively.

Her attention is back on me. "Now why wouldn't I be okay with whatever works for you?"

I don't respond, and my silence is enough of an answer.

"Fucking Kelsey," she sighs, her eyes falling closed.

"I mean, she felt a sense of power making her partner come, I think, so she just didn't get it. So I'd fake and..."

"What?" Hunter asks, her voice biting with anger. But it fades, replaced with a soft, concerning voice just for me. "You faked with the woman you were going to marry?"

I don't know why I told her that. I've never told *anyone* that before. But something about Hunter wants to let her see my vulnerabilities, to be honest with her. Because I think she'd treat them as delicate and precious, protect them like a baby bird in her hand.

"I'm sorry." Her voice is small. "I'm sorry that you..."

"Nope. That's very nice of you, but we're not doing that right now."

Hunter nods. "Got it. Thank you, Giovanna," she adjusts her skirt as I get to my feet. "For bringing me here. For this. I know you're letting me into a private part of your life, and I want you to know I see that."

My heart stutters because she's *right*. Tonight has been my past and present colliding. The first girl I'd loved, in a place I had mourned her and our lost relationship.

She reaches out and squeezes my hand. "I think you're brave too, Giovanna. Do you know that?"

"Thank you," I whisper, voice thick. I've never felt so known, so seen, so thoroughly, unconditionally understood and accepted than I feel at this moment.

I've never felt as at peace with myself as I do with her.

Chapter 24

Hunter

Playlist: Two Queens in a King Sized Bed | girl in red

I was right—Kelsey was indeed pissed when we returned to the party. Jo and I made a quick pit stop in the bathroom and lobby to fix smudged lipstick and mussed hair, hoping it wouldn't be too obvious what we'd snuck off to do. But I know myself, and I know I'm carrying myself differently after coming on Jo's fingers.

"We're not paying for you to leave!" Kelsey says as we re-enter the room.

"Sorry," I say unrepentantly. "Anyone else want pictures in the photo booth?"

A few of the drunk bridesmaids dash over to the backdrop, rummaging through the props laid out on the table.

"They left when they should have been doing their jobs," Kelsey huffs to Becky.

Jo scoffs. "You forget I've coordinated with you before Kelsey. When have you ever worked an event without taking a break?"

That shuts Kelsey up.

Finally, we're the last people in the room.

Giovanna's eyes hold mine, so dark and earnest. "What happens after tonight?"

I bite my lip. "What do you want to happen after tonight?"

"That's the problem. What I want to happen, versus what *should* happen are two different things."

"What do you want to happen?" I repeat.

She searches my eyes. "I want to keep kissing you. Keep making you smile and giggle all the damn time, but especially when I'm making you come."

Jo leans into me, pressing her lips to my neck. My head falls backward, opening myself to her as she continues.

"I want you to give me all the weird music lore, and humor me when I say I don't like our little monster. I want to wake up and hear you clanging pots and pans in the kitchen and help you find your keys and dance in the living room and wonder which of my books you've stolen and if you like it." She nips at the sensitive skin on my neck and I shudder.

"And what do you think should happen?" I somehow manage to choke out. It's a miracle I can speak, I'm so turned on right now.

"I think I should get away from you. Because I can't give you what you deserve, and we'll both get hurt."

I pull away and gently brush a wave of hair behind her ear. "Then let's have tonight. Tomorrow we'll figure out what happens. Let's just take it day by day."

She swallows and nods. "Okay. Then we should get to cleaning, because we only have two hours left tonight and I don't plan on wasting a moment."

"Time is an illusion. Tonight lasts until we get out of bed in the morning. Deal?"

"Deal," Jo agrees easily, pulling me in and kissing me deeply. I squeal when she grabs a handful of my ass and squeezes. "The sooner we're done cleaning, the sooner I get those pretty tits of yours in my mouth."

I've never cleaned as enthusiastically or quickly as I do now. Audrey and her daughter, Piper, join us and help us break down tables and box up photo props.

It's like she can sense my desperation for her. Jo, who's talking with Audrey on the other side of the room, looks over her shoulder at me and smirks.

I stick my tongue out at her.

She rolls her eyes.

I'm horny, I mouth.

She bites back a smile and nods toward the door. *I'll meet you in the room*, she mouths back.

I know for a fact that Kelsey was the one who told Audrey that we didn't need separate rooms. I know she did it to prove we weren't together.

But honestly, a broken clock is right thrice a day or whatever that saying is because I want to *thank* her for being the worst.

When I get to the room, I go over my options. Should I put on something sexy? Or strip altogether and just lay naked on the bed? Should I get room service? Is Jo into food play? I've heard whipped cream is fun...

I jump at the click as the door opens. Giovanna slips into the room and gently closes the door behind her. When she turns, she has a wobbly smile on her face.

"I thought you'd be naked by now, to be honest."

I laugh. "I definitely thought about it. But then I wasn't sure if that was being too forward or too much or—"

Jo steps towards me until we're toe to toe and cups my chin, angling my face so that I'm looking up into her eyes. "You could never be too much, Hun. I can't get enough of you."

I feel myself sway, feeling unsteady and unsure. "You...you can't say things like that," I stammer. "You'll make me fall in love with you."

Goddammit Hunter, I scold myself. *That's how you scare her off. That's why she runs. That's why...*

That's why I know nothing, I suppose, because she doesn't run. She doesn't even look afraid. She just smiles and leans in closer to me, so close that I can taste that damn sparkling water on her breath again. "Fair is fair."

I don't know who kisses who first, all I know is that our mouths are fused together and my head is swimming because what the hell does that mean?

Giovanna gently presses against me until the backs of my knees hit the side of the bed. "Do you know what I want us to do, honey?" Jo breaks our kiss and plants a trail of warm, wet kisses along my jaw.

I somehow shake my head. "No," I squeak as she nips me with her teeth before laving her tongue over the mark and soothing the sting.

"I want to lie down on this bed. And then I want you to straddle me." Her hands are on my hips and I'm grateful that nothing else is expected of me right now because if someone were to, god forbid, ask me the first letter of the alphabet...I wouldn't be able to tell them.

"Making me do all the work tonight?" I ask shakily.

"Not making you do anything you don't want to," she responds simply. "Besides, when you straddle me, I want you to sit on my face."

The power she has over me. My knees are weak and my body is trembling just from her words.

"Oh," is all I manage to say.

"And I want you to eat my cunt, too. Think you can manage that?"

Fuck me fuck me fuck me fuck me fuck me.

I nod jerkily.

"Fantastic," she breathes as she spins us and our positions are reversed. She sits down on the bed, and looks up at me. I cup her face in my hands as she speaks. "Go ahead and get undressed, honey. Let me see all of you."

Chapter 25

Jo

Playlist: Her Body Is Bible | FLETCHER

I watch in amusement as Hunter whips her sundress over her head, standing only in her cowboy boots and lingerie.

"That was fast," I tease, my eyes looking appreciatively down her body. Her curves are a maze I'd willingly get lost in, dimples in her hips, stretch marks along her thighs, textures and markings I want to run my tongue over. Things that the world tells women to change and be ashamed of are things I want to memorize on her. My eyes linger on her tummy, smiling when I see the belly button piercing she got that summer.

"You still have it!" I say, trying to hide my excitement. I reach out and gently touch the dangling pink jewel.

"Yeah," she says shyly. "It's so silly, but I love it. Reminds me of being fifteen and rebellious. And the way you held my hand during the piercing."

"I love it, too," I tell her honestly, looking up and meeting her eyes. "What other secrets do you keep beneath your clothes?"

Her body sways and I bite my lip. I can't get over how much my words have an impact on her, how clearly her desire shows on her face, all over her body. I cup her waist, drawing slow circles over her warm skin as I pull her between my thighs.

"You have secrets too," Hunter whispers. "When do I get to see those?"

"Desperate, are we?"

"We are." Her hands find my face and angle it upwards as she bends down and kisses me. "So fucking desperate for you, baby."

Her words are hot against my mouth, and this time I'm the one shuddering.

"Remember how I told you that you giggle and smile when you come?" I ask breathlessly.

"Mmhmm."

"Remember how I told you I wanted you to see it?"

"Yes?"

"Did you notice the mirror on the closet? The one that we have a perfect view of from the bed?" I nod towards the mirror in question.

Her eyes dart to the side. "I do now."

"I want you to keep your eyes on the mirror when we touch each other, honey," I say gently, turning her face to me again. "I want you to see what I see. Think you can do that?"

She looks dazed. "I'll try."

"Such a good girl." I grin as she absolutely preems under my praise. "Now strip for me."

Hunter reaches behind her back and my hands move to her hips. She unclips her bra and shrugs it off, throwing it haphazardly somewhere behind her, knocking something neither of us care about off the dresser. My eyes are fixated on her breasts. I saw them an hour ago, but seeing her completely topless is a different experience. I drink in the stretch marks on her cleavage, her puckered, pink nipples and areolas. Hers were the first boobs I ever saw and touched, and I always thought the fact they were my favorite was because of nostalgia.

But somehow this perfect woman has perfect tits, too.

"Hunter." My voice is husky, unrecognizable even to myself. "Please, let me kiss you."

She nods, and I wrap my arms around her, pulling her body even closer into me somehow. I swirl my tongue around her nipple and she gasps. Her hands are on my shoulders, nails digging into my skin through my suit jacket. I don't care. She can rip it to shreds if she wants. I'm already in pieces because of her.

"Jo," she chokes out, one hand stroking up the back of my neck until she's cradling the back of my head. "I need you."

"You have me, honey. I'm all yours." I pull her nipple into my mouth and she cries out. I scrape my teeth along the puckered bud before kissing it better.

"So good," she whimpers. "It all feels so good. "

"Has no one ever worshiped these pretty tits before?" I ask, releasing her nipple with a pop.

I feel her shake her head. "No. I was always self-conscious because they're saggy."

I run my thumb over her left nipple. She shivers and, somehow, it tightens even more. "You're perfect, honey. So, so perfect. Do you want to keep going?"

She surprises me by getting to her knees, dressed only in her underwear and boots, and unbuckling my belt. "Yes. But first, I need to see you. Please. I've been wondering and imagining it for months and I can't wait anymore, baby. I don't have to touch you, if you don't want, but *please.* Please let me see you."

Chapter 26

Hunter

Playlist: First, Best, Hottest | Beth McCarthy

Jo is measured as she helps me undress her at top speed. She knows I'm desperate, and I think she likes me that way.

Hell, I think *I* like me that way.

Finally, she's naked in front of me, and I sit back on my heels, scanning her with my eyes and studying every inch of her. She's soft, round, and lush. I reach out and trace a stretch mark on her stomach, marveling at how lovely she is. "You're beautiful, Giovanna," I say earnestly, tipping my head back to look up at her. "Thank you for sharing yourself with me."

Her hands are in my hair. "What does that mean?" she asks shakily.

"It means I'm not taking tonight for granted. That I see you. That I'm grateful you're letting me see you. Touch you. And I want you to know that."

She bites her lip. "That's...thank you. I see you, and I'm grateful, too."

Her hand cups my cheek and I lean into her, unable to take my eyes off her.

"Let me love you," I beg, blushing upon the realization of what I said. "Your body. Love your body. Let me taste you."

Jo letting me love her is the only way she could make tonight better. But I know she's not there yet, so I'll take her body. If that's all I can have right now. I'll worship and love every inch of her.

"You're not naked enough," Jo grumbles, and I reluctantly get to my feet. She runs her eyes over me. "I'm tempted to tell you to leave the boots on."

I grin. "That would be a first, shockingly."

"That is surprising," she agrees, reaching out and running her index finger down my sternum. I shiver at the feeling of her nail between my breasts and she smirks. "I love how you don't hold back and just react. It's the best."

"Maybe I'm a shit liar, too." I take a step back from her. "Boots on or off?"

"Off. This time."

This time. I try to tell my brain not to run with the fact there might be a time she wants to fuck me in my boots. It's fine, I'm cool. Super chill.

I kick off my boots, and then shimmy my underwear down my hips and thighs, letting the lace fall to the ground in a puddle of pink. Jo's kept her eyes on mine throughout my final bit of disrobing, and I keep mine on hers as I step out of the underwear.

"Ta-da!" I lift my arms above my head and cock my hip. "I'm naked!" I peer down at my feet. "Well, almost." The pink socks with tiny disco balls stay on, obviously.

She barks out a loud, snorting laugh and it makes me laugh in return. We move towards one another at the same time, wrapping our arms around each other and pressing our lips together. God, I could stay in her arms forever if she'd let me. Melt into her until all I am is a memory and I'm completely consumed by Giovanna Theresa Quinn.

"Let me taste you, honey," she gasps, breaking our kiss. I whine and press myself further into her before my brain registers her words.

"Oh!" I blush when it clicks. "Yes. That. Let's do that."

She sits down on the bed, shimmying backward before laying down. She lifts her head and arches her eyebrow. "Are you going to sit on my face or not, honey?"

I groan and crawl onto the mattress. "I'll do whatever you want me to do right now."

"See, you say that. But I have a feeling you like breaking the rules. Making me frustrated and working me up, don't you?"

"I plead the fifth." My face is so red. I position myself and straddle her shoulders so that my head hovers above her cunt, all dark curls and glistening wetness.

I did that! I think excitedly. *She's that wet because of* me.

"Don't forget to watch when you come." She licks my cunt with one long stroke.

I moan at the contact. I'm a goner. My thighs are already shaking next to her head and I want to collapse on top of her. I lift my gaze, noticing the mirror is right in front of me. Hypothetically, doing as she says should be easy-peasy. I also have the perfect view of Jo's pussy. Her feet are planted on the mattress, knees spread, and my mouth is fucking watering.

I lower my mouth to her, tentatively circling her clit with my tongue, and almost launching through the ceiling when she moans against me in response.

I slip my fingers into my mouth, then lower them and curl my middle and ring fingers into her, feeling the rough skin I remember from the last time I made her come.

She moans again and I lower my mouth to her, licking her labia. I part her with my free hand and suck her clit into my mouth.

I'm somehow able to focus on the feelings and keep my eyes on the mirror. It's so hot, the way my fingers disappear into her, how hooded my eyes are. It's so fast, but I'm coming in minutes, eyes squeezing closed as I ride out my orgasm.

"Did you see?" Jo gasps, and I whimper from the loss of her mouth against me.

Shit.

"No," I admit, flushing. "My eyes closed."

I gasp and jerk as her teeth scrape against my vulva. "That's a shame," she purrs. "Guess we have to try again. Eyes on the mirror, Hunter."

I haven't fully come down when her lips clasp onto my clit again. She wants to play with me? Fine. I can play with her, too. I force myself to keep my eyes on the mirror as I increase the speed and pressure of my fingers and flick her clit with my tongue.

Her moans and gasps only increase my own pleasure, and as I feel my orgasm building, she tightens around me.

I pull my fingers out from her.

"*Fuck,*" she curses, pulling her mouth away from me.

"I know," I answer sweetly, looking over my shoulder at her and batting my eyelashes. "That's why I stopped. I heard you, baby."

"Such a naughty girl." I squeak and jump as she bites down on my thigh. She says it like she hadn't specifically told me that she loves the wait. "Two can play at this game."

Our mouths are on each other once again, her movements fast, hard, and frantic to my soft, lazy licks and sucks. She likes it this way though, which surprises me. Jo Quinn, with her hard and ragged exterior, enjoys slow, soft, gentle sex. She likes to drag it out, make all her pleasure last as long as possible.

I break contact again and Jo groans in frustration. "This is the cruelest torture," she grumbles.

"No," I correct. "The cruelest torture is knowing we share an apartment and that you couldn't be mine. Imagining you when I made myself come and then biting down on a pillow so you wouldn't know. *That's* the cruelest torture."

Her fingers dig into my hips, and I'm delighted by it.

Her mouth is on me again, flicking and sucking just so that I lift my head and force myself to look in the mirror as she pulls another orgasm from me. My eyes are heavy lidded and my mouth opens as I pant. When I start coming, my mouth slams shut. I think she's delusional. I don't laugh, and I don't smile.

But then as I feel myself beginning to come down, I watch in wonder as my lips turn upward and I let out a giggle.

The *fuck*?

"Did you see?"

I nod, dazed. "That's so weird."

"I freaking love it. I want to make you come a million times a day so I can see that smile a million times a day."

I bury my face in her pillowy thigh, tickled pink and a tiny bit bashful from her words.

"Stop hiding from me, honey."

"No," I whine.

Smack.

I shriek and jump at the stinging sensation of Jo's hand on my ass.

"Did you just *spank* me?"

"Mmhmm." Damn her, she sounds smug. It makes my muscles clench with an aftershock of pleasure. "Remember at that fancy French restaurant Kelsey and Becky took us to and you typed up a list of things I might need to know? I was baffled that you thought I needed to know you liked being spanked. Turns out I needed to know a bit later than expected."

She runs her hand over my ass, soothing the stinging sensation and causing my stomach to swoop with anticipation. "Are you blaming *me*?"

"Sure am. If you never told me, if you behaved, I wouldn't have to do this."

Thwack.

I bite back a moan this time.

"You like that, don't you?" She's amused and unsurprised. "My dirty, dirty girl."

She buries her face in my pussy and I squeal again, this time for the masterful way she uses her lips on me. "You taste so good," she groans into my cunt. "How do you taste so good?"

I smile proudly and grind my pelvis against her.

I bury my face in her, too, trying to decide whether I should tell her that when I'm with her, I'm the best I've ever felt. She curves two fingers into me before I can make a decision.

"Giovanna," I moan, voice low and husky.

"God, I love it when you say my name like that," she gasps from between my legs.

I try to steady my movements, keep my licks and sucks and nuzzles consistent, but she's *too* good at this. When she spanks me a third time, my thighs clench around her shoulders and I explode.

She slows her movements. Her hand is gentle on my backside, slow soothing circles as I come back to this galaxy.

"You're *really* good at this," I manage to gasp, resting my cheek on her thigh. "I haven't done this in twelve years, you're making me look so bad."

She giggles and playfully taps my ass. "You're doing such a good job, honey. Don't be an asshole to yourself."

"You're just saying that because I'm rusty and you feel bad for me," I bemoan.

It's my turn to squeak as she flips us over and adjusts us so that her face is next to mine. My stomach flips, too. She's so gosh darn pretty.

"You're a pain in my ass." She boops my nose.

I boop her nose in return. "Says the woman who spanks me."

"Says the woman who *likes* it."

"Wow. You seemed all too eager to spank me," I tease gently, running my index finger over her lips, her chin, down her neck and between her breasts.

"What are you doing?"

"Dunno. I was told I have to make you come like a good girl. And I'm *such* a good girl, aren't I?"

Jo cups my cheek as I slip my hand between her thighs. "My good girl," she murmurs, her dark eyes on mine.

I gasp and jacknife up as I remember something. "Oh my god! Oh my *god*!" I leap out of bed and rush to the dresser, opening the top drawer.

"Um, hello?" Jo's voice carries from the bed, full of confusion.

"Be patient, baby." I rummage through the contents until I find what I'm looking for. I hold it to my chest and turn slowly back to the bed, unable to stop the mischievous smile creeping on my face.

Jo blinks at me. "I thought you said you packed it away?"

I smirk and walk back to the bed, climbing next to her and pressing a quick kiss to her cheek. "I lied. I might be a good girl, but what's the fun of being good if you don't get to be a little naughty, too?"

Jo's hips jerk as I press the pink rabbit between her thighs and turn it on. I spread her with my fingers and run the head from her entrance to her clit, loving the way her left hand fists the sheets.

"God. You're...you're too much," Jo chokes out.

"I've always been too much," I say, heart in my throat. "I've always been too loud and too excitable and too...just too much. It's always been a bad thing."

She fists my hair and tilts my head up, the green flecks glistening in the lowlight. "You're too thoughtful. Too funny. Too brave. Too beautiful. Too *wonderful*. Saying you're too much in a negative way is like complaining the sky is too blue, a flower too beautiful. You fucking *can't*. I can't get enough of you."

I kiss her, tears stinging the back of my eyes. Because, in this moment, I truly believe she could love me, that she could want us to be real. It feels right, the idea of us whispering what we see in the other in the darkness, in our shared bed. It feels right that I should fall asleep beside her. *She* feels right.

She always has. Finding and falling in love with her again was finding an old favorite oversized sweater from years gone by, putting it on, and realizing it's a perfect fit now. She's my perfect fit.

It seems cruel that the universe would take her away from me, and then bring her back to me just for me to lose her again.

I love you! I want to scream. *And I think you can love me, too. Be brave. Be brave like I know you can. Be brave for me. Choose me. Because I choose you, and I'll keep choosing you, until you forget every time you weren't chosen.*

"I have to make you come," I croak instead, pulling away and ducking my head. "I can't not make...not make you come."

"Hun...*fuck-*" I cut off her words by pushing the vibrator into her. Her eyes close in ecstasy and her teeth dig into her bottom lip.

She's the most beautiful thing I've ever seen.

I slowly fuck her with the toy, pulling it out when her breathing becomes more frantic.

"*Hunter.*"

"Let me tease you, baby. I want to give you the best orgasm of your life, slow and dragged out, just the way you like it. You'll never, ever have to fake with me. Never. You're enough exactly as you are."

Her eyes open as I press the vibrator into her again. I edge her for a few minutes, until she's a writhing and begging mess. "Please. Hunter, *please*," she begs. I don't pull out this time, and it feels like I'm completely surrounded by her as she falls apart, whimpering my name in my neck as her body writhes.

It's everything I've imagined, and somehow much, much more.

"Hun," Jo gasps, as I pull the vibrator from her, her nails loosening their grip on me. "Hun."

"I know, baby." I brush her dampened bangs from her face. "I know. Let it all out."

"Fuck you."

I bark out a laugh. "I beg your pardon?"

"You heard me." Jo lifts her head and presses her lips to the pulse point on my neck, causing my breath to shudder. "Fuck. You."

"You did that already," I tease. "But you can do it again, if you want."

"Don't you want to know why?"

"My sparkling personality, I assume."

"Because you understood exactly what I was saying. You're the only person who got it, who took the time to listen and give me what I wanted."

I push back some hair from her face. "Because you deserve to be listened to, and to get what you want, baby."

We both jolt at the sudden rap on our door.

"Be right there!" I holler, walking bare-assed to the dresser and rummaging for a nightgown and robe. I quickly make myself decent and hurry to the door.

"Hey!" I'm taken aback when I see Audrey at the door. She's taken her makeup off and has a star-shaped pimple patch on her chin. Her dark auburn hair is piled into a haphazard bun, and she's wearing round glasses, completely different from the professional, polished vibes she gave off earlier today.

"Hi," she says awkwardly, her eyes shifting to the side. "I hate to do this. I *really* hate to do this."

"It's okay, Audrey," I tell her, patting her forearm encouragingly. "I believe in you. You can do hard things."

She stares at where I'm touching her arm. "Uh, thanks? Didn't know you moonlit as an inspirational poster."

"Stop deflecting. Do the hard thing."

"We got a few noise complaints."

I stare blankly at her. "I didn't hear anything."

Audrey grimaces, and it clicks.

"*Oh*. We're the noise."

"Yeah, uh, one of the brides called down and asked a manager to talk to you. Nia is dealing with another situation, so you get off-duty me. Apparently they haven't been able to sleep because of, uh, the noises."

My brow wrinkles. "The brides?"

"Yeah. They're in the room next to yours."

I try to hide my smile, knowing that every noise Kelsey heard was genuine, real, and it may very well have been the first time she heard Jo getting exactly what she needed.

"We'll be sure to keep it down," I promise Audrey, fighting back a smile.

We exchange a few more words, then I close the door walking back to the bed. My heart feels like it has wings when I see her sitting against the headboard, sheet rumpled at her waist and a shit-eating grin on her face.

"Did you know Kelsey and Becky were in the room next to us?" I teasingly scowl and plant my hands on my hips.

"I totally forgot." Her face falls for a moment. "This wasn't to get her attention or make her jealous, or anything like that, I swear. I...fuck. I didn't think about her at all, I was focused on us," she says it like she's having a revelation, and in a way, she is.

"I'm so, so proud of you," I tell her earnestly, knowing how much she's wanted to move on and get Kelsey out of her head.

She rests her temple on my shoulder, and I kiss the crown of her head as she inhales raggedly. I hold her there for a few minutes, and then we lay down facing each other. We turn off our bedside lights, and hold each other close until we fall asleep.

Chapter 27

Hunter

Playlist: Silver Springs - Live at Warner Brother Studios in Burbank, CA 5/23/97 | Fleetwood Mac

Beep. Beep. Beep.

I blink awake, disoriented and vision foggy.

Beep. Beep. Beep.

I blearily glance around the room as I sit up. It's still dark, no sunlight peeking through the curtains, and I'm taken aback when my eyes land on the clock next to Giovanna's side of the bed.

3:26 a.m.

Beep. Beep. Beep.

Why is there an alarm going off in the middle of the night? In this economy? Unacceptable.

I grab my phone from the nightstand and swipe up to turn off the alarm. It takes me at least five swipes before I realize the sound isn't coming from my phone.

Beep. Beep. Beep.

"Giovanna?" I whisper, turning my head to look at her.

"Hmmm?" she answers, and I'm not sure why, but I can tell something's not right.

Beep. Beep. Beep.

Oh my god. That's not my alarm, that's not why I recognize the sound.

That's the sound Giovanna's CGM app makes when her blood sugar's low.

My heart plummets. "Jo?" I grab her shoulder and shake roughly. Probably rougher than necessary. But all I can hear is her giving me instructions on what to do if she doesn't wake up.

She turns over onto her side and meets my eyes. She's shaking.

"Hey," I say softly, "is your blood sugar low?"

She's staring at me, but it's almost like she can't focus on what I'm saying. "What?"

Beep. Beep. Beep.

I reach over her and grab her phone, holding it to her face so it unlocks. My stomach sinks when I open the app and it shows that her blood sugar is low, and trending downward.

I jump out of bed and walk to the dresser, where Loretta sits safely in her case. I unzip the case and rummage through until I find what I need and climb back into bed.

She's curled on her side, and is eyeing me suspiciously. "Where'd you get that?"

"Amazon. I thought I should have them on me in case of an emergency." I open the top of the little honey bear and lift the bottle to her mouth. "Open."

Jo obliges, opening her mouth and slowly swallowing the honey as I tilt the bear upward. "You...you bought those for me?" she asks after swallowing.

"Yeah, I know you keep them on you, but I thought it'd be smart for me to have some, too."

We're quiet while she continues to eat the honey. "What now?" I ask quietly, turning to the side to put the bottle on the nightstand when she's finished.

"Usually one is enough, so I'll check my numbers in an hour or two."

I head back to the dresser and grab another honey bear, just in case. When I return, she meets my eyes. "How did you know I was low?" She's still shaky, but less so than a few minutes ago.

"I recognized the alarm," I tell her.

Her brow furrows. "How?"

I blush. "I sort of watched a YouTube video so I'd know what they sounded like. Is there anything I can do to make you feel better?"

"You already did it." She weakly pulls on me, and I lay down on my side, facing her. Her brows are furrowed in concentration as she stares at her phone.

"Do you want me to show you the Silver Springs video?" I ask.

"Hmm?" She looks up at me in confusion.

"I didn't get to show you the Fleetwood Mac performance where Stevie Nicks curses Lindsey Buckingham. Do you want me to show it to you now?"

"Okay," she says quietly. "I feel pretty disoriented right now, but I'll try to follow along with the exclusive Hunter commentary."

I grab my phone from the nightstand, pulling up Fleetwood Mac's legendary performance of Silver Springs and holding it between us.

"Okay, so that's Stevie Nicks, and that's Lindsey Buckingham..." I begin to explain.

"Who's that?" she asks, pointing to Mick Fleetwood.

"He doesn't matter right now. Focus on Stevie and Lindsey. Like look at that tension."

"Do they wanna fuck?" she questions.

"They used to fuck," I explain, "and they had a really messy breakup. So Stevie wrote this song, and legend has it that this live performance is her cursing him."

"Does he deserve it?"

I scoff. "He's a man, Giovanna. Use that pretty little head of yours."

"You think I'm pretty," she says in a quiet sing-song voice.

We're silent as we watch the performance, and when it gets to the bridge, I feel the goosebumps I always feel during this part rise on my arms.

"Oh. Yeah. She's definitely cursing him," she murmurs, checking her phone again.

"Right? It's so fucking powerful. So badass."

"I see why you like this performance so much."

"Yeah?"

Jo rests her head on my shoulder, and I immediately rest mine on the top of her head. "Mmmhmm. You're powerful and badass, too. Like begets like."

My heart skips a beat. "You...you can't say that, Jo. I'll fall in love with you."

Like I'm not already head over heels for her.

"Hmm," she muses. "Would that really be so terrible?"

I don't answer her, I can't. Because then I'd tell her how falling for her again has been the most wonderful and terrifying thing to happen to me. How I've never felt freer, more secure. How I want to continue falling for her all the days of my life.

Once the song ends, we don't move. "Can we watch it again?" she asks after a few silent minutes.

I press play and we silently watch Stevie Nicks perform magic again and again, until Jo's blood sugar is in the safe zone. She falls asleep first, and it feels peaceful. Right.

I want to support her during her lows and her highs, because even though she can take care of herself, I want to take care of her, too. I want to hold her until she feels better, and to love her through it. God knows she deserves to be loved through it all.

And why couldn't it be me?

Chapter 28

Jo

Playlist: Espresso | Sabrina Carpenter

I wake up the next morning to a mouthful of tangled, blonde curls. I sputter and attempt to remove the strands from my mouth, careful not to pull too hard. Hunter's body is snuggled into mine with one arm haphazardly across my chest, like she's protecting me from something in some nightmare she's having.

I found out in the middle of the night how quick she is to do that–protect me, comfort me, support me. Her breathing is heavy in sleep, nostrils flaring with each breath, mouth slightly ajar with a strand of drool dripping from her bottom lip. Despite that, I still want to wake her by kissing her, like this is some fairytale with dubious consent.

Instead I slowly move her arm so I can get up, pulling on a dark purple athleisure set and a pair of sneakers before taking my meds. I check my blood sugar levels on my phone before sending Hunter a quick text telling her where I am going. I want her to know I'm coming back, but I need some time and space to think. To process everything that happened last night.

When I step outside, the sun is rising over the sound and I inhale the salty sea air. The light breeze dances over my skin as I start the one-mile walk to my parents' house.

Port Haven is a small town, just two and a half square miles and a couple thousand year-round residents. It's a nice walk from the inn to the house, and I let myself just be for a moment while I walk. I can process after I steal some of that espresso that my local siblings and their friends steal from my parents.

When I get to my childhood home, I'm a little concerned to discover Poppy was right: the back door is unlocked. I'm more surprised that Ren, Will, Millie, and Poppy are all seated at the counter, at least having the decency to look a smidge guilty.

"Hello, troublemakers." I put my hands on my hips and arch an eyebrow. "Who's gonna show me how to use this fancy-ass contraption?"

"This isn't what it looks like," Ren says, eyes wide as he holds a steaming Best Dad Ever mug.

"We're out of luck. I spilled," Poppy says.

"Why would you do that?" my brother whines.

"She doesn't live here! It's fine! She's not going to tell your parents," Poppy argues.

Will looks between the two of them as they bicker, an amused look on his face.

"Did you miss the chaos when you were at Stanford?" I ask him.

"Surprisingly, yes," he admits, shrugging his shoulder.

"Did you ever see Alex while you were out there?" I ask.

At the mention of my younger sister, Will chokes on his latte. Ren helpfully smacks him on his back, still bickering with Poppy.

"What are you doing here? Ren said you were in town for a bachelorette party or something? Shouldn't you be there?" Will asks when he's finally able to speak.

Of course, that brings everyone's attention to me. I sigh. "We don't have anything for a few hours. I needed to take a walk. And try the espresso. Seriously, can someone help me make some?"

Ren and Millie exchange a knowing look and I internally groan. "Please don't."

"Where's Hunter?" Millie asks, waggling her eyebrows.

"Sleeping. Will, can you help me figure out this machine while my siblings relentlessly interrogate me?"

Luckily, everyone has pity on me. Will shows me how to use the espresso machine, and Ren and Millie stop asking questions.

The five of us fall into an easy, familiar rhythm, laughing and reminiscing about growing up together. Poppy and Will have been a part of our lives so long that they were at the house when our parents brought the twins home from the hospital.

We're surprised into silence by my dad coming into the kitchen in a robe. His red hair is tinged with gray, and there's a five o'

clock shadow darkening his face.

Will, Poppy, Millie, and Ren stare wide-eyed at him. I take a sip of my drink, eyes volleying between the group of them and my dad, who's working the espresso machine.

"Good morning, Dad," Millie says cautiously. "Sleep well?"

"Good morning, offspring," Dad chuckles, his back to us. "I slept fine, until my home decidedly didn't sound like empty-nesters lived here."

"You're not empty-nesters, yet," Ren reminds him. "You can't be an empty-nester till all of us move out, and Izzy and Leo still live here part time."

"Semantics," Dad shrugs. "Your mom decided she wanted espresso, so she's getting espresso."

Millie dry heaves.

"Shut up," I swat her with the back of my hand. "It's cute!"

"And then we're going to have wild, animal sex," Dad continues, watching intently as the espresso machine starts to work its inexplicable magic.

"This is your fault!" Ren hisses, pointing a menacing finger at Millie. "You had to overreact to a cute thing and now I have to picture our parents having wild, animal sex!"

Millie gives him the finger.

"Emilia," Dad chastises, back to us. "Don't be rude to your brother."

"How did he know?" Poppy asks, eyes wide. "How does he always know?"

"Superpowers from seminary." Dad finally turns and faces us, doing a double take when his eyes land on me. "Joey! What a pleasant surprise. Decided to crash the breakfast club over here since you're in town?"

"What's the breakfast club?" Will asks.

"A movie from the eighties," Millie answers helpfully.

"You fools using my espresso machine every morning," Dad clarifies.

"Wait. You know?" Poppy asks nervously.

He gives her a pointed look. "Of course I know. Who do you think wakes up early and unlocks the door for you?" We stare at him in various degrees of shock as he looks between the five of us. "You didn't think your mother and I just...accidentally left the backdoor unlocked overnight?"

There's an awkward silence as it sinks in that that's exactly what we all thought.

He scowls at us. "You think so little of me and I always make sure we have freshly ground espresso in the house. The disrespect."

Millie sniffs, and wipes at her eyes. "Thanks, Dad." Her voice is shaky. "That's nice of you. These mornings mean a lot to me."

Ren and I exchange confused glances out of the corner of our eyes. It's a running joke that bubbly Izzy is the odd one out of the Quinn women. The rest of us are grumpy and harsh, and Millie may be the most menacing of us all.

She and Leo were the only ones to inherit dad's fiery red hair, though Leo's is more muted. She's a tattoo artist, and she has her own artwork all over her body, giving her a rugged look that the old townies in Port Haven don't exactly love. She has a septum piercing and is rarely seen without her winged eyeliner, even this early in the morning.

She's tough, we all are. But unlike Kat, Nic, Alex, and Izzy, who cry at Budweiser commercials, Millie and I are the stoic ones. I haven't cried since before Kelsey left, and I can count on one hand the times I saw Millie cry in her twenty-four years of life.

But here she is, all teary-eyed because our dad unlocks the door early enough so their kids and their friends can think they're sneakily using their espresso machine. For some reason, this show of emotion has me thinking of Hunter. Hunter who wears her heart on her sleeve despite being rejected and hurt. Hunter, who hasn't asked anything of me, just offered me compassion and understanding. Hunter, who smells like magnolias and springtime rain. Hunter, who once told me she loves shooting weddings because she creates a reason for couples to look back at their happiest day.

"I have to go," I say, getting up from the stool abruptly. "Thanks for the espresso." I wince when looking at the mug. I took two, maybe three sips from it, and feel guilty about wasting it.

But not guilty enough to stay.

That Summer
Jo

"Deep breath in..." Darlene, the owner of Sea Wall Ink, says. "Deep breath out."

Hunter whimpers and squeezes my hand as Darlene pierces her skin. I try to squeeze back, but her grip is too tight for any movement.

"And that's it!" Darlene says, rolling her stool away from the piercing table and grabbing a hand mirror from the counter. "Want to see, Annabella?"

I try not to laugh at the poor lady using the name on the fake ID that Hunter had brought with her from Georgia. Our cover story was that Annabella was my older cousin visiting from Georgia. Everybody in town knows me, but not everyone knows Hunter.

Hunter sits up. "Yes, please." She takes the mirror from Darlene and looks at the piercing in the reflection. Her face lights up. "Oh my gosh, I love it!" She squeals happily. "Thank you! Giovanna, can you give me my bag?"

I stand beside her as she pays for the piercing with her dad's credit card—which he apparently never checks the statement for—and then we head out. Hunter digs through her tote bag and pulls out the tiny purple digital camera she's carried around all summer.

"*Take a picture of me!*" *She hands me the camera and tote bag, ties her t-shirt so she exposes her midriff, and unbuttons the fly of her denim cutoffs. My throat is dry as she folds down the waistband of her jeans just below her belly button.*

She looks up at the camera and beams, all squinty-eyed from the sunshine. I can't hide the smile that spreads across my face as I shoot her in a variety of poses.

"What are you going to do when you can't just throw Tanya at me and demand a photoshoot?" I tease, handing her beloved camera to her.

Her face falls. Summer is quickly coming to a close, and we've avoided discussing it.

"I guess," she says slowly, "I'll just have to take lots of selfies, and send them to you so you can see how absolutely lost I am without you."

My cheeks heat, and it's not just because of the summer heat.

Hunter smirks at me and walks toward me. "You're blushing."

"It's a sunburn," I lie.

"You're gonna miss me."

I shake my head. "Nuh-uh. I can't wait for you to come home. I'll never have to hear the word 'y'all' again."

She links her arm in mine and rests her head on my shoulder as we begin to walk towards Queenie's for celebratory shakes and fries. "I'm gonna miss you, too."

Chapter 29

Jo

Playlist: Outlaw For Your Love | Mon Rovla

Walking into our hotel room, I'm greeted by Hunter on the bed. She's laying on her belly, feet in the air and ankles crossed, a wide smile directed to her phone.

"No, I love *you*, baby girl," she coos, not looking up from the screen, and I know she's talking to Dolly over FaceTime.

If this frigid heart of mine was capable of falling in love again, it would have just done so.

"Hey," I whisper softly.

She looks at me over her phone, eyes widening when she sees what's in my arms.

I think she's going to ask about it, but instead asks if I want to say hi to Dolly while turning the phone towards me. Josh holds

Dolly up to the camera, and she's wearing the little crocheted hat I made her.

"Oh my god, hi Dolly!" I squeal. "You look so pretty in your hat!"

Nic grabs the phone from Josh and squints into the camera. "Are you fucking high?"

I scowl. "You're such an asshole."

"I'm sorry, you're cooing over Hunter's pet in a pitch I didn't know you were capable of reaching," my sister argues. "How is that my fault?"

I roll my eyes. "I'm hanging up now. Bye."

I hang up the phone before anyone can say anything and look at Hunter, who's sitting on her ankles in the center of the bed, a shit-eating grin plastered on her face.

"Don't say it."

"You like Dolly! No, you *love* her!" she squeals, bouncing and clapping her hands. "I knew you would."

"No, you didn't."

"Let me have this!"

"Hey, I'm sorry for leaving," I say abruptly.

Hunter frowns and tilts her head. "It's okay. I saw your text and knew you needed space. You communicated that, and I trust you."

A strange feeling grows in my gut. She trusts me not to hurt her. To keep my word. It's a strange thing, to be trusted. To know that someone is choosing to give you parts of themself you can harm.

Hunter's choosing to allow me to hurt her, and trusts that I won't, and it makes me feel so many different things.

"Thank you," I say, lowering myself to sit on the edge of the mattress. "I appreciate your understanding."

"You deserve it. Understanding, I mean. How are you feeling?"

"So much better than last night." I inhale shakily. "Thanks for staying."

Hunter tilts her head. "Where was I going to go?" Her voice is genuinely curious, like leaving wasn't an option she'd considered.

What if she stayed because she *wanted* to? What if she bought jars of honey because she wanted to be able to help in a situation like this?

I swallow roughly, and am suddenly fascinated by my cuticles. "So my CGM app has a share feature—"

Hunter grabs her phone from where I put it on the bed. "What do I need to do? What's the app called?"

"Do you want to know more about what it entails?" I've never shared my CGM data with anyone before. Not Kelsey, not even Nic. I never told Nic it was an option, though I know if she'd known, she would have wanted to share.

Sharing this part of my disease is vulnerable. It means someone is being alerted to my lows and highs, that there's no way for me to just pretend everything's okay. And that's kind of what I do, pretend everything's okay. I don't know if I want to do that with Hunter. I don't know if I *can* do that with her. She sees through the walls I put up and sees who I am at my core. The hurting, scared person, but she chooses to stay with that person, anyway. She waits when I need space, and listens to what I need, in so many ways.

It feels like diabetes has stolen so much of my time, so much of my life. And it's made me want to hide it as much as possible, to keep it away from as many parts of my life as I can.

But I don't want to do that, not with her. I want to be as open and honest and generous as she is, even with the parts of me I want to hide.

She downloads the app and we set up the notifications. I thought it'd feel wrong, the first time I did this. Like I was giving away the last part of myself I could keep for myself.

Instead, it feels freeing, like this part of me was never meant to be kept to myself. Hunter tries out different alert noises and asks all the right questions, like she's excited to support me.

"Thank you for showing me this." She reaches over and gently squeezes my hand.

"No, thank you," I say earnestly, squeezing her hand back. "I've never felt safe enough to use this feature before. You're a safe landing, Hun. I don't really know how to thank you."

"Well," she says slowly, peering curiously at the items I'd placed on the dresser. "You can start by showing me what that delicious smelling bag is over there."

"Oh, I ran to Queenie's and the farmer's market at the seawall." I jump up to get her the paper bag full of greasy diner food. "I hope sweet potato fries take away well."

A soft, slow smile spreads across her face as she peers into the bag. "Sweet potato fries? And is that a strawberry milkshake?"

"Mmhmm."

"Giovanna." Her voice is quiet as she pulls the food out from the bag, almost as if she's in awe. "This is wonderful. Thank you."

"I got you some flowers, too. They reminded me of you." I hand her the bouquet wrapped in brown paper. She immediately brings them to her nose, inhaling the sweet scent.

"Peonies are my favorite," she says softly.

"I didn't know that. I just thought that they were pretty and pink and open. They reminded me of you."

"Do you know why they're my favorite?" she asks, looking up at me through her lashes.

"Because they're pretty and pink and open?"

"Because they remind me of you. You smell like peonies. You always have."

I swallow thickly. "I've used the same body wash since middle school."

"Never change it. Ever." She brandishes the bouquet at me like a weapon. "Or else."

"Yes, ma'am."

"Thank you for thinking of me. No one's ever given me flowers before."

"I've never given someone flowers before," I admit, cheeks heating.

"Not even Kelsey?" She opens the box holding the sweet potato fries, and I sigh in relief when steam rises from them.

"Not even Kelsey. She told me on our first date she thought flowers were tacky and a waste of money, so I never bought them for her."

"Never to anyone before Kelsey either?" she asks around a mouthful of sweet potato fry.

"No. It never felt serious enough."

She inhales shakily as our eyes meet. "Yeah? And this does?"

I take her hand, and intertwine our fingers together. "I'm not sure. But I know it feels different. I want to keep dancing with you, kissing you, making you come, and be held by you during my lows and I don't know what that means. But I like it. I like *you*, Hun. Maybe we could make this a little less fake."

Hunter's returning smile is radiant. "Really? You want me?"

I slowly nod my head. "Is that okay? I can't promise you tomorrow, but today, I want to be yours."

She nods solemnly in return. "*Dale.*"

"Pardon?"

"Do you know how close you were to quoting a Pitbull lyric? What did you expect me to say in response to that?"

"Right, of course." I tease.

"But yes. Today is perfect. And tomorrow we'll re-evaluate." She rubs her thumb over the back of my hand. "Every day is a gift with you, Giovanna. I won't take it for granted."

"Hun." My voice is husky. I've never felt this pure acceptance before. Just the total, complete embracing of who I am and what I need, what I'm ready for.

She reaches up and tucks my hair behind my ear before cupping my cheek. "You mean a lot to me. Always have. That summer was fast and hard and frantic and I loved every moment. But I'm so okay with going slow with you. Savoring each moment we get and taking it day by day."

"Thank you," I whisper.

She rises to her knees and presses her mouth to mine, snaking her arms around my neck. I wrap mine around her waist and pull her tighter into my body. No matter how close we are, it's never close enough. I never can get quite enough of her.

There's a knock on our door and I reluctantly pull away. Hunter sways as I step away from her, like I was the one keeping her steady.

"Don't go," she whines sweetly, pulling at my hand. "Stay here. Kiss me more."

"Jo?" Kelsey's voice wafts through the closed door. "Are you in there?"

"Say no!" Hunter hisses.

"Be right there!" I call, and Hunter groans, releasing my hand and falling back on the pillows dramatically. "I take back everything I said earlier."

"No, you don't."

"No, I don't," she concurs.

I open the door and face Kelsey head on. "Hey, what's up?" I ask casually. While I obviously don't enjoy speaking with my ex-fiance, I don't feel the looming dread I have been for months. All she is to me is a client.

It's freeing.

"Can I talk to you?" she asks, looking over my shoulder.

I lean against the doorframe and cross my arms. "Sure."

"Alone?"

"We are alone."

"Hunter isn't in there?" she asks.

"She's enjoying her sweet potato fries and strawberry milk-shake."

"Hell yeah, I am," Hunter calls from inside the room.

Kelsey's teeth clench. "I really need to speak with you alone."

"Is this a work matter?"

"Of course."

I sigh reluctantly and let the door shut behind me with a *click*.

We walk down the hallway, and once we reach the balcony facing the sound, Kelsey spins around to face me.

"I know you're only pretending to date Hunter to make me jealous."

I blink at her, stunned. "That...is not a work matter."

"Yes it is. Becky's upset because she thinks I'm more focused on you two than us. So tell me the truth, Jo. Why did you want to make me jealous?" She folds her arms over her chest, an expectant expression on her face.

"I have never wanted to make you jealous." It's true. I never pretended to date Hunter to make her jealous. I pretended to date Hunter to prove to Kelsey I was over her. I wanted the complete opposite of what she's claiming I did.

"Jo. Come on. " She takes a step towards me, and suddenly I feel stifled, trapped. "It's me. I understand that what we had was great, but I'm with Becky now."

"Our 'fling' was great?" I say before I can stop myself.

Kelsey raises a brow. "Did that upset you? Me referring to us as a fling? Is that why you're doing this?"

I shake my head. "It doesn't matter, Kelsey. I'm with Hunter, you're with Becky, and we're both happy."

"What if I told you it worked?" she asks.

"I don't..."

"What if I told you it worked. You made me jealous. You have my attention. What would you say then?"

"I'd say you left. You left me and I moved the hell on. I'm not trying to make you jealous, I'm simply existing in my current relationship, and if that's making you jealous...that's not my fault."

"Jo, it doesn't have to be like this," Kelsey says quietly, and for a moment, I almost feel bad for her. "We had good times, you and I."

"You're right." I say. "It *doesn't* have to be like this. Leave me the hell alone and let me do my job without trying to prove Hunter and I aren't dating. It's your bachelorette weekend, and this is how you want to spend it?"

Kelsey glares at me, and it's suddenly like she's a different person, eyes dark and angry. "Leaving you is the best decision I ever made," she spits. "I know you're faking because no one in their right mind would enter into a relationship with you."

I reel back, shocked by her unexpected cruelty.

It hurts to be spoken to like that, but more than anything I feel bad for her. All she's doing is showing me that she's wearing a mask, that I'm still living in her brain the way she'd lived in mine for so long.

"You should go," I say, eyes trained on the ground.

She scoffs, but I watch as she spins on her heel and walks away.

I exhale shakily when she's out of sight. Just two more days and the wedding weekend, and then I'll be able to get away from her forever. Be able to open my own firm and make a difference.

"Hey, baby," I look up to see Hunter walking towards me, the milkshake and fries in hand. "I saw Kelsey walking away while I grabbed ice, so I wanted to check—*oof.*"

I don't let Hunter finish speaking, instead pulling her into a squeezing hug and holding her against me. I'm overwhelmed by her, by the fact that she exists and that she somehow found her way into my life not once, but twice.

"You two seem happy." I look over Hunter's shoulder and see Becky smiling at us.

I look at Hunter as she looks at me. She already looks like sunshine personified, but when our eyes meet, her smile brightens even more, somehow. She's a walking contradiction, an impossibility, and she's mine.

"We are," I finally answer, letting go of Hunter and slipping my hand in hers.

"Anything we can do for you, darlin'?" Hunter asks.

"Yeah. Have you seen Kelsey? She was gone when I woke up, and none of the bridesmaids have seen her."

Hunter and I exchange a knowing look out of the corner of our eyes. *Do I lie? Say I haven't seen her since karaoke? Do I bend the truth and say we talked this morning, but not tell her why? Do I—*

"Yeah she was talking to Jo around ten minutes ago."

God, I love Hunter and her impulsive self.

Becky stares at Hunter before turning her gaze to me. "Really?" she says, voice cool. "That's interesting."

I feel the need to defend myself, to assure Becky that nothing happened between Kelsey and I. But Becky doesn't need my reassurance.

"I'm sorry. I'm not upset with you," Becky sighs, running her fingers through her dirty blonde hair. "Things are just...weird right now."

I nod awkwardly. For a moment, I feel bad for Becky. I know what it's like to see Kelsey's attention on someone else when you thought you were her one and only.

"Hey, I grew up around here, and there's nothing like a walk along the sea wall when life feels overwhelming," I tell her. "You still have an hour and a half until brunch begins."

She smiles wryly. "I might have to see for myself."

"It's crucial you turn your phone off, too, and let your coordinator deal with the hard things."

She pulls her phone out of her waistband and turns it off before looking at me. "I know I don't deserve your kindness, Jo. But I'm grateful for it all the same." She inhales shakily. "Brunch is at eleven, right?"

"Yep," I say gently. "You have plenty of time, and a great day lined up. It's spa day, and we'll head to the bar at nine for line dancing."

"Right." Becky nods her head quickly. "Right. Um, I'm going to take that walk now. I'll see you later."

Hunter waits until Becky's out of earshot to speak again. "Are you okay?"

I shrug and turn my body so I can stare out at the waves. "I'm fine, but Kelsey thinks we're not actually dating."

"And she cares?"

I nod my head, eyes still on the water. It's a beautiful day today, the beach slowly filling up with locals and tourists alike. People walking their dogs, building sandcastles with their kids, heading into the water with their boogie boards. "I guess. But...I don't care that she cares? Like she can believe whatever she wants. It doesn't have anything to do with me."

When I turn to face Hunter, I'm taken aback by the unshed tears in her eyes. "Did I say something?" I ask, reaching out a hand to her.

She grabs my hand and brings it to her lips, kissing my palm softly. "Yeah. You said something, and I'm so proud of you, Giovanna. I'm so, so proud of you."

I wrap my free arm around her waist, pulling her into me. It's the most comfortable silence, standing side by side and staring out at the ocean.

I never want it to end.

Chapter 30

Hunter

Playlist: Never Let Me Go | Florence + The Machine

"I wonder if Kelsey's going to no-show," I tell Jo as we set up for brunch.

Jo shrugs. "Who knows."

Maybe I'm a terrible person, but damn, I hope she doesn't show up.

Alas, my dream does not come true. She crawls out whatever circle of hell she'd been lurking in to make an appearance. She walks into the room alone and announces that Becky would be joining shortly, as she was still styling her hair.

I look at Giovanna, eyes wide. "Maybe *Becky* will no-show. That would be a telenovela level of plot twist, until you really think about it—of course she'd eventually snap."

Becky, however, does not give me the telenovela plot point of my dreams, striding into the room minutes after Kelsey.

I pull Giovanna aside at least five times to make out with her out of sight of the bridal party. Whenever I break the kiss, she blinks at me like she's surprised I did that. A slow smile spreads across her face just before she kisses me back.

Every time we kiss, she tastes like mine.

Finally, brunch is over and we're breaking down the room. Audrey and her daughter, Piper, help us out again, which means we finish quicker than planned. I'm grateful, because while the bridal party is going to a spa in town, Jo and I are on our own until she has to be at Port of Call, the bar in town. It's not a western bar, but she rented out the entire place for tonight to give Becky and Kelsey the southern-themed night of their dreams.

We spend the day at the beach before going into town to grab a bite to eat. She brings me to Poppy's bookstore, where I grab a historical romance by Tessa Dare, who Jo tells me is Josh's favorite author. Millie is with a client when we stop at the tattoo parlor she works at, so Jo leaves a note at the front desk with all sorts of vulgar language and innuendos.

Siblings are weird.

"Oh my god, these are cute," I say as we set up the bar. Jo looks hot tonight, wearing black linen ankle pants and block heels. She wears a classic white button-up, but her sleeves are rolled up and I am *drooling* at her forearms.

"What's cute?" she asks distractedly, trying to detangle a tinsel garland with cowboy boots and hats on it.

"These!" I repeat, placing a pink cowboy hat with faux fur trim on my head. Giovanna turns toward me, a smile spreading across her face.

"It suits you. Is it authentic?"

"Authentic in the sense that I love it? Yes. Authentic in any other sense? No."

She rolls her eyes and snatches the hat from my head, placing it on her own.

I gasp dramatically. "You know what they say about the hat."

She smirks at me, and I feel her eyes running down my body. I do a little shimmy, making the skirt of my sundress shimmy, too. "Whoever wears the hat rides the cowgirl, right?"

"Mmhmm."

Jo steps forward and looks down at me. I'm wearing my white heeled cowboy boots, so there isn't as dramatic a height difference between us as usual. She cups my hip and pulls my body to hers, eliciting a surprised and thrilled gasp from me. "Is that a promise, honey?" she asks, lips brushing the shell of my ear.

I shiver with pleasure as goosebumps spread over my body. "It's more than a promise." I lean forward until our lips brush. "It's a vow."

"Guess I'm riding you tonight," she whispers before capturing my lower lip between her teeth.

I moan. "Thank god."

"Um, sorry to bother you," an unfamiliar voice says awkwardly from behind me. "I was wondering if you needed help setting up?"

Everything in me screams to pull away, to put distance between Giovanna and I. This frightened part of me still rears her pretty little head every once in a while, reminding me that my family doesn't love me anymore and that my attraction to women is thought of as dirty and should be hidden.

I don't believe these thoughts, but it doesn't mean they're not there.

"Hey, Barry. No, thanks. Just direct the rental people back here when they arrive. They might need assistance if you're willing to help them." Jo says smoothly.

The gangly, dark-haired man nods at Giovanna, not giving me a second glance. "I'll do whatever makes you happy, Jo."

My eyes widen as Jo's body shakes with stifled laughter. "I know, Barry. Thank you."

He does a weird little bow before backing out of the room.

"What was *that* about?" I hiss, looking up into her eyes.

"I'll tell you after you tell me why you jumped away from me like I was a live wire when Barry came into the room."

I grimace. "Yeah that was…not my finest moment. I'm sorry. My therapist said I'm traumatized from forcing myself into a closet for so long, and I think my brain can perceive someone seeing us kiss as being caught. Because, you know, that was my worst fear for a good chunk of my life."

Giovanna tucks a wayward curl behind my ear. "There was reason for you to fear that."

I exhale shakily. "Yeah. But I don't want you to think it's you. It's not you. It's me."

"Hey, it's okay." She reaches for my hand and squeezes encouragingly. "I'm not afraid of your trauma. I'm not afraid of your brain, I'm not afraid of *you*."

Somehow, she said the perfect thing. I wrap my arms around her. "Thank you," I murmur as she kisses my hair. "It all feels subconscious, if that makes sense. Like I don't think any of that is true, but sometimes I think these thoughts anyway."

"It says more about you that you recognize these thoughts as inaccurate than you having them in the first place, you know. And sometimes I still have thoughts like that, too. I don't want to, but sometimes it just happens. My therapist gave me some affirmations to remind me that sometimes, what I truly believe is different from what I think. And that sometimes, thoughts aren't precisely truthful."

"It makes me feel better to know that it's not just me. That I'm not secretly a homophobic bigot."

I feel her smile against the top of my head, and I'm a little jealous. I want to see this smile—it feels like a good one. "No, honey. You're not a bigot. You're an imperfect human, and I love you for it."

I feel her body freeze before my brain processes what she said.

I know she means like a friend. A platonic, general love, and that's fine. But my mind runs wild with thoughts of her and I on the beach, at the spot where we had our first kiss, which quickly turned into having sex for the first time as teenagers.

Now, in my present-day fantasy, Jo tucks an unruly strand of hair behind my ear, which immediately frees itself with help from the sea breeze. We both laugh as I try to hold my hair down and she cups my cheek, adoration in her eyes. "I fucking love you," she says, and I smile up at her, reflecting the same adoration in my own eyes as I echo the sentiment. Then we'd ride dolphins away into the sunset or something. I don't know, this fantasy isn't well formed yet.

"Hey, it's okay," I tell her instead. "There are lots of reasons I love you, too. You pretending to not like Dolly for way longer than it was believable, for one."

My voice is light and casual, but my heart is screaming. *Choose me the way I want to choose you. We deserve to be chosen, to be loved and accepted the way we should have been a long time ago. Because I'll do that for you, and I think you'd do that for me, too.*

"Sorry, that...that was awkward," Jo stammers, attempting to step back. But I don't let go of her.

"I like awkward," I say. "And I know what you meant. I promise I don't think you're head over heels for me."

I want you to be. I can't stop myself from thinking about it.

Giovanna exhales slowly and steps back again. This time I let her. "Okay. Okay." It sounds like she's trying to convince herself it's okay.

And she's right. It is okay.

I would love for it to be more than okay.

Chapter 31

Jo

Playlist: Fearless (Taylor's Version) | Taylor Swift

The music is loud, and the bridal party is sloshed, making for a perfect country-western night. Kelsey and Becky insisted on renting out the only bar in town, Port of Call, which the locals have called Port of Alcohol since I was a kid. We rented a mechanical bull, and hired a DJ and dance teacher to teach line dances and two-step. Hunter has sung and danced along to every song, and I've watched her all night.

"You damn Yankees can't do a proper grapevine to save your life," she grumbles, shaking her head in disappointment.

God, her scent is intoxicating. She must have a perfume that smells like magnolias and rain, too, because tonight she somehow smells more like herself than normal. I'm so distracted by her scent that I don't realize that she's continued speaking.

"I'm gonna do it," Hunter says in a tone that somehow pulls me from my trance.

"What?" I ask dully.

She doesn't answer, instead walking away. I feel her absence like a missing part of me.

My eyes follow her as she walks to the bar, hips swaying in that absurdly short dress. Her boots are heeled, but she still stands on her tiptoes as she talks to Barry. It would be so easy to put my right hand between her shoulder blades and bend her over the bartop. So simple for my left hand to slip under her skirt and circle her swollen clit. I'd tell her to be quiet, even though everyone could see. Would I have to move my hand from between her shoulder blades to her mouth to muffle her whimpers and moans? Could I...

"Whoooo!" I snap out of my fantasy and my eyes are immediately pulled to Hunter as she throws a sparkly pink shot back.

I have so many questions. First and most importantly, how did she get a sparkly pink shot? Second, what the hell is *in* a sparkly pink shot?

"Whooo!" A few bridesmaids cheer from the dance floor. Becky laughs and claps from beside Willie Nelson, but Kelsey, who is at her side, scowls, like Hunter enjoying herself is a personal affront to her. Kelsey's been cranky since our conversation this morning, and I'm proud of me for still not caring all that much.

Hunter skips over to me, skirt swaying around her thighs. She's not the male gaze, nor the female gaze. She's a secret third thing: the Jo Quinn gaze.

"Hi," she says, landing on a bounce in front of me, camera clasped safely in her hands. "You owe me a dance."

I tilt my head to the side. "I don't think I ever agreed to a dance, Hun."

She pouts.

"Maybe you thought about it and forgot to ask. Would you like to dance with me?" I ask, knowing fully well she didn't. I am a sucker for this woman.

Her face lights up and she nods enthusiastically. "Yes, please! I'm going to request a song."

She skips over to the DJ booth, and I feel heat in my face as the DJ doesn't even try to pretend not to look down the front of her dress.

"Hi!" Hunter yells over the Shania Twain song, "Hello! My eyes are up here!"

God, I love her.

I mean...I love her positive qualities. How she tells off the DJ for looking down her dress, how she can be vulnerable and admit her perceived shortcomings. How she brought home a fucking bearded dragon and made me love her. How she takes sparkly pink shots. There's just so much to love about her.

You're delusional if you think you just love things about her.

Shut up, brain.

The DJ has the decency to look ashamed at being caught, and I assume he apologizes, because Hunter doesn't punch him in the face. She motions for him to bend down, and he does so, leaning his ear towards her as she cups around it and tells him what song she wants to play. He nods and plays with the knobs on the turntable as Hunter struts away. She has a fantastic ass, and he doesn't look up once.

I wonder how violent her threat was.

The song fades out as Hunter approaches me, a huge grin on her face as a familiar instrumental intro begins to play. She hangs

Loretta around her neck and reaches out her hand palm up. "May I have this dance, Giovanna Quinn?"

"Yes, you may, Hunter Cleary." I place my hand in hers and she turns to pull me out to the dance floor.

She faces me and threads our fingers together as she puts her other hand on my waist.

"Holy *shit*, Hunter." I gasp, eyes widening with realization as Taylor Swift begins to sing.

"Don't worry, it's Taylor's Version," she tells me seriously, pulling me closer into her.

It's a song from that summer. A country song Hunter introduced me to. A song we'd screamed at the top of our lungs while riding our bikes to the sea wall. A song she'd played on her iPod after we'd kissed. A song we danced to on the beach before we snuck home and had sex.

She softly begins singing along to the first chorus and I can't imagine it ever being better than this. Safe and secure and loved in Hunter's arms.

Loved. She makes me feel *loved*.

I pull away and dip her, her surprised squeal filling the bar as I laugh. When I pull her back to a standing position, I pull her into me, capturing her mouth with mine.

I hear various bridesmaids around us *awwing* but I don't care. I don't care about anything else besides the fact that Hunter's in my arms and she's soft and kissing me back and she makes me feel like I'm worth loving, worth choosing.

When we break our kiss, her eyes are immediately on mine, blinking rapidly.

"Why?" she asks simply.

"Because." I don't have an answer. I wanted to kiss her. I could get used to that, kissing her simply because I want to and knowing she'd return it. I remember how, after the bridal shower, she'd held my hand the entire way home. Not once prying or asking me to talk until I was ready. She had let me process and feel on my own, without leaving me alone. While still holding my hand and showing me she was there.

It's remarkable, really, her quiet ability to show support. She's loud and larger than life and flashy and she doesn't tune that down for anyone, but the love she gives me is quiet, subtle.

Love. Shit. Does Hunter love me? Maybe not romantically, but she at least loves me platonically, I think. The way I love Josh, despite him being a dumbass. The way I love Nellie and Tyler and Mom's tiramisu. The way I love the beach at night and...

"Well *that* was a kiss," Kelsey's voice brings me out of my trance. Hunter is scowling expressively at her by the time my eyesight focuses.

"Thanks," Hunter says flatly. "Why aren't you doing the Boot Scootin' Boogie with the rest of your girl gang?"

I suck my lips between my teeth, stifling laughter. Kelsey notices and her eyes are immediately on me, narrowing. "Something funny, Giovanna?"

My face falls. I can smell the alcohol on her breath. Drunk Kelsey is Kelsey at her worst.

"Why don't you have some water?" I suggest, dropping Hunter's hand. "I'll go..."

"You know, Jo and I were supposed to get married," Kelsey tells Hunter.

You could hear a pin drop with how quickly everything seems to go still. The Boot Scootin' Boogie still plays, but no one's dancing, instead staring at us. It feels like the music is coming from another room, muted and faint.

"Kelsey, don't do this." My voice is quiet and shaky, mouth dry as I speak. I look for Becky, who is under the impression we were a silly little fling. I don't see her, and infer she must be in the restroom.

"I do know," Hunter responds to Kelsey's question coolly. "And now you're marrying Becky, so why don't you back the fuck off, blondie?"

Kelsey ignores Hunter as she turns her face back to me. "Don't you want to know why it didn't work out?" she sneers.

"Kels…" McKenna is at her side, pulling at her arm. "Come on. Let's have one more dance before we catch the shuttle back…"

"I know," Hunter snaps, ignoring McKenna. "Do you want *her* to know?" she asks, motioning towards the bridal party with her head.

Kelsey pulls her arm out of her maid of honor's grip. "I just wanted you to know I'm fine with you two dating. I don't care. Have my sloppy seconds. You'll find out soon enough that she's not worth the effort and don't come crying to me when you're ready to…"

"Finish that sentence," Hunter hisses. Her eyes are full of a rage I should be used to by now…but I still find it ridiculously hot. "Finish that sentence and I'll give you a free nose job, I swear to god."

"She was my fiancée first," Kelsey snaps, "and now you think you can have her?"

"Kels?" I inhale sharply when I notice Becky's returned from the restroom, a look of utter confusion on her face.

"It's not what you think," Kelsey assures her, eyes wide.

"So you weren't just saying that Jo was your fiancée?" I expected Becky to be angry when she found out the truth. I wasn't expecting her voice to be laced with betrayal, for her eyes to show her utter devastation.

Kelsey's eyes fill with tears. "Becky, please…"

Becky takes a step backward when Kelsey steps towards her. "God, I am a fool, aren't I?" She laughs hollowly, running her hand through her short hair. "You told me it was a fling, that she was the one hung up on you."

Kelsey shakes her head frantically. "Becky, please. Talk to me…"

"Are you still in love with her?" Becky interrupts, tears welling in her eyes.

Kelsey flounders for an answer, opening and closing her mouth over and over without making a sound.

"Fuck." Becky runs a hand over her face and shakes her head. "I…fuck." She spins on her heel and strides out of the bar, leaving an echoing silence in her wake.

Kelsey is frozen for a moment before pulling out of McKenna's grip and stumbling out after Becky, calling her name.

I clear my throat. "I think since the brides are calling it a night we should too." I make eye contact with McKenna, who at least has the good sense to look away immediately. The bridal party flows out of the bar blessedly fast, leaving Hunter and I alone in the bar.

"Wow," Hunter says. "I—wow."

"You were scary, Hun." I laugh nervously. "It's a good thing I'm on your good side."

"You *are* my good side." My neck snaps to look at her, and I'm delighted by the way the pink flush creeps up her chest and neck. "Sorry, weird thing to say. I…uh. I'm gonna run to the bathroom," she mumbles, dropping my hand and shuffling towards the hallway that leads to the restrooms.

Fuck, I'm tired. I'm tired of Kelsey holding me back, of feeling like I'm undeserving because I couldn't get her to stay.

I inhale shakily and stride to the bar. "Hey, Barry," I say, voice trembling. "Can you pour me one of those sparkly pink shots my girlfriend had earlier?"

That Summer

Hunter

Giovanna is absolutely miserable. When I look at her, she forces a smile and gives me a thumbs up, but I can tell she hates this. Why did she suggest going to this beach party some of her classmates told her about if she wouldn't enjoy it?

"God, this sucks." Giovanna's older sister, Nic, slides next to me, handing me another wine cooler.

"Why did you come?" I ask, twisting off the top of the bottle.

Nic shrugs, lifting her own wine cooler to her lips. "I have deep rooted self-hatred," she tells me before taking a sip.

I look towards Giovanna who's talking with some of her classmates. While she's currently smiling, her body is tense and shows her discomfort.

"Oh fuck me all the way," Nic says. I'm not sure how one would fuck someone less than all the way, but she's shuffling away from me, a look of horror plastered on her face. "If anyone asks if you saw me, say no."

I furrow my brow. "What's happening right now?"

"The worst person to exist is here, and I have to hide from him. You're on your own, kid." And just like that, she slips into the crowd.

I shake my head in confusion as someone stops beside me. He's tall and blond, and big *with some scruff on his face. "Was Nic Quinn just here?" he asks, looking around with squinted eyes.*

"Nope," I answer easily, taking another sip of my drink. I am many, many things. But I ain't no snitch.

"I thought I saw her over here…" he begins to say.

"Must've been someone else," I interrupt, shrugging my shoulders and turning on my heel to head towards Giovanna.

"Hi," she says, "Having fun?"

"No. I wanna go home," I lie.

Giovanna blinks in surprise. "Oh! I…we can go back, if you want. Are you not having fun?"

I shrug. "I'd rather be watching Miss Congeniality *or something."*

Her resounding smile is so bright. "I love Miss Congeniality*."*

Out of the corner of my eye, I see the blond guy I talked to approaching Nic, who looks horrified at his existence. As he takes a step towards her, a girl behind him takes a step backwards, colliding with him. His solo cup of beer ends up spilling all over Nic.

"Asshole!" she yells at him, throwing her almost-full wine cooler at him, drenching him in a sticky red liquid before she stalks off.

Giovanna and I both wince, reaching for each other's hands instinctively. She squeezes our palms together, but makes no move to help her sister. I giggle at the guilty look on her face as she pulls me with her away from the party. "Let's go home, honey."

Chapter 32

Hunter

Playlist: religion (u can lay your hands on me) | Shura

I'm not drunk, but that sparkly shot had just enough of whatever it was made of to make me feel warm, tingly, and uninhibited. Normally this is fun, but tonight, it's dangerous.

I want to tell Giovanna how special she is. Tell her I'm quitting and losing the money and fuck if I care because I'll still get half and so will she. We can run away together to a little cottage in Port Haven and be gay as fuck and in love and...

Fuck. In love. I'm in love with her. I'm head over boots in love with Giovanna Quinn...again. Or maybe I never stopped loving her. Maybe my love huddled up and hibernated until she came back to me.

I want to tell her, because I don't want to pretend anymore. I don't want to kiss her and hold her hand because it'll make her ex and employer believe we're dating...I want to kiss her and hold her hand because she's mine to do so with. Mine to love.

I grip the edge of the counter and lean towards the mirror, eyes narrowing at my reflection. "Get. Yourself. Together," I hiss at myself. "Bitch," I add for emphasis. I stare at myself menacingly in the mirror for about five seconds before that uninhibited part of me comes back full force.

I blow out a breath and fluff my curls. I'm gonna tell her. I'm gonna go out there and tell her how I feel and if that means I have to take the train home and move Dolly and I somewhere else...I will.

But she needs to know that she's worth loving. Worth choosing. That I love and choose her. Even if she doesn't feel the same way, at least she'll know.

I fix my skirt before spinning on my heel and strutting to throw the door open. I can do this. I can be prepared for rejection and tell her anyway because this is for her. She deserves to know how fucking hard it would be for me *not* to love her and...

I stop short, eyes widening as I enter the bar.

Giovanna Quinn is atop Willie Nelson, the mechanical bull, eyes wide with panic.

I should mention that the bull is not moving, and she still looks like this is the most terrifying ride of her life.

"Hey, Giovanna," I say cautiously, sidling up to the operator. "Whatcha doin' up there?"

"I don't know," she squeaks. "I mean. I do know. And it seemed smart before I climbed up here."

I kick off my boots and climb onto the inflatable platform. "Got it. Do you need help climbing down?"

"No. Yes. Yes. Wait. No. Sorry, I can't move. No."

I sigh. "Scooch forward."

She finally looks at me. "What?"

"Scooch forward. If you can't climb down, I'm climbing up."

The operator, some poor college kid that works for the company Jo rented from, sighs heavily behind me. I swivel and glare at her over my shoulder. I was just the recipient of my own death glare, I know how powerful it is. She rightly slumps back.

Jo scooches forward and I hoist myself onto Willie, adjusting myself until my front is pressed to her back. I wrap my arms around her middle and lay my cheek between her shoulder blades. "Hi, snookums."

I feel her body tense. "I don't like when you call me that. That's what you call me when people are around and you're trying to convince them we're together."

I bite back a smile. "Oh yeah?"

"I like it when you call me baby. You only call me baby when you really mean it."

"Is that so?"

"Mmhmm. I like it when you call me Giovanna, too. Giovanna's always been yours."

My heart skips a beat. I know she's only talking about the name, but little does she know Hunter's always been hers, too.

"What are you doing up here, baby?" I ask softly.

She groans. "I wanted to prove I'm not always scared. That sometimes I can do scary, hard things and take chances that make me want to shit myself, but instead I'm fucking stuck, so that went well."

"Who are you trying to prove that to?" I wonder.

"Me. You. Because...because I want to take risks for you, and make myself uncomfortable trying things I don't want to because Alena said that's where growth happens. I'm such a goner for you, but I want to grow for you, Hunter."

"What about growing with me?" I ask gently. "Doing the things that scare us together? I know you feel like you have to do everything on your own, and that people have proven themselves to be unreliable and untrustworthy, but I want to grow with you. I want to change, and learn, and find out that I'm not always right, because I don't really care if I'm wrong when I'm with you." My speech gets faster the more I go on, heart pounding against my rib cage.

She doesn't say anything at first, and my stomach does a somersault. Finally, she speaks. "What happens when I get scared?"

"Then you'll be scared. I'll do what I can to help you face your fear, or diminish it, or cope with it. Whatever you need."

"And if I need to be alone? You said you hated it when I left."

"If you need to be alone, tell me. Maybe I'm a fool, but I wholeheartedly believe you'll always come back when you're ready. You'll take the time and space you need and then maybe you'll come back with a milkshake and flowers. Talk it over with me. That's not leaving, or running."

I feel the movement of her body as she swallows. "What happens now?"

"What do you want to happen now?" I ask.

"I want to get the fuck off Willie Nelson and make out with you."

"You're going to have to either climb down or we're going to ride."

She groans. "I hate this."

"I know."

Giovanna looks at me over her shoulder. "I'm gonna regret this, aren't I?"

"That's a real possibility." I look over my own shoulder at the ride operator who's given up on us and is scrolling on her phone. "Start 'er up!"

"Start what up?" the ride operator asks without looking up.

I sigh. "Willie Nelson. What else would I be asking you to start up?"

She shrugs and begins to fiddle with the control panel. "Dunno."

Willie Nelson begins to move, slowly at first. Jo is chanting, "oh god oh god oh god oh god," under her breath as the movements become jerkier and faster.

"Hand up, baby," I whisper in her ear, covering her left hand with my own and weaving our fingers together. I expect to have to beg her, but she squeezes our hands and lets me lift them into the air.

We last maybe four seconds on Willie Nelson's back, but it feels like a lifetime. Just the two of us, holding space for Jo's fear together. She screams when we're thrown from the bull and tumble to the inflated platform. I thank my lucky stars that I went against my impulse to go commando under my dress, instead wearing bike shorts over my thong.

"Holy shit," Jo gasps, sprawled like a starfish on her back. "Holy. Fucking. Shit."

I push myself off my belly onto my hands and knees. "You did it!"

"I did it."

I crawl over to her and straddle her hips, cupping her face in my hands. I don't care that everyone can see. "I'm so fucking proud of you, Giovanna. Baby," I whisper, tracing her lips with my thumbs.

She wraps her arms around me and pulls me down so I'm laying on top of her. "I hated every second of that."

"I know."

"I never want to do that again."

I bite back a smile and nuzzle my nose against her cheek. "I believe you."

She turns her face and captures my mouth with hers. I taste the strawberry liquor of the pink sparkly shot I'd been served earlier and smile into our kiss.

"Um. Can you get a room?" The ride operator says, voice full of disgust.

"She's onto something," Jo says as I pull away. "Let's go back to the room. I think I promised to ride you?"I reluctantly push myself off her and get to my feet as she sits up. I extend a hand to her and pull her to a standing position. "Later. I have a better idea."

"Better than me riding you?" she asks as we step off the platform.

"Okay, maybe not. But I need to do this first."

We quickly put on our shoes and I put my hands on Jo's shoulders, looking deeply into her eyes. "Do you trust me?"

"Well, I *did.* Until you asked," she answers, eyeing me skeptically.

"Pretend you still do. Because this is a little outlandish."

Her smile is crooked and soft and god, I stopped counting them, haven't I? Her smiles are so much a part of my life that I stopped taking special notice of them.

My breath stutters as she grabs my hips and pulls my pelvis into hers, leaning her face into mine. "You do that to me. Bring out an outlandish side of me I didn't know existed. I like it." Her breath is hot on my ear.

"I need you to flirt with Barry and distract him. Also pay him to break everything down for us."

Jo pulls away, a horrified look on her face. "Oh god. Hun, I kissed him once in the eighth grade and I don't think he's ever gotten over it."

I want to laugh, but I was hung up on Giovanna Quinn for twelve years, so I get it.

"That's why this will work."

"Why am I flirting with him? *How* do I flirt with him? He's a *man*."

I grin at her, and hook our arms together, guiding her towards the bar. "Questions later. I need you to pull out that thirteen year old Jo Quinn charm that's kept him wanting for fourteen years."

I give her a gentle push and she stumbles into the bar.

"Heyyyyy Barry." She sounds *terrified*.

"Hi, Jo." Barry stares unabashedly at her ample cleavage as she leans on the bar.

I duck under the bar top and run my eyes over the shelf.

"You like my boobs?" Jo asks loudly, panic evident in her voice. This woman.

"I thought you were a lesbian," Barry says suspiciously.

"Oh. Right. Lesbians don't have good boobs."

I try to muffle my giggle, but fail. Barry begins to turn towards me.

"Should I get a tattoo between my tits?" She blurts out, leaning further into the bar, pulling down the neckline of her top. "Since you're not into lesbian boobs I figure you're the perfect, non-partisan person to ask."

"Holy shit," Barry breathes, eyes fixated on her cleavage.

"Holy shit," I agree, climbing onto the bar.

Barry begins to turn again, and I grab a bottle of Don Julio 1942 from the top shelf, hiding it beneath my skirt before ducking back to the other side of the bar.

"I could've sworn I heard—" Barry mutters, shaking his head. I press a sloppy kiss to Jo's cheek as he faces us, his frown deepening.

"Ready to get out of here, darlin'?" I smile into her face.

"Never readier. Barry, do you think you could break everything down for me? I'll come by tomorrow to get it." She pulls a handful of rather large bills from her wallet and slaps them on the bar top. "Thank you."

She weaves her fingers through mine and pulls me towards the door, our laughter echoing in the nearly empty bar.

Chapter 33

Jo

Playlist: This Love (Taylor's Version) | Taylor Swift

Pink sparkly shots are fun, but watching Hunter steal a handle of top shelf tequila from Port of Call is infinitely more fun.

As she leads me down the beach, we giggle like we're fifteen again.

"Where are you taking me, you wild woman?" I laugh as Hunter stops and pulls off her boots and socks. Her toenails are painted a glittery pink that shines in the darkness, and it makes me smile. She's so unexpected and unpredictable and somehow as steady as the waves on the shore.

"You'll see!" she says in a sing-song voice, pulling my hand. "Come on, we're almost there."

Finally she stops, and looks at the houses across the street from the bluffs. "Here. This is it." She drops her boots onto the sand with a muted *thud*.

"This is what?" I ask, looking around.

"This is where I realized I had fallen for you fifteen years ago," she says softly, and my eyes snap back to her.

"Here?"

"Mmmhmm."

"How do you know?"

"Because I thought it was funny that we could see the rectory." She points to a white Cape Cod house across the street, which is indeed where Father Gilligan has lived for the past six hundred years, or however long he's been pastor.

I'm overwhelmed by the fact Hunter not only remembered where she fell in love, but brought me back here. "Hun," I whisper, voice thick.

"Hold on." She lifts the handle of tequila and brings it to her mouth. I swallow hard as she tilts her head back and pours a shot's worth into her mouth. As she swallows, she wipes her mouth with the back of her free hand and holds out the bottle to me. I wordlessly accept, keeping my eyes on hers as I repeat her actions.

"I brought you here for a reason," Hunter says as I lower the bottle. I bend down and put it on the sand, steadying the bottle so it doesn't fall. "And...and I'm scared. Because this might be my Willie Nelson, my reckless climb without any guarantee this is safe."

My heart is pounding, a steady *thump thump thump* in my chest. Maybe I'm irrational in hoping that she could be saying the same thing I want to say. "Be brave with me," I whisper, reaching out and taking her other hand in mine, squeezing both. "I'll ride the bull with you."

Her eyes search mine, so earnest and beautiful. "I'm in love with you, Giovanna Quinn." Her voice is quiet, barely audible over the waves. "And you might not be ready to hear that, but you deserve to know. To know that you deserve to love and deserve someone who stays. Someone who sees how brave and incredible you are. Someone who wants to grow with you because you only get better with age. And..." she inhales shakily, eyes searching mine. "And I'm fucking terrified. Because you can reject me and you know how hard that is for me. But I'm willing to risk that for you. Because you're worth the risk, and..."

"Hunter..." I interrupt, voice wobbly.

"You deserve the sun and the moon," she continues, "and all I have is my heart and a bearded dragon and—"

"Hunter. I have to say something."

She looks so scared, and I'm pretty sure she's trembling. Either that she's shivering from the breeze. "Oh. Okay," she stammers.

I reach out and take her hands in mine. "Hunter Cleary, you're a fucking meteorite..."

"Is that good or bad?"

"Let me finish, honey. You're a fucking meteorite and you demolished everything I believed about the world and myself. Remember when I told you I was a bad liar? That people know when I'm trying to lie?"

Her brow furrows in confusion. "Yeah?"

"I've never been dishonest with you. Not once. I've never felt the need to hide the parts of me and my past that have caused so much hurt, because you see me, Hun. And you've let me see you, too, and what a privilege it has been to see you. To trust you and see and love the parts of you that should have always been seen and loved."

"Love?" Hunter whispers, blue eyes watery as they search mine.

"Yeah, honey. Love. I couldn't stop it no matter how much I tried. You and your boots kicked down the walls I put up around my heart and I wouldn't have it any other way.

"I'm so goddamn in love with you that I'm floating away like a balloon in the sky and I'll do whatever I can to never come back. As long as you float away with me and—"

My words are cut off by Hunter lifting herself to her tiptoes, wrapping one arm around my shoulders and kissing me square on the mouth. I relax into her, like my subconscious knows that she's safe.

She breaks the kiss, and I open my eyes. She's wearing the softest smile, eyes screwed shut as she presses her forehead to mine.

"Want to remember this one, too?" I ask.

"Mmhmm. Never wanna forget what you tasted like after you told me you loved me for the first time."

"The first of many," I promise, taking her hand in mine and bringing it to my lips, kissing where her pulse pounds on her wrist. Another kiss, this time to the center of her palm, and then one the back of her hand.

"I love you for who you were twelve years ago, and who you will be in twelve more years. Who you were yesterday, and who you'll be tomorrow. I love everything you are, and everything you'll be." I promise, bringing the palm of her hand to my cheek.

When Hunter opens her eyes, a single tear falls. I cup her cheek and thumb it away.

"I never stopped thinking about you," she chokes out. "I never stopped wishing, hoping you'd come back to me. Then you did, and you told me you felt like you'd lost yourself, and I knew you had to find yourself again. It's been such an honor to fall in love with you while you did."

"I came back to you by coming back to me," I agree, leaning into her palm.

"Kiss me," she demands, pulling my face down to hers. There's still so much I want to tell her, because I still don't think I've properly expressed everything I'm feeling. But maybe it's not possible to put into words, at least not in one night.

Good thing I have longer than tonight to tell her.

"I want you," she breathes into my mouth. "Now. Please?"

"Here?" I clarify.

She nods frantically, getting to her knees and pulling me down with her. "Here. Remember that night we had sex here?"

I nod as I extend my body over hers. "Mmhmm. I strained my eyes to see that pretty smile when you came in the dark."

Illuminated only by the moon, I see that shy blush and smile. I kiss her hard, as she lays down, wrapping her arms around my shoulders and holding me close to her.

"Touch me," she whispers against my mouth.

I nod and get to my knees between her spread legs. I keep my eyes on her as I reach up her dress, running my fingers over the edge of her bike shorts. She pushes herself up to her elbows and keeps her eyes on mine, lifting her hips so I can pull the shorts and underwear beneath them down in one fluid movement.

"You're somehow prettier every time I see you," I say, hearing the wonder in my own voice as I slide my thumb between her labia. Hunter gasps, hips jerking to meet my touch.

"Please," she breathes, eyes illuminated only by the moon. "Please, Giovanna."

"Please what?" I ask teasingly.

"Please everything. *Anything.*"

I lean over her, kissing her as I press into her and curl my middle finger. She moans into my mouth and she tastes distinctly like tequila and *Hunter*. It's my new favorite flavor.

After a few minutes of slow finger fucking, I shift uncomfortably, trying to alleviate the growing numbness in my arm.

"Hey, Jo?"

"Yeah?"

"Sand's getting everywhere," she says. "Like...*everywhere*."

I pull back and look between her legs, like I'll be able to see grains of sand inside her body, only guided by moonlight.

She squeezes her thighs together, like she's self-conscious, and pushes herself up to her elbows. "Can I tell you a secret?"

"I feel like you're going to tell me no matter how I answer that question."

"I kind of hate this. I'm not fifteen anymore and I think sex on the beach makes a much better cocktail." She smiles sheepishly at me.

Then that sweet smile of hers is wiped clean off her face when I press my fingers between my lips, moaning as I savor the sweet, musky taste of how much she wants me.

"My god," she breathes. "You're hot as fuck. I fell in love with the hottest human on the planet? Even more bananas is the fact that the hottest human on the planet fell in love with *me*?" She squeals and falls back onto the sand, dramatically throwing her arm over her face. "This is the best day of my life!"

I laugh, loud and bright. "Get that perfect ass of yours up. I want to go back to the room—I haven't finished eating."

"Auuughhh," she groans, thrashing in the sand. "I can't. I'm being incinerated by how hot you are, let me burn in peace."

I roll my eyes. "You're such a diva."

"I thought I was a brat?"

"Well, yeah," I admit, reaching down and taking her hand in mine. She hoists herself to her feet and I pull her into me, savoring the hitch in her breath when our bodies press together. "You're a diva *and* a brat. More importantly, you're mine."

She stares at me, mouth open. "Well damn, Giovanna. You already took my panties off, no need to seduce me further."

I furrow my brow. "Speaking of, where *is* your thong?"

She pulls around and spins around. "Uh...I don't see it. Or my shorts."

"Shit," I hiss, pulling my phone out of my pocket and turning on the flashlight. "I honestly didn't even think about where I put them..."

Hunter points to where the waves crash on the shore two feet away from us. "So...it's high tide."

I stare at her. "No."

Hunter starts to cackle, full blown belly laughs. "Oh my god. Oh my god, that's too funny."

"I was really horny," I grumble, my cheeks heating. "I didn't like...think to think about the ocean."

"'Didn't think to consider the ocean?' As we were about to have sex on the beach?" She's laughing harder, bent over and clenching her stomach. I can't find any negativity in this moment, because despite the literal ocean stealing Hunter's undergarments, this moment is *wonderful*.

"Wait." Her laughter stops suddenly, and so does my heart. "What do you mean '*was* horny'?" she demands, straightening her back and firmly planting her hands on her hips.

I bark out a laugh and wrap my arms around her, pulling her into my arms. "Don't worry, honey. I'm still plenty horny."

She cups my face and pulls me down for another kiss. "Yee-haw."

Chapter 34

Hunter

Playlist: Holy | King Princess

I push Jo up against the door as soon as it closes behind us. We hustled back to our room, pausing for a moment at Kelsey and Becky's door to see if we could hear any fighting. That was my idea.

The room was silent, so they must have already fallen asleep. I don't know if they'll be sleeping for long.

"I want to make you scream," I tell Giovanna before licking the length of her neck, her breath hitching in her throat. "I want to make you come so hard, teasing and edging you until you can't help but fall apart. Until you can't keep that perfectly composed facade up any more. I want…"

"You want? It sounds like you think you're in charge here honey. That's pretty silly of you." With seemingly no effort, Jo captures my wrists in her grasp and spins us so I'm pinned against the door with my hands above my head.

"Oh, god," I gasp. "That was so hot. How did you do that? Do it again."

She nips at my neck and I'm lucky that she's holding me up, because otherwise I would fall to the floor in a horny puddle of Hunter. "See? All I have to do is talk to you to make your legs shake."

"God I want to make fun of you right now, but I can't. You're too hot," I gasp before she crashes her mouth to mine. She adjusts her grip on my wrists so that she's holding both with her right hand, lightly running her left down the side of my body until she's toying with the hem of my skirt.

"*Jo.*" I don't know what exactly I'm begging for...except I do. I'm begging for her. For all of her. For her tonights and tomorrows, her mornings and nights. Her kisses and touches and orgasms and snort laughs. Her family, her heart, her honey bears.

Her eyes meet mine, and I watch as they soften. "You are magic, honey. Goddamn magic, and you make me a believer."

Tears are stinging at my eyes. "I'd go through everything again if it meant we both ended up at Tyler's wedding."

Her eyes search mine. "Everything?"

I know what she's asking. If I'd lose my family again, go through all the pain and grief and loneliness that followed that loss.

"Everything," I assure her, meaning it with every part of me. Because finding her, finding *myself*, is worth more than anything else in the world.

She drops my hand to cradle my face, kissing me in a way I've never been kissed. She kisses me how only a person who sees, knows, and loves me could.

She breaks our kiss and brushes the tip of her nose against mine. "Me too. I'd go through it all again if I got to plan all of these asinine events. All of it."

Everything happens so fast, it feels like a montage. Our clothes fall to the floor, and we clumsily stumble into the shower.

"Shit!" I shriek as ice cold water comes out of the showerhead.

"Fuck, sorry!" Jo hurriedly fumbles to adjust the temperature before pinning me against the shower wall. She nips and sucks at my neck and I feel like I could fall apart just from this. I trace her CGM with my fingertips, feeling the shape and texture, and, maybe it's silly, but I feel an overwhelming wave of gratitude for the tools that help her take care of herself.

"I've missed you," I whisper, tilting my head back into the hot water. "I feel like I've spent twelve years waiting for you."

"Being with you again is a homecoming. I don't think I've shown the real me since you. I chased after that feeling for twelve years, almost marrying a woman who hurt me so fucking much. All because I never thought I'd get to be with you again. You're home to me, honey."

Tears stream down my face, hidden by the shower stream as I weave my fingers into her hair, holding her head to me. "I was so scared," I whisper after a moment. "I was so, so scared when I left Georgia. I didn't even have a place to live lined up, I lived in my car outside the city while touring apartments." I inhale shakily. "Eventually I found a place to sublet for a few months and Tyler told me they had a friend who was looking for a roommate. I was so grateful. And then...it was you. You opened up your home to me and even Dolly Parton and...you're home to me too, Jo. Wherever you are, it's always been you."

Giovanna presses her lips to the left of my belly button, her nose nudging my piercing. She's silent as she kisses lower, lower, lower until she's lifting my leg up and over her shoulder.

"I might be sandy down there."

She lifts her eyes to mine. "Luckily, the shower head is detachable."

I reach up to grab the shower head and then pass it to her. Our fingers brush as she takes it from me and that small touch is so electrifying, like we're yearning lovers from a Lisa Kleypas novel, brushing hands and exchanging lingering stares from afar. Not like she's kneeling in front of me, my leg strewn over her shoulder while I clutch onto the safety handle.

She keeps her eyes on mine as she parts where I ache for her and aims the shower spray at my pussy.

I gasp at the pressure of the water on me, making me impossibly more wet for her. It feels so good, but it's not enough.

"Looks like we got all the sand," she says after a few moments of intense eye contact, averting her eyes to examine my cunt.

It feels almost clinical, she's so close to where I want her, but her expression is serious, taking my comfort and cleanliness seriously.

She's *so* hot.

"I need you," I plead, knowing how I sound. But I think she likes me when I'm begging and needy and pathetic for her. If we're being honest with ourselves, she's just as needy and pathetic for me.

She smirks up at me before leaning in and licking from my entrance to my clit in one smooth stroke.

I whimper, toes curling and fists clenching at the euphoric sensation. "More."

"I thought we established you aren't in charge in this situation?" Jo says, batting her ridiculously long eyelashes, little water droplets hanging to the ends.

"'I thought we established you aren't in charge in—' oh, *fuck*." I tried to mimic her, tease her, and she went straight for the home run. She thrust two fingers into me, and sucked my clit into her mouth.

It's a dirty move. I'm pretty sure she'd get a red card, or at least be benched, if this were a professional sport.

"Point taken," I gasp, and she smiles against me.

"You gonna smile for me honey? Giggle that precious way you do when you come?" she asks.

I moan. It's all I can do. Her being horny and lovey turns me on *so much*.

She flicks my clit with her tongue, firm, fast movements that have me winding tighter and tighter at an alarming speed.

I cry out loudly as my orgasm peaks, pleasure overtaking my body and mind as I fall apart for her. I try to stay present, to not zone out and to really *feel* all that she's giving to me. I feel when I smile. I can hear the tiniest giggle, and even better, I'm hyper aware of how Jo's nails dig into my thigh as I do.

I'm panting, out of breath, until she's on her feet, pressing her mouth to mine. God, we taste perfect together. It's so soft as I come down, the way she holds me up, thumb drawing tiny circles on my hip. I break our kiss and slump forward into her, resting my forehead against her shoulder.

"Ready to go to bed?" Jo asks.

I growl. "No. Gimme a sec. You...that was...a lot."

"You're so sensitive," she muses, cupping the back of my head and massaging my scalp with her nails. "So responsive to how I...augh!" She yelps and pulls her hand away like my hair is made of fire. "There's sand in your hair."

I can't help it, I cackle. She sounded so disgusted by the fact that she found even more sand on my person, like the beach hadn't stolen my undergarments.

"Ugh, fuck off," Jo grumbles, playfully jerking her shoulder away so we're no longer touching. "I have sand under my nails."

She's so pretty, even as she scowls under the water, trying to pick out tiny pieces of sand from beneath her nails. I can't help but lean forward and steal a kiss. And this grumpy demon of mine can't help but kiss me back.

"I'll wash my hair so you can play with it without being attacked by a million grains of sand," I say against her mouth.

She's quiet for a moment before responding. "What if I wash your hair?"

My heart pirouettes in my chest, and a little plie at the end for pizazz.

"You wanna wash my hair?" I ask, pulling away from her.

She blushes, and goes back to picking under her nails. "I mean, I guess. If you want me to. It's intimate, right? Like washing your hair is something you'd do for someone you love? Or something?"

Goddammit, she's so precious and scared and unsure and she gets to be all of that with me.

What a life.

I usually only wash my hair twice a week, so I didn't bring the curly shampoo I use. But I'm willing to compromise my hair's health for Giovanna Quinn to wash it.

"It's so intimate. You're the queen of intimacy."

She blinks at me in confusion. "Is that...can I? God. I'm embarrassed by how much I want to wash your hair."

"Never be embarrassed by the soft parts of you. I love the prickly bits too, because they protected you when I couldn't, but the soft, sweet parts of you are so special to me."

She kisses me, and it's a sweet, languid kiss that has me forgetting everything besides the fact that I'm *hers* and she's *mine*.

Jo reaches behind me and grabs a travel sized bottle of shampoo. I'm hypnotized by the simple process of her squirting shampoo out of a tiny bottle. The way her arm jiggles with her movement, how her eyes are focused on the liquid as it makes a small pile in her hand. Her perfect hands as they lather the shampoo...well, that has me biting back a moan and squeezing my thighs together.

"Turn around, honey," Jo instructs. I happily obey, and I can almost hear her rolling her eyes.

"I'm only a brat when I'll get an orgasm out of it," I inform her.

Her hands are in my hair, massaging the sweet-smelling shampoo into my scalp and I moan, leaning back against her.

"I figured," Jo answers teasingly. "I like you both ways. When you're naughty, and when you're my good girl."

"Mmm," I moan, having reached nirvana in this hotel shower. I think I black out for the rest of the process, until Jo's taking down the removable shower head again and carefully rinsing the suds from my hair. She kisses my cheek when she's done and it's one of my new favorite kisses, so sure and loving.

She conditions and rinses my hair before turning off the shower. My teeth immediately begin to chatter, and I realize Jo had been out of the spray.

"Aren't you cold?" I ask, wrapping my arms around myself as I shiver.

She offers me a towel, which I immediately wrap around myself.

"Yeah, but I wanted to do that for you. God, I hate hotel towels," Jo grumbles. "They barely cover anything."

"Lucky me," I tease, before realizing that's probably not the best response at this moment. She looks genuinely uncomfortable. "Sorry, you should tell Audrey."

She shakes her head. "Nah, this is just like...how hotel towels are. They're always too small for people with bodies like mine."

To be fair, my tits are squished together to fit in the towel, but it's not particularly uncomfortable or upsetting for me. Annoying? Sure. But for Jo to brush aside the dignity of being able to have a towel that covers her body as the reality of staying in a hotel breaks my damn heart. She might not want to talk to Audrey...but I sure do. Simply because I think it may not be something she ever thought about.

I never had.

I step towards her and rest my head on her chest. Sex with her is incredible, but the ability to have this comfortable, casual intimacy with her is life-affirming.

"You don't have to say anything to her, but I think you know that doesn't mean I won't."

There's a shift in the universe when she smiles, and I feel it now. It feels a little easier to breathe, my skin clears up, etcetera. "I wouldn't ask anything less of you. Who am I to stop you from being a feral guard dog?"

I laugh. "I'm not sorry."

"I don't want you to be. Not for wanting to keep me safe. Even if your methods are fucking terrifying."

Finally, we climb into bed, and she pulls me into her. She's so soft and lush, except for her pod pressing against my hip.

"Hey, Hun?"

"Mmm?"

"Last night you said you weren't sure you were bi. Do you...uh. Do you want to talk about it?" I guess she can feel the way my body tenses, because she quickly amends her question. "If you want and feel comfortable."

"I've been talking in therapy a lot about the fact that I was raised being told I would break boys' hearts one day." I say quietly. "Men in my family made comments about how I'd make a lucky man happy one day at my first communion."

"Christ," Jo breathes.

"Yeah. I came out of the womb and was immediately taught to cater to the male gaze. I never knew a world existed where I could simply not be attracted to men."

It's hard to say out loud. I've talked to Krista, my therapist, about it. I've been unpacking it more and more for weeks, whether me flirting and sleeping with men was out of a genuine attraction, or simply because I was taught that's how things were.

Jo rubs soothing circles on my back. "I understand that."

It feels selfish and silly saying this to Jo, who was raised in the same faith. Whose mom didn't react the way she'd needed when she came out. Who also struggled to accept her sexuality.

"Does this sound selfish?" I ask.

"No, it sounds like you're still figuring yourself out, which makes sense. You weren't allowed to do that before," she answers comfortingly.

I bury my face in her chest, inhaling her floral scent. "It's hard," I admit. "I feel so, so ridiculous saying that, but it's *hard*. Because I always thought I knew who I was. I was secure in the fact I was bi. I'm a Cancer. I'm kind of chaotic and a hot mess, but I'm *me*. Now I don't know if I'm actually even bi."

"Josh identifies as queer, and doesn't identify with a label. One time I asked him about it, and he shrugged and said that he never found a label that felt right to him. He just knew he wasn't straight. Nic's attracted to men, women, and other genders. She identifies as bi, as does my younger sister Alex. My sister Millie's attraction isn't impacted by gender, and she identifies as pansexual. Their labels are what felt right for them. Not because it was owed to anyone else, but because it felt like it was a part of them. What feels right to you?"

"I don't know." It's painful and humiliating to say out loud.

"There's no rush to figure out what, if any, label feels right. You're still you. It's so, so normal for people's sexualities to evolve or for them to realize a label they once used no longer fits. It's okay to grow, to get to know yourself. We said we wanted to do that, grow and bloom together.You're still growing into you."

An unexpected sense of peace washes over me. I wanted a definitive answer, for Jo to tell me how I should identify based on the information I gave her. This kind of inspirational poster stuff was possibly better.

I'm still growing into me.

We're silent, and she keeps her hands on me, continuing her slow circles on my back, and periodically kissing my temple before returning her cheek to its place atop my head.

I inhale shakily, and for once the uncertainty doesn't scare me. Not knowing exactly who I am doesn't scare me, because I'm not alone.

Chapter 35

Hunter

Playlist: me | Taylor Swift

I wake up as the sun rises the next morning. Immediately I feel *awake*, ready to start the day. Jo is spooning me, her body enveloping mine and her arm draped protectively over my hip.

I might be the feral guard dog, but she might commit murder for me, too.

I slip out of her arms and climb out of bed, walking straight to the dresser where I quickly take my meds with a PopTart. I put my robe on and lean back against the dresser as I munch on my pastry, watching Jo sleep. I'm basically Edward Cullen, but with an ass that won't quit.

She's so fucking pretty in this light, the golden glow of the rising sun illuminating her body. She's still on her side, arm in the same position it was when I'd still been in bed. Once I'm done eating, I grab Loretta and take a few steps toward the bed, peering into the viewfinder and focusing the shot. The normal buzz of my brain quiets to a soothing hum when I shoot like this. Not for events, not for anyone else, just for me. I love shooting weddings, but there's a special peace that comes with creating for myself. I move around the bed, shooting Jo from various angles. I climb onto the bed and settle on my knees, focusing the shot on the details of her body I can never get out of my mind. The lines etched into her upper arms, the luscious rolls of her back and way that her hips flare out, dimples and bumps I'm obsessed with. I'm reckless, straddling her hips as I zoom in on her eyelashes. They're so long, even without a touch of mascara, and they deserve to be considered art.

"Are you taking pictures of me?" Her voice is so comforting that her sudden wakefulness doesn't startle me.

I'm silent as I continue to shoot her, hair mussed and eyes squinted in the daylight. She stretches her arms above her head, a quiet groan escaping her mouth.

"Mmhmm. I had a sudden burst of inspiration and had to capture it. If you hate it, I'll delete them and never do it again." I lower Loretta from my face and look hopefully at her. "Sorry, I should have waited for you to wake up."

Giovanna wraps her arms around me and pulls me down into her. "But then the light would have changed," she mumbles, booping the tip of my nose with her index finger.

My hands are trapped between our bodies, otherwise I'd be fanning myself. "You get me."

"I like you," she says simply. "I like getting you. I remember how important capturing memories was for you that summer. How you were always taking pictures, and asking me to take pictures of you..."

One day I'll admit to her how many photos she was the subject of. How many pictures of her favorite places and things I took. How I got prints made of them and have kept them in an old shoe box beneath my bed for twelve years. How I took the box to New Haven, and back to Georgia, and then to New York, without knowing if I'd get to see her again. I want to tell her how I've carried her spark with me all this time.

But right now, her hands are on my hips, grinding me onto her, and she's so fucking pretty and goddammit, I want to fuck her.

I crash my mouth to hers, movements frantic and desperate, but somehow still mindful enough to place Loretta on the night-stand.

"You never rode the cowgirl last night. You just *stole* my hat without paying the rental fee." I try to sound grumpy and un-happy, but how does one sound anything other than positively delighted when they're straddling Giovanna Quinn?

"You made an outlaw out of me, honey." She runs her hands down my back and grabs my ass through the robe. "But if you want me to behave, I'll behave for you."

I squeal as she flips us over. "My lover's a bandit," I breathe. "That's so hot."

She leaves slow, open mouth kisses down my jaw, my neck. She traces the trim of my robe with her fingers. "I hate this robe."

I scoff, affronted by her blunt distaste towards my favorite robe. "You hate fun and fashion and whimsy, you grouch."

"I was *going* to say I hate it because it's covering you up, but wow, just attack me, I guess."

Oops. Maybe I spoke too impulsively.

"I'd rather come for you in another way," I say sweetly, batting my eyelashes and cupping my breasts through the robe.

She moves quickly, and I arch my back as lowers her head and sucks my nipple through the robe. I moan. "More."

She releases my nipple. "So greedy," she murmurs, firmly pinching my nipple between her thumb and forefinger. I whine, a wordless plea for more, and she captures my other nipple in her mouth as she rolls the one between her fingers.

She pulls away and I want to scream and pull her head back to me. Luckily, she's just undoing the bow at my waist and opening the robe. She leans down and makes tight, slow circles around my nipple with her tongue. My hands knot themselves in her hair, tugging at the root to...I don't know. Pull her away? Pull her closer? All of the above? My brain is muddled and I'm confident I'm not thinking straight. She releases my nipple and repeats her torture on my other breast.

"Jo, more," I whimper, desperate for her.

"Not yet, honey. I need to wind you up first. Make you needy and whiny and bratty and achy." She sits back on her heels and I sit up, the robe falling off my shoulders. "But don't you worry, honey. I'm going to pay you your due. Where's that pretty pink vibrator of yours?"

"Reba is charging behind the TV," I tell her.

Jo gets the vibrator and climbs back into bed with me, straddling my hips and slowly running the tip of the rabbit up my belly and sternum. My breath grows heavier with each slow drag, and then she's pressing the head against the seam of my lips.

"Open," she instructs.

My jaw goes slack and she pushes it into my mouth. She keeps pushing until I gag, and then pulls it out, my saliva dripping from it.

"Can you relax your throat for me, honey? I want you to take me deeper."

I nod and let my eyes close, opening my mouth and lifting my head as she presses it in again, until I feel it in the back of my throat.

Instead of gagging, this time I moan, the imagery of me taking *her* too damn much.

She fucks my mouth with the same vibrator I've fucked myself to the thought of her countless times. The same toy I've clenched around as I imagined her touching me.

"Look at you. So pretty," she coos, slipping her hand between my thighs as she fucks my mouth. She thumbs my clit, electricity sparking in every molecule of my body. My skin feels like it's on fire. It's all too much, and not enough.

I whimper when she pulls away, leaving my mouth empty. I've never particularly enjoyed blowjobs, always sort of saw them as a necessary evil. Giovanna fucking my throat with my pink vibrator, however?

Ten out of ten, would recommend.

"I promised I was gonna ride you. I keep my promises." Her words are rough and filthy, but her voice is so soft, woven with tenderness.

I lift my head and press my mouth to hers as she slips the vibrator between us. I gasp and jerk when she powers it up and presses it against my clit.

Her tongue is in my mouth as she adjusts herself so that she's also pressed against the vibrator, her body a delicious pressure on mine.

She starts to grind her hips, keeping her promise and riding me. I grab handfuls of her luscious ass, my legs wrapping around her calves. At this point we're both brazenly panting into each other's mouth, hot, wet gusts of air.

I've never been slow to come. It's always been relatively easy to get there which I recognize isn't exactly the norm for many, many people. But somehow, it's even easier with Jo. There's no build, no fall, just a crack of lightning through my bones and the weight of Jo's body on mine to bring me back.

She breaks contact and pulls her face away, keeping the vibrator firmly between us. I know my next orgasm is inevitable, and wonder if it'll be another sudden explosion, or a slow burn.

"Give me your eyes, honey." Her voice is raspy and deep—she's close. I force my eyes open and when our eyes meet, the softest, sweetest smile slowly grows on her face. The little imaginary mason jar where I've tucked away her laughs and smiles since moving in is shattered on the ground, the sound of her laughter and brightness of her smile too much for it to contain.

We shatter together, eyes locked as we cry each other's names, falling apart with the promise of putting each other back together.

"I love you," Jo whispers after rolling off of me. The sheets are tangled between our legs, and my head is on her chest, listening to the steady beat of her heart. "I love you. I love you."

"That's so weird!" I tease. "I love you too! We have so much in common—are you single?"

Jo laughs, the sound reverberating against my cheek in her chest. "Am I single? Really?"

"I mean you might be. Are you?" I ask it casually, but then my stomach sinks. What if it ends when this weekend ends? What if—

"I hope not," she says softly, and I can hear the hesitation and nerves in her voice. "We don't have to define anything but...I hope you're mine, Hunter. I'm not sure how to do this right, but we're really good co-parents and roommates already, and if the sun ever explodes and we lose sunlight, I'll always be able to see because I have you lighting everything up."

"Of course I'm yours, silly goose," I tease, silencing her with a swift kiss. "I've been yours for twelve goddamned years."

Jo exhales with relief. "I've been yours for just as long."

I kiss her again, my fingers running through her waves. "The historians will be *wrong*," I muse happily.

Jo pulls away. "Pardon?"

"You know how historians are all like *oh these two single women lived together for fifty years, and never married and were buried in the same casket what good roommates these straight women were!*" Jo stares blankly at me. I ignore her and continue. "When I first moved in and had a giant-ass crush on you, I was *distraught* because historians would be correct if they said we were just roommates and..."

I screech and jerk away when Jo tickles my sides. "Oooh, you had a crush on me, honey?"

"We've had sex. Multiple times," I remind her. "We've exchanged bodily fluids and love declarations. Kindly pull yourself together."

Jo opens her mouth to respond, but is interrupted by a sharp rap at the door. Our eyes meet, and hers widen comically.

"I pray to every god who has ever existed that it's another noise complaint," she whispers excitedly, eyes sparkling with mischief.

I groan and roll out of bed, shrugging my robe back on and tying it at my waist. Jo snickers loudly behind me.

"What?" I ask, my back still to her.

"Is that what you're wearing to answer the door?"

I turn toward her, my brow furrowed. "Yes?"

She snickers again, this time having the decency to try to hide it behind her hand. "Nothing. Speaking of, that's what it covers. Nothing. It's a sheer robe."

I look down, making eye contact with the headlights on my chest. It's so see-through you can even see the love bites I hadn't realized she'd left on the tops of my breasts. When did *those* get there?

"Okay. Cool. Thanks," I stammer, my cheeks heating. I feel her eyes on me as I take the robe off and pull my favorite teddy on before putting the robe back on over it.

"Better," Giovanna says decidedly.

I roll my eyes. "You're so lucky I love you."

I hear the smile in her voice when she responds. "Yeah, I really am."

Now I'm the one having to pull it together. I want to do a happy dance, to spin around the room and grab a hairbrush to use as a microphone. This is joy. This is belonging and safety.

But then I open the door.

Chapter 36

Jo

Playlist: Messy | Renee Rapp

"Audrey!" Hunter's tone of surprise carries into the room. "Hi."

I bite my lip and turn to the side, like anyone can see my smile. Of course we got another complaint. Of course Kelsey probably popped a blood vessel. Of course...

"Hey, Hunter. Sorry to bother you so early." Audrey's voice sounds strange, but I can't put my finger on it. "Is Jo here?"

I sit up, surprised that she's asking for me by name. Did Kelsey complain about me specifically?

"Oh!" Hunter sounds even more surprised. "Hey, Giovanna? Audrey needs to talk to you."

I get out of bed and quickly put on my outfit from last night before going to the door.

"!" I say, forcing a cheerfulness I don't really feel. My belly is gurgling with anxiety. "What's up?"

"Hi. Um, maybe you and I should talk alone?" Audrey's eyes dart between Hunter and I, and my stomach sinks. Something's wrong.

I look at Hunter, who reaches out and squeezes my hand. "It's up to you," she says quietly. "I don't have to stay...but I will if you want me to."

"She can stay," I say, turning back to Audrey and meeting her eyes.

Audrey inhales deeply before speaking. "Becky and Kelsey left. They both left their keys with the night manager and checked out."

I feel like I've been slapped across the face. "What?"

Audrey looks so nervous, like I'll be mad at her. "They both asked her not to tell anyone, but she told me, and you should know, too."

"What the *fuck*?" I seethe, dropping Hunter's hand and stalking back into the room.

Hunter calls after me, but I don't turn back. I'm digging through the twisted sheets, searching for my phone, and once I find it, I call Becky.

"Hi, you've reached Becky Coffey—"

"Fuck!" I curse, jabbing my finger on the end call button. Then I do something I never wanted to do again.

"This is the voicemail of Kelsey Williams. I can't come to the phone right now, please leave a message at the beep."

"Kelsey," I snap. "What the fuck is happening? One of you needs to call me back immediately."

My hands shake as I go to McKenna's room and pound on her door. I don't care that they left, not really. I care that I hung my dreams on this and I have no idea what comes next. I have no idea if everything is canceled, if I'll get the money I've worked so hard for.

I'm certain nothing else can surprise me this morning, until Barry opens McKenna's door.

"Good for you, Barry," I say after gaping for a few seconds, reaching out and patting him on his shoulder. "Is McKenna in there?

Upon hearing her name, McKenna appears behind Barry, wearing a Port Haven High School t-shirt, hair tangled and mascara smudged. Wow. Good for *her*.

"Jo," McKenna looks surprised to see me. "What's going on?"

"Did you know Kelsey and Becky checked out?" I'm past niceties. Unless she wants to tell me how Barry was in bed. Only for educational purposes, of course. The curiosity feels like a balm to the anger I feel.

She jerks back like I slapped her. "*What*?"

"Yep. Last night. Do you know where they are? Neither of them are answering my calls."

She disappears into the room for a moment before reappearing, phone held up to her ear. "It's going straight to voicemail." She taps on her phone a few times, her frown deepening. "She...she's at her apartment. In Midtown."

I blink at her blankly. "The fuck? Did she say anything to you?"

"I've barely talked to her all weekend. She's been...fuck. She's losing it. Lost it, maybe. I've never seen her like this." She looks anxiously at Barry, like he'll be able to add to the conversation. He isn't.

"Cool," I say dryly. "Cool. Cool. Cool. This is..."

"Cool?" Barry offers helpfully.

"Will you tell me if you hear from her? Either of them?" I feel like I'm begging. Which is pathetic. But also my clients are fucking MIA and I don't know what I'm supposed to do in this situation, because despite having over a half decade of experience since entering the field, and having plenty of cancelled events and runaway brides...what I'm supposed to do has always been clear.

This is anything but.

"Yeah. I'm sorry, Jo." She sounds genuinely remorseful.

"Thanks," I reply.

I skulk back to mine and Hunter's room, Audrey appearing beside me out of nowhere. "I checked in with the other bridesmaids, one of them had Kelsey's location and said she's back at her place in the city."

I sigh heavily, both grateful that Audrey went out of her way to get this information, and frustrated that it's nothing new. "Yeah, McKenna said that too."

I lift my hand to knock, realizing I didn't grab a key before I booked it out of there. Hunter swings the door open before my hand makes contact with the wood, her phone nestled between her ear and shoulder.

"Yeah, she's right here," Hunter says, eyes wide. *It's Becky*, she mouths, and my stomach churns. She hands me the phone, and as soon as it's cradled in my hand she somehow finds my free hand, intertwining our fingers.

I bring the phone to my ear. "What the hell is going on?"

"Jo, we've decided to cut the bachelorette trip short." She says it so casually, like sneaking off in the middle of the night without telling anyone isn't sketchy as all hell.

"I'm sorry, what?" I feel so many emotions in my chest, a bubbling anger, a twisting confusion.

"Your services weren't what we'd expected, and we ended up fighting over it. So we've decided to spend the rest of the weekend alone at home."

I drop Hunter's hand again. "You've got to be fucking with me. I did everything, *everything* you asked of me, and suddenly it wasn't enough? So you fucking dip? Without giving me a heads up so I can do everything I need to cancel today's events, end our reservations, and coordinate the bridesmaids' travel back to New York earlier than planned? What the *hell*?"

"I understand you're unhappy, but this is what's best for Kelsey and I for now."

"So that's it?" I spit out. "Are you letting me go? I'm out of a job?"

"We're just talking about this weekend, Jo. There's no reason to be so dramatic."

"You left in the middle of the night," I hiss. "Don't talk to me about being dramatic."

She's silent for a moment. "I'm trying to save my relationship, Jo. You of all people should understand what it's like to want to stay engaged to Kelsey..."

I hang up before I say anything I regret, angry heat radiating behind my eyes.

"Jo?" Hunter takes my hand in hers. I try to slow my breath, steady my head. It feels like the world is spinning around me and I'm caught in the motion. I try to focus on how soft Hunter's skin is, how nice her hand feels in mine, not on the constant spinning and indecipherable noise in my head. She pulls me further in the room, Audrey following us, and lowers us to the foot of the bed. My forehead immediately rests on her shoulder.

"They're not coming back," I mumble into her shoulder.

"What did she say?" Audrey asks.

I lift my head shakily. "That she's trying to save her relationship. That I, of all people, should understand why she's doing this."

"What's that supposed to mean?" Audrey asks.

I can hear the vitriol in Hunter's answer. "Jo and Kelsey were engaged. But Becky didn't know that until last night. So I can't think about what she has the audacity to imply or I'll burn everything to the goddamned ground."

"Christ," Audrey sounds stunned. "What the fuck? Why did she ask her ex to plan her wedding?"

"I'm good at my job," I mutter.

I can feel Hunter and Audrey exchanging silent glances. I don't blame them.

I don't know how much time passes, but eventually Audrey exits the room, leaving Hunter and I sitting silently at the foot of the bed.

"You okay?" she eventually asks.

I don't know what to say, how to explain the complexities of how I feel right now, so I shake my head.

"Wanna go to Queenie's?"

I don't. I want to crawl beneath the blankets and dissociate and find the tears that haven't come since before Kelsey left the first time.

I stare at the ground, feeling myself withdrawing more and more into myself. I want to run. As fast as I can, as far as I can, and I promised Hunter I wouldn't.

So I tell her. I open my mouth and tell her everything I'm feeling. The hurt and betrayal that has me feeling shame, because how can two people who have already hurt and betrayed me do it yet again?

Hunter leans and lays her head on my shoulder while I purge and try to make sense of the whirlpool of emotion inside me.

"That's a lot," she says quietly. "I'm sorry."

I laugh hollowly. "You're the last person in this situation who should be sorry. You're the only good thing about this shitshow."

"I'm sorry you're hurting. You deserve better as a human, and as a professional."

"Is it shitty of me if I agree with that?"

She straightens, and gently turns my face, her eyes searching mine. "No, because it's *true*. What can I do to support you right now? Do you want me to take care of talking to the rest of the guests? Working with Audrey to cancel stuff? Then I'll run out and grab Queenie's and we spend the day on the beach or watching *Pride and Prejudice.* Take the train back tonight to see Dolly early?"

That shockingly doesn't sound like the worst idea ever.

"What do I do? While you're taking care of me...what do I do?"

"Whatever you think is best." Hunter stands from the bed and walks to the window, drawing back the curtains. Everything inside me wants to draw back and hiss, like an angry cat.

"I'm sorry, did you just *hiss*?"

Apparently I did it outloud, and not just in my head. Whoops.

"The sun is mean," I argue.

"Okay, but the sun also might help us activate those happy chemicals in your brain. Unless you want to stay in bed and be sad, which is totally okay. What do you want? What do you need?"

"I want to hide...but maybe I shouldn't," I say slowly.

She smiles softly. "What would Alena say?"

"To start small. One thing at a time."

"Why don't you take a shower? I'll get dressed and go talk to the bridesmaids, and we'll reconvene and take it from there."

How do I tell her that showering even feels like too much? That standing up, getting undressed, turning on the water, doing everything I have to do in the shower, drying off, and getting dressed again is *too much.*

I don't have to, because her eyes soften and she gently cups my cheek in her hand. "Hang tight, baby. I'll be right back."

It feels like she's gone forever, and I just stare out the window at the sound, at the boats and ferries and families slowly crowding on the shore.

When she comes back, it's with strawberry milkshakes and sweet potato fries from Queenie's.

We eat in silence, and I appreciate her not pressuring me to talk more. We both take our meds, and I check my blood sugar. While Hunter was gone, she'd updated McKenna, so that takes *that* off my plate.

When we finish eating, she takes me by the hand and leads me into the bathroom. Her touch is gentle and guiding as she slips my shirt over my head. It's not sexual, but tender and loving.

Hunter gets undressed, taking my hand to guide us both under the hot water. She's on her tiptoes behind me, massaging my scalp with shampoo the same way I had last night.

Could I let myself have this? Could I believe I deserve it? Could I let Hunter take care of me, like she is now? Like she says she wants to?

Could I let myself really trust her? It feels too late to be questioning this, wondering this. My heart already lives outside my body, dwelling in Hunter's hands.

But Kelsey leaving once again, in a totally different context, still has me spiraling, wondering what I could have done differently for her to have stayed.

Hunter doesn't force me to speak for the rest of the day. I mean, I do. Just not in-depth. I stay, and she holds my hand while I try to untangle my feelings, despite it being hard as fuck.

Audrey, being the absolute angel she is, insists on working on her day off to take care of breaking everything down and canceling the remaining activities for us. When Hunter mentions going home early, Audrey checks us out immediately, so we won't try to change our minds, she says.

When Hunter and I get home, it feels strange. Not good, not bad, just new. We're in this familiar place, in our new, unfamiliar relationship.

I can't help the smile that spreads across my face when she squeals and rushes to Dolly's terrarium, where our child lounges in a bearded dragon sized hammock. Hunter cradles Dolly in her arms, cooing and kissing her little scaly head.

"I've missed you so much, Mommy's never leaving you again," Hunter promises in between kisses, and I chuckle.

She lifts her gaze and smiles at me, shuffling over to me. I reach out my arms and she places Dolly into them. It's strange to think how much I hated the idea of having a bearded dragon. Dolly's truly somehow wormed her way into my heart and made it bigger.

"So, uh," Hunter sounds nervous, as she picks at her cuticles. "Where do we sleep tonight?"

I blink at her a few times, confused by her question. "Here?"

"Right. But like...do we have to sleep in separate beds?"

I try to fight back a smile, and fail spectacularly. She jokingly punches me in the shoulder.

"I don't *want* to sleep in separate beds." I can hear the amusement in my voice. "Do *you* want to sleep in separate beds?"

She shakes her head, a sweet blush reddening the apples of her cheeks. "I like sleeping next to you."

I chew my bottom lip between my teeth, then shift Dolly in my arms so I can cup her mom's cheek in my hand, tracing that blush with my thumb. "I love you," I say simply. "I know today's been weird, and I don't want to lie to you. Everything in me wants to run and hide to protect myself, but I want us more. I want you to help me shower when it's too much for me, and learn more about who was fucking who in Fleetwood Mac..."

"Everyone was fucking everyone," Hunter interrupts. "Like…"

"Hun."

"Right, sorry. An important, emotional monologue isn't the right time to interrupt for an info dump. Continue."

I smile because goddamn, even her excitement for her hyperfixations is so fucking dear to me. I want to know everything about the things she holds close to her heart.

"Yes, I still want you. Even when I'm depressed, or down. Even when I don't seem like I do, I still want you. I'm not going to be perfect at showing it or giving you what you need, but I promise to work at it and be better and…" I trail off and look at her expectantly. She's just smiling at me. "What?" I ask suspiciously.

"Nothing. Everything. You," she says, like it's not complete nonsense. "I'm just so proud of you. You promised to communicate and not run, and you're doing it! You're harsh on yourself, but you're so wonderful and I see how hard you're trying. I wish you did, too."

She hugs me, sandwiching Dolly between us, and I bury my nose into her sweet-smelling hair. "Giovanna, I love *you*. Not you when you're not depressed or when your blood sugar is perfect. *You*. All of you, and the multitudes you contain."

Later that night, when I'm falling asleep with her tucked beneath my arm, I find myself feeling like maybe, just maybe, everything's going to be okay.

Hunter pretty much shoves me out of the apartment Tuesday morning, and when I get to the office, neither Becky nor Kelsey are there. I haven't heard from either of them since talking to Becky Sunday morning, but it sounds like they're prioritizing saving their shitty relationship. So hooray for them, I guess.

They're not there for the rest of the week, and by Friday morning, it feels like the new normal—the same way kissing Hunter and cooking us eggs for breakfast has become my new normal. Hunter and I are domestic, and Kelsey and Becky don't show up to work.

When I walk into the office, I do a double take when I see the light on in Becky's office.

"She's back?" I ask my coworker, Daniel.

"Yep," he responds, spinning his office chair so he's facing me. "She walked in at 8:36 in sky-high heels. Didn't say hi to anyone, just went right into her office and slammed the door." He gives me a sympathetic look. "So I'd brace yourself."

"Any sign of Kelsey?"

He shakes his head. "Nope."

Dread fills my entire being. Maybe I'm wrong and it's nothing.

But, it doesn't *feel* like nothing. It feels like I'm getting fired. I wasn't exactly professional in our last interaction, and Hunter, god love her, sure made many a threat.

I'm typing in my password to check my email when Becky knocks on the door.

"Jo, can we talk?"

My heart is pounding, and I wish Hunter was here. First, because she would be the feral guard dog I love so much, but also because she would hold my hand and I wouldn't have to go through this alone.

I nod, getting to my feet shakily as she leaves. I follow her to her office where my stomach drops further when I see Janae, an HR representative, sitting across from Becky at her desk.

I shakily lower myself into the chair next to Janae. "What's going on?" I cringe when my voice cracks.

Becky puts her glasses on and looks intently at the papers on her desk. "I'd like to offer you a partner position." She says this without making eye contact with me at all.

I stare at her. "You...what?"

"I want to offer you half of the business. We'd be equal partners and you would receive a much higher salary than your current compensation." Becky still is flipping through papers on her desk, not looking at me, and it feels clinical.

"Why?"

"Because you've proven yourself capable of leadership in this capacity time and time again. Frankly, this is long overdue."

"Then why *now*?"

Becky finally looks at me. She has dark circles under her eyes, and she's breaking out. I've never seen her skin looking less than perfect.

"Kelsey has been separated from Coffey & Co. effective immediately." Becky folds her hands on the desk. " You will no longer be working on the freelance project we assigned you."

Maybe I should be happy to hear they've broken up, that the wedding is canceled.

But the money I'd been paid is gone, taking my hope of freedom with it.

"However, because of your performance while contracted, I've made the decision to promote you and invite you to buy into the firm."

I stare at her.

"I'm...not fired?" I ask, voice shaking.

Becky laughs, the fakest laugh to ever be fake laughed. "Of course not. You're the heart and soul of this firm, Giovanna. We're nothing without you, and it's long overdue for us to show how much we appreciate you."

I don't say anything, my head swimming with a billion different thoughts. There's the thoughts of what I should do, what I could do, and then there's what I want to do.

They're all different things.

"There is a stipulation, however," Becky continues, spinning the stapled papers around so they're facing me. "One Janae and I will be more than happy to explain in full."

I pick up the papers and shakily flip through. This stipulation Becky speaks of sticks out immediately.

"You want me to agree not to get romantically involved with Kelsey Williams?" I'm staring at the words, like if I just look a little harder, it'll make sense.

"Yes," Becky answers, like this part of my employment contract is the most natural and rational thing in the world. "As I said, she and I are no longer involved, however, considering your past involvement with her, I need to ensure that nothing happens between you two again."

"Don't want to work with someone who's dating your ex? Or, worse, engaged to your ex-fiancée?" I sound ugly, I know that.

But this is uglier.

Becky sighs heavily. "I just had to tell my entire family that my half million dollar wedding is off. So yeah. I'm sorry for wanting to feel safe in my workplace."

"Nothing happened between us while you were together." I can't even look at her. I feel sick to my stomach.

"She said that too, but I think you understand why I'm having you agree to these terms."

I flip the page and look at the salary. It's a big increase. Over my first year, I'd make up for what I'm losing by Kelsey and Becky canceling the wedding. More benefits...and I'd own half of the company. There's even a proposed name change: Coffey & Quinn.

But if I sign this contract, I'm signing away any hope of setting myself free. Instead of being under Kelsey's thumb, I'll be under Becky's. I know I'll never be able to move home, open up the firm I want to.

Never have the life I want.

I shakily inhale and meet her eyes. "Can I have some time to think it over?"

Becky's eyes are sharp, but not unkind. "Of course. Take all the time you need. You'll be getting the check with the rest I owe you for the, um. For you know. Hunter is too."

I nod, staring at the wood grain of the desk. I'm off from work the next few weekends, which was something Kelsey and Becky insisted on, so that I could spend time working on their wedding. In fact, I don't have weekend events until after Labor Day because of this.

I wish I did. I wish I had something to distract myself from this.

Because I feel like I'm drowning again.

Chapter 37

Hunter

Playlist: Landslide | The Chicks

I've been singing along to Taylor Swift's *Lover* album all day, leaning into that feeling of being head over heels. I'm finally editing the pictures from this weekend, all the asinine photos of drunk brides, drunk bridesmaids, and way too many photos accidentally focused on Jo.

Who can blame me? She's a smokeshow.

Dolly is lounging on my lap while I hum along, so loud that I don't hear Jo behind me until she's pretty much shouting.

"*Hunter*!" I scramble to pause the music and lower my headphones from my ears. When I spin my chair to face her, I immediately know something's wrong.

"Jo?" I say cautiously, gathering Dolly in my arms and slowly getting to my feet. "Are you okay? You're home early."

"Becky and Kelsey broke up." Her voice is flat when she says it, emotionless. She usually looks tired after work, but today her eyes are empty and her shoulders are hunched, like she's closing in on herself.

Personally, I don't see the problem with them breaking up. No relationship, no wedding, no more having to see Becky and Kelsey. That's a win if I've ever heard one, but something tells me Jo doesn't feel the same way.

"I know it's not surprising," she continues, averting her eyes and staring at the ground. "I know maybe I should be happy. But I'm not getting the full paycheck."

My stomach sinks as I remember why Jo had taken the job in the first place. The income from these events was going to make her dream a reality, give her the freedom she'd been dreaming of.

"Oh, Giovanna," I feel like I'm about to melt into a puddle of tears, so shattered by her palpable hurt. I take a step towards her, and my heart constricts when she takes a step away from me. "Jo?"

"Please, don't," her hands are shaking, and I want to take them in mine. To squeeze them and assure her we'll figure it out, that I'm not going to let them continue to hurt her. That her dream will come through, somehow.

"I want to run again." Her voice is shaky, and she's rubbing the heels of her hands into her eyes. "I want to run and hide and wait it out until it just goes away."

I swallow roughly. "Then run."

She meets my eyes again. "What?"

"You're feeling restless and need to run? Then fucking run."

"I promised you I wouldn't," she shakes her head, and I'm not certain if she's trying to convince me, or herself.

"You'll come back when you're ready." I'm not sure who I'm trying to convince either. "You'll run and then you'll come back when you don't need to run anymore. I'll be waiting...if you want me to wait."

"I do," she says it so quickly, and it makes my heart feel a little less unbearably heavy. "And I will. I'll come back tomorrow—I just need tonight."

"You're overwhelmed and hurt, rightfully so, and you need to figure this out with some space. I trust you."

Her arms are around me and she's pulling me into the tightest hug.

"I owe you."

I pull away, and get on my tiptoes, pressing my lips to her forehead. "You owe *yourself* peace. I love you, and you don't owe me anything."

I stay in the office while Giovanna moves around the apartment, packing things up. I stare absently at her bookshelves, a rainbow of cracked spines. *What do I do now?* I don't have to finish editing the photos from last weekend.

Jo pops her head back in the office. "I'm going to Nic and Josh's. You have their numbers. I promise I'll come back."

"I know." I force a smile, squeezing Dolly tighter to me.

She looks at me for a second longer, like she's trying to memorize my face, and then she's gone. I hear the front door close moments later, and that's when I let myself crumble.

I cry until it hurts a little less, until my eyesight is blurry and I can't exhale out my nose.

By then, the sun has set, and I'm starving. But worse, I understand what Jo meant about hiding, about running. That's all I want to do. To run after her, to run away from this hurt and pain and *rejection* I feel. But I know that's not what it is. I never thought patience was my strong suit, but I waited twelve years for her. I can wait again.

I force myself out of bed and into the office, pulling up Google Docs and writing down my thoughts. I'm surprised at how cohesive it all seems on screen. It makes sense, and slowly, I begin to realize something:

It's possible.

Chapter 38

Jo

Playlist: My Mind Ain't Always On My Side | Molly Grace

"I've never seen her like this," Josh whispers loudly, like I can't hear him.

I can. He's a very bad whisperer.

"Yeah, this isn't good," Nic attempts to whisper back. God, these two shitty whisperers are perfect for each other.

"What do we do?" he hisses.

"I don't know; it's been a minute since she's been like this!" my sister says at practically full volume.

"You know I can hear you right?" I ask. There's no response, and I assume they've resigned to talking with those obnoxious couple looks again.

"Josh," I groan.

I hear some scuffling behind me before he responds. "Uh, yeah?"

"More chocolate milk, please." I thank him a few minutes later when he places a fresh glass of chocolate oat milk on the table.

"JoJo? Do you want to talk about it?" Nic asks softly, placing her hand on my forearm.

"Nope."

It's silent for a moment while I assume Nic and Josh give each other more *looks* over my head.

"Well, that's that," Josh says. "She doesn't want to talk about it, Buttercup."

"Hey Joshy? Why don't you go grab that first edition Lisa Kleypas you found at the used bookstore last week?" Nic's tone is sickly sweet, and I immediately know she's up to something. "Jo would love to see that."

Josh, the sweet, brainless, golden retriever that he is, does not see the signs.

I look at my sister out of the corner of my eye as her boyfriend jogs up the stairs. She's watching Josh as he leaves, her eyes following his movements, and once he's upstairs, her eyes are on me. "That should keep him busy for a few minutes."

I sigh. "What are you doing?"

"Gaslighting my partner so I can get whatever is bothering you out in the open. Spill."

God, she's unhinged.

"Nothing's bothering me." I reach for the glass of chocolate milk, and gasp in horror when Nic snatches it from my grasp. "What the *fuck*, Nicoletta?"

"No chocolate milk until you spill."

I roll my eyes and reach out for the glass. Nic jerks away and I narrow my eyes. "Give. It. *Back*."

She responds by taking a sip.

"You're dead to me." I lunge for the glass and Nic jumps up from the couch.

"If you make me spill on the new couch, you'll end up in the same realm of infamy as Leo. *Leo*. You don't want that. Come on, just tell me what's going on."

"Becky and Kelsey canceled the wedding." I hold my hand out expectantly. "There. Can I have my chocolate milk now?"

I watch the confusion on her face give way to understanding. "The money."

"Yep. I only get fifty percent. It's not enough to open my business." Saying it out loud makes it feel more real, somehow. More concrete.

"JoJo," Nic sits down next to me. "I'm so sorry."

I shrug. "It's whatever."

"It's so whatever you showed up at my house tonight demanding *Miss Congeniality* and chocolate oat milk and watched said movie three times without reacting or saying a word. Totally, completely, whatever."

"I hate you."

"I know. But it's almost midnight and we need to talk about this."

I groan loudly, stomping my foot like I'm a petulant teenager. "I just *did*."

"More," Nic demands.

"I don't wanna," I whine.

"That's why you gotta. Why are you here and not at home?"

"I needed my big sister. Is that so hard to believe?"

"Impossible, actually."

"I'm in love with Hunter." It comes out before I can even think about saying it. it just comes out. "I think falling again made me believe that life could be good, that my dreams were in reach."

I inhale shakily. "I still have my wedding suit, you know. I love that damn thing. I don't think about Kelsey when I look at it, I think about how beautiful I feel in it. I let myself believe the life I wanted for myself was in reach. Then Hunter said she loved me too, and more than that, she showed it. I felt like even the most impossible dreams were at my fingertips.

"She stayed and supported me through multiple lows and now I feel like the rug's been ripped out from me again. Becky wants to promote me to partner, but I don't *want* to be a partner at her business. Even if it's legally half mine. I don't want to work with her in any capacity and..."

"What *do* you want?" Nic asks, a touch of curiosity in her voice.

"I want to move home and do my little beach walks every day and I want to bring Hunter and Dolly with me and...I want to open my own firm. The way I have always wanted. I thought my hard work was paying off and my dreams would be able to come true. Now I have nothing."

"Did you two have a fight?"

I shake my head. "Not even a little one. She encouraged me to take the space I needed to process everything. She..." I try to swallow the lump that manifested in my throat, but it's no use. "...she told me she trusted me. That she knew I'd come back."

I look up and meet Nic's eyes, which I'm taken aback to see are watery. "JoJo," she sniffs. "I think she really loves you."

"I...think she does too." It feels weird to say it to someone else, almost cocky. *Like, hi! The greatest human decided I'm worthy of their love so I can't be a* complete *piece of shit.*

"But what if I hurt her? She's so open and warm and I feel so closed off and cold."

"Have you met my partner and I?" Nic says flatly, and it makes me fight back a smile. Josh is annoyingly happy all the time, and

Nic has an infamous scowl that graces her face ninety-nine percent of the time.

"He loves me just like this," she continues, "all crotchety and complaining and *me*. Maybe he deserves better than me, but he chooses me every day. And I somehow make him even *happier*? Maybe everyone deserves better than an imperfect, human love. Maybe that's why people read that weird alien smut Nellie told me about. But even better is finding the perfectly imperfect person for us. The one who makes waking up easier, makes doing life better. Who sees the real you annoyingly well, and wants to see you even *better*. Is that Hunter for you?"

God, I love Hunter so much, it hurts. I'd loved Kelsey, but now I realize there was something missing. It was Hunter's strength and hope and fiery, righteous anger at injustice. It was our little monster and her mom's loud offkey singing through the apartment.

She's always seen me, and wanted to see me better. When we were fifteen, and even more now.

It was always her.

"I like her. A lot. She makes you laugh that ugly laugh and you seem...more healed. More *you*." Nic's eyes are still watery when she takes my hand in mine and squeezes. "Ever since she moved in with you, I've slowly been seeing parts of you I haven't seen since before Kelsey. Parts of you I'd missed, and I know it's not just her. I know it's so much hard work on your end, and I'm so glad my sister's back." Nic throws her arms around my neck in a tight hug. In a move that surprises even me, I hug her back, long and tight and full of the endless love we have for each other.

I think about how Nic, since dating Josh, has felt almost like a new Nic. She's still the same grouch she's been her entire life, but it's like new facets of her are being unlocked. Maybe I'm getting to experience that for myself, too. Maybe that's why I hug her back—I feel safe softening in my big sister's embrace instead of hiding.

"You're going back to her, right?" she whispers in my ear.

I nod my head. "I'm going to text her tonight, but I'll go back in the morning. Is it okay if I crash here?"

Nic still hasn't let go of me. I can't believe this sentimental woman is the same human who used to karate chop our parents when they attempted to hug her for the sign of peace at Mass.

"Of course it's okay, JoJo. You'll always be welcome wherever I am."

"Even if Josh says no?"

She scoffs as she finally breaks the hug. "Like Josh would say no. He loves you, too."

I bite back a smile. "Do you maybe want to stop gaslighting him and call him back?"

She sheepishly pulls a weathered paperback out from its hiding spot next to the couch cushion. "Joshy!" she hollers over her shoulder. "It's down here!"

Seconds later Josh is sliding into the living room. "Thank god, I was about to disassemble Dad's desk."

I shoot Nic a disapproving look, which she way too naturally ignores. "Here you go, baby," she coos obnoxiously at him, holding the book out to him. This man blushes from his neck to his ears as he takes it from her, an adoring look on his face. I, of course, roll my eyes, despite a feeling of comforting warmth spreading through my entire body. Josh looks the way I feel when I look at Hunter.

Maybe the world is a little better because we can love.

"JoJo's sleeping over tonight, is that okay?" Nic asks, a light pink blush on her two cheeks. These two losers are so disgustingly enamored with each other.

"Of course it is." This simp manages to tear his eyes from Nic and looks at me. "You're always welcome here...Jo."

"Not calling me Josephine looked painful," I tease.

"It was, thank you for noticing." He looks back at Nic. "Why don't you two take the bed, and I can take the couch in the office?"

I try to refuse, "I couldn't..."

"Shut up, Josephine." Josh swivels his head and narrows his eyes at me. "You're family."

"There he is."

A few minutes later, Nic and I are snuggled beneath the clean sheets with *Miss Congeniality* playing in the background. She's pointing out the constellations on the ceiling mural she'd had painted for Josh for their first anniversary.

"You know, I'll miss you if you leave the city," Nic says suddenly, turning onto her side to face me.

I smile, only seeing her by the fuzzy light of the TV. "I'll miss you too. But I think we needed each other more at other points in our life. Don't get me wrong, I'll always need my big sister."

"Considering Kat is useless," she interrupts.

"Exactly. But you have Josh. And I have Hunter and we're moving forward in our lives in ways I didn't think possible, at least for me. I didn't think I'd get to experience love again, let alone a deeper, fuller love."

"Life's funny that way," Nic says with a giant yawn. "It throws you someone from your past and they become your soul's reason."

Nic and Josh had gone to the same elementary school and *hated* each other as kids. When they bumped into each other one night on the train ride back to the city last year, it was the beginning of a comedy of errors, one that ended in where they are now. I'll never forget how angry Nic was after running into him. I've seen Nic pissed a bajillion times throughout my life, but never to that degree. A year later, she looks at this man like he hangs the moon, and she paints him the stars.

She refers to him as corny shit like her "soul's reason."

I think about Hunter, how my heart finally was ready to heal because she believed in me, encouraged me, and took me seriously. How I was finally ready to let myself simply *be* again.

I fall asleep thinking about a certain chaotic blonde as Sandra Bullock and Benjamin Bratt banter in the darkness.

Chapter 39

Hunter

Playlist: State of Grace (Taylor's Version) | Taylor Swift

For the second morning in a row, I'm awake when the sun rises, light streaming between the city buildings. This time, it's because, well, I never went to sleep Friday night. I stayed up all night chugging mug after mug of Jo's favorite tea, and by the time I clicked print, the sun was rising.

I could've gone to sleep. Should've, probably, but I was jacked up on caffeine and hope. Rather than get an appropriate amount of sleep, I got ready for the day, and left Jo a note on the counter, telling her where I'd be.

"Port Haven is next," the conductor says as they check my ticket stub. I nod in understanding, butterflies and a bajillion other insects fluttering in my belly. It's either an orgy or a dance-off, I'm not sure.

I inhale shakily, gazing out the window. This is either going to go really well, or really poorly. Jo might think I'm out of my mind and tell me so.

Or maybe it'll mean something to her, the way I hope it does.

I left Jo a note telling her to meet us at our spot in Port Haven, that I'd wait for her and...

And it just occurred to me that we sort of have *two* spots in Port Haven: the lighthouse and the spot on the shore where the sound stole my undergarments.

Shit.

I rummage through my bag for my phone. I wanted this to be romantic, reminiscent of a historical romance with sweeping grand gestures and letters, but modern conveniences are indeed convenient.

Except my phone isn't in my bag.

"*Fuck*," I swear. God, it's probably on the counter, right next to that gorgeous note I left her. I'd been so distracted by my nerves and anxiety that I haven't looked at my phone once. I kind of just...took the subway to Grand Central, bought a ticket at the machine, looked at the board to find my track, and then dissociated the entire ride.

Krista, my therapist, has been encouraging me to speak kinder to and about myself. To not insult the things I do because of my ADHD.

Right now it's hard as hell.

I feel angry tears prickling at the back of my eyes, and not bullying myself feels downright impossible.

I just want everything to be perfect for Jo. To show her how hard I want to fight for her. How worthy she is of being fought for.

How am I going to do that if she can't find me?

I gather my things and step off the train onto the platform, following the small crowd of people towards the parking lot. I have no idea how I'm going to get to the beach. Maybe I'll talk to someone at the ticketing desk and see if they can call me a cab or something.

"Oops, sorry," I mumble to the human I bump into on the ramp to the parking lot.

"It's fine—Hunter?"

I do a double take when I look up and make eye contact with McKenna, Kelsey's maid of honor. Former maid of honor, I guess.

"Hey!" I look around nervously, worried she might be with Kelsey. "What brings you here?"

Her cheeks darken with a deep maroon blush. "Um..."

Then I see Barry, the bartender, leaning against a beat up car. He beams when he sees her and eagerly waves.

I squeal. "Shut *up*. That's so cute!"

She looks embarrassed. "Is it? I usually talk to Kelsey about shit like this, but my therapist and I decided it was time to go no-contact with her."

I'm surprised by that. It's not that McKenna seems spineless...but McKenna kind of seems spineless.

"They called off the wedding, if you hadn't heard."

"Yeah, she left our bridesmaid group chat and started vague tweeting." She rolls her eyes. "That's exactly what happened last time, too."

"Jo deserves better than being referred to as 'last time,'" I grumble, put off for some reason by the phrasing.

McKenna stops short, and I stop walking too, turning to face her.

"What actually happened between them? Kelsey and Jo?" She doesn't look judgmental, but genuinely curious.

"That's Jo's story to tell. Not mine."

"I liked Jo. When they were dating. And I think Kelsey may not have told the entire truth about their breakup." She says it carefully, like if she doesn't say the exact right thing, Kelsey might overhear and cause further destruction.

I wouldn't put it past her.

I'm about to ask what exactly Kelsey told her when a revelation washes over me like a wave: knowing what bullshit Kelsey said won't help me, and it certainly won't help Jo.

"I don't know what she said, and I don't want to…but the breakup wasn't initiated by Jo. I think she's happy it's over now, but it's taken this long for her to get there. It's been painful for her. Her relationship and breakup with Kelsey were the root of a lot of that pain."

McKenna doesn't say anything, simply nodding before continuing to walk. I follow her, since I'm not sure where else to go.

Barry absolutely lights up when McKenna greets him with a long kiss and honestly, it's cute as shit.

"Barry Bear, you remember Hunter? She was the photographer last weekend…"

I don't have time to gush over Barry Bear being the best pet name *ever*, because Barry's eyes narrow at me, and I know he knows I stole the tequila from Port of Call.

"Can I have a ride to the lighthouse?" I blurt out as he opens his mouth, probably to demand I pay him however much a handle of Don Julio 1942 costs.

"No," Barry glares at me, but how is someone whose nickname is *Barry Bear* supposed to be intimidating?

"Of course!" McKenna says at the same time. I shift my eyes between the two of them as McKenna's eyes widen. "Barry, be nice. We can do that thing in the car you told me you wanted to try about after we drop her off—"

I have no idea what this fantasy of Barry's is, nor do I particularly want to. Whatever it is, it's worth more to him than being angry at me for stealing. His face lights up, and he opens the back door of his car, doing an over-the-top sweeping motion with his arm. "M'Lady."

I expect the ride to be awkward and uncomfortable, but to my surprise, McKenna and Barry are *cool*. Barry tells me about what it was like being in Jo's class without an ounce of creepiness or fawning. This man officially only has eyes for McKenna, and if he hurts her, I'll make sure he's never seen again.

I ask Barry to drop me off at SandPiper Inn instead of the lighthouse so I can say hi to Audrey. Also maybe steal a free cup of coffee from the lobby since I think I forgot my meds this morning.

Audrey isn't in the lobby, but Piper is, playing at the grand piano.

"Hey, Piper," I greet her as I approach the piano.

"What are you doing here? I thought the wicked witches called off the wedding?" She doesn't look up at me, just keeps playing, and I notice she has yellow circular earplugs in her ears.

"Wicked witches?"

"Yeah, that's what Mom called them. Kelly and Betty or whatever."

"Or whatever," I agree. "Yeah, they called off the wedding, but I'm in town and wanted to pop in and say hi. Is your mom around?"

"She's at home," Piper answers easily. "But she's coming by later if you want to see her."

"I don't think I'll be able to, but tell her I say hi." Piper nods as her fingers dance over the keys.

I listen to Piper play for a few minutes. "You're talented as hell," I tell her, impressed by her skill.

"I know." Her tone isn't cocky, but neutral. Like it's a fact that she does know. "I want to go to Juilliard when I graduate, so my teacher at school suggested I take private lessons over the summer with a new teacher. My first lesson is today."

I talk to Piper a little more, before walking to the lighthouse. Somehow, I managed to forget my phone, but remembered bobby pins to pick the lock.

I close the old, wooden door behind me and look around the lighthouse. It looks different in the daylight—the paint is peeling, and honestly, I wouldn't be surprised if a ghost popped out and introduced themself to me.

Maybe it's easier to say that now because she's not with me, and there's no lingering notes of champagne in the air.

I don't bother turning on the lights, the sun streaming through the window panes lights up the place just enough for me to be able to read the words of the Tessa Dare paperback I bought at Tea-Riffic Books last weekend.

Bobby pins and random book? Got it.

Phone which is one-billion percent essential? Don't got it.

I'm only able to read for a few minutes before I hear a loud, snorting laugh I can recognize anywhere.

She's *here*.

She got the note and immediately took the subway—no, a cab because it's quicker—and now she's here.

I should...

Wait. What should I do? Do I fling open the door and throw myself into her arms? Do I let her find me? Do I—

My thoughts are interrupted by another loud laugh and a clicking noise as Jo picks the lock. She says something, voice muffled, and then there's another laugh.

I freeze, blood running cold. I don't know that deep, masculine laugh.

Jo's with a man? At our spot?

Okay, now I'm panicking.

The door opens and I suck in a breath as two figures, neither of which is Jo, fall through the doorway as they grab at each other's clothes. One of them is probably my height and curvy, untamed curls creating a halo around her head. The man whose pants her hand is currently down is tall with broad shoulders and red hair and—

Oh my god.

"Oh my *god*," I say, loud enough to break whatever horny trance Giovanna's parents are in. They have eight kids and they're behaving like they want to make a ninth. They pull apart, and their matching looks of pure horror mirror mine, I'm certain.

"Hunter?" Mrs. Quinn asks, blinking at me. "What are you doing here?"

"Waiting for your daughter. What are *you* doing here? Wait. Never mind. I don't want to know. Did you enjoy pickleball?" I nod to the racquets in Mr. Quinn's hand. I'm rambling and incoherent, but how else are you supposed to react when you get interrupted by the love of your life's parents humping each other?

"Um. Yeah." She looks anxiously at her husband, who's studying the wooden floor like it holds the meaning of life. "I think we'll be going."

"Yeah, this is awkward," I agree. "At least it wasn't one of you walking in on us again, right?"

Shut the hell *up, Hunter.*

That gets Jo's dad to look at me, eyes narrowing.

This dude *hates* my guts.

"What are you doing here, Hunter?" he asks, voice suspicious.

"I told you. I'm waiting for Jo."

"*Why* are you waiting for Jo?" he specifies.

"Because I love her and want to prove it to her. Big, extravagant gestures. Rom-coms." I want to slap myself. I keep saying way, way too much. But I can't help it. I'm nervous. "I don't expect you to understand…"

Mrs. Quinn squeezes my shoulder. "I think it's lovely."

Mr. Quinn is still silently staring at me.

"Mr. Quinn?" I say cautiously. "I, uh. I know you don't like me. And I know why."

Jo's mom looks between the two of us. "Why?"

I don't answer, but keep my eyes on his. "I know I hurt her. That she wasn't well that fall. But I love her. So much. I think some part of me always has, and has been waiting for the opportunity to try again. I was fifteen, and in the closet. I didn't have a family like yours. I haven't talked to my family since I came out, almost a year ago. Unless they change, I never will again."

His face softens slightly, enough that I know he understands what I'm saying. I hope it's enough to prove myself to him.

"She's so damn lucky to have you. All of you. You love her so much." I can't help it, my voice cracks. "My family loved me on the condition that I met their expectations, and when I couldn't do it anymore…their love ran out. I thought I was the problem, until your daughter showed me I'm unconditionally lovable. I want to give her that back. She's the best part of me." I trail off, biting my lower lip so hard I taste metallic in my mouth. I can't look at them, and their silence echoes.

"Thank you." My neck jerks up and I meet Mr. Quinn's eyes. His eyes are the same shade of green as the flecks in Jo's. "Maybe I was wrong."

It's not everything I want to hear from him, but it's a start. If he's anything like his daughter, admitting he's wrong is no easy feat, and means he's making an effort.

I nod, fighting back tears. "Yeah. Um, and I'm sorry for fucking up your post-pickleball rendezvous."

Now would be the *perfect* time for a sea witch to come and take my voice.

They both cringe, understandably, and no sea witch steals my voice, less understandably.

"Um. Okay. Well. I'm gonna just. Wait here for Jo." I hope they get the message—I got here first, so I have a claim to the spot.

Mr. Quinn scowls, and it feels like I've undone all the progress I've made with making him hate me less.

"May I suggest y'all try a shower quickie instead?" I offer helpfully.

What the *fuck* is wrong with me.

Mrs. Quinn laughs uncomfortably.

"I'm so sorry." My cheeks are burning with embarrassment. "I forgot my ADHD meds this morning, and they help my verbal filter work better. When I don't take them, it's kind of like a manual process. I have to purposely stop and think and since I'm nervous, I'm sort of..." I trail off, horrifically embarrassed.

You know what? Maybe I'll let them keep the lighthouse. Have their little midmorning bang and I'll wait outside till they're done. That way I'll be able to catch Jo if she comes, before she's traumatized.

To my surprise, Mrs. Quinn's face softens. "I was diagnosed with ADHD in the spring after Nic encouraged me to get evaluated. I've noticed such a big difference since starting medication."

My whole body relaxes. Mr. Quinn might hate me and think I'm a villainous harlot who hurt and defiled his daughter, but Mrs. Quinn gets what it's like to have a brain like mine.

"I didn't get diagnosed until my fifties," she continues. Isn't that wild?" She laughs again, and it's so much like Jo's it makes my heart ache and bloom all at once. "My two youngest both have it as well. Leo got his diagnosis in elementary school, and Izzy in middle school. But I never thought about it being something *I* could have. It's really something, learning new things about yourself throughout your entire life. I raised eight children, and thought I knew everything I needed to know about myself. Turns out I was wrong."

I feel that way, too. Like I'm still learning new things about myself and life. When I look at Mr. Quinn, I'm thrown off by his expression. Gone is the disgruntled look he was giving me, replaced by pure love and adoration directed to his wife. It makes me feel things, big things. Like maybe Jo and I will look at each other like that in thirty years as we learn more about ourselves and each other. Like maybe, not having all the answers right this very second isn't the worst thing.

"Thank you for telling me that," I say. "Sometimes it feels like I'm the only one with this experience and it feels less isolating knowing you understand."

She reaches out and squeezes my hand, immediately making me burst into tears. It's *such* a mom thing to do, and I never thought anyone would act maternally towards me again. How the hell do I explain to Mrs. Quinn that I thought I'd lost the right to a mother's reassuring hand squeeze? That even though she's not my mom, she's planting seeds in the desert of my heart—a place where I long ago accepted my mother and grandmother's disapproval.

Turns out I don't have to. She pulls me into a hug and lets me cry on her shoulder as she holds me.

I know Jo has a complicated relationship with her mom, that her mom really hurt her. I also know Jo truly believes her mom makes an effort to do better. That she understands the harm she caused, and has welcomed her other queer children with open arms, despite not doing that with Jo right away.

She's not perfect. None of us are. But I can feel how much she loves her children in the way she smooths my hair. The way she tells me over and over again that she's here. The way she doesn't try to stop my tears, but welcomes them as part of the human experience.

Finally I pull away and rub at my face. Mrs. Quinn licks her thumb and scrubs at the corner of my eye, where my mascara must have smudged.

"I'm sorry. Thank you. I'm sorry." I don't know which I want to emphasize: my gratitude for her comfort, or my remorse for having cried in the first place.

She just smiles and nods. "Of course. We'll leave you to your grand gesture. I assume it'll put Jo's beloved Mr. Bingley to shame?"

I explain my plan to them. It's outlandish and quite frankly, likely impossible. But Mrs. Quinn cries when I finish speaking, telling me she knows it'll mean a lot to Jo.

I hope she's right.

Chapter 40

Jo

Playlist: The Architect | Kacey Musgraves

"Agh!" I yelp, shocked awake by cold liquid on my face.

"Get out," Nic says from the doorway. My vision is still blurry, so she's just a short, menacing figure in the doorway with a spray bottle dangling from her index finger.

"You told me I could stay!" I screech, throwing a pillow at her and missing by three feet.

She sprays me again. "I told you you could stay whenever you needed. You don't need it anymore. Now you're avoiding. Call your therapist, and go get your girl."

I scowl at her. "I *will*, Nicoletta. Why must I do so without a full night's rest?"

"It's one P.M., bud."

I do a double take. "No it is *not*."

She lifts the spray bottle again and I duck under the covers. "Josh and I went climbing, grabbed bagels, and cleaned the entirety of the first floor while belting out the Mamma Mia soundtrack, which you somehow slept through. Now we're watering his plants and maybe I want my partner to bend me over our bed. So get the fuck out."

"Gross."

"What? It's Saturday, and you have to go kiss that pretty girlfriend of yours."

"We didn't put a label on it," I mumble, still cowering beneath the blankets. "We never got to talk about it."

"Too busy talking with your bodies," she says sagely.

"What if she decides she doesn't want me?" I surprise myself by saying my fear out loud.

"Jo." Nic's feet pitter-patter on the floor as she walks across the room, the mattress sinking down when she sits on the edge. "She wants you."

"She did. Or maybe she still does, in the present. But what if one day, she decides it's too much...the depression, the diabetes...what if she decides I'm not worth it and leaves?"

"What if she decides you *are* worth it and stays?" Nic's voice is so soft, I can't help but peer out from beneath the comforter to make sure it's really her.

"I think when someone loves you, they don't see the things you perceive as flaws the same way as you. You aren't your lows. Not your low moods, or low blood sugar. You're you, and I think she knows that sometimes your blood sugar might be wonky or you might be depressed. But that doesn't mean you're not worth loving. I know that's not how it's been for you, but not everyone will be like Kelsey. The right person will be different. The right person will be patient, and kind, and see and love the real you when you can't."

"Josephine," Josh says out of nowhere.

Nic and I both jump because this man is six foot something and somehow was able to sneak up on us.

"I know you hated me when I went radio silent on Nic when my grandma was sick." He sits next to Nic on the mattress, taking her free hand in his. "You remind me of myself, you know."

I gasp in horror. "You take that back!"

He doesn't. "I ran, too. I tried to push Nic away and for some reason, your menace of a sister didn't budge."

She beams up at him, and I fight the urge to gag. "Because I knew you were worth staying for."

His returning smile is crooked. "Yeah, but I didn't think that."

I groan. "Okay, okay, I get it. That's enough life lessons from you two. I'll leave."

"Jo." Josh's tone is suddenly serious. "The hardest part of being loved is accepting you deserve it when you feel like you don't. But it's worth it. Letting Nic love me is the most difficult, best decision I've ever made."

I swallow hard as he presses his lips to Nic's temple. Could it be that straightforward? Choosing to allow myself to receive the love Hunter wants to give me?

"How did you know you weren't going to hurt her again?" I ask.

"I didn't. I don't. I go to therapy every week to process my trauma. She's there after and supports me while I learn to prioritize my mental health for the first time. Because I'm responsible for that, and she deserves a me who is able to receive her love."

She deserves a me who is able to receive her love.

He's right. My sister deserves that, and so does Hunter. So does Josh, and so do I.

Suddenly, I know what I need to do.

"I have to go," I say, tossing off the blankets.

"Hell yeah, you do!" Nic cheers, pumping her fists in the air. "Go get your girl!"

I leap out of bed, more energized than I've felt...ever. Hunter's home. At *our* home with *our* bearded dragon listening to *our* records and trusting that I'll come back to her today.

"I love you. Both of you," I say, voice thick.

They both beam at me. "We love you," Josh says. "I'm not even scared of you anymore."

I raise a brow.

"Okay, I'm still scared of you, but only like, a little," he amends.

"Good." I playfully punch his shoulder.

I get dressed as fast as I can and make a run for the nearest subway station to catch a train to midtown.I want to be ready to receive Hunter's love, because her love is precious and deserves to be fully received. To do that, I have to treat myself like I'm someone who deserves her love, who deserves all she's hoped for.

Which is why, instead of unlocking my apartment door, I'm swiping my badge and striding into Coffey & Co, where I know Becky will be in her office, just like she is every Saturday afternoon.

I'll make the changes I need to be ready to receive Hunter's love.

Chapter 41

Hunter

Playlist: Love Story (Taylor's Version) | Taylor Swift

Today has been bizarre. An undetermined amount of time after Jo's parents left—probably to continue their post-pickleball tryst elsewhere—there's a knock at the door. I know it can't be Jo, since she knows how to pick the lock. I don't know who else to expect, but I certainly wasn't expecting to see her brother.

"What are you doing here?" I ask Ren, blinking up at him in surprise.

He holds up a Spiderman lunchbox. "Bringing supplies for the grand gesture, of course. Can I come in?"

I shrug. "Sure. But I am planning on passionately making out with your sister as soon as she gets here."

"I will make myself scarce. Not to worry." I close the door behind him as he steps into the lighthouse and looks around. "Damn, I've never been *in* the lighthouse."

"The only reason I'm here is because your sister is a criminal." I pause a beat. "Also, so are your parents."

"Yeah, I was wondering why they knew you were in here."

He hands me the lunchbox and I unzip it. There are a few juice boxes, packages of apple slices, and Lunchables packed into it.

"Do you think I'm five?" I ask him, trying to swallow the lump in my throat.

"I panicked and had no idea what you like to eat so you're getting what I keep in my mini-fridge at school."

"Why?"

"Because sometimes kids forget lunch, or don't have money to buy it or have low blood sugar or…"

"No, why'd you bring this to me?" I interrupt.

"My dad texted me and said you were camping out here and waiting for Jo. He asked me to bring food."

Mr. Quinn asked Ren tocheck on me? "Thank you, and tell your dad I said thank you, too," I say, blinking back tears.

He squeezes my shoulder and smiles. "You're good people, Hunter. I never thought I'd be happy at the prospect of gaining another sister, but here we are."

Obviously, I'm a blubbering mess as I hug him.

He breaks the hug first, an apologetic look on his face as he readjusts his baseball cap over his curls. "I have a private lesson in a few minutes at SandPiper Inn, but if you need anything, go to my parents'. I'll try to check in on you again, but hopefully Jo shows up and I won't have to."

"Don't text her or anything," I plead. "This needs to be between us."

After Ren leaves, I pull out the historical romance I brought with me. This one promises a road trip between a rake and a wallflower, and son of a gun, I'm an easy woman to please. Give me a rake simping over a wallflower and I'm content.

Throughout the day, I'm visited by the rest of the local Quinns. Millie stops by with Poppy next, handing me a package of adult diapers. She tells me she has no idea if there's a bathroom in the lighthouse, which I also hadn't considered.

Kat stops by a little while later, with a twelve pack of water bottles and two boxes of Saltines. It feels hyper-specific, but I'm not gonna complain.

Today, she seems like the Kat I remember from that summer, instead of the hurt woman I saw at Sunday dinner. She's aloof and composed, but now I can see the crack in her facade. She's trying to convince herself just as much as her family, that she's happy, in a perfect marriage, and has no reason to be hurt.

I thank her for coming and ask if I can hug her. I'm surprised when she consents, but as soon as we let each other go, she leaves without a word.

Izzy stops by with her best friend, Finn, right after. Unlike her eldest sister, Izzy is a chatterbox, telling me all about how she's working as a lifeguard at the community pool while home from college, and Finn's her chauffeur. She brought sparklers, telling me that while my plan is lovely, it needed more sparkle. I love her immediately.

In contrast, Finn is silent. He's tall—maybe a full foot taller than Izzy—and lean, with light russet brown hair and wire-rimmed glasses. I ask him about himself and his eyes widen like a deer caught in the headlights as he stammers in response. Izzy squeezes his hand, like she knows how he feels which is so fucking adorable I want to throw up.

As the sun starts to set, Leo and his girlfriend, Stella, are the last to pop in.

"We got the bubbly!" Leo whoops, handing me a bottle of prosecco.

I eye him suspiciously. "How old are you again?"

He scowls and snatches it back. "If you're gonna be a snitch, you're not getting the goods."

Stella looks at the stairs, an amused expression on her face. "You know, I thought this was just mine and Leo's spot."

I grab back the bottle, able to do so when Leo is distracted by his girlfriend. "You and the rest of this goddamn family."

"Is it Kat and Steve? I always kinda hoped they were secretly freaky," Stella says way too excitedly about her boyfriend's sister and brother-in-law.

"Yeah, it's his parents," I inform her flatly.

Leo sputters as Stella howls with laughter, her head thrown back.

Finally I'm alone again, and a sinking feeling settles in my chest. It's almost dark, meaning it's probably close to eight, and she's not here.

She's not here.

I stumble to the stairs, lowering my trembling body to sit. This is decidedly less fun than the last time I was here.

What if she's not coming? What if this is her answer? What if it's too much? What if...

There's a few clicks as the lock is picked yet again. This time, I know it's not her.

Despite knowing not to expect Jo, I'm still surprised when it's her father.

"Ah, Leo said you were still here," Mr Quinn says, gently closing the door behind him.

"Yep." I pop the p, annoyed by his appearance. "I told you I was waiting for her. However long it took." I don't tell him how I'd snuck up to the SandPiper Inn a few times to utilize their restroom in the lobby, because as effective the diapers Millie brought would have been, I was able to make it there and back within ten minutes. Giovanna would have waited ten minutes for me.

Wouldn't she?

He looks around. "I don't think you should be out here alone." I can tell he's choosing his words carefully, and that only makes me sadder she hasn't come yet. I wish I could prove to him that Jo and I care about each other as much as we do. As much as I hope she still cares for me.

"No offense, Mr. Quinn, but I'm really tired of caring about what you think about me or what I do."

He arches a brow in question, but his eyes are patient.

"Why don't you like me? Why can't you accept that I'm not a closeted fifteen year old spending the summer with her homophobic grandparents anymore?" Tears are in my eyes, again, but I'm so tired of trying to prove myself.

"Maybe she's not coming, and you know what? I'll respect whatever she chooses. But it'll be her choice, not mine. Because I love Giovanna more than I knew I was capable of loving anything and...and she chooses me. Or at least, she chose me." My voice trails off, the heartbreak too big to continue.

"Do you like grilled cheese?"

I blink at him through my tears. Of all the things I thought he might say in response, this didn't cross my mind.

"What?"

"Do you like grilled cheese?" He says it like asking about my sandwich preferences makes any sense in this context.

"Yes?"

"My kids say I make the best grilled cheese. Aria made home-made tomato soup last night and we have leftovers. Come home and eat, Hunter."

"I can't give up on her," I manage to choke out. "I can't...she deserves..."

"Hunter." His voice is gentle and he walks further into the lighthouse until he's in front of me, placing his hand on my shoulder. "You're not giving up on her. I can call her right now so you can talk to her. Or, if you want to continue with the grand gesture...you can keep trusting she'll come back to you. Joey knows to come home to find what she needs."

"Why are you being nice when you hate me?"

"I don't hate you."

"You don't like me."

Mr. Quinn is quiet for a moment before speaking again. "What do you know about that fall?"

"Jo told me some things."

"She was completely different after that summer you spent together. She completely withdrew and...I didn't recognize her. At the time I thought it was maybe because she liked girls. They used to tell us that, you know? That queer people had higher tendencies of mental illness because queerness itself was classified as a mental illness. I know that's not true now, but at the time all I knew was that I didn't know my daughter anymore. And...you were a scapegoat."

"I was a kid."

"Yeah. Pathetic isn't it?" His laugh is hollow, and I turn my head to look at him. Jo looks *so* much like her mom, but she has Mr. Quinn's nose and lips, and the shade of his green green eyes is identical to the flecks of green in hers. "I couldn't face the truth, so I made up an alternative one that was easier to stomach."

"What was the truth?" I ask.

"The truth is that Giovanna is gay and has major depressive disorder. That maybe, she would have still had that experience, even if you'd never met, even if she was straight. That my wife and I didn't give Jo a safe place to be herself. That we were bad parents. *I* was a bad father."

I don't know what to say. Because yeah, I've certainly thought it, but I never expected anyone to acknowledge it.

"I don't think you're a bad father." I'm careful not to blow smoke up his ass or say bullshit to make him feel better. He was real with me, and I want to be real with him. "I think maybe you didn't know exactly *how* to give Jo a safe space. But I hope you know that the way she talks about you, even during that time, is with love and admiration. She knows you did the best you could, even though you hurt her. She sees the work you've done to be a better parent to her and your other kids."

He squeezes my shoulder again. "Thank you. I want you to know I never hated you...I hated *myself*. You being back in Joey's life was a constant reminder of that failure. It's not an excuse, but I'm so sorry I wasn't kinder to you, and didn't give you a chance."

Neither of us says anything more. I want to forgive him, but if I'm being completely honest with myself, I don't know if I'm ready to do that yet. I'm still hurt, and while I see him and his feelings toward me in a new way, I'm not ready to offer him forgiveness.

My stomach rumbles loudly during my self-reflection and I scowl down at it, Mr. Quinn chuckling softly beside me.

"So. Grilled cheese?"

I look around the lighthouse one last time, stomach sinking as I imagine Jo walking in and not seeing me.

"I'll text her, so she'll know you're waiting at the house."

I exhale. "She's found her way back to me before...maybe you're right. Maybe she'll do it again."

Mr. Quinn gets to his feet with a groan. "Deal." He reaches a hand out, and I take it, hoisting myself to my feet. By taking his hand, it feels like I've accepted his apology. I hope one day, I'll feel ready to offer him my forgiveness as generously as he offered me grilled cheese. Because I love the woman he imperfectly raised, and unlike my own family, he's willing to admit his wrongs and do better.

It feels like a new beginning.

Twenty minutes later, I'm sitting at the island in the Quinns' kitchen as Mrs. Quinn worries over me like I'm back from war.

"You should have gotten her sooner, Seanny," she complains, as Mr. Quinn flips the grilled cheese on the stovetop. He doesn't answer, but shakes his head like he thinks it would have been useless to try to get me to come back to the house sooner. He's right.

He slides the sandwich onto a plate and ladles some soup into a bowl from the saucepan on another burner.

"Grilled cheese, extra crispy," he says, placing the food in front of me. He meets my eyes and smiles.

I smile back, and it feels like another part of my heart is fused back to where it's supposed to be. All by Jo's dad's smile and the apron he wears, proudly declaring that he's the proud father of a smartass gay daughter in rainbow lettering.

He notices me staring at the apron and shakes his head. "Joey got this for me for Father's Day years ago. It's dated now, I have multiple smartass gay daughters."

I dip the sandwich into the soup, and take a bite. "Holy shit. This is the best grilled cheese I've ever had."

His grin grows. "The secret is to put mayonnaise on the outside of the bread. Old family recipe."

Mrs. Quinn scoffs and rolls her eyes. "Oh, hush. You saw it on TikTok. But the soup is even better, right?" she says with a wink, squeezing my shoulder in a way I think should make me miss my mom. It doesn't. It makes me miss Jo, miss everything we could have—

"Mom? Dad?" The voice I've been waiting all day for carries through the house, followed by the slam of a closing door. My heart sinks when I realize her voice is shaking.

She's crying.

"Sean. Go," Mrs. Quinn hisses, reaching over her husband to turn the stovetop off before the two of them scurry out of the kitchen.

I slowly stand from the barstool, legs feeling as wobbly and unsteady as a newborn giraffe's as Jo's footsteps get closer.

Chapter 42

Jo

Earlier that Day

Playlist: Good Luck, Babe | Chappell Roan

"Jo." Becky is surprised when I enter her office. "What are you doing here?"

I take a deep breath, trying not to panic. "Hi, Becky. I'm here to give you an answer."

A slow, knowing smile spreads across her face. "Fantastic. I'll have the paperwork drawn up for Monday…"

"Thank you for the offer, but I'm declining. In fact, I quit. Effective immediately."

She freezes, eyes darting to me. "Excuse me?"

"I quit. I can't do this anymore." In a way, I feel bad for Becky. Her engagement and career plans falling apart in one week has to suck.

She scoffs. "Jo, come on. Don't be hasty..."

"I'm not, but maybe I should have been. Maybe I should have hastily refused to plan your wedding, should have hastily quit when the woman I love and I were mistreated. Then we wouldn't be here."

She's silent as she stares at me. Finally, she blinks and shakes her head. She's pissed. I can tell. I want to apologize, but I refuse to do that. Not when I have nothing to apologize for. I slide my badge across her desk, her eyes following the card's movement. "I'm going to clean out my office and get out of here."

She's silent, and I take my leave, knowing that despite the doubts in my mind, the fear about money and finding another job, I'm finally loving myself enough to accept Hunter's love.

Jo: hi hun

Jo: i had to run to the office, but i'm coming home.

Jo: i love you so much

Jo: thank you for waiting.

Delivered.

Dolly's the only one home when I get back to the apartment, but I immediately spot Hunter's phone on the counter. I pick it up and reveal a folded piece of paper with my name beneath it. My stomach flip flops, reminded of another note that had been left for me on my dresser over a year ago. But this one is written in pink ink and has little hearts doodled around my name. Still, I can't stop my hands from shaking when I unfold the paper.

> *My Giovanna,*
> *You're worth waiting for and fighting for and taking chances on, despite what anyone's told or shown you. Meet me at our spot in Port Haven. I'm waiting for you.*
> *Your Hun*

My hands continue to shake as I fold it again. Our spot. Hunter's waiting for me at the lighthouse. I have no idea why, but I don't care. I don't need to know why she's not here and in Port Haven instead. I don't need to know what I'm going to do next for work, or what happens when my savings account is drained. I know I have her, and I have me, and right now, that's enough.

I walk determinedly to the door, flinging it open and then reeling back when a short, blonde woman stands in front of it, her fist raised like she was about to knock.

"Jo." Kelsey's eyes are red-rimmed and puffy, her lower lip trembling as her eyes meet mine. "Can we talk?"

"No." I surprise myself at how easily it comes out, saying no to her. *Finally.*

She's surprised by it, too, eyes widening before they fill with tears. "Please, Jo. I know I hurt you, I fucked up. I never should have left you. I still love you, please…"

I laugh. Not cruelly, or out of amusement, but from complete and utter shock. "No, you fucking don't."

"Yes, I do. Seeing you with Hunter…"

"Don't you *dare* say her name," I hiss, fists clenching at my side. "The only thing you love is having control over me, berating me, and making me feel small and unworthy."

I can tell by her face that Kelsey truly expected me to invite her into the apartment, maybe take her back right then and there. She certainly didn't expect me to say no.

"You won't even hear me out?" Her sadness transitions to anger, and her eyes flash at me.

"No," I say simply. "I've moved on. Even if you did love me anymore, which you *don't*, I don't love you. I love Hunter. Can you move so I can lock the door?"

Kelsey doesn't budge. "This isn't fair."

I shoulder her out of my way so I can shut and lock the door before pocketing the key. "Yeah, well. You expected the impossible and now you're surprised when it is indeed impossible. That's not unfair. That's life."

With that, I turn and walk away, not looking back at her once.

I'm able to get to Grand Central and catch a train that's about to leave in under an hour somehow. Doing so means I have to purchase my ticket aboard the train. When the conductor comes around and I attempt to buy a ticket, I realize why I shouldn't have rushed.

"This is the express train, ma'am," they tell me when I say I'm going to Port Haven. "Our only stops today are Stamford and New Haven."

I guess in my rush through Grand Central, I'd found the soonest northbound Metro North and jumped on without checking to see if it stopped at Port Haven. I've lived in the city for almost a decade, and this is a first.

"Um. I'll get off at Stamford and catch the next train to Port Haven," I mumble.

Before the train gets to Stamford, I check the app and see that there's a train going to Port Haven fifteen or so minutes after I'm due to arrive.

I can do this. I'll make it to the lighthouse and I'll kiss Hunter and tell her all about how I cut ties with Becky and told Kelsey off and she'll be so proud and...

"Attention, Metro North passengers," the overhead speaker announces. "The next northbound train has been delayed by an hour due to a derailment in Harlem. We apologize for the inconvenience."

Of course the train is delayed, because why wouldn't everything that could go wrong go wrong? That would just be boring.

I open a ridesharing app on my phone, and physically recoil when I see the price and amount of time it would take to get to Port Haven. The normally forty-five minute ride is apparently two hours and almost a hundred dollars. After some quick Googling, I'm able to see that both major highways are completely backed up due to construction.

Absolutely on brand for this damn state.

I shuffle to a bench and plop down.

Hunter said she'd wait for me. I just have to hope that she meant that through transportation mishaps, too.

I exhale gratefully as I *finally* step onto the Port Haven train station platform. The sun has almost completely set and god, I'd give anything to be on the beach, holding Hunter and watching the sun dip beneath the waves.

Instead I'm calling my brother.

"So, how's happily ever treating you?" Ren asks when he answers the phone.

"What are you talking about? I need you to pick me up at the train station."

He's silent for a moment. "Wait, you're at the train station? Did you *just* get in?"

"Yes, Lorenzo," I say exasperatedly. "Stop asking questions."

Ren mutters to himself, but I blessedly hear the jingling of his keys.

Ten minutes later, I'm in the passenger seat while he drives to the lighthouse.

"I'm going to wait out here," he calls out the window as I run to the lighthouse. I dismissively wave a hand at him.

"Hun?" I bang on the door. There's no immediate answer, so I knock again. "Hun, I'm here."

Still no answer.

I dig through my bag, finding a single bobby pin at the bottom and hurriedly inserting it into the lock.

I push the door open when I hear the tell-tale click, and my heart sinks to my stomach.

The lighthouse is empty, I can feel it. I turn on the light, just to check.

She's not here.

"*Fuck*," I curse, shoving my hand into my pocket and pulling out the note she'd left on the counter. My eyes scan her writing again, desperately searching for an answer. She said she'd be at our new spot, which made me think of the lighthouse, but maybe she meant the spot on the beach?

I run back to Ren's car and he rolls down the window, his phone in his hand. "Jo..."

"She's not here. I think she might be on the beach, I'm going to check there."

He looks down at his phone and then back up at me. "Please be careful. If you can't find her, go home."

I roll my eyes. "Nothing's gonna happen."

"Just promise me that if you don't find Hunter at the beach, you'll go to Mom and Dad's."

Why are siblings so annoying? "Fine," I agree, just to get him off my ass.

Hunter isn't on the beach near the rectory, either. My heart is pounding in my chest as I look around for footprints, for anything to show me she was here. Maybe she meant the inn?

I sink to the ground, because I know she didn't mean the inn, and I know she didn't mean the beach. She meant the lighthouse, but I was too late.

A sob escapes my throat and I curl into myself, weeping into my hands. This cry is simultaneously relief and pain. Stabbing feelings in my chest, and a lightening of the weight I've carried since the breakup. It's the first time I've cried since Kelsey moved out, and in a way that feels important. Like instead of being numb, I'm feeling again. But the only person who'd understand why this means something isn't here.

I don't know how long I cry on the beach for, but eventually I'm able to catch my breath. I shakily force myself to stand and walk to my parents'. I promised Ren that's what I'd do, after all.

I'm so fucking tired by the time I get to the house. It's not a long walk, just a few blocks, but I guess crying for the first time in over a year really takes all of a girl's energy.

I unlock the front door and walk in. "Mom? Dad?" I wince at how my voice cracks, how my eyes fill with fresh tears.

I follow the sound of voices in the kitchen, furiously scrubbing at my eyes, trying to get myself together so Mom and Dad don't worry too much. So I can make this hurt ache less.

For the second time today, I'm surprised by a short blonde woman as I walk into the kitchen.

But this time it's the exact short blonde woman I want to see.

That Summer
Hunter

"Almost...there," I grunt, pulling the zipper on my suitcase with all of my might. Finally, I get the last inch zipped up. The zipper is at risk of breaking, sure, but everything is contained. My entire summer packed away in my pink suitcase.

I sigh and sit back on my heels, my stomach churning. My grandparents are taking me to the airport in a few hours, and I'll be leaving Port Haven and the rest of the summer behind.

Let's be honest, it's hurting me to leave Giovanna behind. I want her to come with me, or for me to stay here. To be able to hold her hand and kiss her cheek in the school hallway.

To go through autumn, winter, and spring with her, because I'm certain she's just as amazing in every season.

And maybe I will. I think about all the pictures I'd taken of us throughout the summer, pictures of milkshake mustaches and goofy grins. Pictures of laughter and kisses and joy. Giovanna gave me joy.

I'm meeting her at the sea wall to say goodbye. It can't be more than a hug, since it's in public and during the middle of the day, but it doesn't feel right to end the summer anywhere else. I slide on my flip flops and jog down the stairs, coming to a sudden stop when I hear my grandparents' voices.

"She's a homosexual and they're allowing her to teach at the elementary school," PawPaw complains from the kitchen.

"See, this is what's wrong with this country!" MawMaw responds. I can hear the water running, and it sounds like she's doing the dishes. "They just let that deviance around children!"

"That's what they want. They want our children to be desensitized to immorality and evil. That's all this is. Evil. Pure evil."

My body is shaking, my head swimming. I don't know who they're talking about beyond that they must teach at the elementary school, but evil? For simply existing as you are and wanting to teach? I want to interrupt them, to tell them that Giovanna is a lesbian, and that doesn't impact her ability to do anything. She's just Giovanna.

But I can't say that. I can't out her, especially not to my grandparents.

And that's when it hits me.

They can never, ever know about Giovanna and I. They can never know how much I love kissing her, touching her. They can never know that being with her is the closest I've felt to god.

"Did you hear the Harrisons' grandson is engaged to a man, too?" MawMaw says.

"It's such a shame," PawPaw responds, turning the sink off. "I remember when he would visit, he seemed like a good kid. I don't understand why he's acting out on those urges."

"There are camps and therapies that are supposed to help, too," MawMaw supplies. "The Harrisons actually sent him to one, but he refused treatment despite them threatening to take him out of their will. He chose a life of sin over his own flesh and blood."

It takes me longer than it should to realize I'm crying. Big, fat tears streaming down my face.

They will never understand.

Finally I find the strength to move, striding out the front door and letting it slam behind me. I'll get a discussion later about being polite, etcetera, etcetera. And I'll apologize and try to be good enough for them. Quiet enough. Not gay enough.

I get to the sea wall first, and climb up, pulling my legs to my chest and resting my chin on my knees as I stare at the sound.

MawMaw and PawPaw asked me for years to spend the summer with them, and I always declined because...well. They're MawMaw and PawPaw. This summer, after getting caught drinking at a party and humiliating my parents' good name, Mom and Dad booked my flights. I was planning my escape when I met Giovanna.

I don't know who I am yet, but I sure know who I'm not. I'm not quiet, or demure. I'm not well-mannered or ladylike.

I'm not straight.

But I have to do all of those things, because what happens if I'm not? If they find out I like kissing girls when it's something they condemn so strongly? If I'm not the daughter they worked so hard to create?

I don't know what happens, and I'm scared. I'm scared I'll get kicked out, that I won't have anywhere to go. And with MawMaw and PawPaw being friends with people like the Harrisons, who cut their own grandson out completely...how do I know they won't do that to me? I don't.

"Hey, Hun." I jump when I hear Giovanna behind me. I look at her over my shoulder and try to smile, but the act of doing so is physically painful. Her brow furrows in concern when she notices, and she climbs up onto the sea wall next to me. "What's wrong?" she asks gently, wrapping her arm around my shoulder. It's platonic enough that it won't get us in trouble, but I violently jerk away from her touch anyway.

I don't want to hurt her, but we can't keep talking. We have to end this. We'd already talked about continuing long distance after the summer, but it's not safe for either of us.

"What's going on?" she asks, and I can hear the nerves in her voice. I hate it.

"I...I can't do this anymore," I force myself to say. "Now that summer's over, we have to leave this in the past."

Somehow, I feel her heart crumbling in her chest.

Or maybe it's just mine.

"I thought...I thought you wanted to stay in contact and..."

I shake my head vehemently, trying to match my breath to the waves as they crash on the shore. "No, I don't want that. This was fun, but..."

"But what? Where is this coming from?" Her voice is shaking and I want to calm it, to steady it, to make it all better. "You were saying something completely different literally yesterday *and now you're just closing the door on us?"*

"Summer's over, Giovanna. This was fun, I wanted to mess around with a girl, soI did. But let's face it. I'm not you. I'm not gay. I have a life to go back to, one that doesn't include kissing girls."

I hate every word coming out of my mouth, but I know this is the only way to keep us both safe. She'll never want to talk to me again, and as much as I don't want this...I know it's the right thing to do.

"Wow," she finally says. I can't look at her. "I...wow. Okay. Um, have fun being perfect and straight and kissing perfect and straight boys, Hunter. You really fooled me, you know. I thought you were different."

Hot tears sting in my eyes as Giovanna leaves. I want to look back at her, to run after her and beg for forgiveness.

Instead, I apologize to the universe, pray to god, if he's real, that maybe, if I get it right one day, she'll come back to me.

Chapter 43

Jo

Playlist: To Hell & Back | Maren Morris

"Hun," I sob, completely breaking down at the sight of her.

She stares at me, eyes narrowing. "Why are you crying?"

I answer with another sob, lifting a shaking hand to my mouth. She's here. Hunter's here.

She closes the distance between us, wrapping her arms around me and pulling me into her.

"I thought you'd given up," I cry into her hair. "I thought I'd lost you again."

"I'm never giving up, Giovanna. Never, ever."

"I slept till one and then Josh and Nic had to kick me out because they said I was hiding again and then I went and quit and then I went to the apartment and found your note and then Kelsey was there and then I took the wrong train..."

She pulls away, blue eyes wide. "Wait, *what*? You quit? Kelsey? Wrong train?"

"I was supposed to be here hours ago," I bemoan. "But I got on the express train that doesn't stop in Port Haven, so I got off in Stamford and then the next train was so damned delayed, and I asked Ren to give me a ride to the lighthouse..."

"Okay, that explains why you're just getting here now. Please go back, though. What do you mean you quit?"

I inhale shakily. "Nic and Josh said some things..." I pause, looking over my shoulder. "Where are my parents?"

"They skedaddled when you came into the house. Why?"

"And they aren't eavesdropping?" I ask loudly, earning some shuffling noises just outside the kitchen in return. I scoff and roll my eyes as Hunter giggles.

I turn back to her and take her hands in mine. "I quit. Josh was telling me how the hardest part of love is accepting that you're deserving of love when you don't feel like you are, and showing yourself love.

"I don't know why...but that made everything so clear. I quit my job, honey. I quit because it made me miserable and kept me from being able to be fully loved by you."

Hunter's eyes search mine. "Oh my god, Jo," she whispers. For a hot minute, I think she's going to express her disapproval. But then her arms are around my neck and she's pulling me down for a hug. "You fucking did it."

After a few moments, she breaks the hug and takes a step back. "I did something too. Something to show you that I want you. That I'm one-hundred percent, all in with you. But first, what did you say about Kelsey?"

"She came to the apartment as I was leaving."

Hunter pulls away, and she forces a smile. I want to melt. She's so fucking cute when she's fighting the urge to murder my ex.

"I refused to hear her out," I continue, clasping her hand in mine. "Because what's the point? She's not a part of my future, nor my present. She had the audacity to claim she still loves me, and god, Hun. You'd have been so proud. I told her she didn't love me and left."

Hunter bursts into tears, throwing herself into my arms as I pick her up off the ground. I hold her tight to me. "Now that I know what love's supposed to be like, I know without a doubt that whatever Kelsey feels for me, it's not love."

She pulls away from me, cupping my face in her hands. "I do, you know. Love you. " Her eyes shine with tears. Happy, grateful tears, I know, because they're mirrored in mine.

"I do know. It's kind of the only thing I know for certain right now. I have no idea what comes next...but I know whatever it is, it's with you."

She nods frantically, pressing her lips to mine. It's barely been a day, and I've missed her so damn much.

"How do you feel about talking about what comes next?" Hunter asks after breaking the kiss. "I have something to show you. You quit your job to show me you believe in us, and I spent the night on my computer doing the same."

I lower her to the floor and she reaches into her bag, pulling out a file folder. She places it on the counter and opens it. The first thing I see are at least a dozen pictures. My breath catches in my throat as I lift them.

"Are these..."

"From that summer? Yeah." Hunter wraps her arm around my waist and rests her head against my shoulder. "I've kept them in a box under my bed, but I don't want to hide them anymore."

It's hard to breathe as I flip through the selfies of fifteen-year-old Hunter and I, pictures of us on the beach, drunk and young and laughing. The picture I took of her outside the tattoo studio and selfies of us kissing. Then there are the solo pictures of me. Me on the beach, feet in the water and insulin pump clipped to my bathing suit. Me in bed asleep, close enough that you can see the individual hairs of my lashes. Me from behind, watching the sunset. A selfie of Hunter with her head in my lap.

"You're the reason I fell in love with capturing the world. Capturing love. Joy." Hunter's voice sounds far away. "You were my first subject."

"You've always seen the potential in me." My voice is shaky, disbelieving.

"No." She turns and presses her lips to my shoulder. "I've always just seen you as you are. I never saw you for what you could be, and thank god for that, because you were the best surprise ever."

I place the pictures on the island, my vision blurring as I read the heading of a document in the file folder.

Giovanna & Hunter's Port Haven Event Coordinating Business Plan by Hunter Lillian Cleary.

"What's this?" I manage to croak out.

"Is the heading unclear?" She leans over and scans it. "Oh. It's a bit rambly. I titled it at like seven this morning."

"You can't be serious." I flip through the papers, flip through budgets, rental properties, predictions, and graphs. I point to a figure on the paper. "I won't have that money anymore. Not since the wedding was canceled. Also, I no longer have an income."

"That figure is what you and I are making from Kelsey and Becky combined. If we join forces, we could do it. We'd have to find a few investors, but we'd be able to foot most of it. You could open your own business." She squeezes my hand.

I stare in shock at the paper, not quite believing what I see, what I hear. "Hunter, no. I can't let you do this."

"Shut up, Giovanna. I *want* to do this. It was fun getting to use my degree for the first time in years. You have the vision and experience, and I have the business savvy. We could do this. We might have to live in a shoebox for a while, but..." she looks up at me, eyes so hopeful. "I can still take pictures, and you're home for me. Your happy is my happy. Your dream is my dream. And *our* dream is possible."

I cry again and goddammit, when will I stop? "It's risky," I whisper as she pulls me into her arms again. "Most businesses fail..."

"You think I don't know the statistics? I have a business degree from Yale, Giovanna. *Yale.* I know the statistics, and you know what? I still think it's worth the risk. *We're* worth the risk. I want to jump off the ledge with you, ride the mechanical bull with you, steal bottles of tequila with you.

"I love you, Giovanna Quinn. I loved you when I was fifteen, but that love was nothing compared to the love that's grown in the most unlikely of conditions. And still, our love has a lot more growing to do."

"I love you, Hunter Cleary," I whisper. I'll never get sick of telling her. "I love your hope and optimism and your brain. I love how you believe in me, and make me want to believe in me, too. I love that you look at the world not with fear, but with determination. I love how you waited for me to be ready to be loved, to return your love. I'm ready now."

Her eyes sparkle, and she presses her lips to mine for a moment before speaking. "Then let's fucking jump, baby."

Chapter 44

Hunter

Three Months Later

Playlist: Jump Then Fall (Taylor's Version) | Taylor Swift

Momma Quinn: <picture> Hi sweetheart! Poppa Sean and I are ready to go and can't wait to see what you have in store for tonight.

Momma Quinn: We're so proud of you both. <heart emoji>

Hunter: you both look fabulous! we love you and can't wait to see you. <heart emoji>

"Is everything ready?" Jo asks anxiously, rearranging the champagne flutes for the sixth time.

I smile at her. "Of course it is. You planned it."

She attempts and fails to fight back a smile. She turns her head and captures my lips with hers. It's so sweet, but she and I both know she's trying to hide that damn smile of hers.

"I love you. I'm so proud of you," I murmur against her mouth.

These eight words are the chorus of our life: I love you. I'm so proud of you.

We say it to each other multiple times a day, and it has yet to lose any of its power.

"Ready, baby?" I ask, pulling away and fixing her collar. Audrey just enters the room, the same room where a few months ago, Jo realized the meaning behind my favorite song. Audrey's auburn hair is perfectly curled, and there's a heart-shaped bi flag pin on her lapel.

"Never," Giovanna answers. "But you'll hold my hand?"

"Always."

Tonight, we're launching Lillian Theresa, LLC, mine and Jo's event planning and coordination firm. The past three months have been unbelievably hectic as we packed up our lives in Brooklyn and moved into a tiny studio in Port Haven. Sean and Aria are storing most of our shit in their basement, but it still somehow feels like we have everything we need in our cramped space: Giovanna, Dolly Parton, my vinyl and magnet collections, and as many mass market historical romances we could fit on our one bookshelf. Every night, after hours of work, Giovanna insists we take twenty minutes and dance to a record of her choice.

"It's five o'clock somewhere," she declares on a daily basis, flipping through the vinyls stacked haphazardly on the floor next to the record player. "And since it's five o'clock in Port Haven, we are legally required to dance."

And dance we do. To Fleetwood Mac, Willie Nelson, Dolly Parton, Taylor Swift, Olivia Rodrigo, and so many others. It's my favorite part of the day. Not just because we dance and Giovanna holds me, but because she always sings along. She always smiles. Because it's *her* favorite part of the day.

When we told Audrey about our plans for Lillian Theresa, she'd generously offered to let us use an empty office in SandPiper Inn while we launched. We signed a lease on our own office space this week because of all the support our people have given.

The room steadily fills up, music playing in the background. I can tell Giovanna's taken aback by the sheer amount of people here, but I'm not. For the most part, we've been welcomed with open arms to Port Haven. Except for the twenty-eight people who signed a petition saying that allowing a queer oriented and owned business to open in Port Haven would be celebrating grievous sin. The twenty-eight people identified themselves as current or former parishioners of Our Lady of Hope. Including my grandparents.

After I saw the letter, Giovanna held me as I cried into her arms. I've come a long way since I went no-contact with my family, but it still felt like a knife to the heart. And I didn't understand *why* it still hurt.

"Loss of love isn't something that just stops hurting," she told me as I got snot on her favorite jumpsuit. "It's okay that it still hurts. It's okay if it always hurts. The presence of pain is not the absence of healing."

In a way, that's been both of our journeys—learning to live with pain and hurt, letting it coexist with hope and love. Not letting it hold us back from living.

"It's so beautiful, Giovanna," I whisper, taking everything in. It's a fairytale, a dream come true. At least two-hundred people are here, dressed to the nines, including, of course, Jo's parents, siblings, and their partners. Izzy and Leo both came home from college to be able to attend, and I was able to meet Alex, Jo's sister who lives in California, for the first time when she flew in as a surprise. I was talking to her earlier, and I'm not sure if she hates me, because she kept glaring over my shoulder. Nellie and Tyler took the train in, too, and rented a room at the inn. We hired Tyler to cater dessert for the event, which they went above and beyond for, of course.

After she quit Coffey & Co, dozens of vendors who had worked with and loved Jo reached out to Becky for her information. Becky had refused, of course, but Jo's coworker, Daniel, made it his mission to send her info to them. Photographers, caterers, musicians, and entertainers all reached out hoping to work with her again. She was able to reach a mutual agreement with them that our services would be provided to the entire Tri-State area, as opposed to just Fairfield County as we'd originally planned. Our vendors agreed to the same.

Turns out she was truly the heart and soul of Coffey & Co, the reason for their success and why clients and vendors kept working with them. Now, she's our heart and soul, and tonight,
it shows.

We're in talks of expanding even further than we'd ever hoped. It's unreal how well respected Giovanna is in the industry, but also unsurprising. We're hoping to open a second office in Manhattan by this time next year, and recently, a third office in Boston has been brought up as well.

It's beyond my wildest dreams, watching Giovanna shine like the gem she is. She's the best risk I've ever taken.

"Looking good, ladies," Ren says, sidling next to his sister and poking her in the side. She squawks and jumps away from him as I bend over in laughter. I'm wearing the same pink dress I'd worn the first night we danced in the living room. I thought about wearing something black or more professional…but I couldn't. I couldn't imagine wearing anything else tonight.

The photographer we'd hired for the event snaps a few pictures. He's one of the vendors that followed Jo, and drove up from Jersey for the event so I could have a night off. He's trans and like many of our other queer attendees, wears a pin proudly declaring his identity. I'm so proud of what we created, a safe space that she and I didn't have twelve years ago.

"Stop bullying me," Jo whines. She puts her finger in her mouth and then into Ren's ear. He yelps and jumps away, sloshing champagne all over his suit as his phone clatters to the floor. She bends over to grab it for him, but he's faster, swooping down and pocketing it.

I raise a brow at him. "That's shady."

"It's really not. If she was your sister, you wouldn't want her touching her personal belongings either," he counters.

Jo scowls at him. "What's that supposed to mean, Lorenzo?"

He doesn't answer, instead patting the top of his sister's head. She bats at him and pulls away, grumbling something about him fucking up her hair. "Don't worry about it. I'm proud of you."

She rolls her eyes, but her mouth tips up at the corners. "Thanks. Go be annoying somewhere else, please."

"You got it, boss." Ren salutes her before pulling out his phone and typing. "I'll see you guys later." He pockets his phone again and winks before walking away.

I wait until he's out of earshot before turning to Jo. "You know he's sexting someone, right? Ooh, bacon wrapped dates!" I happily snag an hors d'oeuvre from a passing server, thanking them before I bite into it.

My girlfriend sputters in disbelief. "Why the *hell* would I know if my brother is sexting someone?"

"It's obvious!" I say, mouth full of food. "He was so protective about his phone. He's sexting someone."

Jo gags.

"Hey!" Nic and Josh appear next to us. Nic wearing a skin tight black bandage dress with a bi pride pin and fishnet stockings. Josh stands behind her, a progress pride flag on his suit jacket, not even trying to hide the fact that he's ogling her ass. I clear my throat and he meets my eyes, smiling bashfully. I wave him over.

"Are there chicken tenders?" I overhear Nic asking Jo.

Jo points to a server across the room. "Yup. Mini pizzas will be coming out next, too. I made sure you had some of your safe foods as options."

"Ren's sexting someone," I tell Josh.

His eyes widen. "No shit? Our Ren? Spill."

I tell him my theory, and he nods along thoughtfully. "And that's how I know Ren's sexting someone," I conclude.

"Oh, for sure," he agrees, taking a sip of his mocktail.

"Augh!" Giovanna exclaims, and we both turn to her. Nic must have gone off in search of chicken tenders, because Jo's alone and glaring at us, her hands planted on her hips.

It's hot as hell.

Brandon, Josh's friend from high school and our accountant, pops in before she can say anything, shaking Josh's hand.

"The event is fantastic," he says, turning to me. This is the first time we're meeting Brandon in person. He lives in Jersey and we've been meeting with him virtually for the past few months. He's about an inch taller than Josh, who's already a foot taller than me, and has graying temples and scruff. He's also a former football player, a big, broad guy. "I'm so sorry to do this, but I have to head out early."

He waves at us as he makes his way to the exit, and Jo tries to speak again.

"Could we—"

"Shut up, Josephine," Josh says, pointing towards the entrance. "Hunter, you see that?"

I look to where he's pointing and gasp. "Oh my god. Is that..."

"Yep."

"Leaving almost exactly two minutes after..."

"Yep."

We exchange a knowing look. I grab a champagne flute from a passing server and we keep eye contact as we sip from our respective drinks.

"Um, hello?" Jo waves her hand in front of our faces. "Anyone care to fill me in?"

"Right." I'm glad Josh answers first, because that makes it easier for me. "Your brother is fucking the lady who owns the inn."

"Audrey," I supply helpfully.

"Audrey?" Jo laughs. "No the hell he's not."

Josh and I exchange another knowing look.

"Oh my god, stop doing that," she complains. "You two aren't allowed to be friends anymore."

"I mean, it makes sense. He's Piper's piano teacher so he's here a lot, and more importantly, she left the room exactly two minutes after he did," I say.

"So?"

"*So* it's the perfect amount of time to not raise suspicion when having a bathroom quickie."

Josh nods in agreement.

"What are we talking about?" Nic asks, rejoining us with a plate piled high with mini pizzas and chicken tenders.

"Ren is fucking Audrey," I tell her.

Nic gags violently. "That's disgusting, Hunter. He's your brother, too."

This family is wild, and I love being a part of it.

"I hate to break it to you, Buttercup, but your mom re-entered the room two minutes after your dad." Josh at least has the decency to look like he truly regrets having to be the one to tell her this.

Nic responds by lobbing a mini pizza at his head.

We mingle for a little longer, trying to make conversation with Leo and Kat, who are huddled in a corner. Kat and Steve were listed on the petition as well, which Jo just rolled her eyes at. Kat surprised us by showing up alone tonight, hugging us both and telling us how proud of us she is. Stella wasn't able to make it either, and I realize I've never been around Leo without her. He's checking his phone repeatedly.

"It's perfect, Joey," Sean, as he insisted I call him, tells Giovanna as he hugs her. I try to forget what Josh said and how much I know about Sean and his wife's sex life.

"Thanks, Dad."

"And you." He points at me with his Guinness bottle. "You get in here, I know you worked hard, too."

I smile and hug him. Sean and I have talked since that night in the lighthouse. He likes me now, texting me whenever he sees an article mentioning Dolly Parton.

I've forgiven him. Forgiveness didn't feel like a conscious choice, rather a steady build. While I'll never have my dad back, Sean made a comment at Sunday dinner a few weeks ago that he had ten kids. When we stared at him in confusion, he looked at us like we were missing something obvious. "Hunter and Josh?" he'd said. I didn't know someone would *want* to refer to me as their child again.

Towards the end of the night, I clink my champagne flute with a butter knife as I climb onto the stage. "Twelve years ago, I fell in love in Port Haven. With the town, and with a girl I didn't realize at fifteen would become my future. It means the world that I'm back, creating something beautiful with the person I fell in love with."

I wink at Giovanna, and she blushes. "It means everything to us that you're here," I continue, "and we look forward to working with the queer community in Port Haven and beyond. Giovanna and I didn't have that twelve years ago, and I know I speak for us both when I say that while we can't rewrite history, we can make a better world. Thank you for welcoming us back, and embracing Lillian Theresa. Please join me in a toast to new beginnings!"

I think there's applause after I finish, but I'm too busy hopping off the stage and throwing myself into Giovanna's arms to take it in.

"Did you notice," I whisper in her ear, "that thirteen minutes after Audrey left, Ren re-entered the room? And then *exactly* two minutes later..."

"Can we not? I want to dance with my pretty girlfriend, not think about my brother having a bathroom quickie."

"Well," I say, grinning up at her as I let her lead me onto the dance floor. "It *is* five-o-clock somewhere."

She rolls her eyes, still smiling. Then she dips me, kissing me square on the mouth and this time, I'm enveloped in the cheers erupting around us.

I wish I had a time machine so I can go back and tell fifteen year old Jo and Hunter that it's worth the wait. That everything turns out okay, better than okay. That one day we don't hide and people cheer for and celebrate the way we love, *our* love, because that never felt possible.

"Let's get out of here," I tell her as she pulls me back to a standing position.

"Great. I'll follow in two minutes…"

I laugh and thwack her shoulder. "Not for a bathroom quickie."

"Well, what else is this event for, considering Josh just left three minutes after Nic?" Giovanna scoffs and shakes her head. "He thought he could throw us off."

"You've learned quickly, young padawan," I say proudly. "But no, we're leaving together."

We exit the building, and I pull her along the beach until we get to the lighthouse.

"You're such a romantic," she teases me as I pull a bobby pin from my hair and pick the lock, and then I pull her into the lighthouse. It's dark, and moonlight is the only thing illuminating the room.

"We're going to live here one day," I say definitively as Jo wraps her arms around my waist and rests her chin on my shoulder.

"Where?"

"Here."

"The *lighthouse*?" she asks incredulously.

"Mmhmm. Think about it: you, me, Dolly, maybe some scaleless siblings for her. It's gonna happen."

She laughs. "You're ridiculous."

Maybe I am ridiculous. I am, after all, a dreamer. Always have been. How could I not be? The woman I've spent most of my life dreaming of loving is holding me as we celebrate the start of our new business. I have a family who loves and accepts me, without me having to pretend to be someone I'm not.

I turn to her and take her hands in mine. "I think I've earned the right to dream ridiculous dreams."

She cups my face and brushes my nose with hers. "Yeah. I do too. If you want the lighthouse, honey, I'll buy you the lighthouse one day."

I kiss her in the moonlight, the sound of the waves crashing faintly in the background. I kiss her the same way I kissed her over twelve years ago, with all my love and hope.

This time, I'm kissing her knowing that she's my tomorrow. My next year and years to follow. Knowing that the future is a risk, and knowing that we're worth it.

Thank you for reading *Back to Me*! If you enjoyed Jo & Hunter's story, please consider leaving a review.

Reviews play a huge part in the success of indie books, and an honest review left wherever you talk about books (Amazon, GoodReads, Storygraph, TikTok, Instagram, etc.) can impact an indie author's life greatly!

And be sure to follow me on social media (@KatieDuggan-Writes) to keep up with me and the Quinns!

Acknowledgments

Holy shit, y'all. She's here! I wrote this book during a time of extreme upheaval in my life, but also a time of immense growth and healing. I hope all of that is evident in Jo & Hunter's story, the pain and the goodness I've gotten to experience while giving these girlies the love story they deserve.

First, I'd like to thank myself. I'm so proud of how hard I worked for this. For not giving up and throwing in the towel. For believing in myself when it was really, really hard to do so. But *obviously*, this was not done all on my own, and I have a bajillion other people to thank.

To my family: thank you for your support and never-ending love. Thank you for believing in me when I have trouble believing in myself, and for the inspiration for the familial relationships I write about.

My beta readers: Olivia, Jillian, Colleen, Ricki, Emily, Cait, Vic, Kae, Sarah, Ellora, Izzy, Brooke, and Jenn. Y'all keep me young with your unhinged comments. I appreciate the honesty and love you've given *Back to Me* and me. It's a better book because you decided it was worth spending your time reading.

My sensitivity readers, Kristen and Izzy. Thank you for your honest and informative feedback regarding the Type 1 Diabetes Rep. Making sure I got it as close to right as I could was one of the hardest, and most important, parts of the writing process. Thank you for your vulnerability and willingness to share your experiences.

My fellow ADHD Leo, Jenn. Thank you for beta reading, proofreading, and sensitivity reading for Hunter's ADHD. Your feedback made Hunter even better and me a better writer. Also, thanks for teaching me that Jose Cuervo is *not* a top shelf tequila.

My alpha readers and girl gang, Cait and Kae. You are the best hype squad, both in my professional and personal life, and I love you for it. You both go out of your way to make people feel supported and important, and I hope you know how wonderful and special that makes you. Thanks for loving the girlies from the beginning, and fangirling over the Quinn family.

My editor and one of my all time favorite people, Cheyenne. You've been by my side since the inception of Josh freaking Henry, and I couldn't do this without you. You make my writing better, and my characters stronger. I'm so grateful for everything you've done, and for the friendship we've built. I'm so excited for everything else we'll get to create together.

I can't believe I get to say this...but Chloe Liese and Jillian Meadows, two authors I admire immensely, went out of their way to support me by blurbing my books. They say never meet your heroes, but I think it's pretty dang cool that I not only met, but became friends with two of mine. And yes, their work is truly a reflection of the incredible humans they are. Also, thank you, Chloe, for the Bergman family, and Jillian, for Drafting Daddy Gavin.

Everyone who donated or shared my GoFundMe. It's a weird feeling, realizing you need help. For me, it's embarrassing, but with the encouragement of my friends, I made a GoFundMe to raise money for publishing costs. I love self-publishing, but dang she's pricey y'all! I didn't think much would come of it, but I was proven embarrassingly wrong. I'm so grateful not only for the money, but for the outpouring of support I received. It's incredible to realize how many people are in your corner and genuinely want to see you succeed.

Vic, designer, beta reader, and friend extraordinaire. Thank you for *everything*. For the gorgeous branding, the sticker designs, for beta reading, and just being an all-around freaking great human.

My artists, Paige and Emily. Paige is always able to portray my characters in such a beautiful way, and I'm so lucky to have her as my cover artist. Emily created the gorgeous family tree and page break graphics, both of which I'm *obsessed* with. Thank you both for your talent and generosity!

And of course, you, my lovely, brave readers. Thank you for spending time in my little world, with my silly imaginary friends. Each message I get, each post I see, means the world to me. Every time someone says they relate to a character, or feel seen by one, my heart grows a size. I wanted to write stories that gave readers the feelings I get from my favorite books. Feelings of belonging, of worthiness, of hope, of healing, of *joy*. Thank you for taking a chance on me, and my books. See you for book three!

About the Author

Katie Duggan (she/they) is a New England transplant currently living in Northern Virginia. She writes romance novels that give fat, neurodivergent, and queer characters spicy happily-ever-afters. When Katie's not writing or being kept up at night by her characters, they can be found drinking root beer, going to therapy, convincing people to read her favorite books, and doing whatever hobbies give their neurodivergent brain the most dopamine at the moment.

Email: KatieDuggan.Writes@gmail.com
Instagram & TikTok: @KatieDugganWrites

The Quiblings Series

From the Start
Back to Me
Book 3 (Coming 2025)